HEADFIRST

A NOVEL OF THE 60s

TIM PELTON

For absent friends

The 60's are gone; dope will never be as cheap, sex never as free, and the rock and roll never as great.

Abbie Hoffman

ONE

The warm September sun poured in through the window and made Jamie squint. There wasn't much to look at on his side of the bus, only the mind-numbing sameness of the Boulder suburbs. The show was on the other side-the Colorado Rockies that suddenly jumped out of the plains and stacked themselves on top of one another in ever-deepening shades of blue and purple. To see them, Jamie had to scrunch down in his seat and look past the bald guy across the aisle. Even then, he couldn't see the snowcaps on the highest mountains.

The Greyhound he'd ridden to Colorado from Iowa was built high with broad windows so you could see for miles. Unfortunately, there had been nothing but endless, unchanging Kansas on the other side of those generous acres of Greyhound glass. Now that there was something to see, the old bus he had changed to in Denver had small, grimy windows that were more like portholes.

Jamie sighed and sat back up in his seat. He figured it wouldn't be much longer until the bus got into Colton anyway. After that, if he wanted he could stare at the mountains until he fell over.

Jamie's trip to Colton began about four months before. Then-Pfc. James Shipman had walked into the office of the Post Discharge Counseling Officer at Fort Bliss and asked for information about an early out for college. The PDC Officer wasn't an officer at all, he was a Staff Sergeant named Jones and one of Jamie's racquetball buddies. Jamie had enlisted at 17 (his mother had dabbed at her eyes with a tissue and then signed the permission form proudly) and still had six months to go on a three-year hitch. He wasn't, in fact, that hot to go to college, but as he told Sgt. Jones, "If it'll get my ass out of here early, then sign me up."

He needed a Letter of Acceptance from an accredited school, not an easy thing to get given the short notice and some mediocre grades in high school. After a raft load of rejections, there came a letter from Colton College in Colton, Colorado. "It is our pleasure to inform you that your application has been accepted…"

Jamie took Sgt. Jones down to the bowling alley and bought them both a pitcher of beer to celebrate.

* * *

The bus stopped. There was a brief hiss of air from the brakes, then the driver threw open the forward doors. "Colton! Thirty-minute meal stop, everyone continuing on must be back on the bus in thirty minutes. This is Colton."

A few minutes later, Jamie, a green canvas duffle bag in one hand and a faded plaid suitcase in the other, pushed the front door open and entered the bus station. Most of his fellow passengers were already perched on stools around a chrome-edged counter. They were eating their bowls of chili and hot beef sandwiches in a hurry so as to have time for a cigarette and a trip to the john before reboarding.

A heavy lady in a pink, polyester uniform stood behind the counter adding up guest checks. As she did so, she absently pushed loose strands of bleached yellow hair back up into a sagging beehive hairdo that was held together with hairspray and bobby pins.

"Um, 'scuse me," Jamie said, then added, "ma'am".

Gladys, for that was the name on her tag, looked up at him expectantly.

"Would you tell me how to get to Colton College?'

"Well, y'could sleep with the Dean o' Women. That'd git you in."

She stared at him grimly for a few seconds and then broke into a barking laugh that featured uneven, brown teeth.

"Just funnin' ya. Don't pay me no mind. New student, eh? Where ya from?"

"Ottumwa," Jamie said, "It's in Iowa."

"Well, welcome to Colton, Iowa. Just go out the door, turn left, turn right at the corner, go about six blocks. You can't miss it."

"Thanks. I appreciate it."

"Come back in and see us sometime."

* * *

After his discharge, Jamie had had about a week in Ottumwa to spend with his family. A week was almost too long.

Jamie's father, Ralph, had been a mailman for many years. One day he went to work at the post office, sorted out the mail for his route, slung his bag over his shoulder, and dropped to the floor screaming in pain.

"Threw my back out" was the explanation. After a short stay in the hospital, they brought Ralph home and deposited him on the couch. Ten years later he was still there. Any suggestion that he might get up and do something was met with an incredulous look.

"What? And risk losin' my Disability? They got them hidden cameras, you know." And there he lay.

"Hey soldier boy," Ralph yelled from the living room when Jamie first came in the door, "Get me a beer, willya?"

Jamie's mother, on the other hand, was constantly in motion. Her chosen occupation was selling hand-painted sweatshirts at Craft Fairs.

Every little town in the Midwest had a summer celebration, whether it was "Krazy Daze", or "Pioneer Days", or "River Days", it always involved a parade, a cheap little Carnival, and a Craft Fair in a park. To Rosie Shipman's credit, the sweatshirts actually were hand-painted, just not by her. Thirteen-year-old girls being paid about nine cents a day painted them in various sweatshops in Singapore. Rosie, unaware of this, blithely bought the sweatshirts by the gross and accepted compliments from her customers on her painting skills with convincing modesty.

As Jamie helped his mother load the station wagon for a trip to Dubuque scheduled for the next morning (Steamboat Days), his older brother Jack pulled into the drive.

Jack was at the wheel of the "Dune Buggy" he had bragged about the last time Jamie called home. Looking at the car, Jamie couldn't see how removing the motor cover and the back half of the rear fenders from a homely Volkswagen could turn it into the "chick magnet" his brother claimed, but he swallowed his objections and walked over to say hello.

After pumping Jamie's hand, Jack showed him his new car; proudly pointing out the "performance features" he'd added. These consisted mainly of a chromed Glaspak muffler and a couple of bolt-on taillights. The fact that there were no sand dunes within seven hundred miles of Ottumwa didn't seem to faze his brother, so Jamie just smiled and agreed that Jack had himself a "fine set of wheels".

During the next week, Jamie did his best to enjoy his family's company. He went down to Romano's with Jack for a Stromboli Sandwich, watched baseball on TV with his father, and spent a Sunday with Rosie hawking sweatshirts at Steamboat Days. And every day he felt a little more uncomfortable and a little more anxious to leave.

Once on the bus, he had plenty of time to ponder this lack of loyalty. His first conclusion was that his family hadn't changed one iota in the nearly three years he'd been in the Army. The message remained the same. "Keep your head and your ambitions down. Big dreams are dangerous." No wonder he'd wanted to get away.

Hours later, as Jamie stared out into the passing darkness, a second conclusion came paddling up unannounced and bit him on the ass. It wasn't how little his family had changed that was spooking him; it was how little he himself had changed. His main reason for joining the Army had been to test himself, to find meaning and direction in life, to be "made into a man". And here he was-more than a boy, but not yet what anyone would call a man.

* * *

He snapped on the reading light and opened a well-thumbed copy of Sports Illustrated. Thinking about his life gave Jamie the creeps.

Two coeds, one in a plaid skirt, the other in jeans and a windbreaker, were walking toward him. Jamie set his suitcase down on the sidewalk and switched the duffle bag's strap from one shoulder to the other.

Plaid Skirt was nicely put together, Jamie decided, with long legs and wavy blonde hair that bounced in rhythm to her step. Windbreaker, on the other hand, was a plodder with a sour look on her face.

"Excuse me," Jamie said, "I'm new here and I'm looking for Fulton Hall."

Plaid Skirt stopped and looked puzzled.

"Fulton Hall?"

"Um, yeah. The Administration Building."

"Oh. Big Red. That's it right there."

She pointed to a three-story brick monstrosity.

"Oh, I see," Jamie blushed, "The one with the "New Students Check in Here' sign out front."

Plaid Skirt grinned and nodded her head, then hurried after her companion.

Kinda Cute. Oh please, let there be hundreds more like her around here and fewer humorless duds with dishpan butts like old Windbreaker there.

* * *

Jamie picked up his suitcase and made his way down the sidewalk toward Big Red.

After climbing half a dozen worn, sandstone steps and struggling his luggage through the front doors, he stopped in the lobby to get his bearings.

"New student here at Colton?" said an overly hearty voice behind Jamie's right shoulder.

Jamie turned to face a chubby young man wearing a crew cut and a J.C. Penney suit. His hand was out, so Jamie shook it and nodded.

"Howareya?" the fellow said, "The name's Ralph."

"Ralph."

"Election's coming up, you know. We're just spreading the word. Got any questions about Mr. Nixon?"

Jamie looked over Ralph's shoulder to see a life-size poster of Richard Nixon; arms spread wide, two fingers on each hand raised, and a toothy grin shining on his face. Bright red letters across the poster announced, "NIXON'S THE ONE IN '68." In front of the picture, two more earnest-looking young people sat behind a table skirted with red, white and blue. Across the skirting, a sign was pinned that read "Young Republicans of Colton College".

Jamie shrugged and picked up his suitcase. "No, I'm not really interested. I'm not real political and too young to vote."

"But not too young to have some influence," Ralph yelled after him. "Think about it. We'll be here."

I'm sure you will. I wonder if the Democrats secretly pay these pinheads to sit here and drive people, screaming, to vote for whatsisname-Humphrey Dumpty.

* * *

Jamie followed the signs up the stairs and into a huge ballroom. After waiting in the "R-T" line for twenty minutes, periodically kicking his suitcase and duffle bag ahead of him, he was finally standing in front of a nondescript middle-aged woman who sat behind several open boxes of 3X5 cards.

"Name?" she asked.

"James Shipman"

"In-state, or Out-of-state?"

"Out."

Passing over the rows of white cards, her fingers began to dance down the rows of yellow ones.

"Seldon, Selkirk..." she muttered to herself, "Shepherd, Shipman. Here you are."

She pulled out a card and laid it on top of the filing box.

"Incoming freshman. Tuition and first month's residence fees paid. You're assigned to Hargreaves Hall. Your room assignment will be posted at the front desk there. Make an appointment with Mr. Feiger, the Head Resident at Hargreaves, to discuss your work/study request. Registration for freshmen begins at three o'clock tomorrow afternoon in the Fieldhouse, but as a military veteran, you may go in at 2:30 with the 2nd-semester freshmen. Here is a packet..."

She reached behind her to a table stacked with fat manila envelopes, picked one up and handed it to Jamie.

"...Inside should be all the information you need. Any questions?"

"Yeah. How do I get to Hargreaves Hall?"

"There's a campus map in your packet. Welcome to Colton, Mr. Shipman."

* * *

The following afternoon, Jamie sat by himself in the Student Union Coffee shop with a pile of textbooks on the table in front of him. The bindings on the books were frayed here and there and each of them had a "used" sticker glued to the spine.

He'd managed to talk his parents into paying for his tuition for the first semester, not an easy task what with his mother wondering why he couldn't just go to Ottumwa Junior College and his father droning on about how <u>he'd</u> never gone to college and yet blah blah blah. Getting them to spring for books too would have been out of the question. So he'd emptied out his slender little savings account and cashed in the $25 Savings Bonds that Grandma put in with the fudge she sent every Christmas. It had been enough, but barely.

Ah, what the hell. I'm here and I'm <u>not</u> there.

He tipped a tall paper cup up to his mouth. The Coke that had been in it was long gone, but Jamie was still working on the ice cubes. He let the ice slide down in a pile and hit him in the face, with two or three chunks falling into his mouth. He batted these around with his tongue for a while, and then noisily chewed them up. He had Introduction to Geology open in front of him and he thumbed through the pages, looking at the pictures.

"Shipman, right?" said a voice and Jamie looked up.

A young man carrying a plastic cafeteria tray was standing across the table. He was slender, pretty-boy handsome, and had a shock of light blonde hair that fell down over his forehead, hit his eyebrows, and made a hard right turn toward his ear. His eyes had that blinking, watery look of contact lenses. He set his tray down on the table and stuck out his hand toward Jamie.

"I'm Mike Harding"

"Jamie Shipman," Jamie said as he shook hands, "Nice to meet you."

"I just pulled in this morning," Mike said.

He dunked a french fry into a little paper cup full of ketchup, and then looked up into Jamie's slightly confused expression.

"Oh, I'll bet Feiger didn't tell you about me."

"No."

"I'm your new roommate," Mike tossed the ketchup-laden fry into his mouth.

"Ah. Well, good," Jamie said. "How did you know it was me sitting here?"

The guy across the hall told me to look for the only guy on campus wearing an "Ottumwa Bulldogs" sweatshirt.

Jamie looked down and grinned sheepishly. Mike gestured at Jamie's computer punchcard that lay next to his books.

"Already registered, eh? What did you get?"

Jamie picked up the card. There were small, square holes punched, seemingly at random, across it. A list of classes had been printed several lines below the warning not to "fold, spindle, or mutilate." Jamie looked at the card and shrugged.

"Boredom 101, Introduction to Dullness, Freshman Tedium… the standard stuff. I only got one elective."

"What was that?"

"I was looking for some kind of gut course. They weren't offering basket weaving, so I took Debate. I figured it's just getting up and arguing with some guy. I can do that."

"Let's hope you're right. What'd you get for P.E.? I heard all the fun classes like Golf and Bowling get snapped up by upperclassmen and what's left for the rest of us is shit like Calisthenics."

Jamie was intrigued by Mike's easy self-assuredness and decided he might be a pretty good guy. Unless he pushed it too far.

"Well, actually," Jamie said, "I don't have to take P.E. I just got out of the Army and they gave me credits for some of it. I couldn't convince them to get me past Freshman Math, though."

"Were you in the Nam? "

"No, stateside my whole hitch." Jamie stood up. "Don't mean to run off so soon but I've gotta lug this stuff back to the room. I still have to hunt down my Advisor's office and sign up for an appointment."

"And I've still got to go through the meat grinder over there," Mike added as he stood up. "Catch you later, okay?"

Jamie started away but then turned back after a few steps. "It was good to meet you, man. I think we're gonna get along pretty well."

Mike grinned and nodded, and they walked off in separate directions.

Two

The sounds of a large and busy kitchen in full swing echoed off the tile floor and walls as Jamie walked past banks of ovens, by a row of potato peeling machines, around racks of cookware, and entered an alcove on the far side of the room. Kenny Walsingham stood in front of a line of deep commercial sinks. A number of grimy pots and pans were piled on the drainboard to his left.

"Hey, Waltz," Jamie said, "Doughboy said you could use some help."

"Yeah, no shit. Look at this. "

Kenny tipped a deep pot over so Jamie could see inside. A hard, black layer of what was once beef stew covered the bottom. "They either gotta stop burning this crap or get me an air hammer." He went back to chipping at the mess with a short spatula.

Kenny, though not tall, was sturdily built with brown hair that dropped into sharp sideburns. His pink, apple cheeks sat atop a toothy grin.

Jamie had met Kenny on his first day in the Hargreaves/Johnson kitchen and he liked him almost immediately. Kenny had grinned, stuck out his hand, and said, "Call me Waltz. Pretty much everybody else does."

Kenny had grown up in Colton, his father stuccoed houses or worked on cars, depending on the season. Kenny was a "townie", one of several hired full-time for kitchen work.

Jamie plucked a pan from the top of the pile, ducked it into a sink full of hot, soapy water, picked up a copper scrubbing pad, and began to scour off the remnants of Tuna Surprise.

"You drink beer, don't you Shipman?" Kenny's voice had a hollow sound coming from inside the pot.

"Yeah, I've been known to hoist a few. What have you got in mind?"

Kenny grabbed the overhead sprayer and rinsed the scrapings out of the pot into the disposal sink. He righted the vessel and kept the sprayer on until there were two or three inches of hot water in the bottom of it, then pushed it aside.

"Fuck it. Let it soak overnight. Me and Lyle and some other guys are talking about pitching in on a keg this weekend. You want to come?"

"Sounds like it could be kinda fun. Are most of these guys townies? Am I gonna be the only college guy there?"

"Sure. We gotta have somebody we can pants."

Kenny looked at Jamie seriously for a moment and then laughed.

"Nah, the only guy who ever got pantsed at one of these did it to himself. He wandered off in the bushes to take a crap and passed out. Most of the guys all graduated from Colton High last fall and several are up at the U now."

"Okay, count me in. How much am I supposed to chip in? And where is this going to happen?"

"A couple of bucks should do it. We'll be up at the old quarry just up in the foothills. There's a nice picnic spot next to the water. Tell you what. Be out in front of Hargreaves about noon on Saturday and we'll pick you up. Lyle's got his old Mercury running."

"All right. I finally get to meet this Lyle," Jamie set the pan he'd been working on upside-down on the drying rack. "I was beginning to think he was your imaginary friend."

* * *

Jamie walked out of the dorm and down the steps to the sidewalk. He looked up and down the street, and then turned around when he heard his name called. Mike was coming down the steps carrying a guitar case.

"Hey, Mike."

"What are you hanging out down here for, Shipman? The trolleys stopped running years ago."

"A couple of guys are supposed to pick me up. We're off, I'm told, to a kegger. Want to come along? I'm sure there's room."

"Nah, thanks anyway. I'm supposed to go play with some guys. Sort of an audition."

"I've seen the guitar case in the closet," Jamie said. "Who is this band you're auditioning for? Have I heard of them?"

"Maybe," Mike said, "They're just a local outfit that plays around campus. The Daffodils. Yeah, I know, dippy name. Their guitarist got drafted last month so they're looking for fresh meat. Well, gotta roll."

"Good Luck."

Mike walked off down the street. Jamie watched him go and wondered, not for the first time, what was really going on in Mike's head. He'd only known him for a week or two, and he was probably way off base, but Jamie had the feeling that there was a small, tightly-locked compartment deep inside of the guy. In it was something dark and maybe dangerous. But all-in-all, he liked him a lot. Nearly everybody did.

THREE

Jamie stood up and began to pace. It was twenty minutes past twelve. Although it was a sunny day, it was, after all, September in Colorado and the concrete planter in front of Hargreaves Hall was not a warm place to sit for more than fifteen minutes.

He was so wrapped up in wondering if he'd been ditched that he was surprised when a 1950 Mercury four-door sedan turned off Main Street and headed toward him.

The car was blue with one white fender and sported numerous dents and primer spots. It hit a small pothole, bounced once, and continued wallowing down the street, a motion unmitigated by shock absorbers.

The Mercury stopped in front of him and Kenny stuck his head out of the passenger side window.

"Hey, sailor. New in town?"

"Not new enough," Jamie opened the back door and piled into the back seat.

By the time he'd slammed the back door and turned around, the driver had his hand over the seatback.

"Lyle Kirk. Good to meet you."

Lyle had sandy blonde hair, broad shoulders and a ruddy complexion.

Jamie shook Lyle's hand. "Lyle, I'm Jamie. I appreciate the ride."

"No problem, man."

Lyle pulled down on the gearshift. The gears ground together for a moment before clunking into First. Lyle took a quick glance over his shoulder, made a U-turn, and headed back the way he had come.

* * *

Several hours later Mike was sitting cross-legged on his bed, a Gibson Les Paul guitar in his lap. He was picking 16-note scales up and back, his eyes half-closed as his fingers fluttered up and down the fretboard.

The door swung wide and Jamie slouched against the doorframe.

"Home is the sailor, home from the sea," he said.

Mike stopped picking and thought for a moment.

"…And the hunter home from the hill. That's a poem about a dead guy, you know. I take it the kegger was a snore."

"It was okay, I guess. Not a big whoop."

"I'm disappointed, I was looking forward to seeing you on your knees and hugging a toilet."

"Three-point-two-beer, my friend. The Governor of Colorado's gift to us easy barfers. I'm still a little too blitzed to study. Guess I'll go down to the TV room and watch Bonanza. Maybe Hoss will finally kick the shit out of Little Joe."

"Oh, hey Shipman!" Mike called after him. "There's something I want to ask you…"

But there was no reply.

* * *

Jamie sat at a table in the Union crunching up ice cubes as he noodled away at a page of math homework. Mike walked up and laid some books down on the table.

"I need a cup of coffee," Mike said, "want anything?"

Jamie shook his head. Mike started away, and then quickly turned around.

"Hey, I was gonna ask you something last night. See, I got the gig with the Daffodils…"

"All right. Congratulations, man."

"Thanks. It shouldn't be too tough to catch up; I already know a lot of the stuff they play – *The Letter, Spooky, High-heel Sneakers.* They even want to do some Buffalo Springfield and were pretty gassed when I played *Rock and Roll Woman* for them.

"Anyway, they asked me if I knew anybody who'd want to run lights and sound and help set up and all that shit. You interested?"

"All I know about sound and lights you could stick in a gnat's ass with two grains of sand and a lieutenant's brain."

"Piece of cake, it's just flipping switches and pulling slides, I can teach you in about five minutes. The shitty part is they'll only pay you fifteen bucks a night, twenty-five if it's out of town. What do you think?"

"Well…"

"There'll be chicks at these dances."

"Okay, I'm your guy. When do I start?"

"Saturday night we've got a gig at the Gamma Delta house. But come by practice sometime this week and you can meet the guys."

"Sounds cool. Thanks, man."

Mike turned away and walked toward the Snack Bar.

* * *

The door of Giacomo's Pizza swung open and Jamie, Lyle, Kenny, and Mike walked out into the cool night air.

"Not bad Pizza, I'd say," Kenny said, "not bad at all. What do you think, Mike?"

"Well, it beats hell out of whatever that crap is they call pizza over at the cafeteria, plus they don't give you a pitcher of beer over there to wash it down with."

"Now there's a thought," Jamie said, "I say we stuff the suggestion box."

"Hah. Fat chance," Lyle said. "Speakin' of which, when do Waltz and I get to hear this band of yours? Shipman keeps telling us that you can play a little bit, but so far it's all been, like, private parties – common rabble not invited."

"How about next Saturday at the Student Union Ballroom. It'll cost you. I think it's three bucks to get in. Five if you bring a date."

"Whaddya say, Waltz? Your Mom got a wig you can borrow?"

"Forget it, Lyle," Kenny shot back, "even if she did, I doubt she'd let you wear it.

"Droll, Waltz, very fuckin' droll."

"Aw shit," muttered Mike suddenly stopping, "I left my gloves back in the pizza joint. Walk slow and I'll catch up."

He turned around and ran back the other way.

The remaining three were soon ambling along in front of a Texaco station when a Volkswagen bus pulled in front of them and chugged up to the pumps. The bus was white, at least the front third of it was. Part way down the side the solid white was broken into hundreds of little hand-painted white flowers that flowed across a sky-blue background. On the rear of the bus, the flowers coalesced again into a large, white, peace sign.

"Hey, it's a hippie wagon!" Kenny grinned, pointing out the obvious.

"California plates," said Jamie, "I wonder if they're from Haight-Ashbury?"

"Hate what-berry?" said Lyle.

"You've never heard of Haight-Ashbury?" Kenny rolled his eyes in wonderment, "It's in San Francisco, where the hippies drink Kool-Aid mixed with LSD and see God or whatever. Geez, Lyle, you oughta try reading a newspaper sometime instead of those crotch-mags you keep hidden in your bottom drawer."

They had reached Kenny's car, a blue 1960 Chevrolet.

"Fuck you, Waltz." Lyle pulled unsuccessfully on the passenger-side door handle. "And unlock this fucking door and get the heater going, I'm freezing my ass off."

Once the car door was opened, Jamie slid into the back seat and turned sideways to get a good look at the VW bus. A man had gotten out and was examining the gas pump. He was tall, with thick brown hair that hung down past his shoulders. He wore a fringed leather jacket and a pair of Navy surplus bell-bottom pants.

A young woman got out of the other side. There was a blanket wrapped around her body, but she had a lovely face adorned with a pair of wire-rimmed glasses and a beaded headband. After a few words with the driver, she scurried into the station.

Jamie found this very interesting and studied the hippie. As an almost invariable rule, beautiful women were always in the company of attractive and confident men. The alpha-wolf always got the best of the she-wolves. A funny looking dude like this guy, with his beaky nose, droopy mustache, and bowed legs shouldn't be with a stunner like the one that just went looking for a pee. Jamie decided that the guy must have a fat wallet tucked into those bell-bottoms.

"Here comes Mike," Kenny said, "Looks like he found his gloves."

Noticing Mike as well, the man in the fringed jacket grabbed a leather pouch out of the bus and hurried over to intercept him.

"What the hell is that all about?" Lyle said.

"I'll bet he's gonna try and sell him some LSD." Said Kenny.

"Nah," Jamie put in, "they put that stuff on sugar cubes. I don't see any sugar cubes."

"Well, whatever it is, the deal is made."

Mike was walking toward the car and the hippie was headed back to his van.

"Maybe it was 20 minutes in the back of that van with that guy's hippie chick," said Kenny with a leer.

"Dream on, Waltz." Lyle said, "Besides those hippies believe in Free Love."

Mike opened the rear door of the Chevy and jumped in. The other three looked at him.

"Well?" said Jamie.

"I found my gloves." Mike held up his hands to show them. "They were right under my chair."

"Yeah, yeah. Congratulations," Lyle said, "We want to know what that hippie sold you."

"Oh, him. He said he and his old lady were driving to Boulder to meet some people and they'd run out of money and nearly out of gas. I offered to give him five bucks, but he wouldn't take it. Said he'd feel better if I bought this."

Mike held up a little pair of locking tweezers with some beads and feathers attached to it.

"It's a roach clip."

"Yeah, right," Kenny put the Chevy in gear, "there's no way you can catch one of those little fuckers with that thing. Unless you stomped on him first."

The other three laughed, which puzzled Kenny.

"A roach is the butt-end of a marijuana cigarette, Mr. Expert-on-everything-there-is-to-know-about-hippies," gloated Lyle.

"I knew what it was. I was just makin' sure you did."

"The guy was broke?" Jamie asked.

"Apparently."

"Huh," Jamie digested this. "At first we were thinking he was trying to sell you some LSD."

"If he had," Mike said, "would you have wanted to take some?"

"Oh no, not me. I might want to have kids someday and I've heard that LSD can mess up your chromosomes. I don't even want to see a two-headed baby, let alone try to raise one."

"Yeah, you may be right," Mike slipped the roach clip into his jacket pocket, "But then, on the other hand, that chromosome stuff could be another big bag o' lies made up by some asshole Ph.D. just to scare people. To the Man, a scientist is easier to buy than a Fudgesicle."

"Just the same," Lyle said, "I think I'm sticking to beer. If I'm goin' out a window, I'd rather fall out by accident than jump. Right, Waltz?"

"If you're gonna jump out the window, lemme speed up first. It'll give you a good bounce."

Lyle slowly raised his middle finger.

The Chevy made a right turn onto College Avenue and headed toward the campus.

* * *

Jamie repeatedly turned his ballpoint pen end-for-end. In the front of the room were two tables. A pair of students sat at each table and faced the rest of the class and a few drop-in guests. Off to one side, Mr. Honeywell, a paunchy man with a close, Marine Corps haircut, sat at his desk and read a critique of the debate that had just taken place.

On the chalkboard behind the debaters, the 1968 National Debate Question had been carefully lettered-"RESOLVED: THE UNITED STATES SHOULD IMMEDIATELY BEGIN WITHDRAWING ALL OF ITS ARMED FORCES FROM THE COUNTRY OF VIETNAM."

"The Affirmative side," Honeywell said in a thick, Texas accent, "presented its arguments in a well-ordered and fairly understandable manner. The logic was thin, however, and easily attacked by the Negative."

Jamie wrote, "Affirmative-thin logic" in his notebook. Jamie was a note-taker. When the lecture was interesting, it kept him listening, and when what was being said made little or no sense, like in this class, it kept him awake.

"If your arguments are thin, people, the more you need quotes to back them up," Honeywell went on. "Research, people, research! For the Negative, Miss Drake and Miss Runcitter – B plus,"

The two girls smiled at each other and began to reinsert a pile of 3X5 cards into a tin file box.

"For the Affirmative, Miss Swanson and Mr. Wiebel,-C minus. You can do better. Next Thursday Mr. Krenovich and Mr. Shipman will take the Affirmative; Miss French and Mr. Stone will represent the Negative. That's all for today."

* * *

Jamie ambled down the hall slowly, giving Doug Krenovich, his debate partner, a chance to catch up.

"Sorry, man," Doug said as he puffed up from behind, "I was trying to sweet talk Kerry Swanson into giving us her quote cards to copy. Cunt. All she had to do was say 'no', not give me a fucking lecture."

Doug was slender bordering on skinny. He had a thick mop of un-ruly, curly hair, a perpetually confused expression, and the biggest feet Jamie had ever seen on a guy of average height.

"So what're we gonna do?" Doug went on. "We haven't done shit for research, we got squat for quotes."

The dejected frown on Jamie's face suddenly shifted to a sly smile.

"What?" said Doug, "You think of something?"

"Sort of. But it's pretty half-baked, let me leave it in the oven for a while. Meet me at the Library at ten next Tuesday morning. If it looks good, I'll tell you about it; if I'm just kidding myself, we'll spend the time trying to scrounge up some quotes."

They went out the door and down the steps. Jamie turned left and headed toward the quad. Doug watched his retreating back.

"At least give me a fuckin' hint or something," Doug yelled.

"My Uncle Amos was a prizefighter when he was young," Jamie yelled back, "He always used to say, 'If you can't outpunch 'em, then dazzle 'em with footwork!'"

FOUR

In the semi-darkness drumsticks started banging a syncopated rhythm on a cowbell.

Five-six-seven-eight.

A staccato electric guitar line wrapped itself around the cowbell sound.

Five-six-seven-eight. Break.

Total silence.

Five-six-seven. Now!

Jamie mashed down four switches and banks of colored lights lit up just as the full band hit the downbeat and tore *into Gimme Some Lovin'.*

Gary the bass player caught Jamie's eye and subtly jerked his head up. Jamie reached over to the mixer and pushed a slide up from 5 to 6.

"How're you doin', guy?" said a voice from behind him.

He turned and saw Lyle standing there with his hands in his pockets, smiling, looking a little uncomfortable.

"Hey, Lyle." Jamie pulled out the empty chair next to him, "Take a load off. Where's Waltz?"

"Out there dancing. He brought a date." Lyle gestured out at the crowded dance floor and sat down.

"No shit? Where are they?"

Lyle pondered the crowd a minute and then pointed off to the right.

"There they are," he announced, "She's the blonde hair and the white boots. Her name's Kimberley or Kathy or something. Nice tits and doesn't wear a bra."

Jamie looked where Lyle was pointing and saw a pair of white go-go boots. The girl dancing in them had straight blonde hair, a blue mini-skirt, and a light blue sweater. Inside the sweater, a generously sized pair of breasts swayed gently back and forth as she danced.

"I see what you mean about the tits," said Jamie. "So where's Waltz? Oh, never mind, There he is."

With no apparent sense of rhythm and less grace, Kenny awkwardly shuffled out from behind the girl.

"Dances like Fred Astaire," Jamie said, "if Fred was stinkin' drunk and having a seizure."

Lyle chuckled. "Yeah, that's pretty close. He figures if he dances with her, it'll raise his chances of gettin' something."

"Oh, yeah? Does she roll over fairly easy?"

"Nah. She says she's 'saving it for her future husband'. But she gives a pretty good hand job."

A mental picture quickly took shape in Jamie's mind – a picture of Waltz sitting in his car with his eyes rolled back in his head. Cuddled up next to him was Go-go Boots with her free hand groping in the open front of Waltz's jeans.

Jamie quickly let the thought go. "So how come you didn't ask her out first?"

"Not my type."

Jamie wondered what kind of girl was Lyle's type. He wasn't a bad looking guy, as far as Jamie could tell, with a comfortable air about him and an easy sense of humor. He wasn't queer or didn't seem to be. Lyle just preferred the company of guys. Exclusively. His best friend had found a date for the dance, but Lyle seemed happy to sit on the sidelines and watch.

Come to think of it, I haven't exactly been Social Joe.

He remembered admiring the legs on a pretty brunette in his Geology class a few days before. When he glanced up and saw that she was smiling at him, he couldn't wait to scuttle out the door to safety.

"Hey," said Lyle, "look at that. I didn't know Colton had hippies."

Right in front of the band, seven or eight colorfully dressed people cavorted to the music. They didn't dance with partners, but all in a group. And their movements were more improvisational flailing and leaping than dancing.

At their center, a tall girl with long, flying brown hair whirled like a dervish. She had strips of brightly colored cloth tied to her wrists and elbows that made arcs through the air as she swung her arms. The worn pair of Levis that hugged her ample hips was dotted with sewn-on patches. Below the knee, the jeans sported large triangles of red bandana cloth sewn into the side seams making them into funky, homemade bell-bottoms.

"Boy those people are nutjobs, man. Half the place is staring at them," said Lyle.

Jamie watched the hippies writhe and twirl. He nodded and said, "Yeah, but they seem to be having more fun than anybody else in here."

Then a particular phrase in the music caught Jamie's ear. "Oh shit!" he sat up with a jerk, "Mike's solo."

He reached for the light board, waited two beats, and then pulled three slides down as he shoved one up. A bright, white spot hit Mike as he started his solo.

Jamie had heard Mike play this line a dozen times in the last few weeks and it was always satisfying, but tonight there was an urgency and a sense of power in his playing that had not been there before. He seemed to be driving it directly at the hippie girl who, because she was right in front of him, shared the spotlight with him. Her dancing became an improvisation on the guitar music she was hearing. Mike played a quick circular riff and she whirled, streamers flying. The notes danced up an octave and her spine seemed to arch up to meet them. She clutched her hair and punctuated the final power chord with a hard thrust of her hips.

Jamie slid the lights back to their original level, the girl was once again lost in the crowd, and the band played to the end of the song.

* * *

Jamie stood behind the table coiling up cables, snapping rubber bands around them, and dropping them into a hard-shell case. The house lights were up, but about half the crowd still milled around the ballroom, some looking for word of a party, others hoping for a last-minute pick up. Lyle had left some time before, Kenny and his date had disappeared not long after.

As Jamie opened the case for the mixer and light board, Mike and a tall, barrel-chested man walked up.

"Jamie," Mike said, "I want you to meet Big Dan. Jamie's our light and sound guy. He's okay."

Jamie put out his hand and it was enveloped by Big Dan's paw.

"A pleasure," Dan said in a deep baritone, "You're comin' over afterward, aren't you? A little get-together at my house."

Jamie glanced at Mike who was nodding his head vigorously.

"Sure, I guess."

"Good. I'll introduce you to a friend of mine. His name's Red."

Mike and Big Dan shared a grin and Dan walked away.

Mike turned back to Jamie. "The gig went pretty well, don't you think?"

"Yeah. People seemed to like it, especially that hippie chick in front. She was having a good time."

"Who?" Mike looked puzzled, "Oh, you must mean that bunch of wackos spaz-dancing by the stage. What with the lights I can't make out faces that well. As soon as we get the van unpacked, we'll drop off my guitar at the dorm, and walk over to Dan's house. He only lives a couple of blocks off campus."

Mike walked toward the backstage door. "So who's Red?"

"You'll find out,"

Jamie went back to packing up and within a few minutes had all the P.A. and light equipment stowed in various cases and sitting on the table. He picked up an armload, turned, and there was the hippie girl from the dance floor standing right in front of him.

Her hair was stuck to her head and neck in sweaty curls and perspiration had soaked the armpits of her peasant blouse. Now up close, he could see her face clearly. Her right eye was dilated to the point he could barely tell the color of it, while the left eye, appearing a regular blue, focused on a point above and behind him. As well as the mismatched eyes, she had large, sensual lips coated with a brilliant red lipstick.

"Far out, man," she said, "Are you, like, with the band?"

Jamie resisted the urge to look behind him to find out what her left eye was staring at.

"Sort of. I do lights and sound."

"Tell them I really dug it, okay? I mean it was like… wow, you know? And give them this from me."

She held his head with both hands, bent down, and pressed her mouth against his. Jamie was nearly lost in the sensation of her lips sliding against his own, first closing then opening, coaxing him to follow. As his mouth opened, her tongue slipped between his teeth, slid up and down his own surprised tongue, then withdrew leaving the taste of her saliva hot in his mouth. She pulled her head away, smiling happily, and skipped in bare feet toward the exit doors.

"I have to go," she yelled, "I have to go find Christopher Robin!"

Jamie, stunned, just stood there with his mouth sagging open, his arms still loaded with cases, and his rock-hard penis pressing painfully against the back of his zipper.

* * *

The door opened as far as the chain latch would allow. Inside, Jamie could see an eyeball checking them out. The door closed again. Jamie felt a little embarrassed and foolish standing out on the step. He could almost hear the question being muttered inside, "Sure, Mike's okay, but who's that other guy?"

Then the door opened wide and Big Dan stood inside, waving them in.

"Get in here, Jesus Christ!" Big Dan slapped Mike and Jamie on the back as they stepped into the little front hall. "Glad you made it through, it's a fuckin' blizzard out there!"

Jamie remembered a few snowflakes falling, but that was about it.

"Come on in and meet some folks," Dan said as he escorted them into the living room.

Jamie had been to some parties in his three months at Colton – beer busts and a few frat parties – but this was a whole different thing. Sure, there was music on the stereo, but not at deafening volume and some of the people there were actually listening to it. Most of the lights were off and the room was lit by a few candles here and there and a lava lamp on the mantel. No one was shouting, breaking things, or picking fights. There was smoke in the air, but it carried the sweet smell of incense as well as something earthier. Jamie sat on a big pillow on the floor next to the couch.

Big Dan sat down on the couch between two pretty women.

"Everybody knows Mike, right?" Big Dan said, "This is a friend of his, works with the band, named... uh..."

"Jamie," Mike said from across the room.

"That's right, this is Jamie. Mike says he's okay. Jamie, this is Theresa my Old Lady, Mindy, Jake, Um,,, um, fuck it. If you want to know who somebody is, ask 'em."

Big Dan reached into the breast pocket of his shirt and pulled out a hand-rolled cigarette.

"And this is Red. Full name-Panama Red. In the South of Mexico, when the dirt and the weather are all just right, a marijuana plant will grow so heavy with cannabis oil that it looks red along the edges. They cut this stuff, hang it upside-down to dry, and then..." Dan paused, "they sell it to me."

There was scattered laughter and cheering from around the room.

Dan lit what Jamie had realized was a "joint", took a long drag, and then, holding his breath, passed it to the woman he introduced as "Theresa my old lady". She took a short drag, then another, and then a third, and also holding her breath, passed the joint along. And so it came to Jamie.

Most of the turning points in a person's life come and go without notice. We choose without thinking, without weighing the rights and wrongs of a thing, without wondering where this road might lead or that one might not. Why bother? As far as we're concerned, there is no choice. What we do has been dictated by all the results of all the choices we've already made, by all the events we've experienced and by all the experiences we hope someday to have. And so, unthinking, we do what we do.

But every now and then the forces that pull and push a person this way and that through their lives come to a momentary kind of equilibrium. And we stand at the point where two paths diverge, looking both ways, trying to decide. Jamie knew he could just smile and pass the joint along. That path was straight, comfortable and safe. The other path was not. The other path twisted down into shadowy, dark woods that concealed possibilities of adventure, beauty, and lurking danger.

Barely hesitating, Jamie put the joint between his lips and took a deep drag. Then, holding his breath like the others, he passed the joint to the fellow to his left.

He tried to peg the taste of the smoke that had filled his lungs. It didn't have an acrid edge to it like cigarette smoke, but was gentler and rounder, somehow. He decided it tasted like plowed fields, freshly cut lawns, and licorice. Then he let his breath go with a "whoosh".

He saw Mike's face, grinning at him from across the room. Jamie smiled back and nodded his head as if to say. "Yeah, man. I can dig it."

Jamie felt a tap on his shoulder. He turned to see another smoldering marijuana cigarette being offered to him by the pretty blonde girl who perched on the arm of the couch. He gave her the same smile and nod he'd just given Mike, took a hit on the joint, and passed it on.

The first joint soon came back around, now much shorter and with a feathered pair of locking tweezers attached to it. Recognizing Mike's roach clip, Jamie caught Mike's eye, held up the clip, and mouthed the words, "very cool". As he took a hit on the roach, Mike left his place and crawled across the room toward him.

"I managed to catch one," Mike said, "And I didn't even have to stomp it first!"

Jamie blew up with laughter. Blowing smoke and coughing, Jamie fell backward in a giggling heap. Hilarity being contagious, quickly the whole room rocked with merriment.

"What'd he say?" several voices demanded.

"I think Mike told him," Big Dan tugged at his beard, "that he'd decided to change his major to agriculture!"

Another wave of unbridled glee rolled around the room. Jamie, weak from laughter, pushed himself back up to a sitting position. "Damn," he said to Mike who was leaning back against the couch, "Those jokes aren't even that funny." Jamie and everyone around him howled again.

Jamie decided he liked laughing. It felt good. He also liked the room and the people around him. But mostly, he liked the feeling inside his head and body. Later he would tell Mike that it was as if someone had upholstered his thoughts with a soft, silk lining.

Jamie was slightly troubled by something. All the moisture in his mouth had disappeared, and his tongue was sticking to his soft palate.

Just as he was thinking about finding a bathroom faucet he could stick his mouth under, Theresa My Old Lady and two other women came out of the kitchen. Theresa MOL carried two large pitchers. Ice cubes floating in the pitchers clinked together musically as she walked.

"Well, people." Big Dan's deep voice rumbled, "No expensive French wine for my guests – it's not good enough. I serve only the best. Strawberry Kool-Aid!"

Everyone cheered as paper cups were filled and passed out.

Jamie took a swallow and quickly decided that this was the most amazing thing he had ever put in his mouth. He had tasted Strawberry Kool-Aid before, of course, but this was in full color and 3-D. He poured half the cup into his mouth and let the liquid roll back and forth across his tongue and swish between his teeth.

Someone bumped something against his shoulder. Jamie swallowed the Kool-Aid and opened his eyes. Mike, a conspiratorial grin on his face, was holding out a large stainless steel bowl. Jamie looked inside to see a huge pile of M&M's twinkling back at him.

Not being much of a candy-eater, Jamie took a few of them out, passed the bowl on, and tossed them into his mouth. It was, he decided later, a near-religious experience. His taste buds began singing, in close harmony, "Hallelujah! Hallelujah!" and the minister's voice demanded, "GET SOME MORE OF THESE!"

Obediently, Jamie lurched after the bowl and scooped up a large handful.

"S'cuse me. Sorry. But these are... these are really good!"

A wave of laughter rolled around the room as Jamie happily filled his face with the crunchy little chocolate candies.

* * *

Later that night, Jamie and Mike walked back to the dorm. The wind had died down, the temperature had dropped, and light snow was still falling. Jamie turned his face to the sky to feel the tiny snowflakes hitting his warm skin.

"Got high, huh?' Mike said.

"Boy, did I. That's like amazing stuff. So how long have you been smoking this and only got around to telling me now?"

"It's the guitar, man. People love to stone the band."

"I'd like to get Waltz and Lyle loaded. Those two are funny enough as it is. Can you imagine high?"

The two looked at each other and laughed.

"Yeah," said Mike, "It'd be a hoot."

"Do you think Big Dan would sell us some of his weed?"

"Not a chance. He doesn't sell to anybody. He says he doesn't have that much or that he doesn't want to get busted as a dealer, but I think it's more of an ego thing for him. He wants people to come and sit at his feet and genuflect a little, you know?"

"Yeah, I can see that. So where else in Colton can you buy marijuana?"

"The term is 'score a lid', my man, and I think I know a dude. I'll check it out for you."

"Cool."

FIVE

Doug Krenovich sat, or rather slumped, at a library table cleaning his fingernails with a penknife. Jamie pulled the chair out across from him and waited for Doug to sit up and pull his big feet in so Jamie could sit down.

"Okay, Shipman," Krenovich put away the penknife, "What's this hot idea of yours that's gonna get Old Honeywell excited enough to give us an A?"

"You want an A, huh? I suppose you could lick your lips, bat your eyelashes, and smile at him a lot. He doesn't seem like the type, but you never know."

"C'mon, man. Spill it. What's this plan of yours?"

"Okay, it's like this." Jamie opened a spiral notebook to a page filled with notes, arrows, and exclamation points. "The teams taking the Affirmative have all gone down pretty much the same path. We should get out of Vietnam because guys are getting killed, no progress is being made, huge amounts of money being spent, etc. etc. Then the Negative trots out all their quotes saying 'If we don't stay Vietnam falls to Communism' and 'Domino Theory" blah blah blah."

"Yeah. So?"

"So we open with 'for a dirt-poor country, Communism can be a good thing Look at China.' I've got some quotes about what a hellhole China was before Mao and the Communists took over. Now they all have 3 squares a day, everybody has a job, and everybody has a place to live. Look at Russia before and after the Revolution-same thing. So the Vietnamese will also be better off. As for the Domino Theory, we say that's bunk. Communism has only ever taken root in poor countries with a huge, starving underclass. We take the money we're spending in Vietnam and instead use it to beef up the U.S. economy. Everybody lives better, Communism gets no foothold."

Krenovich thought about it and then began to nod and chuckle. "I like it. It's pretty far out there. You say you've got quotes?"

"A few," Jamie said as he laid five 3X5 cards on the table. But we've got a little time, maybe we can find some more."

"Okay, man. You're on. I'll try to look up something on modern-day China. This might be kinda fun" Krenovich barked out a sudden laugh. "Kathy French is gonna shit when she realizes that all of her carefully-prepared arguments ain't gonna be doodly. We might get that A after all!"

Jamie stopped for a moment at the end of his final rebuttal in what he hoped was a "dramatic pause" then went on. "The Affirmative asks only that you weigh these arguments we have made unemotionally and objectively; points that our opponents have failed utterly to refute, and I'm sure you will agree with us. As John F. Kennedy said. "Ask not what your country can do for you, but what you can do for your country." And the best thing we can do for our country is to get out of Viet Nam. Thank you."

There were a few spectators in the back of the room and one of them, a scruffy guy in a fatigue jacket, slapped his hands together four or five times before being stared down by the others.

Jamie sat down next to Krenovich who leaned over and muttered, "What the Hell was that last thing?"

"You said we didn't have enough quotes. It was the only one I could think of."

Mr. Honeywell cleared his throat, and the two looked up expectantly.

"Mr. Weibel and Miss French-although you were hesitant and a little wobbly, it was understandable in view of the bizarre and wrongheaded arguments you were having to deal with. B's for both of you. As for you, Mr. Shipman and Mr. Krenovich, the thoughts you expressed are totally contrary to what this Nation and the Universities within it bravely stand for. This kind of thinking is symptomatic of the cancer that is eating away at the foundations of Democracy. At the first meeting of this class, I said I would not fail anyone who at least got up behind the podium and gave it a good try. You two have given me grounds to regret that statement. Against my better judgment, I'm giving each of you a D."

* * *

Jamie walked slowly along a blacktop pathway and muttered to himself. "Stupid, pinheaded idea…"

He kicked a pinecone savagely, briefly considered throwing his *Collegiate Debate* textbook after it, then remembered what the thing cost and put it back under his arm. He thought he heard someone yell "hey!" but he ignored it and kept walking. Again he heard "hey!" this time closer and followed by a "wait up!" He looked back over his shoulder and saw that the guy in the fatigue jacket who'd sat in the back of the room was now hurrying toward him and waving. Jamie stopped and waited for him.

"Hey, Dude," said Fatigue Jacket when he reached Jamie, "I don't mean to bother y'all, but I wanted to tell you how much I dug your Vietnam riff back there. Doug's still in that fat fascist's office whining for a better grade so I thought I'd come on ahead. The name's Schumacher, Winslow Schumacher. But call me Shoes-it's easier."

Jamie was intrigued. This guy had the full-on Young Revolutionary look-the long, stringy hair, the wispy mustache, the fatigue jacket. Everything seemed to fit, except perhaps for the hiking boots-but who could expect sandals in Colorado in October anyway? What was fascinating was how Shoes' appearance and lefty politics clashed hilariously with his deep Southern accent.

If, for no other reason than to keep him talking, Jamie asked, "How do you know Krenovich?"

"We share a microscope in Botany Lab. He told me about this debate thing and it sounded at first like about as much fun as watchin' snow melt. Then he told me what your argument was going to be and I got interested."

"Some argument," Jamie said, "Honeywell hated it."

"Damn straight! What more proof do y'all need that you've got a good argument? No shit. Look at this guy Honeywell. Right-wing Fascist America from the top of his flattop haircut down to his shiny, black cop shoes. He and several million stiff-necked pinheads just like him are the main and only reason guys are gettin' killed over there in Vietnam. The first thing we've got to do is to get these people's attention. And y'all couldn't have got any more of his attention if you'd stuck a cattle prod up his ass."

Suddenly Shoes was hopping up and down, playing the agonized Debate teacher.

"Ow ow!" he yelled, clutching at the crack of his ass, "Get that thing out of there! Christ, that really smarts!"

Jamie doubled over laughing and then, unable to remain upright any longer, dropped to the ground. Shoes grinned and took a deep, theatrical bow as Jamie, still lying in the snow, applauded.

Shoes was helping Jamie to his feet just as Doug Krenovich came up looking more than usually confused.

"What the hell are you guys doing?"

"Making snow angels, what does it look like?"

Krenovich looked at the shapeless dent in the snow and then back at Jamie.

"Amputee snow angels," said Jamie, "How'd you do?"

"Nothin', I even told him it was all your idea and I was just a helpless dupe. He didn't buy it. What an asshole."

At the word "asshole" Shoes made a "bzzzt" sound and yelped. Jamie guffawed.

"You guys," said Krenovich, "are weird."

"Cup of coffee at the Union?" Shoes aimed the question at both of them.

Krenovich shook his head. "Nah. I've got Economics. Big lecture class. I'd cut it but I need the Zs. Tell me what you think..." he put on a pair of dark glasses, "am I asleep or awake? Cool idea, huh?"

"A brainstorm, dude."

"Not today, man," Jamie said to Shoes. "I already told my roommate I'd meet him downtown. But I'm cool for tomorrow. I'm usually in the Union around two. I'll look for you and you can tell me about the dirty deeds of the military-industrial complex."

"Those cocksuckers."

"Right on!" Jamie yelled militantly as he turned away. He held up a clenched fist in a final salute.

* * *

As Jamie moved down the sidewalk, he watched his breath form clouds of steam in the cold autumn air and listened to the heels of his boots thump against the concrete. Then he realized he was singing some Army-issue doggerel marching song to himself,

"I've got a gal in Boston, Mass.

She's got freckles on her ass..."

He immediately tried to change the cadence of his footsteps to something less military. He put a little bounce in his stride and sang under his breath.

"Sugar-pie Honeybunch..."

It occurred to Jamie that despite his best efforts at ignoring the whole noxious mess, he was forming the beginnings of an actual political viewpoint. In the Army, nobody cared much about politics and he had been no exception. He didn't want to know why guys were being shot at in Vietnam, he was just relieved not to be one of them. But now he found himself starting to think about it.

Damn that Honeywell and his stupid Debate class. It's his entire fault, that... what did Shoes call him? That fat fascist.

He felt a little better as he turned down Third Street and headed for Melvin's Music Shop two blocks away.

* * *

Jamie had been idly flipping through the album bins for about ten minutes when Mike slapped him on the arm.

"Hey, Ship. What's goin' on?"

"Oh, just sitting here wonderin'," Jamie pulls an album out of the bin and shows it to Mike. "How come they shoot Jack Kennedy and not Petula Clark?"

"Too short, I'd guess. The bullets keep flying over her head. There's Harvey. Come on."

Mike led Jamie over to the front desk where a guy with long, brown hair and a pair of rectangular granny glasses was ringing up a customer and putting her purchases in a slim paper sack.

"Thanks," the clerk said to the retreating customer, then turned his sleepy gaze to Mike and Jamie.

"Harding. Far out. What's goin' on?"

"Hey, Harvey. Wanted you to meet my roommate, Jamie Shipman. He does the lights and sound for the band."

Jamie said, "Nice to meet you." and stuck his hand out horizontally, then realized Harvey had put his hand up higher for a "Power to the People" style handshake. Jamie quickly put his hand up, just as Harvey was putting his down low. This went on for one or two more tries until they managed to weakly grab each other's hand somewhere in the middle and shake once.

"Sorry," Jamie said, feeling foolish.

"It's cool, man," Harvey said, almost smiling.

The awkward moment passed as a middle-aged, bald man came up to the register followed by a woman and a twelve-year-old boy. The man put a trumpet in an open case on the counter and began punching buttons on the register.

"I'd like to look at some guitar picks," Mike said to Harvey loudly enough for the older man to hear.

"Sure," Harvey said, "right over here."

The three of them walked down to the far end of the counter. Harvey got a display tray of picks out and laid the tray on the counter. Mike picked out several and one-by-one flicked them experimentally on the edge of the tray. As he did so, he spoke to Harvey.

"Jamie here is looking to purchase a little weed. I told him you might be able to fix him up."

"Well, hmm. Tell you what. I'm about to go on my lunch break. Gimme about twenty minutes to score a sandwich, and then come down the alley behind the store. You'll see an old milk truck parked back there. Knock on the door. Cool?"

Back out on the street, Jamie wondered whether or not Harvey's lack of expression and monotone voice were a natural result of smoking lots and lots of marijuana. It was a concern for Jamie, but not a big one because he only intended to smoke maybe a few joints on the weekends and that would be about it.

* * *

Mike rapped twice on the passenger-side door of the milk truck. Coming from inside the vehicle Jaime could make out the muffled sounds of Cream playing "White Room." Then the music stopped and a voice yelled, "Yeah?"

"Mike and Jamie!" Mike said in reply.

While they waited, Jamie stepped back and looked at the old truck. The original paint seemed to have been bright yellow and red; Jamie could see a little bit of it peeking out along the seams and corners. But someone, probably Harvey, had painted it all over in white. With a brush.

Harvey's face appeared briefly at the window, and then the door rolled back. Mike and Jamie climbed into the truck and followed Harvey into the back. Paisley carpeting in several different colors had been glued to the ceiling and walls; there was red shag carpet on the floor and a cushioned platform in the back. Most of the platform was taken up by a large German Shepherd,

"That's Hendrix," Harvey pointed to the dog as he settled himself into a beanbag chair. At the mention of his name, the dog's tail pounded the platform. Mike wedged in next to Hendrix and Jamie sat cross-legged on the floor.

Harvey pushed the eight-track cassette back into the machine and Clapton picked up his solo where it had left off.

"Lookin' for some herb, huh?" Harvey asked loudly over the music, "Let's see what we've got." He popped the last bite of sandwich into his mouth, rolled up the paper wrapping and threw it in a corner. Then he reached up under the back of the driver's seat and pulled down a cigar box that had been wedged there.

When Harvey opened the box, Jamie could see several plastic baggies containing some dried, green stuff that looked a lot like Oregano. One of the bags contained half as much as the others and this was the one Harvey picked up along with a corncob pipe.

"I'm thinkin' a bowl right now will put a nice glow on the afternoon. You cool with that?"

Aware that this was something of a test, Jamie nodded and said, "Far out."

Mike smiled and said, "Stoned in the afternoon? I can dig it."

In a few minutes, the pipe was making its way around the truck.

"This is Mexican weed," Harvey blew out a lungful of smoke. "Not Red or Gold, but it'll get you loaded."

Harvey picked up one of the rolled baggies and held it out toward Jamie. "Ten bucks?"

Jamie, who had been listening to Jack Bruce singing about Ulysses and the Sirens and wondering how the sirens managed to sing with a wa-wa pedal, found himself staring uncomprehendingly at Harvey. He knew there was some reason this man was holding this thing up and speaking to him but his thoughts were like wandering kittens that he had to find, pick up, and put safely back into a box.

"Uh...what?" Jamie said, his mouth hanging open.

Mike guffawed causing a ragged puff of smoke to blow out of his nose.

"Oh! Oh yeah. Sure. Thanks." Jamie dug his wallet out of his pants. He slipped a glance at Mike to see if he was chipping in, but Mike was suddenly preoccupied with scratching Hendrix behind the ears.

"I hope you dig that shit, man." Harvey tucked the money into his shirt. "But if anyone asks where you got it, say it was, like, from some freaked-out Vietnam vet who was hitchhiking through town, okay?"

"Oh yeah, I remember the cat," Jamie said, "Tattoos and shit, right?"

"That's him. But if you're looking for another lid, like, down the road, come by my pad after dinner some night." Harvey turned to Mike, "You've been to my pad, haven't you?"

"If I have, I was too stoned to remember."

"Knotty Pine Apartments on 23rd. Ground floor right. Bring your ears, man. I just scored a new Altec receiver. Joplin through that is a heavy trip, no shit."

After they'd left the truck and Harvey had gone back to work, Mike and Jamie walked slowly back toward campus.

Jamie smiled to himself as he let his senses run from one sensation to the next as if they were kids in a toy store. Birds chirping on the telephone wires, the rich smell of the exhaust from a passing bus, the prickly warmth of the wool scarf around his neck.

"Nice," Jamie said.

Mike raised one eyebrow. "Excuse me?"

"It's like they invented the word 'nice' just to describe how I'm feeling right now, y'know? Except for maybe a little cottonmouth."

"Yeah, I could use a cold Coke, for sure. Student Union?"

"Man, I don't know if I could handle the Union." Jamie made a sour face. "How about we just go down to that little off-campus grocery store, buy some chips, and get Cokes out of the machine at Hargreaves. Besides, I think they sell cheap pipes at that store."

"Gonna buy a pipe?"

"Have to. Don't have the faintest idea how to roll a joint."

* * *

Lyle, in the shotgun seat of Kenny's car, had just taken a long drag and was holding the pipe out to Kenny who turned slowly to look at him, a benign smile on his face.

"Want a hit?" Lyle asked in the high, squeaky voice of someone holding his breath.

Kenny just smiled and idly fingered some loose skin above his Adam's apple. "What a good feeling this is. I like this very much."

"Take the pipe, asshole," Lyle squeaked and poked Kenny in the shoulder with it.

"For me? Why thank you. Don't mind if I do." Kenny took the pipe and grinned at Jamie and Mike in the back seat. "This is getting high, huh? Well if this is high then I been low for way too long."

Kenny put the abbreviated pipe in his mouth and drew in.

When Jamie had first shown his new pipe to Mike, Mike had immediately pulled the black plastic mouthpiece off and chucked it in the trash.

"There, that's a dope pipe."

Jamie had looked puzzled.

"You want that shit coating your lungs, man, not the inside of some plastic tube."

Jamie took the pipe from Kenny just as Lyle let his breath go with a whoosh. Lyle put his hands up in front of his face, rubbed his fingertips together, and giggled.

"Wooh. Heeehee," His voice turned suddenly mock-serious. "Gentlemen, I am fucked up."

"Well, yeah," Kenny said, "But did you get high?"

Everyone laughed, even Lyle.

About time they got off.

They had gone through more than half the lid before Lyle and Kenny could say they were feeling the effects of the pot. Jamie and Mike, on the other hand, had been stoned by the end of the first bowlful. Determined to give his friends a good experience, Jamie kept refilling the pipe. Now he was so loaded he felt like a hippopotamus was sitting on his head. Weirder yet, whenever he would look from one side of the car to the other, rather than panning over and refocusing, his eyes would roll to their new destination like marbles down a rain gutter.

He would have liked to tell the others about this, but Jamie knew that by the time he was reaching the end of the first sentence, the thought that had triggered the whole thing would have already waved goodbye and slipped out the nearest exit.

"Hey Waltz," Mike said, "you cool to drive?"

"Any time, any place," Waltz replied, "where did you have in mind?"

"Frosty Muggs."

Kenny had put the Chevy in gear and was pulling out onto the street before the grunts of agreement had died down.

Kenny looked down the road, then at the dashboard and his hands on the wheel. He grinned a toothy grin. "Hey, you know what?"

"Chicken's butt?" Lyle said.

"Nope. What I was going to say is that driving this car is... well, pretty fun!"

"Being that you're the only one of us that has a car," Mike said, "I'd say that's a damned lucky thing. What time does that place close, anyway?"

"Wouldn't it be the shits to get there and the doors are all locked?" Lyle said.

"And my mouth all set for root beer," Jamie moaned.

"Maybe they'll let you suck the snot out of Frosty's nose," Kenny said.

There was a general reaction of "Eww. That's gross, man. Yuck."

Frosty Muggs was not only the name of a Drive-in that specialized in root beer served in cold, frosted mugs; but also the name of the cartoon that served as the business' logo. Frosty was an elfin character with snow on his shoulders and icicles hanging from his chin and nose. It was common knowledge in the town that the stalactites that hung from Frosty's long proboscis were, in fact, the liquid results of a bad cold.

Kenny made a right turn onto Main Street. Up ahead at the next intersection, Police cars and an ambulance surrounded two wrecked cars in the middle of the street. Red and yellow lights atop the emergency vehicles lit the scene with a pulsating, eerie glow.

"Ooh, shit," Lyle said, "it looks like a bad one."

"Bummer," Mike added.

Kenny slowed down as they approached the wreck.

"I'd say the blue car ran the stop sign," Jamie said, "hit the white one and spun it around end-for-end."

"Hey, look! It's Sherm the Sperm!" Kenny cried.

On the edge of the accident scene and directly ahead of them, stood a uniformed Policeman waving traffic around. As they passed, Kenny smiled and waved. The Policeman gave him a chilly smile and a perfunctory salute, waved them along, and then turned to the next car.

"Who was that?" Mike said.

"I told you. It's Sherm the Sperm."

"Good, Waltz," Lyle rolled his eyes, "that clears it up for 'em."

"His name is Larry Sherman. He was in High School with Lyle and me. We got drunk a few times. Nice guy. I hadn't seen him since we graduated."

Although he'd only had a quick look at Sherm the Sperm, Jamie couldn't reconcile that cold look of implacable authority with the term "nice guy". He knew it had more to do with the uniform than the man, but he still couldn't quite get his head around it.

"So you and the cop are pals, huh? Mike said. "Maybe we should go back and ask him if he wants a hit or two."

"Oh yeah," Kenny said, "That's a great idea."

Conversation in the car tapered off as they cruised down Main Street. Jamie relaxed and let the thoughts of Policemen and accidents drift away so he could get back to the business of being stoned.

After a while, Kenny broke the silence. "Uh... I sorta forgot. Where was it we were going again?"

* * *

Later, the four of them sat in a booth in the back corner of Frosty Muggs. Four baskets of fries and four mugs of root beer had quickly disappeared in an orgy of mouth-stuffing punctuated only by grunts of pleasure and the occasional belch. Jamie was using his spit-moistened fingers to pick up and eat the little crunchy bits still hiding in the bottom of the basket.

"You know what the weird thing about that was?" Kenny's question, coming out of nowhere, prompted only puzzled looks.

"Excuse me for asking, Waltz my boy." Lyle finally said, "But just what the fuck are you talking about?"

"Oh. I was talking about Sherm the Sperm. Last Spring he told me he was thinking about going down to Denver to the Police Academy. Tried to get me to sign up too."

Jamie said, "I'm guessing you didn't do it."

"Oh yeah, I did. And now you're all busted."

Lyle threw a soggy French fry at him.

"No, really," said Kenny, "the weird part is that I thought about it. But in the end, I didn't go and because he'd knocked up his girlfriend and had to get married, he did."

"So what you're saying," Lyle said, "is that if you had stayed awake that night on top of Betty Sturdevant, we might be sitting here with Sherm the Sperm, and you could be standing in the street back there in a cop uniform."

"And writing in your little notebook," Mike said. "Sherm and Lyle just drove by. Bloodshot eyes and giggling. Very suspicious."

Six

Jamie sat alone at a table in the Student Union and tried to read a paragraph in his American History textbook for the third time. He knew it was about Daniel Webster and some pre-Civil War rah-rah, but by the time he'd gotten to the second or third sentence, his eyes would still be obediently looking at the words, but his brain would have its feet up, staring into space, and wondering how houseflies stuck to the ceiling.

He regretted buying a used textbook. At the time, he was thrilled not only to get the book at a lower price but that the previous owner had hi-lighted passages all the way through. It would be, he thought, like getting a quick-study version of the text. Unfortunately, the markings made little or no sense and seemed to have been put there only out of spite or whimsy. In the paragraph he was trying to read, the hi-lighted phrases were "Senator from Massachusetts", "wife", "three times", "disappointment and sense of futility".

Jamie knew that if he were to put these tidbits together into a logical sequence and regurgitate them in an exam, it might provide some graduate student with a good laugh, but would kick his chances for a decent grade right in the balls.

At times like this, he toyed with the thought of strangling his roommate, Mike. The guy never took notes in class-at least those times when he deigned to show up-and never studied in the evenings or between classes. The only times he would open a textbook were on the days of the exams when he'd sit down in the library and skim the relevant chapters for an hour before class. He'd then take the test, stroll out with a B, and go listen to music. In order to get a B on the same test, Jamie would have to take copious notes, pore over them for hours, read and re-read the text, then sweat bullets over every test question.

Jamie, by nature, was not a jealous person. He didn't mind Mike's musical talent or even his ease with women. But this studying thing, or lack of the need for it, made Jamie's teeth grind together.

A pile of books suddenly dropped onto the table and Jamie looked up with a jolt. Shoes stood there gesturing at the stack.

"There it is-a great, steamin' pile of useless bullshit. Y'all enjoy the aroma while I go get a cup of coffee."

Jamie chuckled to himself as he watched Shoes wend his way through the tables toward the snack bar. He turned back to his History book ready to give it one more try.

A few minutes later another set of books hit the table, this time without the drama, and Doug Krenovich dropped into a seat.

"Hey, man," Krenovich said, "Have you seen Shoes? He said he was gonna be here."

"Over getting coffee even as we speak. How's it going?"

"It could be better, but it could be a hell of a lot worse." He looked dubiously at Jamie's open History book. "You studying? I'm impressed."

"Nah. I like to open the book now and then to air it out. Keeps that mildewed smell down."

Shoes reappeared carrying a cup of coffee and sat down.

"Neither of you two is twenty-one, right?"

"What's it to you?" Jamie said, "looking for someone to buy you some beer?"

"Just wondering if you were going to vote."

"Vote for what?" Krenovich looked puzzled.

"It's Election Day-the first Tuesday in November. Didn't you see the demonstrators out front on the Quad?"

"No, I came in the side door," Krenovich said, the befuddled look on his face growing. "Colton has a demonstration? You're shittin' me."

"If you consider half a dozen lunatics carrying bizarre signs and walking around in a circle a "demonstration", then yeah."

"This I gotta fuckin' see."

Krenovich grabbed his jacket off the back of the chair and headed for the main door. Jamie and Shoes followed.

The main entrance to the Student Union sported columns and arches and half a dozen wide steps that cascaded down to an even wider cement slab. Enclosed by the wings of the Student Union on three sides with the street on the fourth, this expanse of concrete was called "the Quadrangle" or more usually, "the Quad".

Jamie and Shoes came out of the door and walked over to stand with Krenovich on the top step. In the middle of the quad were the demonstrators just as Shoes had described them. Six or seven hippies in bright-colored clothes that bordered on theatrical walked in a circle and chanted "Get Their Goat, Don't Vote!" Several carried signs that read "Express Yourself, Don't Vote!" and "A Vote for Anyone is a Vote for Them." The demonstrators were oblivious to the heckling and catcalls that came from a knot of onlookers wearing boots and Stetson hats.

"Get a haircut!"

"Get a Job!"

Suddenly, from right behind him, Jamie heard Shoes yell, "COWBOYS SUCK!"

Shoes quickly stepped away from Jamie and gave him a shocked look as if he couldn't believe Jamie would yell such a thing out loud.

Everyone in the quad was staring at Jamie. The Ag boys had daggers in their eyes.

"Hey, fuck you!" one short, thick-necked cowboy yelled at Jamie before he turned and followed his friends to class.

Jamie looked at Shoes and Krenovich who were giggling merrily.

"Thanks, assholes. You trying to get me killed?"

He turned back to look at the demonstrators and noticed one of the women was smiling at him. He recognized her as the hippie chick who had kissed him after the dance a month before. She wiggled her fingers at him, winked, and went back to chanting.

Krenovich, who'd watched this happen, was goggle-eyed.

"You know her?"

"Her? Not really," Jamie turned to go back inside, "But her tongue and I are old friends."

Seven

Jamie walked past an old sign with chipped paint that announced "Knotty Pines Apartments" and up to the first door on the right. The chill that hung in the dark night air made the steam of his breath linger for a while before it dissipated. He knocked on the door.

A moment later the porch light went on and Jamie saw the blinds move in the nearby window. Then the door opened and Harvey, dressed in a checkered bathrobe, pj's, and slippers, waved Jamie inside.

"Come on in, man. It's cold out there."

"Thanks, man," said Jamie as he stepped inside and shut the door behind him. "I hope I didn't come over too late."

"No, no, It's cool. Take off your coat, have a seat, want a cup of tea?"

"Lipton's?"

"No, not that shit. This is herb tea. Some guys down in Boulder mix it up and display it in big glass jars. They sell it by the ounce. It's pretty far out. Want some?"

"Sure. Yeah."

While Harvey banged around in the kitchen, Jamie sat on one of the big pillows that lay in a pile on one end of the room. He had been to Harvey's apartment before, but both times it had been just to buy a lid, say thanks, and leave. He'd never really gotten a chance to look around the place till now.

The posters that covered the walls seemed to be of three different general types. There were Op-art pictures of undulating checkerboards and swirls of intricate design that flowed into or back out of an infinite point, depending on how you looked at them. There were also posters that Jamie could only categorize as "Message" posters. These consisted of marijuana plants, naked men and women having sex in different positions, and, of course, peace signs. Finally, there were the Rock and Roll posters-Hendrix, The Doors, Quicksilver Messenger Service, and Mountain. What most of the posters had in common were their loud, Day-Glo colors. Jamie glanced up at the ceiling and, sure enough, there was a fixture with an unlit black light bulb in it.

It must be pretty trippy in here when the black light is on.

Harvey came back into the room carrying two mugs that had little chains hanging over their sides. He also carried a small bowl that he set down on the floor before handing a mug to Jamie.

"When the tea is like, steeped enough, you can drop the tea ball in there." Harvey indicated the bowl as he settled onto one of the other pillows.

Jamie pulled up on the little chain in his mug. On the end of it was an egg-shaped metal ball with holes in it. He moved the ball up and down and the tea seemed to get darker with every dunk.

"I like your posters," said Jamie, the dutiful guest. "They're pretty far out."

"Yeah, wait till you dig it with the black light on. I gotta get a new bulb, that one crapped out, but when it's on it gets pretty trippy in here."

Since he'd said it without a trace of irony, Jamie just nodded in an "I can dig it" kind of way and grinned into his mug as he sipped his tea.

"This herb tea is kinda tasty," Jamie said as he took another sip. "Oh, and speaking of herbs in general..."

"I imagine you're looking to score a lid, right?" Harvey said, "me too and a bunch of other guys. The dude that was selling to me got busted down in Mexico last week. The Federales stopped him with eight keys hidden in his door panels. Mexican jail is a bum trip, man."

"Ouch. The poor fucker."

"Yeah, ouch. No shit. And the town is dry, man. I smoked the last of my personal stash two days ago. Of course, if you and your friends are into it, I know a dude who is selling Orange Wedge right now."

"What's that?"

"It's STP. Psychedelic shit. STP is like LSD's big brother; I mean like a twenty-four-hour trip, man. Very far out. You interested?"

Jamie chewed on his lip while he thought about it and was surprised to realize that he was indeed interested. Up to this moment he'd been content to be an average-Joe kind of guy. Given, he had recently begun to smoke a little pot now and then, but he'd never seen himself as some acid-headed hippie. Now, suddenly, here he was-ready to "get psychedelic".

"I am interested, yeah. I'd like to meet the dude."

"You got it. Get your coat."

"We're going there tonight?"

"He's crashing upstairs for a while. I thought we'd just run up there. You cool with that?"

"Sure."

Within minutes the two of them were bundled up and out the door.

"The cat's name is Random," Harvey said as they climbed the stairs, "At least, that's what he tells everybody to call him. He's kinda spacey, but going around with a bagful of Orange Wedge, what do you expect?"

They'd reached the upper landing and Harvey knocked on the door to the right. After a long wait, Jamie heard a muffled voice come from the other side of the door.

"Uh... who is it?"

"Harvey"

"Harvey lives downstairs, man."

"No, it's me. I'm Harvey and I brought a friend."

"Oh, okay. Come on in."

The door opened and Harvey and Jamie quickly stepped in and shut the cold out behind them. A tall man with bad posture and a drooping Fu Manchu mustache looked at them through blood-shot eyes.

"Random, this is Jamie, a friend of mine who's looking to get high. Jamie-Random."

Jamie got the handshake right this time. Random gave him an assessing look as he scratched the back of his neck.

"Okay, cool. Take off your coats, have a sit."

Jamie sat on a ratty couch and Harvey perched on the opposite arm. Random left the room. In a few minutes he slouched back in carrying a small ceramic jar, which he placed on the coffee table. He sat cross-legged on the floor, took the top off the jar, and took a clear, plastic bag full of bright orange pills out and laid it on the table.

"It's Orange Wedge, man. It came from San Francisco. Five bucks a hit."

Jamie looked closely at the pills in the bag. He'd been expecting them to somehow look like wedges from a real orange but they were regular-looking pills, smaller than an aspirin but proportionally thicker."

"STP, right?' Jamie said.

"You got it, dude. They last a looong time. These even can be splitters if that's your trip, half of one is enough to get you off really good."

"Well, I want to get four, for my friends and me, but I can't be sure that they'll want theirs, you know?"

"I'd say buy them, man," Harvey said, "If those cats don't want them, let me know and I can guide you to some people who'll take them off your hands."

"In that case," Jamie said as he dug out his wallet, "what the fuck, let's do it."

A few minutes later, Jamie was standing back out on the walk in front of Harvey's apartment as Harvey unlocked his door.

"Good night, man," Jamie said, "Thanks for the tea and for turning me on to this stuff."

"Stone groove, man," Harvey replied. "You and your friends are gonna dig it. In fact, some people are coming over Friday night. We'll all be tripping. Nothing too heavy, you know, some music, a mellow scene. You guys are welcome to slide by if you like. Don't knock, it'll freak people out. Just come in."

"Yeah, that might be cool," Jamie said, "Maybe we'll see you."

* * *

Jamie, Lyle, and Kenny sat around a table and looked down at three orange pills in the center of a plate. The table was in the dining room of Kenny's house. The rest of the Walsingham family had left the day before to visit relatives in Nebraska and wouldn't be back until Sunday evening.

Lyle glanced up at Jamie. "Is Mike gonna take his?"

"He said he was going to drop it after he finishes a gig at the local High School."

"How come you're not doing the lights?"

"The high school kids are doing their own. So, are we gonna do this, or what?"

"It's not LSD, right?" Kenny said, "I might want to have kids someday."

"Nah," Lyle said, "it's STP, whole different stuff. And look at it this way-you might <u>want</u> to fuck up your chromosomes, then your kids could have a chance to come out normal."

"Oh, that's reassuring. Fuck you very much. I say let's drop 'em and get it over with."

"Tell you what," Jamie said, "this dude, Random, said they were splitters. So let's each do half. If we like it, we can drop the other half later. Have you got a razor blade, Waltz?"

Kenny got up and headed into the kitchen. Lyle yelled after him, "And bring a glass of water. I don't want to choke this thing down dry."

* * *

Ten minutes later, the three sat in the living room. Disappointment hung heavy in the air,

"Nothin'," Lyle said, "Not even a little buzz. You got anything?"

Kenny just slowly shook his head.

"Maybe the dude was full of shit about them being splitters," Jamie said, "Let's drop the other half."

"May as well," Waltz stood up.

"Where the hell are you going?" Lyle said.

"To get another glass of water. For me. You may choke if you wish."

"Asshole."

* * *

Another ten minutes later and the air of disappointment was deeper with tinges of anger.

"We got ripped off!" said Lyle. "That fuckin' Random, or whatever his name is, is probably sitting around, counting our money, and laughing his ass off."

"Is there anything we can do?" Kenny asked Jamie.

"Well," Jamie said, "I know where the guy lives, but I don't know if I'm up for a heavy confrontation scene. We could go over to Harvey's and ask him. He said some people were coming over to drop this stuff and trip out over there. Right now they're probably as pissed as we are. It couldn't hurt to show up and join the mob."

"That's better than anything I can think of. Waltz?"

"Let me get my coat."

Jamie stood up with them. "Hey Waltz, you got any pitchforks or torches?"

His hand on the doorknob, Kenny turned and gave Jamie a mystified look.

"It's from Frankenstein, nitwit," Lyle said," I'll tell you in the car."

"I knew that," Kenny said.

* * *

Colton being as small as it is, within a few minutes Jamie was leading Lyle and Kenny up the walk to Harvey's apartment. There was only a dim light that leaked around the edges of the curtains, but the stereo inside was playing loud enough that certain bass notes were making the window panes buzz. Jamie was mentally rehearsing what he was going to say. *"We never got off..."* No, too weak... *"It's been over a half hour since we dropped, man...'* Better."

Jamie opened the door, stepped across the threshold, and his brain and body exploded in a geyser of brightly colored fireworks. It was as if whoever had been in charge of keeping the intake of sensations and the outflow of thoughts and feelings all damped down to a manageable level had waited until Jamie came in the door and then thrown the floodgates wide open. He stood at the center of a maelstrom. At that moment, everything in the room had developed great depths of meaning, of presence, and of beauty. Beauty especially-more than he had ever before thought possible.

His vision had changed. Anything he looked at soon became a minutely detailed collection of colors and shapes. Each color seemed to move and pulsate at a slightly different rate than all the colors around it. But when he looked closely at a certain color, it would dissolve into a myriad of other colors.

The music coming from the Stereo speakers was Jefferson Airplane's "Crown of Creation". It was creating intricate sonic shapes that moved and danced together in the air. But there was another presence amid this dance and he suddenly knew it was total silence, wrapping itself around the music and vibrating in quiet counterpoint. Just before the symmetry of it overwhelmed him, he realized he could back away just by focusing his attention on something else.

A girl danced alone in front of the stereo. She was thin, with mouse-brown hair, and wore thick, round glasses. Her dancing was free form and without particular grace or rhythm. And yet the effect was mesmerizing. Every time one of her arms would sweep through the air, a dozen af-ter-images of an arm would chase behind it. A quick hand gesture looked like a fan made of fingers.

Jamie turned to Lyle and Kenny. He wondered if the STP had af-fected them as suddenly and as dramatically as it had him. One look gave him his answer. Both of them had hugely dilated eyes like pairs of big, black dinner plates. A look of shocked wonder was on both their faces.

All three of them looked at each other and the communication was instantaneous. "Yes, we got off! And hot-damn, what a ride!" Simulta-neously, they burst into laughter-deep, joyous laughter propelled by the surges of energy within them.

"Hey, check this out," said a voice at Jamie's elbow.

The voice belonged to a tall, boney teen-ager with a baby face. The boy held a coffee can in his hands. There were four switches on the side of the can and three colored light bulbs on top of it. The boy snapped one switch and Jaime, Lyle, and Waltz all watched as a red light bulb came on. It went out just as another switch was snapped. After a pause, a blue light came on. Snap. Both the red and blue light came on. Snap. The blue light went out and after a moment, the red went out as well. Snap. The yellow light came on. Snap. The yellow light stayed on and was joined by the blue. Finally, the boy snapped the bottom switch, all the lights went out, and he put the can under his arm.

"It's a science project for school. Flashy, huh? Heh-heh. I'm McNulty. Jack McNulty. This Orange Wedge is pretty far out stuff, don't you think? Like..." McNulty put his hand flat on the top of his head, and then flung it into space like a fighter plane catapulted off an aircraft carrier. "pzzzZZZzzz! Y' know what I mean? Like... Wow!"

"Wow." Jamie, Lyle, and Kenny all said at once. Flying on the drug and mesmerized by McNulty's frenetic actions and monologue, "wow" seemed to be the only word their mouths felt capable of saying.

"What a great word 'wow' is if you think about it," McNulty went on with barely a pause, "Kinda puts the whole experience into one single syllable. Wow! Woooowwww. wow. See what I mean?"

"Oh wow," Jamie said.

"Exactly! Are you guys Harvey's friends?"

"Yeah. Sorta. Is he around?"

"That's him in the chair over there. He doesn't talk or do much when he's on acid. We call him the Mad Skulker."

Jamie followed McNulty's gesture and saw Harvey in the far corner of the apartment; he sat in a shabby armchair, his knees pushed together and his hands shoved under his thighs. He stared at a poster on the wall. Harvey must have bought a new black light bulb because the posters were glowing with garish, Day-Glo colors. The op-art ones that had seemed to suggest movement when he'd seen them two days before were now definitely moving and Jamie felt drawn into this endless march of checkerboard patterns.

When he finally pulled his attention back-it could have been two minutes or twenty-he was standing alone. McNulty was across the room talking animatedly to a chubby blonde woman. Kenny stood next to him, nodding and laughing at nearly everything the boy was saying. Not far away, Lyle stood at a low bookshelf carefully examining a small rubber dinosaur. Jamie went over to him.

"How's it goin' man?" Jamie said and then pointed to the dinosaur, "Found a new friend?"

"It's a Stegosaurus. See, on his belly it says 'Stegosaurus' in raised letters. Makes me wonder, what if I woke up one day and it said 'Man' on my belly in raised letters."

Lyle looked up at Jamie and his eyes began to twitch and then a short, sharp shudder ran up his body and it seemed to Jamie as if something blew out through the top of Lyle's head.

"Jesus Christ," Lyle said, "What the fuck was that?"

Jamie held his hands out, palms up, and grinned his incomprehension.

"Well, now it's official," Lyle said, "I'm fucking crazy. And you know what? I don't care!" And he began to laugh.

At first, Jamie joined in the laughter because Lyle made such a merry sight-whooping wildly as he clutched the little dinosaur. But then Jamie had to admit to himself that he, too, had pretty much lost touch with reality, and how funny that actually was.

Soon both of them were sitting on the floor, still laughing, too weak to stand up. Kenny and McNulty were standing over them.

"What's so funny?" Kenny said.

"I'm totally nuts," Lyle said as he tried to catch his breath.

"No, no, no," Jamie said. "He's just mildly deranged. I'm the one who's completely out of my mind."

"Bullshit! I'm probably the craziest motherfucker that ever... well, except for Waltz. He's crazier than both of us put together."

Another round of raucous laughter burst out. Other people in the room happily laughed along with them. Not because they had heard what had been said, only for the sheer joy of laughing.

* * *

Jamie sat in the back seat of Kenny's car and rolled a flashlight battery back and forth from one palm to the other. He'd sat on the battery when he'd gotten into the car. Now he felt its amazing smoothness, hefted its weight, and wondered how it had come to be where it was when he sat on it. McNulty sat next to him, elbows on the back of the front seat, and swapped stories about John Krauter with Lyle and Kenny.

Earlier, McNulty had slapped himself on top of the head and said, "Hey, Krauter's playing tonight at the Full Moon. You guys want to go?"

"Krauter? You mean Crazy John Krauter?" Kenny said.

"Yep. That's him. He's going to play guitar and sing folk music and shit."

"I didn't know he could play."

"He can't, actually. He's terrible. But he's really serious about it. Should be hysterical."

The whole procedure of putting on coats and hats and walking out of the apartment was just too much hassle for most of the people there to even consider. Lyle, Jamie, Kenny, and McNulty were the only ones who left.

Once they were in Kenny's car, Jamie said, "Who's this Krauter?"

"Krauter was in our class at Colton High," Lyle said.

"Class of '67. Woo hoo!" Kenny shouted.

"Still got that old school spirit eh, Waltz?'

"Bet your ass. You know what they say-be true to your school."

"Thank you, dumbass Beach Boy."

"That's mister dumbass Beach Boy to you."

After a short silence, McNulty said, "Wasn't he the Student Body President or something?"

"Who?"

"Krauter."

"Oh yeah, Krauter. And Quarterback of the football team, and National Honor Society, the All-American boy."

"After he graduated, he traveled to San Francisco."

"1967-The Summer of Love."

"He got psychedelicized." Kenny slowly rolled the word off his tongue. "He came home one freaky dude."

"I heard he moved out of his bedroom and into the basement," McNulty said. "His only furniture was a mattress and a candle."

"Yeah, that's true," Lyle said, "and he changed his name and wouldn't answer to any name but his new one. And he wouldn't tell his mom what the new one was."

"Can you hear her standing at the top of the basement stairs? Oh, Frank! George! Uh... Pascual!"

The roar of an 18-wheel rig going by in the opposite direction interrupted their boisterous laughter. The truck had all its running lights on, so even after it had passed, long trails of orange were still going by.

"Wow," they all said together.

"Hey, we could go out to the airport," Kenny said, "and lay down on the runway and watch the planes land right over us. Wouldn't that be far out?"

Everyone stared at Kenny, dumbfounded.

"I mean if Colton had an airport."

Lyle chuckled as he shook his head. "Yeah, that does put a little hitch in your plan, there Waltz. But if Colton did have one, and it wasn't so cold, and if airport security didn't come out and beat the crap out of us, and if the planes didn't touch down too soon and smear us across the pavement, then yeah, I suppose it'd be pretty far out."

Kenny just grinned and said, "See? I told ya."

While the other three tried to remember where they were going, Jamie looked down at his feet. He noticed that little pinpoints of colored light were floating up out of the darkness. They moved at a stately pace as they twinkled in and out of view. The longer he watched, the more intricate their patterns and color shifts became. Just as he began to see gossamer threads of light writhing slowly among the colors, McNulty shouted, "Full Moon!"

Everyone looked at him, startled. Then Jamie said, "Oh yeah, Full Moon Coffee House. That's where we were going. Is it far?"

"Actually, we're close. Turn left on Orchard, a couple of blocks," Lyle said, "On the right."

"This STP stuff is great!" Kenny made the turn, "You don't have to worry if you don't remember where you're going, it'll get you there anyway."

"And in Technicolor." McNulty added, "Hey, did you guys each drop a whole one?"

"We did a half," Jamie said. Kenny pulled into a parking space. "But then we thought we weren't getting off so we each did another half."

"Good news for you. Do you know what Random said about them being splitters? That's bullshit. They're actually four-ways! Look at Harvey, he dropped a quarter and he's a zombie. You did four times too much!" McNulty laughed himself out of the car.

Jamie, Kenny, and Lyle looked at each other. A slightly worried giggle quickly turned to a what-the-hell laugh and they piled out into the night.

Jamie had to stop and make sure he hadn't left his battery in the car. He found it in the pocket of his jacket, squeezed it once, and hurried after the others.

* * *

The four of them sat on mismatched folding chairs around a small table. Their attention was on a tiny stage in a corner of the room. On that stage, a young man with a wispy beard and long hair struggled to replace a broken string on his guitar.

It had been something of an adventure just getting in the door. Jaime hadn't realized how odd it would be to deal with people who weren't, as

McNulty had put it, "ripped out of their skulls." A tall, skinny guy with a dark goatee had been standing at the door requesting a $2 cover charge for each of them. Kenny realized he hadn't any money, Lyle only had a Twenty, and McNulty had a handful of quarters. Jamie had a couple of singles in his wallet, but they felt weird and greasy to the touch and he got into a whole what-if-they're-counterfeit and who-cares-if-they-are-it's-just-stupid-pieces-of-paper thing that had him standing there rubbing the bills between his fingers and staring at them blankly.

They eventually got to a table and were able to focus on the performer. It was difficult for Jamie to tell if Krauter could carry a tune or not because the song, obviously self-written, didn't seem to have a tune to carry. The final chorus was the line, "Negroes, Indians, and Jews-I love you." repeated four times. Each repetition got louder and the guitar strumming more strenuous until, on the final "you", one of the guitar strings broke with a discordant "twang".

There was a round of polite applause and Jamie slapped his hands together a few times so as not to stand out. That was the challenge, Jamie had quickly realized, of being this stoned in public. Staying unnoticed among the crowd while all of your senses were being lavishly overwhelmed seemed to be a manageable thing, but just barely.

He was congratulating himself on how well he was blending in when a female voice at his elbow said, "Can I get you anything?" He turned to find a girl standing there holding a pad and pencil expectantly while she chewed lazily on a wad of gum. Instantly, all the possible permutations and combinations of who she was and what she meant by the question went careening through his head. He felt a bolt of energy climb up his spine, crash through the blizzard of thoughts and blow out the top of his skull. The girl stopped chewing her gum and stared at him, as did everyone at the table. Jamie managed to squeak out, "What have you got?" and followed her gesture to a large blackboard with menu items scrawled on it. Jamie's intention was to quickly scan the board, select something, and be done with it. But it was difficult when the chalk-line letters and numbers were wriggling and changing into other letters and numbers. Add to that the thought of putting anything solid into a stomach that had been queasy and fluttery all night and he was completely stumped for an answer.

He heard McNulty say, "I'll have a Coke, please," and knew he only had moments to come to a decision. When he saw two words near the bottom of the board that seemed to spell out "herb tea" he remembered the pleasant, earthy drink Harvey had given him and croaked out his order.

The girl made a note on her pad and said, "Chamomile okay?"

The word was totally meaningless to him, but he nodded and she went around to the other side of the table to take orders from Lyle and Kenny.

McNulty leaned toward Jamie and said, "Nice rush."

"What?"

"You know..." McNulty put his elbows out and faked a rising shudder that ended with his eyes bulging. Jamie tried to protest but McNulty just pointed at him and laughed. Kenny and Lyle, having placed their orders, turned and wanted to know what was funny. So McNulty repeated the pantomime for them.

Several people shushed at them from around the room and the four had to stifle their giggling and focus on Krauter, who was glowering at them from the stage.

When it was quiet, Krauter cleared his throat and pushed his hair back behind his ears.

"For this next tune, I'd like my friend Geraldine to come up and sing. Come up here, Geraldine."

He gestured toward the back where a tall, dark-haired woman was making her way toward the stage. When she got there, she waited while Krauter adjusted the microphone for her. She had a thin face and thin shoulders and arms. Below that, the thinness quickly gave way to ample, then out even further. She looked, to Jamie, like a longhaired bowling pin.

"We took this old, and very heavy, poem," Krauter said, "and put it to music. It's called Desiderata."

Krauter sat down on a tall stool and began to softly strum his guitar. Geraldine closed her eyes and nodded her head in rhythm. Then she began to sing.

"Go placidly amid the noise and haste..."

The woman's voice had an operatic quality with a forced vibrato and the melody was erratic, wandering haphazardly up and down the musical scale. It wasn't just this, but the utter seriousness of how the song was being presented that tickled Jamie and made him want to laugh.

"As far as possible, without surrender, be on good terms with all persons..."

But the desire to keep a low profile and not be rude made Jamie bite his lip and keep his face straight.

"Avoid loud and aggressive persons; they are vexations to the spirit..."

Jamie noticed something startlingly odd. It seemed as if Geraldine, straining to hit a run of high notes, had crossed her eyes. Just as he was ready to discount it as some kind of hallucination, she did it again. A huge barrel laugh tried to force its way up Jamie's throat but he fought it back. Mustering up all his strength to deny the laugh, he began to shake and sweat.

"For always there will be greater and lesser persons than yourself..."

Jamie was in serious pain by now, but he was hanging on. Then he heard the tune start climbing toward high notes again and saw her eyes begin to slide together. He quickly looked away only to see Lyle in as much agony as he was suffering. Lyle squirmed in his seat, his jaw muscles flexing, and a tear rolled down his cheek.

"Exercise caution in your business affairs for the world is full of trickery..."

Jamie closed his eyes and breathed heavily through his nose, determined not to give in. Then he felt McNulty's knee bump against his own and, knowing it was a mistake, he looked over. McNulty's eyes were crossed.

Jamie, along with everyone else at the table, exploded. Within a few seconds, Jamie was lying on the floor squealing helplessly. Lyle had his head in his lap and he was making odd clicking sounds, his face bright red and his mouth drooling. Kenny's head was hung over the back of his chair as he clutched at his ribs and cackled. McNulty bounced up and down in his chair, slapping the table as he howled.

A few minutes later and moaning "Oh my God", Jamie finally managed to get to his feet. The music had stopped, Krauter and the woman looked upset. Everyone in the room stared at the four of them angrily.

"Well," said Jamie, "I guess I don't get my herb tea."

Laughing and hanging on to each other, the four weakly stumbled out of the Full Moon Coffee House and into the cold night air.

* * *

They drove out of the city limits to a little picnic area and got out of the car to pee while they looked at the night sky. It was a moonless, cloudless night and the stars were breathtaking.

When his bladder was empty, Jamie sighed with pleasure, shook his penis two or three times and shoved it back in his jeans. It was small and shriveled, partly from the cold but mostly from the drug,

"Just as well," he said aloud, "I can't imagine using it for anything else tonight."

"Using what?" Lyle said.

"My dick. It's shrunk to about half the size of a Vienna Sausage."

"Thanks for the graphic, man. Now instead of peace, love, and flowers, I'm gonna spend the rest of the night picturing your wrinkled little dick."

"Hey," Kenny said as he opened the driver's side door, "speaking of wrinkled little dicks, shouldn't Mike be finished playing?"

"Who's Mike?" McNulty said as soon as they were all in the car.

"My roommate. He plays lead guitar with the Daffodils."

"The Daffodils were playing a dance at the high school tonight. He's your roommate, huh? Cool."

"He had one of these hits of Orange Wedge. He was going to drop it after they got the equipment packed up."

"Let's swing by the school," Waltz headed the car back toward town, "maybe he's still there."

* * *

Kenny's car cruised slowly by Colton High School but the place was dark and deserted. He stopped next to the curb.

"Nobody here," Kenny said, "The dance must be over."

"Really, Waltz?" Lyle lit a cigarette. "You sure about that?"

"Just as sure as a mouse grows hair."

Lyle snorted a laugh that turned into a coughing spell. He looked at the cigarette, said "yuck!" and threw it out the window.

McNulty said, "Anybody got a watch?"

Jamie did have a watch, but it was too dark to see and he said so. Kenny snapped on the dome light, Jamie said, "almost one", and Kenny turned the light off again. A few moments later, everyone in the car said "wow."

Although he had pushed his sleeve down and put his arm back in his lap, Jamie could once more see the watch on his wrist, almost with enough detail to see the hands and numbers. Evidently, everyone in the car was having a similar experience.

"Do it again!" everyone clamored. Jamie added, "Focus on something and don't move your eyes while the light is on."

Once more the light snapped on, stayed on for a few seconds, and then went out. A few seconds after that everyone again said "wow."

Jamie had turned and was looking at McNulty. When the light came on, McNulty was looking at his own wide-open hands. And a few moments after it went out, the same image reappeared to Jamie, even though he was looking in another direction.

"This is very cool," said Kenny, "it's like taking pictures with your head."

"Do it again!" everyone cried, and so they did. And again. And again.

After about ten minutes of this, Lyle said, "You know, I don't mean to sound paranoid, but if a cop came by and saw us parked here at one o'clock in the morning flashing the interior lights on and off, he might think that something was a little strange."

"Yep, that's true. And you know what?" Kenny put the car in gear and pulled out into the street, "He'd be right! So where are we off to now?"

"We could drop by the Music Room," said McNulty, "and see who's there."

"Music Room?" Jamie said.

"It's up on campus. You know the cafeteria between Hargreaves and Johnson? Underneath it, they've got recreation rooms and TV rooms and like that. And there's a smallish room marked Music Room that has a stereo in it. It's open all night and after midnight the only people in there are acid-heads tripping out. Especially on weekends."

"What the hell," Lyle shrugged, "I suppose if we don't like it we can always bolt. Jamie?"

"Sure, yeah."

"Then let's go."

"Wait a minute," said Kenny, "don't I get a vote?"

"You don't want to go?"

"No, I want to go, I just want a vote."

"Okay, Waltz. You can vote while you drive."

* * *

The trip down the stairs and through the hallways under Hargreaves had been just that-a trip. And for Jamie, not an entirely pleasant one.

To his dilated eyes, the lights in the building had been harsh and glaring, and to his sensitive ears, the usual sounds of college life had jagged edges to them as they echoed from the hard tile walls and floors. Adding to his nervousness were the close proximity of the kitchens where he and Kenny worked and the danger of meeting and actually having to have a conversation with one of the cooks.

When they finally got to the Music Room, Jamie was relieved to find the lights were low and the music-Jimi Hendrix-was not overbearingly loud.

The room was furnished with comfortable chairs and couches in conversational groupings. There were twelve or fifteen people scattered around the room, some talking animatedly, and some just listening to the music. In one corner, a young woman with pigtails danced by herself with slow, languid movements.

Jamie settled himself on the arm of a couch against the far wall, pulled the battery out of his pocket and began to quietly play with it. He rolled it on the back of his hand, then flipped it, caught it, and spun it around; all the time watching the trace lags chase his fingertips.

"What've you got there?" Kenny was sitting on the couch next to him.

Jamie shrugged and held up the battery. "Ray-O-Vac," he said, "I've been sorta carrying it around."

"All night, right?" said Lyle, who stood to one side.

Then Lyle held out his hand, opened it, and showed them the little stegosaurus. He and Jamie chuckled at each other then turned to look at

Kenny who had just cleared his throat. Kenny blushed, then reached into his breast pocket and pulled out a spoon, one obviously stolen from the coffee house. Their mutual laughter was interrupted by a familiar voice from across the room.

"Hey, Shipman!"

Jamie looked up to see Mike striding across the room with a grin on his face. One look in his eyes was all Jamie needed to know that his roommate was as stoned as they were.

"This shit is fuckin' wild, isn't it?" said Mike, "I may not ever smoke pot again."

"We got to wondering where you'd got to," Jamie gripped Mike's hand. "McNulty suggested we try here."

Mike turned to look at a short, balding man next to him. They both whooped, "Synergy! Synergy!"

"Dig it. I was wondering where you were, and Aaron said, 'Let's try the Music Room.' Aaron is the station manager at KCCS, I met him over at Harvey's. This is Jamie, Lyle, and Waltz."

"Aaron," said Jamie, "Far out. This is McNulty; he's been our Pied Piper most of the night. We ran into him at Harvey's too, only earlier."

Mike and Aaron looked at each other and said "Synergy!"

Jamie and Lyle looked at each other and shrugged their shoulders.

"Aaron has a theory," Mike said, "that there's this energy thing, that's like everywhere. What did that Psychologist dude call it?"

"The Collective Unconscious," Aaron said.

"That's it. And that people on acid are, like, really wired into it. So when two acid-heads want the same thing, even if they're miles apart, then that's what's going to happen!"

"On acid, the whole is always greater than the sum of its parts." Aaron said, "That's Synergy!"

Aaron and Mike slid their palms of their hands together and snapped their fingers.

As happy as he was to meet up with Mike, he couldn't help but feel a twinge of resentment toward this Aaron who suddenly seemed to be Mike's best friend.

Mike suddenly held up his hands, "Third Stone from the Sun! I gotta hear this."

Mike hurried over to a position right in front of a speaker and shut his eyes. A guitar riff soared and Jamie was suddenly entranced. It seemed as if Hendrix's playing was reaching out of the speakers and picking each of them up like a kind of sonic helium. He gave up trying to understand "synergy" and went along for the ride.

"Hey, you," said a distinctive female voice, and Jamie opened his eyes.

There, standing directly in front of him, was the girl with the unmatched eyes who'd kissed him after the concert and then waved to him at the "demonstration."

"It seems like everywhere I go there you are, man. It's very heavy," she said.

"It must be... synergy!" he said, pleased to have remembered the word.

"What's that?"

"I don't really know. You'll have to ask him," Jamie gestured to Aaron, "Hey, did you ever find Christopher Robin?"

She looked surprised and then started to laugh. She tended to snort when she laughed which Jamie thought was a little bizarre but kind of charming.

"Oh, man," she snuffled, "You are a trip. That did my head. Whew. That guy over there with the overcoat, he's Christopher Robin. So, yeah, I guess I found him."

She waved at a handsome young man in a long, black overcoat and signaled him over. He just rolled his eyes disdainfully and turned back to the conversation he was having.

"He's so cute when he's being an asshole," she said, "I'm gonna go over a grab his butt. He hates that when he's tripping."

She turned back to Jamie and said, "Oh yeah, my name's Patty."

"I'm Jamie."

"Hi, Jamie." she grinned over her shoulder as she walked over to the guy she called Christopher Robin. Jamie watched to see if she was really going to grab him, but then McNulty stepped into his field of view.

"You know Patty, huh?"

"Just met her. What's she like?"

"Can't say, personally. But I've heard she's kee-razy-if you catch my jive, if you dig my drift."

McNulty snapped his fingers beatnik-style, and then bobbed his eyebrows like Groucho Marx.

"There are some maniacs still up playing ping-pong, "McNulty said." Aaron and I are going to go stroll around the tables and watch the trace-lags. You want to come?"

"Nah, I think I'm gonna just sit here and lurk for a while."

Jamie slid down onto the couch next to Kenny. Then he felt someone was staring at him and he turned to see Kenny with a very serious expression on his face and a spoon hanging from his nose. Jamie burst out laughing which made Lyle look and then laugh. Kenny couldn't hold a straight face any longer, and when he joined the laughter, the spoon fell into his lap.

Their laughter quickly subsided to chuckling, and Jamie realized that they must have come down somewhat. A few hours before, all three of them would have been on the floor.

He settled down to watch the color layers in the carpet undulate and crawl,

But I'm still pretty damned loaded.

A few minutes later he had an idea and turned to the other two. "When Mike comes back over, let's do his head. Here's the plan..."

Not long after that, the last chord of "Are You Experienced?" faded out, and Mike walked back over to the couch. Jamie, Kenny, and Lyle sat there solemnly staring straight ahead.

"You guys okay?"

Simultaneously, Jamie covered his eyes, Kenny covered his ears, and Lyle covered his mouth. Mike's eyes bulged, and then he laughed, hard.

"Very fucking cute. Thank you. Oh, shit, here come the other two. Shove over and we'll do it to them."

By the time McNulty and Aaron had arrived at that end of the room, there were four faces lined up staring into space.

"Uh oh," said McNulty, "zombies."

Aaron looked over his shoulder to see if something was going on back there, then looked back.

"What the Hell are you doing?"

Jamie put his hands over his eyes, Kenny covered his ears, Lyle covered his mouth, and Mike cupped both hands over his crotch.

After the laughter had subsided Aaron said, "I particularly like 'Fuck No Evil.' I wish I'd thought of that before I crawled into bed with that weird chick last month."

* * *

Morning sunlight filtered through the blinds that covered the windows in Harvey's apartment. Jamie's butt was a little sore from the hard floor and he leaned back further on the pillow under his back. Mike, Lyle, and Kenny were similarly strewn about the living room. Buffalo Springfield's "Expecting to Fly" was on the stereo.

Harvey came out of the kitchen carrying a saucepan.

"I only had three mugs so a couple of you get jelly glasses."

He put the mugs and glasses down on the floor and filled each of them with a hot brownish liquid from the saucepan.

"I put the tea balls in the pan and let it steep for longer. Should work."

Jamie reached out and took one of the jelly glasses. "Thanks, man," he said to Harvey, "It smells really good."

"Stone groove, man," said Harvey as he settled into a chair with one of the mugs.

* * *

Several hours before, they had drifted back over to Harvey's. Around five o'clock Aaron said he had to go open the station and get the morning show started. McNulty asked to bum a ride back to his house.

"My father always gets up way early on Saturday morning to make pancakes," McNulty said, "If I'm not in my bed pretending to be asleep, there'll be massive freaking out. Nice trippin' with yiz."

"Same for me," Aaron said, "Laughed my ass off."

"I was wondering what happened to your ass," said Mike.

Aaron rolled his eyes and gave Mike a good-natured finger.

"Let's talk about that Nighthawk Show idea." Aaron wrapped a muffler around his neck.

McNulty stuck his head back around the door. "Oh, hey Mike," he said, "Don't forget we're gonna jam sometime. I'll call you."

The door shut behind them.

Lyle looked over at Mike. "What was that about?" he asked.

"McNulty plays the bass. He talks a good lick. I'd like to see if he could play one."

"No, I mean the Nighthawk Show. What's that?"

"Well, it's just an idea. Aaron runs the campus radio station. Very small potatoes, I don't know if you can pick it up more than a block off campus. It's mostly boring Student Affairs crap and then they shut down every night at eleven. He wants to get the okay to stay up for three more hours and have me DJ a Progressive Rock show."

"Sounds pretty cool," Kenny said.

Harvey stopped staring at his thumbs and said, "Do you have to bring in your own records?"

"Nah, the record companies all send out free copies of their latest releases. They've got stacks of albums up there they haven't even listened to yet."

"What about school?" Jamie said, "and the band?"

"I don't know. Fuck it, I'll figure something out. Meanwhile, Am I the only one who's starting to feel tired and shitty?"

"Not tired," Kenny said, "But shitty is definitely coming on."

Jamie was feeling achy twinges along the edges of his bones as if they were somehow trying to force their way up through the skin.

"Is Random still up there?" Mike gestured at the ceiling, "I'm thinking maybe we ought to do another."

"It wouldn't do you any good," Harvey said, "You have to wait twenty-four hours after you come down before you can drop again. Otherwise, you don't get off."

"Well, that's a drag."

"Yeah, it's a bummer. Especially with no pot to smoke to take the edge off."

* * *

The five of them listened to the stereo, sipped their tea, and watch dust motes float through the beams of sunlight that slipped around the window blinds. Jamie's bones still ached, his eyes stung, and he wondered if he would ever sleep again.

There was a knock at the door.

Harvey peeked through the blinds before sliding back the bolt on the door and opening it.

A girl bounced in and grinned at everyone. Jamie decided she was about fifteen. She had long, wavy, dark hair that surrounded a vaguely Mediterranean face.

"Hi," she said, "My name's Rachel. Do you like my new sneakers? I got them in Tel Aviv!"

Rachel bounced up and down several times.

"So who are you guys?" Rachel asked as she dropped her coat on the coat pile in the corner.

"I'm Jamie. That's Huey, Dewey, and Louie."

"Don't listen to him." said Mike, "I'm Louie. That's Sneezy and that's Grumpy."

Rachel looked at Harvey. "I take it there was some LSD being eaten here last night."

"No," he replied, "It was actually STP. Orange Wedge to be precise."

"Well in that case!" Rachel yelled and ran into the bedroom. She re-emerged with three socks rolled up into balls.

"Watch this!" She threw the three balls into the air, caught two of them and began juggling. She wasn't very good and was only able to keep the balls up for a couple of minutes, but everyone cheered and applauded. She caught the balls and put them behind her back.

"Now, how many balls are there? Stick up fingers!"

Everyone held up three fingers except Kenny, who put up six.

"Correct!" Rachel pointed at Kenny, "You get the prize."

She tossed him the three sock balls.

"Where'd you learn that? Jamie asked.

"I was on a kibbutz for two weeks last summer and my friend Ari taught me how to juggle. I should practice, I guess."

As she spoke, Rachel examined a coffee can with light bulbs on the top and switches on the side.

"What's this?"

"McNulty brought it over last night. He said it was his science project."

She turned it over and looked inside. "Some project," she said, "only one of the switches is hooked up."

She snapped on the bottom switch and set the can down. The three Christmas lights on top began to blink randomly. Jamie, Lyle, and Kenny looked at each other and snorted.

"Jack and I have a couple of classes together. We're both Seniors at CHS."

"Jack?" said Kenny, "Who's Jack?"

Rachel threw a meaningful look at the blinking tin can.

"Oh, Jack <u>McNulty</u>. I never caught his first name."

Upon hearing that she was a high school Senior, Jamie decided that she was either fifteen and really smart, or seventeen and still waiting to grow tits.

"It's common knowledge," she said, "that the best thing for being strung out is breakfast. Harvey, have you got eggs? Bread? Milk?

Harvey spread his hands out and said. "No idea. I suppose you'll have to check."

Rachel groaned her disapproval as she headed for the kitchen.

Lyle looked at Harvey and shook his head. "How cool is that? Drop acid with the guys and the next morning some cutie-pie chick shows up, puts on a little show, and then cooks breakfast."

Rachel put her head back in the room. "Oh, don't forget. There's a party next Saturday night at my parent's house and you're all invited."

"Are your parents going to be there?" Harvey asked.

"Well, sure. It's their party."

"Oh good," said Mike. "We're gonna drink martinis and talk about our bowels."

"So, Jamie," Lyle said, "How are your bowels?"

"My bowels haven't moved since the Battle of Gettysburg."

"That's a bummer."

"It saves on toilet paper."

Mike, Lyle, Jamie, and Kenny chortled merrily. Harvey looked, at best, mildly amused. But Rachel, fists on hips, was not laughing.

"If you guys are about finished, I'll explain. We live in a split-level house. While my parents and their professor friends are upstairs..."

"Talking about their bowels," Kenny said.

"While they are upstairs, Angela and I and our friends will be downstairs. Now if I can find some syrup or powdered sugar or something, I'll make French toast. Will that be okay with everyone?"

There were nods and grunts of approval all around, and then Kenny sat forward on the edge of the couch.

"I don't mean to rush you," he said, "but Jamie and I have to leave in twenty minutes."

"What?" said Jamie.

"The cafeteria, dude. You and I have to work the lunch shift."

"No, you're kidding. Aagh. It's Saturday, isn't it? Crap."

"I think we can make it," Rachel said. "If someone will come help me."

Jamie shrugged, got up, and followed her into the kitchen.

"Who's this Angela?"

"Angela Tucker. She's my best friend. Her family lives in Denver, but she can't stand her mother and my mother loves everybody, so Angela lives with us and goes to Colton High. You'll probably fall in love with Angela. Everybody does."

EIGHT

Jamie sat cross-legged on the floor next to the stereo and read the backs of album covers. Not that he was so enthralled by the music that was playing that he just had to read about the band, he was there because the alternative was to get up and go talk to the other people at Rachel's party. Jamie tended toward shy and most of the people there were strangers.

Lyle and Kenny were listening in on a heated discussion that included Rachel. The subject was whether the upcoming Nixon Administration was either going to be bad for the country, or a total disaster. He was even less interested in the conversation McNulty was having with Mike-all augmented seventh chords and jazz-fusion.

What Jamie really wanted to do was to sit and talk with Angela Tucker.

Rachel had been right on the money about Angela. Although Jamie would never admit to "in love"-he had only met the girl twenty minutes before-the word "infatuation" was definitely in play. She wasn't beautiful, she was cute-almost cartoon cute with curly, auburn hair and freckles dusted over her apple cheeks. But it wasn't how she looked, or even how she could swear in a sweet, musical, high voice so fiercely that your hair would stand on end. What totally disarmed Jamie was her absolute lack of pretension. Until he met Angela, it had seemed to Jamie that everyone had some kind of filter in their head between what they thought and what they spoke. "Is this an offensive thing to say?" "Am I going to be held accountable for this if I say it?" "Maybe it would be better to keep quiet and just smile." Whether by luck or design, Angela was filterless.

Whatever bubbled up in her head came out of her mouth unaltered. And, fortunately for everyone, what came up in her head was usually endearing, quirky, and frequently very funny.

When Rachel had introduced them, Angela had stuck out her hand and grinned, "Hey you! Aren't you the little cupcake?"

Jamie looked into the biggest pair of green eyes he'd ever seen and gaped like a deer in the headlights.

"Whoa, look at you" Angela giggled, "You're blushing!"

She tapped him on the end of his nose and said, "Must be a strawberry cupcake."

Jamie mentally reached for his stash of clever comebacks, found the container to be completely empty, and so just stood there with an idiotic grin as Angela was introduced to Lyle and Kenny.

A few minutes later Angela and Mike were chatting as if they were old friends. Jamie watched them talking and marveled once again at Mike's easy charm with women as if he knew there was nothing they would rather be doing than talking to him. Had he learned it or was it a natural gift?

As he was standing by the stairs, Jamie heard the doorbell ring and a few moments later several voices, one of which was Shoes' unmistakable southern drawl.

Oh shit, I spaced it.

Jamie turned and headed up the stairs. He had told Shoes and Krenovich about the party earlier in the week, given them the address, and told them he would call and square it with Rachel. But then there were a couple of out-of-town gigs with the band and he'd forgotten.

Halfway up the stairs, he met Krenovich and Shoes coming down.

"Hey, glad you made it past the guards," Jamie said. "Were they armed?"

"Who? Mrs. Berman?" Shoes laughed, "She's a sweetheart. She took one look at my I.D. badge here, and rolled out the ol' red carpet."

Shoes pointed to the lapel of his fatigue jacket where he wore a large white button with a red fist printed on it.

"A fellow revolutionary among the faculty wives set?"

"Yeah, she seems okay," Krenovich said as they got to the bottom of the stairs, "Not to mention she's got a pretty nice rack on her too!"

"Who's that?" said a voice behind him.

"Oh, you know, Mrs. uh..." Krenovich turned, his finger still pointing back up the stairs, and looked into Angela's impish grin.

"You must mean Grace, Rachel's mom. Yeah, I suppose she does have some pretty nice boobies, not that I've ever taken a shower with her or anything. Hi, I'm Angela."

Shoes and an embarrassed Krenovich had barely blurted out their names when someone called to Angela from the far corner. She apologized for running off and with a "We'll talk later" scurried across the room.

"Who was that?" Shoes enquired.

"Angela?" Jamie said, "I'm told she's the human icebreaker cruising merrily along, leaving crushed and broken hearts bobbing in her wake. And that girl over there, in the red turtleneck and vest, is Rachel. C'mon, I'll introduce you."

The conversation between Shoes and Rachel quickly turned political and within a few minutes, Jamie found himself once again on the floor in front of the stereo studying the back cover of *Love: Forever Changes*, peeking over the top edge periodically to see what Angela was doing and who she was talking to.

Jamie decided he was being an idiot. If he wanted to talk to the girl, he should just get up and go over there and talk to her. Lurking behind record jackets was getting pretty creepy anyway.

He put the cover down and slowly got up, trying to come up with some sparkling conversation starter. Then it occurred to him that a clever line wasn't necessary. If he just stood in front of Angela, she'd immediately make some goofy remark. Then all he'd have to do was respond.

Jamie had barely located Angela when Mrs. Berman came down the stairs.

"Yoo-hoo! Rachel!" Mrs. Berman said, "You forgot to bring down the refreshment tray I made up for your guests."

She came into the room carrying a large two-handled tray mounded up with munchies. Jamie could see three different kinds of cheese and four different varieties of cracker, apple slices with caramel dip, carrots and celery with ranch dressing, and a variety of cookies. And that was just the top layer.

Rachel cleared a space on a coffee table.

"Thank you, dear. Now you and Angela go get the sodas, potato chips, cups, paper plates, napkins-all that stuff up on the kitchen counter, okay?"

As Rachel and Angela ran for the stairs, Mrs. Berman put the tray down. She straightened up and smiled as she looked around the room. "I'm Rachel's mom if you haven't figured that out. A week from tomorrow at ten o'clock we're going to gather in front of the Post Office. I'm hoping most of you will come and help us protest. Call us if you want to make signs."

As she headed back toward the stairs, Lyle caught her eye,

"Excuse me, Mrs. Berman..."

"Call me Grace, dear. Everyone does."

"Okay, um..." Lyle pulled a pack of Old Golds half out of his pocket for illustration. "Is it okay to smoke in the house?"

"Well, sure. Anything you want to smoke is just fine."

It wasn't long until the tray on the coffee table was nearly empty and everyone in the room was sitting down and picking the last crumbs from their plates. Across the room from Jamie, Mike and Angela sat together, quietly talking and laughing. There had been no overt "cutting the heifer out of the herd" on Mike's part, but by the time Jamie had put a few crackers on his plate, he looked up and it was done.

"Hey Rachel," Krenovich held up a fat joint, hand-rolled in yellow paper. "Your mom did say 'anything we want to smoke,' right?"

Rachel just grinned and shrugged. The joint was soon lit and making its way around the room. Jamie noticed that only a few of the people were just passing it along. Most were taking deep hits, having obviously done this before.

Jamie felt someone tap him on the shoulder, turned, and a pretty girl with golden copper hair was proffering a smoldering joint. As he took it, he looked back to see Krenovich and Shoes, grinning at him like idiots. Jamie pointed at the joint, gave them a broad, animated wink and a silly thumbs-up, finally taking a deep drag.

An hour later a lot of the partygoers had left. Those remaining sat with eyes half-closed, enjoying being stoned. Even McNulty was subdued, only the bouncing of one heel giving away his restless energy.

"Hey, Doug," Jamie said. "Where did you get the weed? I thought the town was dry."

"My brother sends me a lid now and then. He lives in Northern California; does a little farming on the side."

Mike called from across the room, "Tell him 'Eeyi-eeyi-o' for me, willya?"

Mike had an arm around Angela and she, in turn, had snuggled into his chest. Jamie quietly sighed and put his attention on the music. *In the Court of the Crimson King* was on the stereo and Jamie waded into the cascading waves of sound. But then he noticed a discordant phrase in the music that suddenly stopped and then started again a few moments later. He was about to make a comment about it when he heard Mrs. Berman say "hello" upstairs and he realized it was the phone he'd been hearing.

"Oh, Rachel," her mother called, "Telephone for you."

Rachel got up and plodded up the stairs. She returned a few minutes later.

"That was Harvey. He said that Random is back at the Knotty Pines. He's got a bag of purple LSD that he says is pretty far out."

People looked back and forth at each other and slow smiles spread around the room. In as much time as it took for them to put their coats and hats on, they were all trooping up the stairs.

As people were spilling out of the door, Mrs. Berman came to the landing. "Oh Rachel," she said and her daughter turned around. "Where are you off to?"

"Don't worry, Mom. We're just going to go drop some acid."

"Oh, okay Honey. Have a nice time."

Once they were outside, Shoes looked at Rachel.

"That was pretty bizarre."

"What?"

"We're gonna drop acid. Oh, okay. Y'all have a nice time."

"That's just Mom. She's mostly pretty cool."

The girl with copper-gold hair who had been sitting next to Jamie stopped him.

"Do you know this Random? Is he all right?"

"I think so. I bought some Orange Wedge from him last week and lived to tell the tale."

"Okay, cool. But watch out for me, okay? If I get flippy, will you talk me down?"

Jamie hunched his shoulders and tried to look like Humphrey Bogart. "Schtick with me kid and everything will be hunky-dory."

The girl smiled at him, which wrinkled her nose like a chipmunk's, and got into a car, leaving the door open for Jamie. As he got in after her, it occurred to him that even though he may have lost out on Angela, perhaps this was the consolation prize.

The girl's name turned out to be Lisa Cunningham and she, like Jamie, had only done psychedelics one previous time. As the night went on, he was surprised, pleased, and a little mystified by this lovely creature. She was smart, she was funny, and she was open to almost any adventure. The big head-scratcher was why she seemed to prefer his company to anyone else's. It was the middle of the night when he finally figured it out.

Everyone had gathered at an old, abandoned factory out on the edge of town and a mad game of hide-and-seek was in progress. Jamie and Lisa were both holed-up behind a big rusty tank and trying hard not to giggle and give away their position. She reached up, squeezed his shoulder, and suddenly made a dash for home base with Shoes in hot pursuit. Still feeling the touch of her hand, Jamie had his "aha moment."

I'm her stegosaurus. I'm her good luck charm, her trusty companion for the night. I can do that. And she can be my Ray-O-Vac battery. We'll be trippin' buddies.

Several hours later, they found themselves sitting on the still-warm hood of someone's car, rolled up in blankets, their backs against the windshield, watching the sun come up out of Kansas.

Jamie and Mike loitered on the sidewalk in front of Hargreaves Hall. Around them, the sidewalks and parking lots were almost deserted. The sound of an approaching car caught their attention and they turned expectantly, but it was a late-model Lincoln that cruised on by without slowing.

"You'd think those two knuckleheads would show up on time just once," Mike said, faking disgust.

"Whippersnappers!" Jamie replied in a Grumpy Old Coot voice. "Someone oughta take 'em out behind the woodshed and teach 'em some goddamn manners!"

Mike grinned, and then looked back up the street.

Jamie tipped his head back to soak in the sun. It was a warm day for late November, few clouds and no breeze. The dry, brown grass and barren trees added a pleasantly melancholy edge to Jamie's mood and he let himself be carried along by it.

"Poor fuckin' Lyle. He's pretty well screwed," Mike said.

"What? 'Cause he got drafted? Even he is saying it might be a good thing."

"Crawling through the jungle dodging bullets?"

"Not necessarily, man. I did my whole hitch in Kansas and Texas. Not that that's so great, but nobody was shootin' at me. Chances are, Lyle'll be fine."

"Yeah, well, let's hope."

Jamie noticed a Volkswagen van turn left and head toward them.

"Hey man, check out the old bus," Jamie said, "Maybe Waltz traded in his Chevy for it."

"Not fuckin' likely."

But Mike's words faded in his throat as the van's lights began to flash, its wheezy horn beeped, and it pulled over to the curb in front of them.

One of the passenger-side windows slid back and Waltz's round face appeared in the opening. His fingers came up and wiggled at them.

"Hello-o,' he chirped.

The side door of the van rolled back and Lyle's voice came out of the dark interior.

"Come on you fuckers, get your asses in here. We got a meal to cook!"

Jamie scooped up a brown paper grocery bag as Mike grabbed up the two large baking pans that had been sitting on the wall next to the bag. They jumped into the van and flung themselves into the middle seat.

McNulty, a cigarette clamped in his teeth, turned around in the driver's seat and grinned at them.

"Ya like the new wheels?" He said as he put the bus in gear, "Hang on and don't let the molten rubber splatter on your clothes!"

Then he made a quick U-turn as Lyle struggled to slide the door closed without falling out.

"Where did you get this?" Jamie and Mike said almost simultaneously.

"For his birthday two months ago," Waltz answered for McNulty who was checking for traffic before pulling out onto the main street.

"The pieces, anyway," McNulty said.

Lyle, sitting in the rear seat, leaned forward, put his forearms on the seatback behind Jamie and Mike, and explained.

"His old man..."

"That's Professor McNulty to you," Waltz interjected from the front seat.

"His old man bought it for peanuts because it had a blown engine and some other stuff wrong. He knew some old greasemonk up at the college motor pool and paid him to rebuild it in his spare time."

McNulty slid open his window, tossed out the cigarette butt, and slid it back. "It took him two months, but what the hell."

"It's very cool, man. I dig it," Mike said.

"What?"

The van was now up to thirty miles per hour and the clattery engine sound made normal conversation difficult.

"I dig it!" Mike yelled.

McNulty, a maniacal grin on his face, turned completely around in his seat and bounced his eyebrows up and down, then turned back around in time to swerve out of oncoming traffic.

* * *

As they were getting out of the van, the door to Harvey's apartment opened and Rachel and Angela came out on the porch.

"Happy Thanksgiving!" They yelled together and Angela added, "tooo yooooouuuu!"

Jamie and Lyle grabbed their pans and bag, Lyle and Kenny got some things out of the back of the van, and they all trooped up the walk and into the apartment.

"Bring the food into the kitchen," Rachel said, "let's see what we've got."

As Jamie carried his bag toward the kitchen he waved to Shoes and Krenovich who were sitting next to the stereo talking to Harvey. Next to the kitchen door, Mike was already sweet-talking Angela. When she saw Jamie, Angela pushed away from Mike and came over to talk to him, an action that Jamie noted with some interest.

"So what did you bring?" Angela said as she pulled down a corner of the bag to look inside.

"Mac and Cheese," Jamie said. "It wouldn't be Thanksgiving without Mac and Cheese, at least not at the Shipman's. I'm gonna make it from scratch."

"I tried to get him to just buy a few boxes of Kraft's," said Mike, "but he wouldn't go for it."

Angela threw a mock-contemptuous look at him and then turned back to Jamie. "Let's just ignore him for a while. So, is Lisa coming?"

"Umm... no, I don't think so. She had to go back home for the Holiday. A farm somewhere in Kansas, I think she said. Benderville? Does that sound familiar?"

Angela had that "Don't give me that crap, I know there's something going on" look in her eyes as she smiled and said, "She's kinda cute, isn't she?"

"Who... Lisa? Yeah, she is..." Jamie could feel his face heat up and take on a crimson hue. "As cute as a bug's bazoo," he garbled and fled into the kitchen.

As he unloaded the paper sack, Jamie tried to make sense of this sudden emotional overload. He was disturbed at how freaked out he was. On the one hand, having Angela standing that close and looking up at him with those big, green eyes bordered on wonderful. The downside was her assigning him a romance. It meant that he would not be in the "Possible Relationship" category-a bummer-but also not in the "How Do I Let this Guy Down Easy" category-probably a good thing.

Welcome to the "Just a Good Friend" category.

By then he had piled a chunk of cheese, half a dozen eggs, a quart of milk, and a bag of macaroni on the table. He looked up to see Rachel, Lyle, and Kenny, staring dubiously at a small, uncooked turkey sitting in the middle of one of the large baking pans he and Mike had "borrowed" from the cafeteria kitchen.

"They had some bigger ones, but they were all frozen rock-solid. This little guy was the only thing thawed out that we could afford."

"Harvey said he thought about sixteen people were coming," Rachel said as she prodded the bird, "this 'Little Guy' isn't much bigger than a chicken."

"Aw, c'mon," Lyle said, "It's almost ten pounds. Plus, people can fill up on spuds and gravy." He held up a large, mesh bag of red potatoes.

"Don't forget there's Mac and Cheese," Jamie said.

Rachel sighed. "Okay. I'll get the 'Little Guy' ready for the oven while you two peel potatoes."

Both Lyle and Waltz just stared at her.

"But... uh, we wanted to go out in the front room and drink beer with the other guys," Waltz said in a near-whine.

"And let the women stay in the kitchen and do the cooking, I guess."

"Well..."

"It's a brave new world out there, boys,"

Rachel rooted through a drawer. She found two paring knives and handed them to Lyle and Waltz. "Better get used to it."

"But I'm going in the Army in a week," Lyle said.

"Think of it as practice for KP. Here," she set a large bowl down on the table, "put the peelings in the garbage and the potatoes in here."

This was a side of Rachel Jamie had not yet seen and he hesitated a bit before speaking.

"I don't mean to be a buttinski or anything, but..."

Rachel affixed him with a steely glance.

"Back home, my mother never peeled the potatoes. She just cubed them up with the skins on, boiled 'em and mashed 'em. It made little red spots in the potatoes, but they tasted just fine."

"They did?" Rachel asked uncertainly.

"Oh, yeah. Mom said all the vitamins were in the skin. And the lumps, but that's another question."

Rachel looked at Lyle and Kenny. "Do you mind if the potatoes have red skin-speckles in them?"

The two allowed as how that was okay with them and Waltz added that it might be "kind of groovy". So Rachel told them to wash the potatoes well, cut out any bad spots, dice them up and put them in the bowl. Then she left the kitchen to ask Harvey if he had any spices for the turkey.

"Man," Lyle emptied the potato sack into the sink, "only seventeen and she's already got a pair of brass clangers on her. Women's Lib. Jesus."

"It's the Revolution, man. The whole world is changing," Jamie looked through the cupboards for a pot to boil the macaroni.

Kenny suddenly looked up and grinned. "You mean it's like Christmas morning."

Lyle stopped washing potatoes. "What?"

"You know, you get some stuff that you really wanted, and some stuff you didn't-like an ugly sweater from Aunt Rose. But you just take it all anyway and say 'thanks'".

"Deep, Waltz. Very fuckin' deep."

"Thank you," Kenny ignored the sarcasm, "Man, I sure could do with a beer, right now."

"Synchronicity!" yelled a voice from the doorway. They looked up to see Aaron standing there, holding a cardboard box with "Coors" written on the side of it.

"Far-fuckin'-out," Lyle said, "Just say 'beer' and a case of it appears."

"It was a case when I came in the front door. Now it's just a couple of six-packs."

"Here," Jamie said, "let us relieve you of some of your burden."

Within a few minutes, the water was heating on the stove, the potatoes were being diced, the turkey was being stuffed, and everyone except Rachel had a beer in their hand.

"Sure you don't want one?" Aaron asked Rachel before he put the last six-pack in the fridge.

"No, thanks. I'm going riding this afternoon, and then Angela and I are going back to our house for family Thanksgiving."

"Riding?" Kenny looked impressed, "You own a motorcycle?"

"No, a horse. My daddy-he lives in Florida-bought her for me for my birthday last year. Her name is Missy. We keep her at a stable North of town."

"Could you trade her in for a motorcycle?"

Rachel flicked a small wad of wet stuffing at Kenny. He picked it off his shirt and popped it in his mouth.

"Needs salt."

"Hey, Rachel," Aaron tried to look nonchalant, "Who's that girl with the short, curly hair and freckles?"

He was standing near the kitchen door sneaking glances out into the front room. Rachel came over and followed his gaze.

"The one in the tan bell-bottoms?"

"Yeah. Who is she?"

"I have no idea. But I do know how you can find out."

Aaron waited for the answer.

"You walk up to her, put out your hand and say, 'Hello, my name is Aaron... Jesus.'" She shook her head in disgust and left the kitchen.

"You'd better do as she says, man," Lyle laughed, "otherwise there'll be a terrible punishment."

"Or even worse." Added Kenny.

"Bailiff!" Jamie yelled, "Whack this man's peepee."

Aaron laughed along, not sure how to take this.

A hubbub began in the front room and grew closer and louder. Everyone in the kitchen turned to look.

Big Dan, followed by Theresa My Old Lady, came through the kitchen door seeming to push the air and noise before him like a tugboat pushing a bow wave. He was holding a large cardboard box that he set down on the table. He turned with a dramatic flourish.

"Lafayette, we are here!" he bellowed.

From out of the box came a large, pink turkey, stuffed and ready for the oven. He set it down next to Kenny and Lyle's turkey, overshadowing it by at least twice.

"But wait," he said, "there's more."

He lifted another bird out of the other side of the box. This one was much smaller, flattish, and darker brown.

"A duck, by God-Daffy himself. And Theresa brought everything to make Orange Sauce."

"Here, light this." Big Dan reached into his breast pocket and pulled out a fat joint, which he handed to Lyle and said, "I think we need an appetizer."

Lyle quickly lit the joint from the gas flame under the potatoes and started it making its way around the room.

A tall, thin fellow with a dark goatee stuck his head in the kitchen door. He was carrying a gallon glass jug.

"Excuse me," he said, "anywhere I can park this?"

"Quentin, come on in," Big Dan smiled. "A fine table wine, right?"

"Yep," Quentin said, "the best, man. Red Mountain wine-two bucks a gallon."

He deposited the jug on the table, accepted the smoldering joint, took a big hit, and stuck out his hand to Jamie.

"Name's Quentin," he squeaked as he held his breath.

Jamie shook Quentin's hand as he let go of his own lungful.

"Jamie. Nice to meet you." Jamie felt a soft fog climbing up his spinal column as the cannabis entered his bloodstream. "I think it's gonna be stoned out today."

"Oh yeah," Quentin said, "with a strong chance of far out."

* * *

Jamie sat, cross-legged, on a pillow; his back slumped against the wall. He slowly surveyed the room. There were at least fifteen people strewn around the makeshift low table. He wasn't sure exactly. He'd lost the ability to count shortly after finishing dessert. He had been very drunk, very stoned, and completely stuffed before Theresa My Old Lady set the large pan still warm from the oven down on the table. Those marijuana brownies were the finishing touch. Now he felt like a water buffalo was sitting on him. It was a warm, soft, comfortable water buffalo but it wasn't allowing him to move, let alone lean forward and pick up that last bite of turkey with gravy on it that his mouth wanted so badly.

"Just as well, I guess," he said to himself. With a stomach so full that taking a deep breath sent a stab of pain through him, he was afraid another bite might rupture something.

So his eyes drooped to half-closed and he let his foggy brain try to pin down a thought that had been dancing around the edges of his consciousness for the last hour. Something to do with peace. Or peacefulness. That was it.

"Peace" is too big a concept. But this room, these people, this peacefulness-this has meaning, and depth, and weight...

Suddenly, someone outside was banging on the door. It was loud, sharp, and terrifying. Several people screamed.

The adrenaline that was pouring into his bloodstream made Jamie thrash around like an overturned cockroach. Images of being clubbed senseless, dragged through the snow, and thrown into a wagon scorched his already-addled brain.

Jamie managed to sit up. Some of the people around him were gaping in confusion, others were crawling and stumbling into the bedroom and kitchen. Harvey was at the window peeking through the curtains.

"It's not the Pigs!" Harvey yelled over the ruckus, "Be cool. It's just some farmer-looking dude. He's grinning and waving."

"What do you want, man?" Harvey yelled at the window glass.

Jamie heard a reply from outside. He couldn't understand what was said, but the voice seemed somehow familiar.

Harvey turned from the window and looked at Jamie. "Hey Shipman," he said, "You got a brother named Jack?"

Jamie sat at a table in Ziggy's Saloon and watched condensation drops run down the sides of the mug of beer in front of him. It was all he could do to keep his eyes half-open and his mouth half-closed. Across the table, his brother Jack was slurping the last of his own mug and keeping an eye out for the cocktail waitress to order another.

"Jesus," Jack said as he looked closely at Jamie, "Are you sick or something? Your eyes are really bloodshot."

"Nah, it's nothing," Jamie said and shrugged. "A gust of wind blew some dirt in my eyes earlier. I rinsed 'em out. So why did you drive here all the way from Iowa on Thanksgiving?"

"Because..." Jack paused for dramatic effect, "I'm moving to Australia."

"What?"

"I'm moving to Australia. You know-'Down Under'. Kangaroos and stuff."

Jamie could only gape in astonishment. This was his brother Jack, the same brother who, every year, resisted driving down to Missouri for the Shipman Family Reunion. Jack maintained it was just "too far to go". And now he was moving to Australia?

"The Australian government has this program," Jack said, "I saw it on a poster on a bulletin board at school. If you have training in certain skills, they'll not only pay your way down there but set you up with a good job as well. If, after three years, you want to move back to the States, they'll pay for the ticket. If you want to stay, they'll pay for a vacation, anywhere in the world. Pretty nifty deal, huh?"

"Yeah, it sounds pretty cool I guess, But what's this skill you have that they want?"

"Irrigation Technology. That's what I've been studying at Ottumwa Junior College. Plus, I've been working for AgriSystems for the last four years. If that doesn't make me an expert, well, don't tell the Aussies."

Jack laughed and took a hefty swallow of beer. Jamie tentatively sipped at his own mug.

"So, okay," Jamie said, "Australia. Far out. I mean, I gotta hand it to you, Jack. It takes a lot of guts to make a change like that."

"Thanks, Bro," Jack replied as he slowly rotated the beer mug on the tabletop with his fingertips. Then his voice took on a more somber tone.

"There's another reason too. I just don't want you to be mad or anything. I mean, you went into the Army and did your hitch and all, and I'm proud of you for doing that. But I just don't want to go. To Vietnam, I mean. And I don't think they can draft me if I'm living in Australia. You're not mad at me or anything are you?"

Jamie hadn't seen that look on Jack's face since his brother had borrowed his fishing pole and accidentally dropped it in the creek.

"No," Jamie said and then grinned, "Absolutely not. In fact, I'm the one that's proud of you. Fuck the Army. And Fuck Vietnam."

Jaime held up his beer mug, clinked it with Jack's and they both took long swallows.

"So, have you applied yet?"

"Oh, yeah. That was a month and a half ago. Signed all the papers, even went up to Chicago for an interview with the Australian Consulate."

"What was that like?"

"Kinda weird, actually. The guy asked me a couple of questions that I'd already answered on the forms, shook my hand, and told me he hoped I enjoyed his country. That was it. The only thing I could figure is that they wanted to make sure I wasn't a nigger."

The use of the word made Jamie cringe, but he covered his reaction with a sip of beer. Jack, and his Father for that matter, had always used the term without a second thought. Jamie felt it was like holding up a sign that announced, "I'm an ignorant asshole!" to the world. Suddenly a mental picture of his brother marching down the street, proudly holding up such a sign, popped into his head. He started to giggle.

Jack was in the middle of an explanation of how he'd found Jamie.

"...So there was this folded note taped to your dorm room door... What's so funny?"

"It's like I saw you in this parade," Jamie tried to think between giggles, "and you were... uh... coming down a gangplank off a ship in Sydney. You know, there to save Australia!"

"Ah, okay. Pretty funny," Jack said, "Don't try to get a job with Bob Hope as a joke writer, okay. Anyway, I'm taking the plane. It leaves San Francisco Sunday morning. So I want to get you to drive me down to the Denver airport tomorrow. Is that okay?"

"Sure, man. No problem. But what...? I'm sorry. I'm confused a little bit. You drove out here in the Volkswagen..?

"Dune buggy. Yep."

"And you're flying to San Francisco tomorrow...?"

"That'll give me a day to visit with Aunt Wilma in Palo Alto."

"So what happens to your car?"

"You get it."

Jamie just stared at his brother as his brain, mired in marijuana molasses, tried to process the information.

"I get it? Do you mean the car? You're going to give me your car?"

"Well, sorta." Jack looked off into a corner of the bar, "I'll sign it over to you, but if I decide to come back home then you've gotta give it back. I mean, if I want it then. Is it a deal?"

"Well, sure." Understanding slowly dawned, "Thanks, man. That'll be pretty cool. I'll take good care of it, don't you worry."

They shook hands and slapped each other on the back, and then Jack went to bum a pen from the barmaid while Jamie just sat and grinned to himself. A car! Wheels! What if Jack was right and the VW really was a "chick magnet". Probably not, but he couldn't help feeling like he was back in the Angela Sweepstakes. Maybe not a Front Runner, but definitely moving up.

When Jack returned with the pen, he pulled a folded piece of paper out of his breast pocket.

"This is the Registration. There's a place on the back for Transfer of Ownership. Give me a dollar."

Jamie pulled a dollar out of his wallet and handed it over.

"For good and valuable consideration," Jack read, "blah blah blah, one dollar." He filled in the blank. "Now I just sign it and date it, so..."

After signing, He pushed the document across the table to Jamie.

"You sign there..." He pointed to a line and Jamie signed his name. "Okay, you now own the coolest of the cool, dune buggy. Keep that in the car. Then in a couple of months, when the tags are about to expire, you can use that to get a Colorado Title."

"Cool. Very cool.' Jamie said, "And if you, like, knock up a kangaroo or something and have to come running back home, I'll give it back, but at twice the price-two dollars."

"Shrewd, brother, very shrewd."

* * *

The next afternoon, Jamie was happily driving the Volkswagen back to Colton. The radio didn't work, which Jamie decided was just as well since the engine noise would have drowned it out anyway. So he sang all the old "car songs" he could remember-*409, Little Cobra, Shut Down,* even *Dead Man's Curve.* He tried to fit his new car into some of the lyrics but "Volkswagen" and "Dune Buggy" were too ungainly. The best he could come up with was changing "Little Deuce Coupe" to "Little VeeDub."

He looked over at the empty passenger seat several times and tried to picture Angela sitting there. And every time he did so, the girl riding next to him would not be Angela, but Lisa.

Feeling a little rattled, he decided to go back to singing.

NINE

Patrolman Larry Sherman pulled his squad car into a parking slot behind the Colton City Police Station and shut off the engine. He stifled a yawn, and then slapped himself on both cheeks.

"Man," he said, "I gotta get more shut-eye; all I need is to fall asleep and run into somebody. Wouldn't that look great on my record?"

He dropped his ticket book into his open briefcase, got out of the car, locked it up, and headed toward the back door of the station.

I can't blame Jeanie. As soon as the Bink starts to cry, she's up and picking him up out of his crib. But the little meatball has to shriek until he's sure Daddy's awake before he'll take the tit.

He made his way into the squad room, dropped his briefcase onto an empty table and pulled up a chair. There were several desks grouped along three of the walls, but those were assigned on a rank and seniority basis, of which he had neither.

As he plucked the various report forms he needed out of their bins, the thought occurred to him that he might be able to make up some lost sleep when he started on Graveyard the following week.

I just have to get Jeannie to take the Bink over to her Mom's during the day when I'm asleep.

The thought of it made him smile as he arranged his ticket book, log, and report forms in front of him. Then he got to work.

Forty minutes later, he was just finishing when John Krall, the Duty Sergeant, put his head into the room.

"Hey, Sherm," Krall said, "The Old Man wants to see you."

Sherman's eyebrows shot up.

"Me? Why?"

"Well, I don't know. Maybe it would be a good idea to waddle your ass down the hallway and ask him, hmm?"

Sherman, ignoring the sarcasm, dropped the completed forms into the Department in-basket and headed for Chief Gaskin's office.

It's the damned quota. I only wrote forty-two tickets last month. Shit.

Sherman wiped his sweaty hands on his pants, straightened his shoulders, and knocked on the door.

"Come in!" yelled a gravelly voice.

Sherman walked in and came to attention in front of the desk. He started to salute, but The Chief waved it away.

"No saluting. Didn't I tell you that? This station is too small for all that formal crap," the white-haired man said over the top of his reading spectacles, "Wait until I'm dead. You can salute at my funeral. Sit down."

Relieved, Sherman took a seat on a red leather sofa. If it were to be a dressing-down, he would have been left standing.

"I got a memo the other day from the State Attorney General's office," Gaskin said as he picked up a paper on his desk.

"It seems they are 'highly concerned about the trafficking and consumption of illegal drugs in the state of Colorado, especially in and around Universities and Colleges.'

Well, maybe in Denver and Boulder and some of those places. But in Colton? Horseshit." He dropped the paper on his desk and leaned back in his chair.

"So what does this have to do with you? Well, they are 'strongly suggesting'-a nice way to say 'do it or else'-that every police department in cities over 20 thousand or towns with colleges send a representative to a three-day seminar on 'Techniques in Anti-Narcotics Law Enforcement'. I've decided to send you."

Sherman could only sit and blink his eyes.

"And now you're wondering Why Me?" Gaskin said, "Well, it's mainly because you're the youngest man I've got. You understand kids these days better than those old farts out there that sit and swap World War Two stories and pine for the days of Harry Truman. As I said, I don't think there's anything more going on in Colton than maybe some kid buys a Marijuana cigarette on a street corner in Denver and then brings it back here to smoke with his buddies. But if there <u>are</u> any drug pushers in Colton, I think you're the one with the best chance to nail 'em."

"Well, that's... I mean..." Sherman stammered, "Thank you, sir. I'll do my best."

"I'm sure you will. Give my regards to your wife and little... what's his name?"

"Larry Junior, Sir."

"Him, too. I'll let you know about dates, travel vouchers, and all that stuff, okay? Now go home."

Yes, sir. And thank you, sir."

TEN

Jamie sat, cross-legged, in an overstuffed chair and looked around at the farmhouse's living room, and especially the people in it, and marveled at how he had got there. A farm on the plains of Kansas would not be high on anyone's list of Road Trip Destinations, least of all in January with the temperature at fifteen degrees below zero and a wind moaning around the corners of the building.

But there they were In Lisa's parents' farmhouse. They'd brought a case of beer with them, which with nine people wasn't going to make for a drunken brawl. Off in the hallway to Jamie's left, Aaron, Madeleine (the girl who'd worn the tan bell bottoms to Thanksgiving dinner), and Catherine and Sandy-a couple of Madeleine's friends-had found the family board games stash and were trying to decide between Parcheesi and Clue. Mike had helped Lisa drag her stereo out of the bedroom. They had The Rascals on the turntable singing about "Good Lovin" and were comparing their Kansas relatives. It was the discovery just this morning that they had this common tie that had been the starting point of the entire trip.

Lisa had mentioned that she came from a farm near Benderville, Kansas. Mike, overhearing this, said that his mother's sister, Aunt Madge, and her family lived in Benderville and he hadn't seen any of them since he was little. Within minutes, it was decided that everyone should all go to Benderville.

It was Semester Break-a four-day weekend-and it didn't take long before seven people were jammed into Lisa's parents' '61 Thunderbird and cruising out of Colton. The plan was to drop in on Mike's relatives for an hour or so, then spend the night at Lisa's. Her parents had, shortly after Christmas, hitched their Airstream trailer to their pickup and driven down to a trailer park south of Phoenix. There they would remain until mid-March.

On the old western-style couch that shared a coffee table with Jamie's chair sat Mitch, Mike's cousin. Curled up against Mitch was a blonde girl with too much eye makeup. Mitch had not introduced her, and she showed no interest in anyone but Mitch.

Jamie liked Mitch, almost from the first minute he met him. Mitch was open, non-judgmental, laughed a lot, and liked to listen to good stories almost as much as he liked to tell them.

Jamie had just told Mitch about the last time he'd dropped acid. It was the night before Lyle had to go into the Army and since Waltz had gotten a job on a mining survey crew in Wyoming, he was leaving the next day as well. So they bought the last three hits of what Random swore was "Purple Haze". About three in the morning, still ripped to the eyeballs, they remembered the peanut butter rolls that were coming out of the oven at the Bus Station. It took them half an hour in the parking lot to screw up their courage enough to go in. Just as they were a few feet inside the door, Gladys the waitress had snapped her head around, recognized them, and bellowed, "Hey! Look who's here!". Screaming, all three spun around and ran out into the night.

Mitch laughed. "Man, I can completely relate. People come up with some far-out shit when they're tripping. It's like some cats I know who were walking around stoned in the middle of the night just before Christmas and they found the bottom part of a Christmas tree someone had cut off. They were all into a 'fuck Christmas' trip but there was this messed up tree. Acid logic, man. They figured this had to be some kind of cosmic sign. So they took it home, set it up in an empty coffee can, and decorated the fuckin' thing with dog turds in twist-tied baggies."

While they were still laughing, Lisa came up to them with Mike trailing behind her, his eyes rolling.

"All right, Mitch," Lisa said, posing with her fists on her hips, "There's a couple of mysteries here and I need answers. Capiche?"

"Wow!" Mitch said, "You spoke Italian. I think I'm in love!"

The girl next to him sat up and punched Mitch in the ribs. He winked at her and stroked her shoulder and she snuggled back down against him.

"Mike says you grew up in Benderville and you're about a year older than me," Lisa went on, "but I don't remember you in High School and I'm pretty sure I would."

Jamie didn't doubt it. Mitch had wavy hair, a pug nose, and slanted, roguish eyes. Girls probably all went a little nuts over him.

"When I was 15," Mitch said, "Bert and Madge found me on the front porch one night, drunk as hell and barfing in the garden. A couple of guys down at the granary had given me some rotgut whiskey. Thought it was funny. Well, the next day Bert and Madge were throwing around the phrase "military school", so I packed up my little suitcase and split. Went to live with my sister in Lawrence for the next three years."

"It was Colonel Mustard in the Living Room with a lead pipe!" Aaron's voice came bellowing down the hall and growing closer. "All I need is another beer to lubricate my intuition and I'll prove it."

Aaron stopped in the doorway and leaned into the room.

"We seem to be out of beer. I propose an expedition into town. I have no money or car, but I am, provably, over twenty-one. What? No takers?"

"It's cold out there, dude," Jamie said.

"I tell you what," said Mitch, "it's Aaron isn't it? I'll not only put up the money, but I'll drive you into Benderville myself, but only on one condition..."

Jamie had heard the term "sparkle in his eyes" many times before and had always felt it was just a metaphor, but damned if Mitch's eyes didn't seem to actually sparkle as he explained his "condition". Probably, he decided, because Mitch wore contact lenses.

"When we came in," Mitch said with a smile playing at the corners of his mouth, "I saw a bicycle on the front porch. All you have to do is ride it down to the main road and back. Naked, of course."

"Naked?" said Aaron.

"In fifteen below weather. With a stiff breeze."

Amid the laughter that erupted, Aaron squinted and tapped his lower lip. He was clearly considering it.

"Wait a sec," Lisa said, "The liquor store in Benderville closes at eleven. Disappointing, I know, but state law is state law."

"Counterproposal," said Aaron. "I'm not too crazy about the bicycle on this ice, so how about I run down to the road and back wearing nothing but my sneakers? My reward being twenty bucks for my date next week with Madeleine."

"Don't I get a say in this?" came Madeleine's voice out in the hallway.

Aaron quickly stepped back to let Madeleine enter the room.

"Since we're going on this date together, I think I ought to run with you."

"Under the same conditions?" Mitch grinned at her.

"Fair is fair."

"In that case, I accept!" Mitch pulled out his wallet with a flourish, extracted a twenty dollar bill, and slapped it down on the coffee table. "But just to make sure you don't cheat, I guess I'd better go with you. What do you say, Mitz?"

The girl with the heavy eye makeup just looked at him like he'd proposed a quick gargle of broken glass and shook her head from side to side. Everyone else jumped to their feet with shouts of "Me too! I'm in! Far out!"

Within minutes seven people were gathered next to the front door wearing nothing but shoes.

A few minutes later Lisa came downstairs wearing only a bra and panties and carrying an armload of towels. "Everybody take one!"

The towels were passed out as Lisa stripped off her underwear and tied up her sneakers.

"So what are the towels for?" said McNulty, "we're not going to get wet are we?"

"No, silly," Lisa jumped up and headed for the door, "They're to tie around our necks. We can't be Superheroes without capes, can we?"

With a cheer, everyone ran out the door, down the steps, and out onto the drive.

* * *

It was only later, as everyone slouched around the farmhouse kitchen, sipping hot chocolate, and softly giggling at each other, that Jamie could remember the Run with any clarity. During that crazy dash, it was a wild melee of butts, elbows, knees, and hair. Uncontrollable laughter and wild yelling nearly drowned out the crunching of feet on hard-frozen snow.

There was Mitch, up front, urging everyone on; Aaron chuffing along as fast as his short legs could go; Madeleine deliberately limiting the stride of her long legs in order to stay next to Aaron; Mike leaping forward every few steps in a kind of awkward skip; and ten feet in front of Jamie, there was Lisa. Her elbows were held high, a ponytail of her blonde hair bounced at the nape of her neck, her improvised cape billowed in the breeze. Jamie marveled at the easy, comfortable stride Lisa had fallen into.

The sharp cold stung Jamie's skin, his breath poured out clouds of steam, and he exulted as waves of laughter rolled up and down the group. He knew that laughing was taking his wind and making running difficult, but there was nothing to be done about it. The only thing more absurd than watching a group of naked people running through the cold and snow is actually being one of those naked, running people.

Mitch reached the road first, tapped the mailbox marked "Cunningham", turned around and began running back up the drive. Shouting encouragement, he held up his left hand for the others to slap as they went by. Following suit, everyone did the same. Jamie tapped the mailbox, slapped the hands of Aaron and Madeleine, and followed Lisa's pretty little bouncing butt back up the drive to the house.

* * *

Jamie sat at the kitchen table and wrapped his hands around a mug of hot chocolate, letting its warmth seep into him. He turned and smiled as Lisa slid into the next chair. She grinned back at him and said, "That was fun."

He nodded, took a sip of the sweet warmth, then gave her an appraising look.

"You never told me you were a runner."

"I think if I had tried walking I'd still be out there."

"No, I'm serious. All the rest of us were just scuttling along as fast as we could go. You were actually running."

Lisa looked at Jamie with a bemused smile for a moment. Then she stood up, put her cup in the sink and said, "Come on, I want to show you something."

Jamie followed her up the stairs and down a short hallway. She opened a door and Jamie followed her into a bedroom. It was her bedroom, obviously, with a pink comforter on the bed over a crocheted dust ruffle, and posters on the wall of the Beatles and the Rolling Stones.

Lisa walked over to a wide, shallow cabinet that was hanging on the wall and opened both doors. There were thick layers of ribbons-some pink, red, and white but most of them were blue. Several gaudy trophies with little sculptures of running women on top stood in the center section, on the wall behind them were 8 X 10 photos of Lisa poised in the blocks waiting for the starting gun, Lisa in full stride, Lisa lunging past another runner to break the tape.

Jamie walked up to the cabinet to get a closer look.

"Wow," he said, "Just like... wow. My mind is officially blown."

"I was in Sixth Grade when I first started to run competitively. I liked it. I liked running and I liked winning. So I worked at it, listened to my coaches, and tried to get better. My Mom had this cabinet made and set it up like some kind of shrine. It's all kind of embarrassing now."

"You've given up running?"

"I don't know. Track Season at Colton doesn't start until the snow melts. I'll go out for the team, I guess," Lisa closed the trophy cupboard, "But I'm fully expecting there to be a dozen women there who will all be faster than me. I know it sounds kinda stupid but... I don't like losing."

Jamie looked around the room. Something didn't quite look right and he was right on the edge of figuring out what it was.

Lisa sat on the corner of her bed.

"Jamie," she said, "there's something I want to ask..."

"This is it?" Jamie interrupted. "Your bedroom I mean. A bed, a desk, a dresser... and that's it? No stuffed animals? No collections of little unicorns? No bean bag chair for you to snuggle in? If there was a big cross on the wall, this could be a cell in a monastery."

Lisa tried to put a hurt and angry look on her face, but she couldn't get it to stick. She shook her head and laughed.

"How many girl's bedrooms have you been in any way? Oh well, go through the closet door there. On the back wall is a short door-only about four feet high. There's a light switch just inside on your right."

When Jamie opened the little door, crawled in and switched on the light, he began to laugh.

"This," he gestured as Lisa crawled in after him, "is what I'm talkin' about."

It was a tiny little room, about 10 feet long and six feet wide, with the ceiling sloping down from five feet on the door side to less than three feet on the other. There was a little foam mattress covered with a flowery quilt and big pillows along the wall for backrests. A giant stuffed Panda was at one end of the room and a small table with a pile of books and a reading lamp at the other.

"It was just a little storage space under the eaves," said, "But when I was little I used to slip in here to hide so often that my Dad finally put up insulation and wallboard and a carpet on the floor. Twelve years later and I still think it's kind of magical."

"Oh, it is," Jamie agreed. He was sitting on one foot in the middle of the room. "Magical. And very cool. Where did you get that?" he asked, pointing at a cartoonish mask of an American Indian.

"That's Little Bear, she said, pink appearing on her cheeks. "When my father finished this room, he put it up there. He said his name was Little Bear and his job was to look out for me."

"Good work, LB," Jamie said to the mask.

"Now," Lisa said, "snap off the light."

As soon as Jamie did so, the ceiling began to glow with the soft blue light of a thousand little stars.

"Wow, what a trip. Just when you think it can't get any farther out-it does."

Lisa clicked the reading lamp on. The stars disappeared, replaced by the lamp's warm glow.

"There's something I want to ask–"

"So who put all those stars up, you or–"

"Shhh. Don't interrupt. I've been getting up the courage to ask you this so now you have to listen."

Jamie caught her serious tone, just nodded, and slid over onto the other end of the little mattress.

"Jamie... do you like me at all? I mean, you know, really like me?"

Confused, Jamie stared at her. "Uh, sure. Sure I do. I like you a lot. I think you're kind of wonderful."

"Then what's the problem? Look, for the last three or four years, ever since I started to grow these," she looked down at her ample bosom, "I've been listening to lines, dodging sweaty, groping hands, going out with losers who only want to ball. Then here you come-someone fun and interesting, someone I feel a connection to-and what do I get? Brotherly hugs and little peck kisses goodnight. So I'm asking... what's the problem?"

He reached out and took Lisa's hand. "I've just... well, I'm the sort of... Okay. Cards on the table. I've been scared."

It was Lisa's turn to look confused.

"I really like being with you and we've had a lot of fun together," Jamie said, "I didn't want that to end. What if you were thinking of me as this 'fun friend' and I suddenly grab you and stick my tongue down your throat. I could picture that-you gagging, pushing me away angrily, and telling me to get lost. I didn't want to risk it."

Lisa tightened her grip on his hand and then pulled him to her.

"Come here, you"

The kiss began softly, their lips barely touching, their tongues reaching out to each other, probing, and then sliding. Then their mouths pressed tightly, hungrily together. Jamie's heart was racing, his senses thrilling at the touch of her fingertips as they roamed over his body.

Lisa, breathing heavily, pulled her mouth back from his and whispered, "Clothes."

They unwound from each other and hurriedly undressed. Lisa had stripped down to her bra and panties and was tossing pillows off the little mattress to give them room to lie together. Jamie looked down at himself to see his stiff erection poking his boxer shorts straight out in front of him. Deciding that keeping them on would be ridiculous, he stripped off the underwear and, letting his hard penis lead the way, he went to the mattress and laid down next to Lisa. She quickly wrapped both arms and a leg around him and kissed him deeply as their bodies strained together.

He gently squeezed her breasts through her bra and then reached around behind her. He fumbled with the hooks for a few moments before whispering, "Sorry, I don't know the combination."

She laughed, reached behind herself and in seconds the bra came loose. He swept the straps off her shoulders and caught her beautiful, ample breasts in his hands. She had large areolas and he kissed them tenderly letting his tongue curl around the nipples until he felt them harden.

As he kissed her mouth, his hand slid down over her stomach, beneath the elastic of her panties and into her thatch of pubic hair. She moaned, and raising a leg, allowed his hand to close over her. Her head fell back and she groaned, "Oh... oh yes." Her hips began a slow rhythmic push against his hand and he allowed his finger to slide deep within her with every thrust.

Her hand closed around his manhood and she squeezed. Jamie felt a climax begin to build and he pushed away from her. He knew when he came it was going to be quick and if he was going to dump a load, he'd much rather it be inside of her than in her hand.

Breathing hard, he sat back on his heels and just let the wholeness of her fill his vision.

"You," he said, "are indescribably beautiful."

He reached out, grabbed her panties and slid them down over her thighs. She kicked them off, put her legs around him, and sat up. As she held him close she whispered, "Do it, Jamie. Do it to me now."

He laid her back down and crawled between her legs. She reached down and guided him home. As he began to move she gripped his buttocks hard to keep him still, shifted her hips a little, then put her arms around his back.

"Oh God," she whispered, "that feels so good." And they began to move together. Slowly at first, then quickening.

Jamie felt gooseflesh starting at the small of his back then come roaring up his spine like a breaking wave. Much too quickly and impossible to stop, he came. He grunted as every muscle in his body stiffened-from his curling toes to his tightening jaws. The little pump at the base of his cock was spewing semen as fast as it could. His body thrilled at the sensation but guilt flooded his mind.

Lisa gripped him with her legs and arms and picked up the pace. Determined to please her, Jamie tried his best to keep up but soon his now-shriveled member was squeezed out of her like a pimiento out of an olive. Movement stopped and they were still for some time.

Still wrapped around each other, they lay together, breathing heavily, soaked in sweat. After a while, Jamie carefully rolled off to one side. He looked into her face, expecting to see disappointment there. Instead, she was grinning at him. The grin became a giggle, then a full-throated laugh as she planted big wet kisses all over his face.

"Wow," she said, "that was fun."

"You're not disappointed?"

"Disappointed? How could I be disappointed? I got laid! And so, my furry friend, did you."

With the last word, she slapped him on the ass for emphasis. Jamie laughed.

"Yeah, I did, didn't I?"

With merry laughter, they held each other tight and rolled around on the little mattress.

"Oops," Lisa said as she pushed him gently away, reached into a drawer in the nightstand and came out with a Kleenex that she tucked between her legs.

"What goes in must ooze out."

"Oh... I guess I should have asked... y'know before, but are you...?

"On the pill? Yes. I got a prescription as soon as I got to Colton. For months I've been wondering if it was a wasted effort. But then suddenly-wow! You know?"

* * *

The conversation flowed along so smoothly that Jamie lost all track of time. Lisa was smart and witty and seemed to enjoy his company as much as he enjoyed hers. At one point she was talking about a Philosophy class she had been sitting in on.

"You didn't take it for credit?" Jamie asked.

"No, just for fun. It was a third-year class and you have to have taken Intro to Philosophy before you can officially sign up. But Willoughby is the head of the department and really good. Also really old and about to retire. He only taught one class last semester and that was "Existentialism" so I sat in just because I may not get another chance to hear him teach."

Her hand had scooped up his flaccid penis and now held it gently as she talked. It occurred to him that at any other point in his life, if someone had touched him there he would have shouted, jumped back, maybe taken a swing at them. Now here he was practically purring.

"Willoughby, huh?" he said, "was it worth it?"

"Oh absolutely. The man is so far out. He's like a talented mimic or something. He doesn't just quote Nietzsche, he becomes Nietzsche."

She let her back hunch up, twitched an imaginary walrus mustache, and said with a German accent,

"I could only beleef in a Godt who knew how to dance!"

As she said this she jerked her hand several times for emphasis. His laughter faded into a groan and he pressed his hips tighter toward her body. She smiled at him slyly.

"Ooh, is something stirring? Let's see if we can wake him up."

She cupped his testicles with one hand and began to gently caress his penis.

"Come on, Thumper," She crooned, "Show us what you've got."

Jamie felt himself begin to twitch and stiffen.

He tried to say something like, "ooh wow, that feels great!' but it came out of his mouth as "uuhngrrugggh..."

Lisa seemed to know just when to squeeze and when to stroke. A few minutes later he was standing up stiff and tall. His heart pounded wildly against his ribcage and his erection throbbed to the same rhythm. She threw one leg over his hips and slowly lowered herself onto him. Then she began to rock. Slowly and softly at first then faster and deeper. Her breath was coming in short gasps that became high-pitched, soft moans as the tempo quickened. Jamie was, by turns, very proud of himself for lasting so long, worried about himself that he might be doing something wrong, and ashamed of himself for constantly checking in to see how he was doing. Lisa, without slacking the pace, bent over, clutched his body, and buried her face in his neck. Jamie grabbed her ass with both hands and worked his pelvis in the same rhythm. Just as he felt himself slip beyond the point of no return, every muscle in Lisa's body seemed to go through quick, stuttering spasms as she quietly screamed into the pillow. Jamie moaned as he pumped the second load of the night into the still-twitching girl.

They lay together in a sweaty heap, their ragged breathing slowly returning to normal. Finally, Lisa rolled away, tucked a Kleenex between her legs, and snuggled up to him. They looked into each other's eyes for a long moment.

"Oh..." Jamie said in a near whisper.

Then both said, "Wow."

"Quick," said Lisa, "pinkie shake!"

She put out her fist with the little finger sticking out in a hook. After a moment's confusion, Jamie put out his own little finger. Lisa hooked it and pumped their hands once up and down.

"Pinkie shake?" Jamie said with a slightly scornful face.

"Well, of course. When two people say the same thing at the same time, you pinkie shake. It's good luck if you do. If you don't, well..."

"In Iowa, you yell, 'Jinx! You owe me a Coke!' Then count to ten real fast. If the other person doesn't say 'Jinx' before you get to ten, then he, or she, has to buy you a Coke."

"Iowa, huh?" She sat up. "At what point does one of the people punch the other in the shoulder?"

"No, no, no. That's a completely different game. You see, one person makes this little 'O' sign with his fingers and... OW!"

"See? One pinky shake and you're getting luckier already."

"How does you punching me in the shoulder make me lucky?"

"Well, you're lucky I didn't punch you in the nose."

They mock-scowled at each other, then burst into fits of giggling. Wrapped in each other's arms, they fell back onto the little bed. They pulled the comforter up around their chins, snuggled together, and within moments they were asleep.

* * *

Jamie and Lisa came downstairs and the smells of breakfast cooking got more enticing as they approached the kitchen. As they walked through the swinging door, conversation abruptly stopped and six faces turned to look at them. Then everyone cheered.

Mike looked at his watch and said, "Well it's about time... in more ways than one!"

Jamie, felt heat rising up his neck, and looked over at Lisa to see she was glowing a bright strawberry red. To cover her embarrassment she went to the stove where Madeleine was turning hotcakes in two frying pans, while bacon was burbling happily in a third.

"Where did all this come from?" Lisa said, "My parents emptied the refrigerator before they left."

"Aaron and I volunteered our twenty dollars and Mitch drove us into town for supplies," Madeleine said. "The flour and baking powder were in the cupboard, and-'Ta-Daa'-these were in the back of the freezer."

She reached into the trash can and pulled out two empty boxes of Birdseye frozen blueberries.

"Oh, wow. Blueberry pancakes! I was hungry but now I'm drooling."

Just then Mitch came through the swinging door holding a joint in one hand and a match in the other.

"I'm thinking before we eat," the match flared, "a little somethin'. You know what I mean."

As Mike held a lungful of the smoke, he proffered the joint to Jamie who took a long hit and passed it to Lisa. From Lisa, it started around the room. Within a few minutes, Jamie felt that old familiar stone come creeping up behind his eyeballs. Jamie slipped his arm around Lisa, pulled her close to him and they shared a silly grin. Then he turned back to Mitch who had pulled another joint out of his shirt pocket and was in the process of lighting it.

"Where, my man, did you get this righteous pot? Colton has been bone dry for it seems like weeks. Even old Harvey, who's been carding out seeds and saving them to plant next spring is grinding them up and smoking them."

After they had both toked from the new joint and passed it on, Mitch said he knew a guy in Boulder.

"I'm no big-time dealer, but this dude'll sell me a few lids at a good price whenever I want to drive over there. He says he digs turning on the Villagers. Makes him feel like Santa Claus or some shit. I sell some to my friends and it keeps me in smokes for free."

"Have you got a couple of lids? I've got twenty bucks that I've been sitting on 'til my government check gets to me next week."

"Not on me, man, I never carry more than I can eat-small town, you know. Everybody knows everybody-but I think I can fix you up. We'll take a ride later."

* * *

An hour later, Jamie, Mitch, and the blonde girl-Jamie thought he remembered Mitch calling her "Mitz"-were zipping up coats, putting on hats, and heading for the door. Lisa had found a jar of instant coffee on a back shelf and everyone not leaving was sitting around the living room hugging warm mugs and listening to music.

"Oh my God," Lisa suddenly cried out. "Look at this!"

She was holding a Who album and pointing to a picture of the band on the back cover. Catherine and Sandy came over to look. Then they looked at Jamie, then back at the picture, then back at Jamie.

"Far out," said Catherine.

"Cool!" said Sandy, "like they were twins or something."

"What?" Jamie said as he walked over and took the album cover that Lisa held out.

"There on the back cover," Lisa pointed out, "the drummer, Keith Moon. You look just like him."

Jamie had thick, straight, dark hair that he hadn't had cut in six months. His hair was settling into a sort of "Dutch Boy" look that he kind of enjoyed. And he had to admit that the round, nebbishy face under that same haircut in the photo looked a lot like his own.

"Nah, yer daft! Oi don't look a bit loike 'im," Jamie said in an awful English accent, "But 'e looks a lot loike me!"

There was general laughter as they walked out the door.

* * *

Mitch's car, a '62 Impala ragtop was parked, motor running, on the shoulder of a small country highway. Mitch was making his way across the snow-covered ditch to the line of fencing beyond. After only about ten minutes' drive from the farmhouse, the heater had just begun to warm the interior of the car. The girl was sitting in the middle of the front seat staring straight ahead while Jamie, next to her, watched Mitch's progress toward a particular fencepost.

"So, your name is 'Mitz', right?"

Without looking at him, she nodded her head.

"Is that short for 'Mitzi' or like a nickname because you have large hands?"

She held up her normal-sized hands, snorted, and rolled her eyes. By then, Mitch had dug a metal lunchbox out of the snow, extracted some of the contents, replaced the box and was sweeping snow back over it. Then he headed back to the car.

"Here he comes, like a pirate returning from the treasure chest with gold doubloons in his pocket." Jamie said before adding, "Arrrr."

Mitz wordlessly turned her head to look at him out from under the eye makeup, and then watched Mitch make his way around to the driver's door.

Back behind the wheel, Mitch handed two marijuana-filled Baggies across to Jamie who handed a twenty dollar bill back.

"You know those are pretty fat lids, Mitch said. "You could divide them into three, sell two for ten bucks each, keep one and still get your 20 bucks back."

"As a matter of fact," Jamie looked at the two bags, "I was thinking along the same lines myself. Thanks, dude."

"My pleasure."

Mitch turned his car around and headed back to the farmhouse.

"One thing," Jamie pulled the little sawed off pipe out of his coat pocket and began packing the bowl with some of his newly-purchased weed, "Since you don't make it up to Colton very often, how would you feel about introducing me to your Santa Claus friend in Boulder? So he knows I'm not a narc or anything."

"You're not are you?"

"Nope. Just a college student with a few friends who like to get high."

"Okay, cool. I'll give him a call and then, if he's up for it, I'll get hold of you and see what we can work out."

"Sounds like a plan."

Nicely loaded by now, Jamie was enjoying skimming through the snowfields in the Impala. Mitch popped open the glove box, snatched out a cassette, and plugged it into the stereo.

"Man, you think rock 'n' roll is good when you're stoned, dig this!"

Loud, wildly intricate jazz began to pour out of the car's speakers. It was Dixieland, and it was compelling, amazing, and hypnotic. As the recorded clarinet danced and shimmied through the piece, Jamie watched Mitch's fingers dance and shimmy against the steering wheel. Then Jamie sat back and let the music carry him away.

With a grin on his face, his head bobbing to the beat, Jamie decided that if life had a soundtrack, for his story, at this moment, this music was perfect.

ELEVEN

There were thirty-four other men in the classroom besides Larry Sherman, all of them dressed in different police uniforms, depending on what jurisdiction they came from. There were eight uniforms from Denver as well as several plain-clothes guys, five representatives from Boulder and several from each of the other mid-size cities-Fort Collins, Pueblo, and Colorado Springs. Most everyone else was there, like Larry, by himself. There were no women in the room.

Agent Slocum of the DEA was finishing up his presentation.

"Just remember, Gentlemen, information is the name of the game. Just as the Army runs on intelligence, drug enforcement is no different. Develop your sources. If you bust some kid with half an ounce of pot in his pocket, you've wasted your time. He'll get probation and if it's a small town, you'll never get another collar. But if you can turn him, find out where he got it, and then find out where that guy got it, your first bust can have a very heavy impact."

As Slocum scooped up his notes from the lectern and put them into his briefcase, the cop in the seat next to Sherman leaned over and said out of the side of his mouth, "Slocum laying on top of his wife seems like 'very heavy impact' to me."

Sherman glanced at the DEA agent trying to button his suit coat around an extremely ample gut. He looked at the cop next to him and rolled his eyes.

"Weak, Anderson, very weak."

Sherriff's Deputy Jack Anderson was from Gunnison. Tall and thin, with curly red hair and a spray of freckles across his nose, he seemed to be always looking for the next great joke and always finding it was just out of reach. But after sitting in the classroom next to him for three days, Sherman had decided he liked the man's company, bad jokes and all.

"Okay, Don Rickles, what'll it be?" Sherman stood and closed his notebook. "Lunch in the cafeteria? Or run across the street for one of those Reuben Sandwiches?"

"Need you ask?" said Anderson, also standing, "The Reuben, for sure. Also, french fries and an iced tea which we can pretend is the cold beer we should be drinking with it."

Sherman dipped a couple of fries into a little cup of ketchup and gave his tablemate a serious look. "Tell me something Patrolman Anderson, just between you and me and the shithouse door, have you ever smoked pot?"

Anderson quickly glanced around the room to make sure no one was listening, then grinned conspiratorially, "I toked up a couple or three times before I joined the force. I've been cool about it since then, what about you?"

"No, never have. Did it turn you into a dangerous lunatic?"

"Well, there was that old lady that I beat up. Then I stole her purse and threw her under a bus."

This made Sherman chuckle.

"Actually," the red-headed cop went on, "it was sorta fun. I laughed a lot, ate a big chocolate fudge sundae and went to bed. End of story."

After taking a moment to chew and swallow a big bite of corned beef and sauerkraut, Anderson gave Sherman a level look.

"Doesn't it sometimes seem weird to you that we're going to all this trouble for no real reason?"

"One good reason, my friend, it's against the law. That's all I need."

"Say farting was against the law," Anderson said, "and your mother cocks a leg and lets a loud rattler go, would you arrest her?"

"In a heartbeat. Handcuffs on, down to the station for booking. And that night I'd sleep like a baby."

"I bet you would. And wake up every two hours with wet pants, crying your head off."

TWELVE

There was a soft knock at the door. Jamie marked his place in his Geology textbook and threw a questioning glance at Mike who was sitting on the upper bunk running scales on his guitar. Jamie shrugged and opened the door. Big Dan stood there in the hallway, grinning, his hands in the pockets of a leather coat with long fringe running down the sleeves. Behind him stood a tall, thin dude with lank hair that hung down to his shoulders. Jamie was sure he had met him, but couldn't put a name to the face.

From behind him, Mike said, "Hey Dan. Get in here. What brings you to our little dorm room?"

Jamie stepped aside, let the two visitors in, and taking a quick peek up and down the hallway, shut the door behind him.

"Hello Mike, hey Jamie. How's it hanging? You know John Krauter, right?

"I don't believe so," Jamie said, hoping that Krauter didn't remember him. "But I've heard of you. Musician right? I'm Jamie."

Krauter only said, "Cool, man." and they shook hands.

"I heard you've got some Psilocybin," Big Dan said, "that true?"

"Thinkin' about doin' up a little Magic Mushroom, eh?" Jamie grinned, "Sure, I can probably fix you up. Five bucks a hit, I think I've only got six left."

"Far out, man. One for Theresa, one for John, and two or me... how about four?"

Jamie went to the closet, dug around in the back, found a little wooden box, and took out a baggie that had a few pills in it. He counted out four largish gelatin capsules that contained a gray powder and then put the remainder back in the closet.

Mike laid his guitar down and said, "Two, dude? Seriously? I mean, just one of those 'shrooms is a pretty flashy trip. I laughed so hard and so long, the next day my ribs had bruises on them. Both sides, man."

Big Dan smiled and shook his head. He handed a twenty to Jamie and took the pills. "Now, don't go telling everybody 'cause I'm not sure myself what's going down, but it's like... I had a vision, man"

"A vision? Like what?"

"I was ripped to the gills on some very pure window pane acid when suddenly there was this brilliant light all around and a golden voice. Yeah, I know, sounds don't usually have colors, but this voice was like, just pure gold, man. And it told me to 'prepare myself'. No shit, that's what she or he-couldn't tell-said, 'prepare yourself."

Dan's eyes took on a faraway look as he told his story. "I had about half a key of the red weed left. I took it out to the highway and laid it on the first hitchhiker I came across. No more smoking for me, just psychedelics. I have to stay sharp. So thank you Jamie, my man, you may have done the world a big favor."

"Always happy to help," Jamie said as he opened the door. He was not feeling comfortable and just wanted to get the two out of the room.

"Keep it cool, man"

Krauter left but Dan stopped to shake Jamie's hand.

'Tell me something, Jamie. Did you ever want to be President of the United States?"

"Well no. That's a little too much work for me."

"No work at all, man. You'd be like a figurehead. The country would be run by a religious government."

"Oh, okay. Let me know how that works out."

Jamie watched as the two men headed down the hallway to the elevators. Feiger, The Head Resident, watched the two hippies go by and then turned to give Jamie the stink eye. Jamie returned the look with a big grin, held up two fingers and yelled, "Peace, Dude!' before going back in the room and closing the door behind him.

As soon as the door closed, Mike burst into laughter.

"Ooooe. Good ol' Dan seems to be on that slow train to Flip City."

"Seems like, doesn't it? I hope I'm not around when he gets there. I don't think I'd deal well with full-on batshit crazy."

"But look on the bright side. You could go from being a lowly drummer for the Who to President of the United States."

"Are you still on about that Keith Moon shit? You and Lisa are making me nuts with it. So I've decided to grow a mustache."

"Oh yeah?" Mike said, peering at Jamie's upper lip. "C'mere and let me see."

Jamie reluctantly obliged and Mike inspected from several different angles.

"I suppose," Mike said as he picked up his guitar, "you could let those two hairs grow to about a foot long, then glue them on your lip running back and forth."

"Droll, my friend. Very fucking droll."

"Think of it as a 'stache combover'."

Jamie gave Mike a sour look, and then reopened his textbook.

* * *

A warm, Spring breeze was blowing outside the Colton Post Office as Mike emerged, carrying a small package. He stopped to watch a pair of robins fly after each other around and through the new young leaves of a pair of cottonwoods. He got to Jamie's Volkswagen, saw Jamie was still in the phone booth against the Post Office wall and sat on the car's front fender to wait.

The birds swooped down to a puddle in the street left by a recent shower, splashed around a bit, then resumed their game of "I might consider mating with you, but you'll have to catch me first".

Jamie came out of the phone booth.

"Well, that sucks," Jamie said, "my guy in Boulder left town in a hurry. The chick who answered the phone said his mother was sick or some shit. But the guy once told me his mother had died when he was little."

"So you're not driving down to Boulder today I take it."

"Nope. No reason to. And it looks like the Easter Egg Party over at Harvey's tomorrow night is going to be a drag. A lot of people were looking forward to getting loaded for it. Me included."

"Well," said Mike, "Sometimes when that big ol' bummer is coming straight at you, out of nowhere comes a tidal wave of peace and love that knocks that bum trip right off the road and into the ditch. Pow!"

"And what, my guitar-strumming friend, the fuck are you talking about?"

"In a second, Dude, in a second. First I want to ask you something."

Mike tossed the package through the open passenger window onto the seat, and then walked around to the rear of the car.

"I noticed this when I came out of the Post Office. It's April, right?"

"Yeah..." Jamie said, puzzled.

"Down there in the bottom corner of your license plate, that's the month it expires, right?"

Jamie looked at the plate and saw three capital letters there-M.A.R.

"Oh shit. What the fuck am I gonna do?"

"You got a rag of some kind?"

"There's an old towel on the floor of the back seat."

"Get it for me will ya?"

As Jamie crawled into his car, Mike crossed the sidewalk to a puddle that had formed in the dirt under a lilac bush. He scooped up a handful of mud, took it back behind the car and threw it at the plate. Jamie handed him the towel and he began to clean his hands with it.

"Well," said Mike, "what do you think?"

Since the license plate was lettered in Brown paint on white, the mud had rendered the expiration month all but illegible.

"Hey, how cool is that?" Jamie said, pleased, "Thanks, Man."

As they got into the car, Mike said, "It's only temporary. The next rain storm will wash it off."

"Okay, cool. Now, what is this tidal wave of love and fucking peace, Man?"

As Jamie drove Mike was tearing the brown paper wrapping off the little package. He tossed the paper into the back seat and sat there admiring an old, scruffy book. Jamie leaned over to look.

"Treasure Island?" Jamie scoffed. "This is your tidal wave? What are you going to do, go over to Big Dan's and be pirates together?"

"Maybe," said Mike enjoying the moment, "or maybe not. Let's see..."

He opened the book. The centers of many of the pages had had a square cut out of them and inside of the small compartment they formed lay a pile of pink pills. Jamie goggled.

"Holy shit. Is that...?"

"LSD, my Man. Pink double domes. About 150 micrograms apiece."

"Far out, Man. It is a tidal wave! Who sent them to you?"

"Remember that gig in Denver the 'Dills played last week? The one where you and Lisa were balling and you didn't go?"

"I told you I had to study. I had a Poli-Sci midterm coming up."

"Yeah, right. Anyway, there was a dude there who said he was holding and he could fix me up. So I gave him thirty-five bucks and told him to send it General D and whaddya know, he didn't rip me off."

Mike began counting the little pile.

"How many did he send you?"

"Thirty. Take out five bucks for shipping and handling and that's a buck a hit. If it's as good as he said it was-you know, Owsley's Recipe and all the usual bullshit-but if it's at all good and I sell for two bucks a hit, that's a pretty cheap high."

"You know," Jamie said, "maybe you ought to sell it for four or five bucks. At two bucks a hit, people will drop two or three each. There could be some massive freaking out. Remember Willy, that kid from Nebraska who dropped two of those Lemon Drop caps?"

"Oh yeah, I remember. He thought the back of his head had fallen off and his brains were leaking out. Spent the whole night trying to get somebody to take him to the Emergency Room."

"If I remember right, you got him to tie a dish towel around his head so he wouldn't bum anybody else's trip."

Mike looked at Jamie out of the corners of his eyes and started to giggle. Jamie felt a big guffaw boil up out of his chest and he let it go. They laughed together for a full two blocks.

"You, my friend," Jamie said after wiping his eyes, "are one cruel motherfucker."

* * *

"No, I told you, Jamie Shipman, I'm not dropping anything tonight. I'm in training."

Jamie knew from experience that whenever Lisa used his full name she was serious and wouldn't be swayed. He folded the pink pill back up in the little paper envelope he had made and put it back in his pocket.

"Do you still want to go, tonight?"

"Yes, of course. Just because I'm going out for track doesn't mean I can't have any fun."

Jamie put the Volkswagen in gear and pulled out into the street.

After a few minutes of silence, Jamie said, "What if someone should light a joint and start it around?"

"Oh, I'll probably pull a couple of butcher knives out of Harvey's kitchen drawer and go berserk. Nothing like a blood bath to convince a few hippies of the error of their ways."

"Or you could just pass it along without taking a toke."

"That too."

* * *

By the time they walked into Harvey's Apartment, Jamie was flying. Whatever his eyes rested on quickly became oversaturated with color and seemed to crawl apart. Since he had been dropping acid regularly over the last few months, he no longer found himself in a semi-hysterical state, clinging to his sanity.

I may not be the engineer on this train but it's nice being able to kick back and enjoy the ride.

Doug Krenovich, his eyes dilated and his cheeks flushed, appeared in Jamie's field of vision.

"You tripping?" Doug asked.

Jamie considered the question. "I'm on the train, man. But I'm not stuck out there on the cow catcher. This time I'm ridin' inside."

"What? Huhh..."

"Think I'll go up in the Vista Dome and have a look around."

To illustrate his point, Jamie began to make railroad noises and to bob to the imaginary click of a railroad car's wheels.

Doug's body began to twitch and then shake. The movement ran up his spine to his head which flopped around for a moment like an Aspen leaf in the wind.

"Fuck, man!" Doug said, "You just did my head. Fair warning, Shipman, I owe you one."

"I'm looking forward to it, my freaky friend."

Noticing that Lisa was talking to Madeleine and several other girls, Jamie wandered into the kitchen. There were a handful of people, Jamie knew them only vaguely from the music room, gathered around Patty who was regaling them with a wild story of her days in Venice, California. At the stove was Aaron, working with several large, steaming pots. The kitchen table had been cleared off and covered in newspapers and Harvey was arranging a row of mismatched bowls and cups on the papers. In the air was the slightly sulfurous smell of boiling eggs and vinegar.

Jamie stepped over to Harvey.

"Well, Howdy there, stranger."

Harvey turned slowly and looked up.

"No stranger than you," Harvey said and held up his hand. Jamie gripped it.

Jamie held up a carton of eggs he'd brought in from the car. "Eggs you wanted, eggs you got. Where should I put them?"

"Over there next to Aaron. He's the egg-boiler on this trip."

Jamie crossed over to Aaron, put his carton of eggs on a pile next to the stove, and complimented the egg-boiler on his work.

Aaron dipped a slotted spoon into the water, brought out an egg, and slowly rolled it around.

"Think about it, man. A chicken pops one of these out about five times a week. Each one is bigger than her head and weighs about a sixth of her body weight. That'd be like you shitting out a twenty-five-pound bowling ball every other day for like two years, man. Kinda painful to think about, you know?"

Jamie felt his sphincter twinge a little bit.

"Thanks for the sunshine, man."

Jamie went back over to see what Harvey was doing. He had bottles of dye, some white vinegar and a kettle of boiling water. He was mixing some of each liquid in every cup or bowl.

"What's that?" Jamie pointed to a small bowl of yellow liquid.

"Melted Margarine."

"What do use that for?"

"Watch and dig it, man."

Harvey dropped about a teaspoon of the margarine into the cup of blue dye, then put a cool, hardboiled egg on another spoon and dunked it into the cup. He rolled it around for about fifteen seconds, then drew it out and put it into the empty bottom of a cardboard egg tray to dry.

Jamie stared at the egg and muttered, "Wow."

Instead of the solid blue he was expecting, the egg was covered with swirling blue and white shapes like something by Van Gogh.

"Look at that. Psychedelic eggs! You weren't shittin' us, man. Lemme go get Lisa."

A few minutes later, a very impressed Lisa was at the table and begging to dye a few eggs of her own. Another few minutes and a crowd of people had gathered around the table relegating Harvey to getting cartons of freshly cooled hard-boiled eggs out of the refrigerator.

Just as Jamie was leaving the kitchen, the front door of the apartment banged open and another crew of giggling acidheads rolled in. Jack McNulty was the first one through the door, followed by Rachel and Angela, with "Shoes" Schumacher, trying hard to look like Che Guevara in a black beret, coming in last.

"Happy Easter!" Rachel and Angela crowed together.

"He is risen!" McNulty intoned, "and hath dropped a pink double dome!"

All, including Jamie, laughed and applauded.

Lisa came out of the kitchen and greeted the two girls with hugs, then slipped her arm around Jamie's waist.

Shoes started to close the door behind him, but stopped and opened it again.

"Hey y'all, look who's comin' up the walk."

A moment later, Kenny Walsingham came through the door. He was wearing a big, Hoss Cartwright-style black hat with a broad, flat brim. Behind him, a beautiful girl with long, wavy, blonde hair stepped into the room and Shoes closed the door behind her.

"Waltz!" Several people all shouted at once. Jamie, McNulty, and Shoes were all slapping Kenny on the back while Angela and Rachel hugged him.

Kenny grinned and blushed, then stepped back to introduce the girl who'd come in with him. He lightly placed his hand in the small of her back.

"Okay everybody," Waltz said, "this is Nancy Traynor. She's from Casper. She goes to school at Casper JuCo, but she's thinking of transferring down here to Colton. Nancy, these are some of the crazy people I've been telling you about."

Nancy touched Kenny on the shoulder and whispered something to him.

"Oh, yeah," Kenny said, "she likes to get high so don't think she's a narc or something."

Nancy playfully punched him in the shoulder and turned to the group. "I just didn't want anybody to get paranoid about me, that's all."

Jamie was looking at Waltz and Nancy together as a couple. With his acid-enhanced vision, he could almost see the lines of force that tied them together. Then he realized Waltz was looking at both him and Lisa together and knew the same thought was passing through Waltz's head.

Well, well. Look who has himself a girlfriend. How cool is that?

Jamie shook himself back to reality and realized Rachel was talking to Krenovich. He turned to listen.

"..two weeks ago, no it was three weeks ago" Rachel looked at McNulty. "You didn't tell him? It was so bizarre!"

He didn't answer, just pushed his shoulders up, bugged his eyes out, and made that McNulty face that said, "Don't know-can't say!"

"So a bunch of us had dropped and we were just riding around in Jack's van trying to think of something fun to do when someone remembered..."

"That was me," Shoes cut in, "I just said 'I think 2001 is playin' in Boulder' and that was it. Off to Boulder we went."

"Well, where was I?" whined Krenovich.

"Y'all weren't in the van, dude. That's all I know"

"So here we were in the third row of this theater," Rachel picked up the story, "blasted out of our skulls, and then the really flashy part near the end starts."

"Where he's, like, zipping through this wormhole in space?" said Aaron.

"No, man," McNulty said, "he's traveling through the barrier between parallel universes."

"No, that's not it," Lisa said, "It's all in his mind. He's breaking through his reality to a higher state of consciousness."

"Whatever he's doing," Rachel said, loud enough to regain everyone's attention, "Some guy came walking down the aisle toward the screen. He got past the front row and just kept walking. He went up three or four steps and right into the screen! And he disappeared!"

"What?" said Waltz, "What happened to him?"

"I don't know! He was just gone!"

Jamie looked at McNulty and Shoes. "No shit? Just disappeared?"

McNulty said, "Poof." and made his hands pop open.

Shoes said, "Completely cooked our heads, man."

"Okay, well you win the far-out trip story of the night prize," Jamie laughed, "Go out in the kitchen and get yourself an egg."

* * *

It was after midnight and Jamie sat on a big body pillow, with his back against the wall. A crush of thoughts was banging around inside his skull. He was doing what every acid-head knew was something you should never do when you were stoned. He was trying to figure out his life. Sometime before, as much as half an hour or as little as five minutes, Lisa had left the apartment with Waltz and Nancy.

She had said, "It's getting late and I've got to get back to the dorm and get to bed. Waltz is going to give me a ride back. Okay?"

Jamie wasn't sure what to say. Should he ask her to stay for a while? Then he'd have to go out later in the cold, still completely loaded and try to drive her home himself. But if he said, "Sure, okay. Go with Waltz" would she think he was pleased to be rid of her? Should he go with them now and then ask Waltz to bring him back?

He couldn't decide so instead of saying anything, he just stared at her and gawped like a beached trout.

Waltz and Nancy, standing by the door with their coats on were staring at him. Lisa gave him an impatient look.

Jamie finally forced some sounds out of his mouth, but they consisted of "Uh... uhh... uh"

Lisa said, "Never mind. I'll just go. I'll talk to you tomorrow." Jamie could hear a steely edge in her voice.

As she walked out the door, he sank into the big pillow on the floor and started replaying the scene in his head, trying to figure out what he should have said or done that would have made the whole thing come out better.

Mike had come in earlier, bringing a friend named Lefty that he'd been hanging out with lately. Now Lefty was in the kitchen and Mike was sitting in an old overstuffed chair with Angela curled up in his lap. Mike was playing with a lock of Angela's hair and talking softly to her. The girl was almost purring.

Now, Mike would have handled that easily. He knows how to rap to a chick.

Then Jamie looked at Angela with her big doe eyes and he couldn't help imagining what it would be like if he were the owner of the lap she was cuddled up on. That thought sent his mind careening down another well-worn path.

Lisa was, he'd realized some time before, the perfect girl for him. She was smart, funny, confident, almost unaware of how beautiful she was, and best of all, she liked him. She seemed to prefer his company to any other's, and when he thought about her he got kind of squishy inside. He was pretty sure he loved her, but could not bring himself to tell her so. And maybe he didn't love her really, if he was all giggly in love, why did he keep thinking about Angela? Maybe if he told Lisa he loved her, maybe by saying it he could convince himself. To some guys, he knew, "I love you" was nothing more than a casual phrase used only to get a girl into bed and nothing more. But in his mind, the words meant you had signed the contract. You were in it, forever and ever, worlds without end, amen. And that was a step he just couldn't bring himself to take. Or was it Angela? If he committed himself to Lisa, any faint hope that Angela would one day be his would disappear. Or did the phrase "settling down" have, for him, the finality and resonance of a jail sentence? Was he just not ready to stop having fun?

Jamie was tumbling down this rabbit-hole ass over teacup when Lefty walked into the room and, inadvertently, pulled him back.

"Hey, you hippies!" Lefty announced, "While you were out here being psychedelicized, we were getting robbed in the kitchen!"

"Everybody gaped and yelled "Huh? What?" and "What happened?"

"Three Chinamen slipped in the back door, held a knife to Harvey's throat, and stole all the eggs. Eight dozen eggs, gone just like that."

Mouths agape, everyone in the room just stared and tried to make sense of what they had just heard. Chinamen stealing eggs? What?

Then Lefty mimed a two-handed cast with a fishing rod and began turning the imaginary reel.

"Hey Harvey," he yelled back into the kitchen, "I just hooked about a dozen on one cast! Heh heh heh."

Mike and a few others laughed, Krenovich said, "Fuck you, man. Fuckin' Chinamen. Jesus Christ."

Lefty put his hands on his hips and chuckled with sheer delight.

Harvey came into the room and said, "All the eggs are dyed. They look pretty far out. Now, what do we do with them?"

"Well, what do you think you do with eggs?" Angela asked and then answered herself, "You go and hide them of course."

"Bentley Park is only a few blocks away." Rachel said.

"Cool. Let's do it!" said Aaron.

"And then after the sun comes up," Jamie said, "we'll go back and look for 'em!"

Jamie was surprised that within about forty-five minutes, everyone in the house had got their coats on, had divided up the eggs equally, and had gotten themselves sorted out into three different cars.

Amazing. For a bunch of loaded hippos, this must be a new speed record.

It was approaching four o'clock when Krenovich came limping back to Jamie's car. Everyone else, coming down off the night's high, had packed into Jack's van and Lefty's old Studebaker Station wagon and left the park, promising to be back at ten.

"Krenovich?" Jamie called into the darkness. "What happened to you, man?"

"I fell out of a fuckin' tree. What I thought was a good, thick branch was actually a little dead twig."

"Bummer, dude. If you hadn't hurt yourself, I'd be laughing."

"Nah," Krenovich looked at his foot and turned it this way and that, "It's not too bad."

"Okay, cool," Jamie said, then burst into giggles.

"What's so funny?"

"You fell out of a tree, man."

Then Jamie switched his voice to a TV announcer's cadence, "That's what's wrong with America's Youth. They take drugs and fall out of trees."

"The bummer was that I hadn't hidden the egg yet when I fell. So I had to climb the god-damned tree again."

"Why didn't you just stick it in a bush or something?"

"Hey, when Doug Krenovich hides an egg, he hides a fuckin' egg!"

By the time most of them regrouped in the park it was well past ten o'clock. A warm sun had chased most of the morning chill from the air. Few had slept, none of them well, and they looked it-strung out and pallid, with dark circles around their eyes. The only animated one was Patty who wore a long, loosely pleated skirt consisting of several layers of colorful fabric. Where everyone else trudged, she danced. And the skirt twirled as she did so.

"Hey wait before you start," Krenovich hurried up to the group, still limping, "Sorry I'm late, but I figured I'd better roll up the prize."

He held up a fat joint. It had taken at least four papers to roll it, and Krenovich was justifiably proud.

"So whoever finds the most eggs..."

"Hey, can I see that?" Lefty interrupted, taking the joint.

He quickly produced a lighter, fired it up, took a deep toke, and passed it to Aaron.

"Hey, man," Krenovich protested. Then he shrugged and took a hit.

"Whoever finds the most eggs," Lefty said, "Gets to eat the roach."

As they passed the joint around, Patty danced into the group and took a hit.

"Oh, I didn't tell you," she laughed, "On my way over here I passed a little kid coming the other way. He was holding a purple egg with yellow and white swirls all over it. His eyes were as big as dinner plates, man. It was so far out."

When the joint was smoked, the searchers spread out across the park, except for Patty who noticed two little girls playing on the monkey bars and went over to join them.

Fifteen minutes later, Jamie was standing under a tree near the playground. He heard Mike call and turned with a grin as his roommate and Angela walked up.

"Find anything?"

"Nothing, zero. How about you?"

"No eggs," Angela said, "I found something but Mike wouldn't let me keep it."

"It was a dog turd. She just wanted to put it down my neck."

"Now would I do that?" Angela looked up at him with all the innocent cuteness she could muster.

"Ah. Okay, here she goes," Jamie looked over to the playground. "Those two little girls have been trying to get Patty to hang by her knees from the monkey bars. They both did the trick and then flipped over backward to land on their feet. Now she's finally gonna try it."

Patty had found a higher bar, grabbed it and was pulling her feet up. As she got her legs up and bent over the bar, her skirts slipped down and covered her head. The two little girls stopped giggling and stared, open-mouthed. Patty was not wearing underwear.

Jamie looked at that thick, dark bush of pubic hair and muttered, "I know what I'm seeing, but I don't quite believe it."

"Believe it, brother," Mike chuckled.

Patty grabbed the bar again and back-flipped over to the ground. She cheered for herself as she pushed her skirts back down, and then looked around for her two little instructors, but they were a good half a block away and walking fast.

Not long after, the hunters regrouped at the cars.

"Did anybody find anything?" McNulty inquired.

"Not a whole one," Madeleine said, "we found a few broken ones."

No one else had found an egg. Even Krenovich said that the one he'd hidden in the tree was gone.

"So a bunch of kids must have combed this park earlier and found every egg we hid, right? And the eggs they didn't take home they threw at each other," said Jamie.

Everyone nodded in disappointed agreement.

"Well, we had some fun. The kids had some fun. I'd call this Easter Egg Hunt a complete success!"

The group looked at each other, and then smiles broke out. Then cheers.

* * *

Jamie and Mike came out of the Salvation Army Thrift Store carrying an old, green sofa with worn-down spots on the arms and back.

"Jesus," Jamie said, "this thing weighs a ton. What's it made of? Bricks?"

"It's a sofa-bed, man. It's an uncomfortable sofa that folds out into a really uncomfortable bed. Not bad for five bucks."

Jamie heaved his end of the sofa up onto the tailgate of an old Chevy pickup that was parked at the curb. Shaking his hands to get some circulation back, he went around to the back end to help Mike push the sofa into the truck.

"I dig the truck." said Jamie, "Do I know the guy who owns it?"

Mike pushed up the tailgate and hooked the chains that held it.

"Interesting guy, kind of a cowboy-hippie-Jew. Rachel put us together. He's not much older than you or me but he inherited the stable where she keeps her horse, Alpo."

"She calls that horse Alpo?"

"No, but I do. Pisses her off."

Mike opened the driver's door and then said, "Malcolm Tingley."

"What?"

"The dude's name. I think it was something like 'Tinglestein' but he changed it to Tingley because it sounded more country. Loves country music. Plays a mean rhythm guitar."

"A cowboy-hippie-Jew who loves country music," Jamie said as he closed the passenger door, "Sounds bizarre, man. Is he bizarre?"

"No, he's pretty cool, actually. Wants McNulty and me to play with him. That's why he loaned me the truck."

"You want to play country music? 'Okie from Muskogee' and that shit?"

"No man. Think 'Nashville Skyline' and Bob Dylan."

"Cool album."

"And," said Mike as he pulled into the street, "Dylan's a Jew."

* * *

Forty-five minutes later they had struggled the sofa bed into the living room of the little gray house on 5th Street. The woman who owned the place had bought it with a dining room and a single, generously-sized bedroom. It now had no dining room and three small, oddly-shaped bedrooms. Waltz, Shoes, and Mike had scraped together a hundred dollars each-half for the deposit and the other half for a month's rent-and moved in.

Mike was giving Jamie the Grand Tour.

"On the left, we have my room," Mike said. They put their heads through the doorway. "Notice the deluxe mattress on the floor-in case I ever fall out of bed I won't hurt myself. Bathroom down here. Nice big tub in there. If Mrs. Gorton figured she could raise the rent by dividing it into two little tubs, she'd have done it. And here's the kitchen at the back. Angela noticed that Mrs. Berman had an old refrigerator in her garage and sweet-talked her into letting us have it."

"Where is it?"

"Over in the Berman's garage waiting for you, me, and Malcolm's truck to go pick it up."

"A freakin' refrigerator?" Jamie rolled his eyes, "That hash you said you have better be damned good."

"For you, brother, even the best is not good enough. Plus, if you and Lisa ever get tired of the back seat of that Volkswagen, you can come on over here."

"Where?" Jamie asked, looking around, "Is there a basement?"

"Actually I think there's a root cellar under there somewhere, man, but I was referring to the uncomfortable sofa bed."

"Oh, thanks, man," Jamie said. He went out on the back stoop and surveyed the dirt and weeds.

"We could pull the truck into the alley and back it up almost up to the steps here. With a couple of boards and an old carpet, we could just slide that fridge right on in."

"Woo, dig it" Mike held his hand out palm up. "Give me five, my man."

Jamie slid the palm of his own hand across Mike's and both snapped their fingers. With a laugh, they walked around the house to get the truck.

THIRTEEN

Larry Sherman listened to the reply on the radio, and then thumbed the button on the microphone.

"Copy that. Initiating 10-61. Unit Seven-out."

He reached over and flipped the switch that activated the lights on the roof. He could see the reflection of the flashing red lights in the rear window of the red Volkswagen ahead. The little car's brake lights came on, and it slowed to a stop at the curb. Sherman pulled his cruiser in behind it.

The policeman checked for traffic, got out of his car, and walked slowly up to the driver's side window of the VW. As he walked he noted the modifications that had been made to the car to make it into a "dune buggy" and smiled to himself. He had a secret game he liked to play he called, "Guess who's driving?" Just by the car, he tried to figure out who the driver might be before he got a look at them. This one was easy-a student, male, liked to drink beer and watch football, probably in a fraternity.

He reached the rolled-down window and bent over a little to get a good look at the young man behind the wheel.

"I'm sorry, officer. Was I speeding?"

"License and registration, please."

Yep, just as I thought. Hair is a bit long for a frat boy, but that's getting to be the style these days.

Taking the license and registration, he straightened up to examine them. The license was from Iowa as was the Registration, but the names didn't match. The license was for James Shipman, but the Registration, which had expired two months ago, was for John Shipman.

"You're James Shipman?"

"Yes, sir."

"I stopped you because the number on your license plate turns out to be for a 1964 Cadillac registered in Des Moines. It's a common practice to remove license plates from a vehicle, use them to replace the plates on a stolen vehicle, and then drive the stolen car out of state. Please wait here while I call this in."

In Training, Sherman had learned that it was often helpful to intimate a much more serious charge might be coming down. It tended to get a suspect to agree to the lesser charge without putting up much of a fuss.

In a few minutes, he walked back up the VW's driver's side window.

"Mr. Shipman, may I ask you to get out of the vehicle? I need to ask you some questions."

The driver nervously complied and followed him around to the front of the car. Sherman kept the stern, but friendly look on his face (his wife referred to it as his "cop face").

This guy looks like someone I should know.

He cleared his throat and said, "We have several problems here. One is that this registration is two months expired. The second is that you are James Shipman, and the name here is John Shipman, and the third is the way it was signed over to you is not recognized in the State of Colorado. Can you explain any of this to me?"

Shipman said that the car had been sold to him back in November by his brother Jack, who then moved to Australia. Jack had assured him at the time that the information and signature on the back were sufficient to get a Colorado title. He then apologized for letting the plate expire and said he would pay the fine and get Colorado plates as soon as possible.

"That's pretty much what I thought," Sherman said, "but we have to be sure. It would help a lot if we could find the chassis number on the car and see if it matches the number on the registration. Any ideas where it might be?"

"No, sir."

"It's probably on some kind of plate attached to the body somewhere. You look inside while I look in the engine compartment."

Sherman took his flashlight off his belt and shone it around inside the open back end of the car.

From inside Shipman yelled, "Nothing in the glove compartment or on the firewall."

"Sherman heard the radio in his Cruiser blurt out, "Unit Seven? You copy?" and he went to answer it.

When he came back he said, "One of the guys at the station owns a VW and says it's stamped on the body pan under the back seat."

The two of them got a grip on the back of the back seat cushion and pulled. It snapped up and out and there on the floor was a plate with a long number stamped into it. Sherman examined the number on the floor and the number on the registration.

"Okay, he said, "they match."

Shipman's smile of relief was short-lived, however, when Sherman said, "I'm going to have to ask you to lock it up and come with me down to the station. We have to get confirmation from Iowa that the plate was not stolen."

Fifteen minutes later, the patrol car was headed down the avenue that went by Washington Park. The bridle path that went all the way around the park was next to the street on this side and as they stopped at a stoplight, Sherman noticed a thin girl on a bay horse trotting toward them. When the horse drew abreast of the patrol car, the girl reined it to a stop and stared at the car. Shipman raised his left hand and waved just as the light changed and Sherman accelerated away.

"Friend of yours?" Sherman asked.

"Yeah. Her parents loaned us a refrigerator."

* * *

Sherman sat at his desk and while he waited for the phone to ring, filled out some back paperwork. Suddenly he sat up, stared at the wall for a few seconds, and then started to grin.

"Hey, Corky," he said to the Sergeant-on-duty, "Come here a sec, I just figured something out."

The Sergeant walked over and half-sat on the corner of Sherman's desk.

"The guy I brought in," with a short whip of his head, Sherman indicated the young man sitting on the wooden bench across the hallway staring at his shoes, "he looks like somebody I know and it's been driving me nuts trying to place him. I finally figured it out."

The Sergeant sighed and said, "And..."

"My wife bought the new album 'Tommy' by the Who last week. And guess what? You know the Binker-the baby-cries like an air raid siren half the night. He has for months. But all we have to do is put on 'See Me, Feel Me' from that album and two minutes later he's fast asleep."

"And the point is..."

"The point is that that guy looks just like one of the guys in that band. The drummer or something."

"The drummer is named Tommy?"

"No, no, that's the name of the album. It's like a Rock Opera... never mind. I guess you had to have been there."

"Yeah, I guess," the Sergeant said as he walked back to his chair.

The phone began to ring and Sherman picked it up. He talked for a bit, then walked out into the hallway.

"Mr. Shipman?" he said and the young man looked up, "The Cadillac has only had that plate number for a month. Prior to that, it was owned by your brother. So no problem there, but do you mind stepping into this room for a couple of minutes? There are a couple of things I want to hash over with you."

Sherman opened a door and allowed Shipman to precede him into the room. Inside, there was only a table and four chairs.

"Have a seat, Mr. Shipman"

Sherman sat on one side of the table and Shipman the other. Sherman tore a traffic ticket out of his book and passed it across.

"I'm going to ticket you for driving with an expired plate. There are several other charges I could throw at you and I could impound your car. But I don't think that's necessary. Do you have somewhere off the street you could park it for a while?

"Yes, sir, I think so."

"Because what you're going to have to do is write to your brother in Australia and see if he has the Title to the car. In Colorado, the Title and the Registration are two different things. If he doesn't have it, then he'll have to make out a Bill of Sale that has all this information on it."

He passed the Iowa Registration back to Jamie.

"He'll want to make sure there is a "Quit Claim" clause included. Then he needs to get that Notarized-or whatever it is they do down there- and send it back. With all that in hand, you should be able to get a Colorado Title and then Colorado Registration and plates. Is all that clear?"

"Yes, sir, and thank you."

"No problem," Sherman pushed his chair back, slumped a little, and crossed his ankles. "There's just one more thing. It's probably stupid but the State Drug Enforcement Agency seems to think that our campus is crawling with drug addicts and dealers. Personally, I don't think it's near as big a deal as all that, but I promised some people I'd keep my ear to the ground. Do you ever come across any of that sort of thing?"

"No, sir, not really," Shipman said, "but the other day I was walking across campus and I saw some people-two guys and a girl-trading puffs on a funny looking cigarette. They were in the shadows under a tree and I thought about getting closer to see who it was, but they disappeared."

"Hmmm" Sherman nodded, "I tell you what. Here's my card. If you come across something maybe a little more serious, like if somebody's selling stuff, and you can get me a little hard information, give me a call. You'd be doing a service to the town and the school."

"Okay, sure," the young man said.

"But don't take any chances, okay? Some of these hippie dealers can seem all peace and love, you know, but if they feel threatened they can be dangerous."

"Don't worry. I'll be careful."

FOURTEEN

"Holy shit!" McNulty was peering out the back door of the 5th Street House, "It's Jamie. And look who's behind him."

Waltz and Mike leaned across the sink and pulled the curtains on the back window apart. They watched Jamie turn the Volkswagen past the garbage cans and park it in the back yard. He got out of the car, waved at the police cruiser that was still in the alley behind him. The cop waved back and then sped away down the alley.

"Well, fuck me," said Waltz, "it was Sherm the Sperm."

Jamie shut and locked the door of the VW, then turned toward the house only to see half a dozen hippies come spilling out of the back door and down the porch steps. Lisa raced past the others and threw herself into his arms.

She was squealing happily and yet her cheeks were wet with tears.

"You scared the shit out of me, Shipman!" she half-cried, half-laughed, "just don't ever do that again."

Jamie felt a hand squeeze his shoulder to see Mike smiling at him.

"We thought you were busted, man. Rachel came galloping up on old Alpo..."

"Her name is Missy," Rachel said, kicking Mike in the ass with one of her riding boots. "It was quicker than trying to find a telephone."

Jamie looked around and sure enough, there was a horse tied to a crabapple tree on the side of the house away from the street.

"It really wasn't that big a deal," Jamie said. They headed back toward the house, his arm still tightly around Lisa. "He stopped me because my license plate had expired."

Near the back steps, Jamie thought he smelled gasoline and stopped. Six or eight glass pop bottles were on the ground in a cardboard box. A gas can sat in the grass nearby. Jamie looked at the bottles, then up at Shoes who just shrugged. Krenovich stepped up next to Shoes.

"Molotov Cocktails, man. We figured we'd throw them in the back door of the police station, and while the fuckin' pigs were freakin' out, some of us would run in the front and drag your ass out."

"Well, on the one hand," Jamie shook his head, laughing, "that's probably the stupidest plan I think I have ever heard. But on the other hand, I think it's very thoughtful of you. I'm touched, guys, I really am."

Soon afterward, all were in the little living room, a joint was making the rounds, and Jamie was telling the story.

"When those red lights came on, I was shitting in my pants. See, I'm holding-big time. In the glove box, I had a dozen hits of mescaline, several big horse caps of Psilocybin, and three grams of hashish. I was wondering about eating all of it and if I did would I even survive when he came back and told me it was because of the expired plates. After that, I figured if I was really respectful and cooperative, I might get by. And that's pretty much what happened. I was even helping him look for the chassis number. He's digging around in the back and I'm in the front seat- 'Nope. It's not in the glove box'."

"But how come I saw you in the cop car on your way downtown?"

Jamie grinned at Rachel-mostly because everyone was laying around in patched jeans, flowered halter tops, and tie-dyed T-shirts and she was wearing riding pants and boots and had a black, velvet-colored helmet on the floor next to her feet.

"My brother signed it over to me in a wacky fuckin' way and they had to check to make sure it wasn't stolen. In the end, they gave me a ticket I have to pay and told me to park it off the street until I could write to Australia and get brother Jack to send me the right paperwork. Oh yeah, check this out."

Jamie reached into his breast pocket, pulled out Officer Sherman's card, and held it up.

"I am now an official Narc!"

Conversation stopped dead as everyone stared.

"Old Sherm the Sperm told me he was lookin' out for drug dealers on the Colton Campus and how did I feel about helping him out?"

"Sure thing, Officer Sherman!" Jamie said in a little kid's voice, "We'll get those bastards!"

When the laughter died down, Rachel got to her feet and picked up her helmet.

"I'd better get Missy back to the barn." She turned to Jamie and said, "Stand up you. I need a hug." Jamie complied and patted her gently on the back as she squeezed him.

She started for the door, then turned and announced to Mike and Shoes, "Don't forget. Saturday Night. We'll be expecting you at eight o'clock."

"Wouldn't miss it," said Shoes.

"We'll be there," said Mike.

After she had left, Mike looked at Shoes, "Shit. Did you remember?"

"Nope. Forgot all about it."

"About what?" several people said.

Mike looked down at his shoes while a red flush colored his cheeks.

Lisa whispered to Jamie, "Have you ever seen Mike blush before?"

"Nope," Jamie whispered back, "this is a first."

"We," Mike finally said as he threw an arm around Shoes' shoulders, "are taking Angela and Rachel to the Colton High School Prom."

The girls went "Aww" as the boys hooted.

"And there's supposed to be a party afterward," Mike returned to his comfort zone, "at a cabin somewhere up in the mountains. Get high as you get high, I suppose."

While everybody else laughed and cheered, Lisa was giving the two an appraising look.

"Do either of you two own a suit?"

Mike made a "Who me?" face and shook his head.

Shoes took a defiant stance. "If a man who wears suits and ties isn't already a Fascist, it's only because he's still in training."

Mike looked at Shoes. "Hey Mr. Mussolini, nice tie. Oppress anybody today?"

"Yep, And I didn't even get my suit wrinkled."

"Very funny," Lisa gave them a hard look, "If you two do anything to spoil those girls' Prom Night, like wearing Bozo clown outfits or fig leaves, I'll have my sadistic boyfriend kick your asses."

"Ooh, better do what she says," Jamie said, "that guy is a mean sumbitch".

Mike held his hands up in helplessness. "What can we do?"

Lisa looked at Waltz, McNulty, and Krenovich. "Do any of you guys have a suit?

Krenovich just shrugged. McNulty offered his old Marching Band uniform and Lisa, after considering, asked him to bring the jacket.

"I think the suit I had for graduation is in a closet at my parent's house," Waltz said, "Nancy is pretty good with a sewing machine."

"Good. Give me her phone number, okay. I'll get Madeleine to ask Aaron and the other guys at the Perkins Street house. As for you two," she gave Mike and Shoes a calculating eye, "We'll need measurements-chest, waist, inseam, that sort of thing. And start thinking about corsages!"

After Lisa had spent a little time on the phone, Jamie asked her to come out on the front porch with him.

The porch was small and needed paint, but it did have railings on each side where people could sit and have a private conversation. Sitting on one of these railings next to Lisa, Jamie took her hands in his.

"The cop thing earlier, getting pulled over and all," Jamie said, "I was making jokes about it in there, but it really freaked me out, you know?"

Lisa looked down and squeezed his hands tightly.

"So I decided to stop dealing. School will be out in a couple of weeks, so after I get my last Government check, I'm going to get a job."

"What will you do?"

"I dunno. Lefty says that the sawmill is hiring."

"Jamie…" Lisa hesitated, and then plunged in, "have you ever thought about what you might want to do as a profession? You know, like teaching, or writing, or being a Geologist, or something. Maybe you could find a job that would help get you started."

"Maybe I want to be a professional Board Stacker, did you ever think of that?"

"Now don't get all huffy, Shipman, I'm trying to be helpful."

"I'm not huffy, okay?"

Jamie stood up and walked to the other side of the porch.

"I don't know what..." Jamie thought for a second, "I don't want to end up as some middle-aged fart trapped in a dead-end desk job who wishes he'd thought about it a bit more when he was young-when there was a possibility that he could help change the world."

"So the best thing is to hang around with your buddies and get high. That's how you change the world?"

Oh, come on. You know there's a lot more going on than that. The drugs are just... entertainment."

Lisa started to fling a retort back at him but bit it off before it could leave her mouth. She looked away down the street and her eyes began to get misty.

"I'm sorry Jamie. I was out of line. Mainly, I'm relieved that you're not going to be dealing anymore. I love you, Jamie, whatever you decide to do."

Jamie took her head gently in both hands, kissed her, and then held her close.

"I'm crazy about you too, Lisa."

Nice, Shipman, "I'm keerazy about you." Seriously? That's the best you can do?

Lisa pulled her head back, dug a wadded-up tissue out of her pocket, and wiped her eyes.

"Are we okay, Jamie?'

He kissed her on the top of the head. "We're okay."

"Good. Now here's the plan. I won't be able to spend as much time with you as I'd like for the next few days. I'm committed to helping those two knuckleheads get ready for Prom. And we've both got finals to study for. But if this Prom is like my Prom was, there's a thing before the actual dance when friends and family can go and see the participants promenade."

"Do what?"

"Promenade, that's where the name comes from. Didn't they have Prom in Iowa?"

"Well sure, but I didn't go."

"You've seen movies where there's a Royal Ball? And couples walk in together and some Major Domo-type calls out their names?"

Jamie looked a little confused and Lisa, affecting a deep voice with a British accent, called, "The Duke of Wisteria and the Lady Maxwell!"

"Oh yeah, sure. And they go down a long staircase into the ball-room."

"Exactly. Only instead of a staircase, they walk around the lobby of the High School in front of the trophy case, and instead of a ballroom, they walk into the gym. And that's the part we get to watch."

"Okay, cool. Can we make fun of them as they go by?"

"As if I could stop you. But try to have a little dignity, okay?"

"Well, obviously." Jamie was unable to conceal a grin.

"And afterward I have to go back to the dorm and for the next two weeks we can't see each other."

"Why not?"

"The Small College State Track Meet is in Fort Collins two weeks from Saturday. I'll be running the 600, 800, and the 1600 meter relay. 'School, train, and rest,' the Coach says, 'No distractions and no boys.'"

"Can I come and watch?"

"I'd be pissed if you didn't. How loud can you cheer?"

"You won't be able to hear the starting gun!"

Lisa laughed. "Madeleine and Aaron are coming. You can catch a ride with them."

* * *

"Mr. John Anderson and Miss Jane Wilford"

A tall boy with a blonde flat-top haircut and a much shorter girl in a purple formal gown came through a double door and into the High School Lobby. The girl's gloved hand was in the crook of the tall boy's elbow. Two or three people in the back of the small crowd of watchers cheered and a camera flashed. The girl smiled and blushed as she and her date followed the fifteen couples that had been announced before them.

Jamie nudged Lisa and asked, "What do they call that guy who announces the names? Sergeant Major Domo Dude, or what?"

"Herald"

"Yeah, okay. But what's his title?"

"Ha ha."

"So when are they coming out?" Waltz craned his neck to see around the other parents and well-wishers. He and Nancy were on Jamie's left and Aaron and Madeleine stood to Jamie's right.

"Soon as the Haha says their names, I guess," Jamie said. "Mike said they were all going to drop acid before they got here. What if they got too freaky with all these people? They may have already run off screaming."

Lisa gave Jamie a squinty-eyed look. "They'd better not after all that work we did, right you guys?"

Nancy and Madeleine nodded their agreement.

"Where's McNulty? Shouldn't he be here?" said Aaron.

Waltz shook his head. "He couldn't get a date. He said he'd meet us at Harvey's house after. He knows the way up to this cabin."

Jamie glanced around them. They were perfectly safe because the little crowd was giving them a four or five foot space in all directions. Of course, the fact that he and his friends were dressed so differently than the rest of the onlookers might be a contributing factor. He was wearing blue and white striped floor-length bell-bottoms over a pair of cowboy boots and had on a tie-dyed, long-sleeved T-shirt with a cowhide vest. The others were similarly dressed in headbands, beads, long scarves, and fringes. Waltz had added copper Conchos around the crown of his black hat.

"Here they come!" Aaron said and they all turned to look at the doorway as Shoes and Rachel stepped up. The Herald quietly asked them their names, then intoned, "Mr. Winslow Schumacher and Miss Rachel Berman!"

The hippie contingent waved, cheered, and jumped up and down which caused the surrounding crowd to step back even further.

Shoes was wearing a dark suit with bright paisley fabric cut in long triangles sewn into the legs to make them bell-bottoms. The same fabric was around the bottom hems of the legs and around the cuffs of the jacket. He wore an open white shirt.

"Is that my suit?" Waltz asked, "Great job, Nancy."

She smiled with pleasure as everyone patted her on the back or gave her a squeeze.

Rachel was wearing a long, flowing black skirt with a high waist over a ruffled long-sleeved blouse fastened at the neck with a cameo brooch. The Victorian look happily clashed with a long, pink and orange scarf that was tied around her head and dropped to one side, almost to the floor.

Shoes and Rachel grinned at each other and their friends as they joined the parade around the Lobby. As they drew even with the gang, Handfuls of confetti were thrown into the air over them, and plastic horns and kazoos were blown merrily.

As soon as they had passed by, Jamie looked back and saw Mike and Angela in the doorway. Mike and the Herald were arguing.

Finally, the Herald seemed to give in, shook his head sadly, and intoned, "Mister Funky Michael Harding and Miss Moonbeam Tucker!"

Mike strode into the lobby with Angela practically skipping at his side. He was wearing the tight, tan bell-bottom pants that Jamie had seen him wear frequently at band gigs. Over that he was wearing a dark green Sergeant Pepper-style jacket with gold braid and a high turtleneck collar. On his chest was pinned a large, yellow and red plastic flower.

Angela wore a matching green strapless gown that was cut so long in back it dragged on the ground and as short as a miniskirt in front. On her feet, she wore a pair of calf-high, brown combat boots.

As they came up to the group of their friends, who waited with handfuls of confetti and noisemakers, Jamie quietly asked Lisa, "Did you make that jacket out of McNulty's old band uniform?"

"Well, we all worked on it," Lisa said, "The gold braid came off and went back on pretty easily. And Madeleine got the dye color pretty close, don't you think? After we cut the lapels off, it was hard getting the collar to stand up like that. We finally stitched some cardboard in there."

"It looks really cool, Babe. I hope Angela and Rachel appreciate it."

"Oh, they do. In fact, they helped. We had a lot of fun."

Nothing more could be said because Mike and Angela had pulled up, and the noisemakers were drowning out any conversation. Covered with confetti, Mike suddenly turned and stopped in front of Jamie.

"Dude! Quick! Smell my flower!"

Mike seemed to push the plastic flower on his chest up toward Jamie's face. Jamie shrugged and bent down to smell it. Mike's hand jerked and a stream of water came out of the flower and hit Jamie right between the eyes.

Everyone was laughing hard as Jamie wiped his face with his sleeve.

"Asshole," Jamie said to Mike in mock anger, "Move along, you're holding everybody up."

The couple got back into the promenade and left their friends still laughing. Waltz and Nancy waved white handkerchiefs like two people seeing their relatives off on a cruise. Before they went into the gym, Angela looked back over her shoulder, caught Jamie's eye, and winked.

* * *

Jamie skipped down the steps of Hargreaves Hall, opened the back door of Waltz's car, tossed his old Army surplus parka into the back seat and climbed in after it.

"It's May," Nancy said, "Why are you taking that heavy coat?"

"McNulty said the cabin was pretty high up in the mountains. It's probably colder up there than down here. And if I'm going to get wrecked on acid up there, I'll want to be walking around outside diggin' the mountains, not cooped up in some little cabin with a bunch of freaks. Present company excepted, of course."

For the past few months, Jamie had grown tired of acid parties with too many people jammed into a little house listening to loud music and laying weird little head trips on each other. He still liked getting stoned, especially if the visuals were good, but he found himself more and more outside in the cool night air, walking the streets of Colton.

"Too bad Lisa couldn't come," Nancy said, "she's pretty nice. I like her."

"Yeah, I'm kinda partial to her myself." Jamie replied, "But the Track thing is important to her so I can get behind it. And, like I told her when we dropped her off, if she starts feeling like a prisoner she can rattle a tin cup on the bars and I'll come over and bust her out."

Jamie pulled a square of folded paper out of the watch pocket in his pants and unfolded it carefully, revealing two tablets of acid. They were the last of his stash. He'd sold the rest to Mike and a couple of others for what he'd paid for them. He had kept two out-one for himself and one for Lisa in case she changed her mind about going. He looked at the two light blue tablets, shrugged, and tossed them both into his mouth.

When they got to Harvey's apartment, Cream's *I Feel Free* was rattling the window panes. Remembering not to knock, they went in.

McNulty, Lefty, and Krenovich were standing in front of the stereo shouting a conversation. Aaron, Madeleine, and some other folks were out in the kitchen, and in the far corner of the living room, Harvey and a slender woman with waist-length brown hair were talking to Big Dan and Theresa My Old Lady.

As Jamie closed the door behind Waltz and Nancy he quietly asked, "What's the name of Harvey's new squeeze? I can't remember."

Waltz gave him a quick "I haven't the faintest idea" look, but Nancy whispered "Jacqueline".

Jamie led them over to Harvey's end of the room.

"Hey Harvey," Jamie said, "What's goin' down? Jacqueline, nice to see you again. Dan, Theresa, and these folks are Waltz and Nancy." Everyone shook hands all around.

Jamie had led his friends over to meet Dan hoping the big man would say something way off the wall. Dan did not disappoint.

"Hey, Jamie. Lemme tell you something, man. Now dig it, that new religion I was telling you about? It's happening, man, it's coming on like a freight train. Am I lyin? Huh?"

From his chair, he looked meaningfully at Harvey, Jacqueline, and Theresa. They solemnly nodded their heads. Jamie couldn't tell if they were afraid to disagree or if they actually believed what he was saying.

Dan put his hand on Jamie's shoulder and pulled him down close.

I've heard the term crazy eyes before but this cat has Crazy Eyes!

"I've been having visions, man. Just little ones here and there, just gettin' me ready for the Big One, the Breakthrough, dig? You don't have long to wait, man. It'll be so far fuckin' out."

Just as Jamie was wondering when Dan was going to let him go, the door opened and the two Prom couples walked in.

Dan jumped up and yelled, "Mike! Goddamn! Where you been, Dude?"

Jamie assumed he was going over to tell Mike about his "visions". Jamie looked down at Theresa who sat and fiddled nervously with the fringes on her purse.

"You okay?"

"Oh I'm fine, no problems," the worried look in Theresa's eyes did not match her words, "It's just... he can be so intense sometimes."

Jamie decided that Nancy must be a born nurturer because within moments she had squatted down next to Theresa's chair and was holding her hand and talking softly. As Jamie moved away, he glanced at Harvey and Jacqueline who were looking across the room at Dan. He'd seen that kind of look before.

It's how Waltz looks at a warm Peanut butter roll from the bus station.

"Hey!" Lefty yelled, then reached out and turned the volume down on the stereo which drew a cold look from Harvey. "Hey!" he yelled again and everyone stopped talking. "Whattya say let's get this row on the shoad. You ready?" he looked at Krenovich, "And don't say 'groovy' or I'll slap the shit out of you."

Krenovich put up his hands and tried to protest, but most everyone-including Lefty-were going out the door. Krenovich blinked, shrugged, and followed them.

Jamie was last out the door. He turned and looked back at the four who were staying-Harvey, Jacqueline, Theresa My Old Lady, and Big Dan. Already in conversation, they ignored him and Jamie left.

* * *

Jamie stood in the cold air of the Colorado Mountains and slowly looked around the little valley of Eagle Park. There were seven or eight log cabins here and there, none with lights on or cars around them.

"Vacation cabins." Waltz had said as they were driving up the dirt road that wound through the valley, "The people who own them live in the cities down on the flat and come up here on weekends, mostly in the summer."

The cabin they had been directed to was fairly large and built into a hillside. McNulty and Waltz were duck-walking around under the porch with Waltz's flashlight looking for the key while everyone else stood around and waited. Many of the partiers had worn only light jackets or sweaters and were hugging themselves or hopping up and down to keep warm.

"Why don't we just break a window or something?" Lefty called to the guys under the porch, "I'm freezing my ass off out here."

"He said the key was hanging on a nail behind the second step." McNulty said, "There isn't even a nail there."

"Maybe he meant the second step from the top," Waltz said as he lifted the beam of his flash.

"Aha!" McNulty cried and in seconds he was out from under the porch, up the stairs, and unlocking the door.

Lights were going on and people were trooping in as Nancy said, "Are you coming in?"

"No, you go ahead," Jamie said, "The acid rush is coming on pretty strong. I'd better stay out here for a while until I've got a handle on it."

He waited until Waltz and Nancy had gone into the cabin together, then he started down the road at a brisk walk. In a sky with only a few clouds, a nearly-full moon spread a pearly light over the little valley and outlined the pine trees with a subtle silver glow.

Jamie thought he saw brilliantly-colored wildflowers in among the sagebrush, and then realized they were acid patterns forming among the plants. The more he watched the brighter and more distinct the colored patterns grew until they began to move together. The fact that these apparitions weren't really there didn't interfere with his enjoyment and wonder at the dance they were doing. They moved to the rhythm of his boot heels striking the dirt road and the hiss of the breeze blowing through a million pine needles. Distantly at first, but growing in volume was a rollicking, roaring sound.

He topped a small rise and saw below him the source of the noise. A river tumbled down out of the forest, splashing and swerving its way around and over rocks and boulders as it made its way down the valley. The road Jamie had been walking on crossed over the river by way of a sturdy wooden bridge. He stepped onto the bridge and felt the pounding of the water through the soles of his feet-as if the wanderlust in the water was calling to the bridge, "Come with us! We're going to the sea!" and the strength of the bridge answering, "No. I am here and will not be budged."

The little imagined conversation made him smile as he leaned on the wooden railing and looked down at the river surging underneath.

As he stared, once again the drug began to add color and light and movement to his field of vision. Little specks of light reflecting from the water quickly became a myriad of colorful sprites surfing on the strong currents. Lines of light spiraled up and out, then dived back toward the water and blew apart in a spray of water over a rock.

Jamie's already stimulated imagination seemed to shift into a higher gear as he became a miniature surfer sliding down the face of a giant surge. No surfboard was necessary; he was maneuvering across the face of the wave on his bare feet. First high, then low, then up over the top where he flipped twice and caught a flume of rushing water that swelled in the opposite direction. Jamie suddenly realized he was not in the water but standing on the bridge, bouncing on the balls of his feet, and shaking a fist in exultation.

Jamie pulled his attention away from the river and looked up at the sky where filmy, iridescent clouds trailed across the edges of the moon. Within seconds, songs about the moon began cascading through his perception-"Bad Moon Rising" followed by "Blue Moon", then "Mister Moonlight". All in perfect fidelity and stereo sound.

One of the many benefits of LSD is you never get a song stuck for long in your head. Before you can get through the second verse of it, another tune comes along and elbows its way past the previous one.

Before he could chew on this musical cud any further his attention was drawn by a faint and unusual sound. A soft, steady crunching sound, it was too measured to be natural. He turned his head and peered up the road where the sound seemed to be coming from. In the darkness, he thought he saw something moving, but then everything was moving. At a distance, all details were doing a slow, colorful gavotte with each other.

Maybe I should get off this bridge. If it's a Sherriff's Deputy I can run. But where would I run to? Everyone back at the cabin will be in handcuffs. Probably being beaten with rubber hoses.

Jamie's heart rate was way up and his hallucinations were pulsing wildly. Then Krenovich stepped out of the throbbing patterns.

"Hey, Shipman," Krenovich yelled, "Is that you?"

"Yeah, it's me." Jamie's voice quavered with relief, "What's happening?"

"Not a lot, man. People are wondering what you've been doing out here for the last two hours."

"Well, for one thing, having the shit scared out of me by you."

"Me?"

"With all that fuckin' hair up there, I thought I was being attacked by a giant dust mop."

Krenovich poked at his curly hair which, over time, had become a large and unruly blonde afro.

"This shit? Yeah, it's a hassle. But the chicks dig it. And if it gets me laid, I'm cool with it, you know?"

Jamie turned and started back to the cabin. Krenovich fell in beside him.

"It's all about the sex for you isn't it?" Jamie said.

"Well, yeah. And the drugs. To tell you the truth, if all the Hippie chicks took a vow of celibacy, and the clean-cut kids over at the Christian Youth Center were fuckin' each other's eyes out, I'd be shouting, 'Hallelujah, brother! I've been saved!'"

Jamie laughed, and then remembered something Krenovich had said.

"Two hours? No shit?"

"About that, yeah."

"Seems like about twenty minutes."

Jamie put his hand up to his nose. It felt like a little round icicle.

"I'm wondering," he said with a smile, "if whoever owns that cabin has some instant hot chocolate stashed in a cupboard. Usually, I can't eat anything when I'm tripping, but a warm mug of hot chocolate right now would be out of fuckin' sight!"

"Only one way to find out."

When they came within sight of the cabin, Jamie stopped.

"Now that's a postcard, isn't it?" Jamie said, "warm light coming out of the windows, smoke from the chimney. Very pleasant."

"Yeah, it looks peaceful out here," Krenovich said, "but fuckin' crazy inside."

"Oh yeah? How are the Prom couples doing?"

"Shoes and Rachel are playin' tonsil hockey in the back bedroom. Lots of sweaty groping but she's keeping her clothes firmly in place. Shoes' balls must be bright blue by now. Angela, on the other hand, really wants to ball Mike, but McNulty and he are yuckin' it up in the living room and Mike's ignoring her."

"In other words, pretty much the usual."

"Pretty much. There's a side door that goes right into the kitchen if you don't want to get involved in all that."

"Lead on, my freaky friend."

* * *

Jamie stood in the corner of the kitchen and tried to be as inconspicuous as possible. Krenovich, on the other hand, was standing on a chair and rummaging through an upper shelf of a kitchen cabinet.

Jamie kept flicking his gaze from one thing to the next. If he spent more than a second or two looking at any one thing, that thing would dissolve into a shimmering play of colors moving and yet not moving. Various shapes would resolve themselves, grow into almost three-dimensional images, and then dissolve back into the morass. When he'd been wandering around outside, the darkness and moonlight had desaturated the colors until everything was in a kind of grayscale. Any colors he saw he knew were added by the drug. Inside, all colors were brilliant. And constantly shifting. If he looked too long at the linoleum floor it became a seething, blue-green mass.

This shit is way too bizarre. Am I warm enough yet? I gotta get back outside.

He heard a voice coming from above him and looked up.

"Hey, man!" Krenovich waved a brown canister, "Scope this shit out. Hershey's fuckin' Cocoa. You're supposed to mix it with warm milk, which we don't have, but we could heat up some water and I saw a bottle of coffee creamer down on a lower shelf."

"What?"

"Hot chocolate, dude. You said you wanted some hot chocolate."

"I did?"

"Man, I thought I was fucked up, you're about two orbits out past Pluto." Krenovich jumped down. "I'm gonna find a saucepan."

He went around the corner into a walk-in pantry just as Angela came into the kitchen, saw Jamie, and ran to him throwing her arms around his neck. She was wearing pantyhose, her combat boots, and a man's flannel plaid shirt.

"Jamie, Jamie. I wondered where you were." she said in a throaty voice, "Have you ever been so horny that you knew if you didn't ball someone, you'd just flip out?"

As she spoke she wrapped a leg around one of his and began to grind her crotch against his thigh. Jamie started to sweat and his pulse hammered. She pulled her head back and he looked at her face. Even with smeared mascara and bloodshot eyes, she was dazzling. Then her face slowly began to distort, the colors of her skin to crawl apart and back together and her eyes to jump up and down on her face. They were on her forehead, then down on her cheeks, then back to their normal places.

Jamie gently pushed her away.

"I'm sorry," he mumbled, unable to look at her, "I can't... I mean, I gotta get back outside. I'm too stoned to be in here."

Krenovich came out of the pantry holding a frying pan and looking confused. Jamie only saw Angela's lips trembling as he stepped backward out onto the porch and closed the door.

Jamie took off down the road and didn't come back to the cabin until the gray light of morning was coloring the sky in the East. He would think back on this night many times in the future and wonder what might have happened. Usually, he would decide that he'd been very lucky to have been, as Krenovich put it, "out about two orbits past Pluto".

On the way home later that morning, Angela sat between Jamie and Mike in the back seat of Waltz's car. She had her left hand looped through Mike's arm and in her right hand she held a condom, still carrying a load of semen and knotted off at the top. She giggled as she twirled it around and hung it off the end of her nose like a giant booger. Mike looked out the window and tried to ignore her.

FIFTEEN

"Where the hell have you been, dude? It's been more than a week since that whole fuckin' Prom trip went down."

Mike pulled two cans of Coors out of the refrigerator and handed one to Jamie.

"Some of us are still in college, you know," Jamie pulled the ring top on his can, "I had a Philosophy final on Wednesday, and a Math final this morning. A week ago I got up Monday morning and realized I couldn't remember anything I've learned this whole fucking semester. All of it gone-roasted in the fires of LSD. I'm just hoping that what I crammed during the week got me by. I've got Geology in a couple of days so I can't stay long. I dig what you've done with the refrigerator."

"All I did was paint it black. One of Madeleine's friends is an Art major and brought over a big stack of partially-used tubes of acrylic paint and some brushes. So we had a 'paint the fridge' party."

Mrs. Berman's refrigerator was now a flat black color that featured an impressive array of decorations. Giant pink spiderwebs, multi-colored paisley designs, a cartoon of a moose that had "Nestle" written on it, lots of flowers of different colors, the Blue Glove from Yellow Submarine, and a bright red, clenched fist above the lettering "OFF THE PIG!".

Jamie tapped this last one and chuckled, "Shoes must have jumped in, right?"

"You gotta like a man who's dependable."

"He had Rachel with him, I suppose?"

"Au contraire, my friend. She dumped old Shoes like a pair of old shoes. Angela says she's gettin' into Malcolm Tingley."

"The Cowboy Hippie?"

Mike finished his beer, took aim, and tossed the can in a long arc into the garbage.

"See what happens when you go all academic on us?" Mike grinned, "You miss out on all the gossip. Like me moving back to Arizona for the summer."

"Wait. What? No shit? I thought there was some pregnant girl with a heavily-armed, angry father?"

"Didn't I tell you about that? Psycho chick. Met some Army Lieutenant and suddenly she wasn't pregnant anymore. Daddy put his guns away and my little pink butt was off the hook."

"When did you decide to go back?"

"I didn't. My old man decided. He needs help on a new golf course and told me to get my ass home for the summer."

"Does he have a hitch in his backswing or something?"

"He builds golf courses, I told you that, didn't I? You've seen, like, pictures of rocky desert landscapes with strips of green grass running through them? Beautifully manicured putting greens amid the boulders and cactus? My old man. I don't mind going, really. I'm a Cat Skinner so the bread is pretty good and I've been itching for a new Marshall amp. Maybe a stack. Wouldn't that be far fuckin' out?"

"A Cat Skinner? You mean you...?"

"Yeah, right. I catch cute little pussycats and tear their hides off to make hand warmers. Come on, dude, I drive a bulldozer. Started when I was sixteen. I can also blow up big rocks and shit with dynamite. Now that's a trip."

"Dynamite is pretty scary shit, isn't it?"

"Hang on for a second, let me show you something."

Mike went into his little bedroom and Jamie walked into the living room, set his beer down, and picked up a well-thumbed issue of The Fabulous Furry Freak Brothers. He was chuckling at Fat Freddy when Mike came out of the bedroom, yelled "catch", and lobbed him a nondescript, brown paper-wrapped cylinder. Jamie dropped the comic and caught the object, then read what was printed on the paper cover.

Dynamite. High Explosive. Handle With Care.

"Jesus H. Christ!" Jamie's hands shook a little as he gently laid the stick down on the coffee table, "I think I just shit my pants."

Mike was laughing so hard he had to lean against the wall for support.

"Man, the look on your face. I thought your eyes were gonna come popping out like Daffy fuckin' Duck. Don't worry, without a blasting cap attached, this shit is harmless."

So saying, he picked up the dynamite, flipped it up in the air, caught it after a couple of spins, and headed back toward the bedroom.

"I suppose you've got a blasting cap hidden away somewhere too," Jamie yelled after him.

"I'll never tell," came the reply.

"So what the fuck do you have a stick of Dynamite for?"

Mike stuck his head back around the door jamb.

"A Statement, man," Mike said, "sometimes when shit seems to be slidin' away, a dude has got to make the Big Statement. And this…" he held up the dynamite, "is a hell of an exclamation point."

"You're fuckin' crazy, you know that," Jamie yelled at the now-empty doorway then went back to the Freak Brothers.

In a few minutes, Mike came back out of the bedroom.

"So," Jamie said, looking up, "What else did I miss? Did McNulty get laid?"

"Ha. Doesn't he wish? Now, let me lay something on you, see what you think. How'd you like to rent my room for the summer?"

"This room?"

"No, a closet down in the basement of Big Red. Of course, this room. I've talked to Waltz and Shoes, they're both cool with it. And you and Lisa can have someplace to ball besides under the bushes in Roosevelt Park."

"I'm not even going to dignify that with a response," Jamie said, "But I'll take the room. Thank you. Speaking of Lisa, did you know that big State track meet she's been training for is tomorrow? I'm riding over to Fort Collins with Aaron and Madeleine to watch her run."

"That's pretty cool. I hope she kicks ass."

"Yeah, me too. You know I haven't seen her since the Night of the Squirting Flower."

"You guys okay?"

"We're fine," Jamie said, "I think. Like I said, she's been in Training."

"Want another beer?' Mike asked as he headed for the kitchen.

"Still working on this one, man. Thanks," Jamie wiggled the half-empty can at Mike, and then took a swallow.

"Oh, one more thing," Mike stopped and turned around, "and don't take this the wrong way, okay, but just in case things don't work out between you and Lisa and you, like, want to get it on with Angela, I'm cool with that."

Jamie was still clutching his beer can and staring into space when Mike came back into the room. Jamie refocused.

"What?"

"What what? Oh, what I said about Angela. She and I talked, you know. About Arizona and gone for the summer and all that shit. And we decided that it'd be cool if we both saw other people while I was away and then next fall we'd get back together and, like, see how the wind blows, you dig?

In other words, you'd figured out this whole trip, laid it on her, and since she was too proud to beg, she agreed. Poor kid.

"Ah, okay, I dig," Jaime said, "but what's all this about me wanting to get it on with Angela?"

"Oh come on, man. I've seen you making those mooney eyes at her when you thought nobody was looking. I don't blame you, dude. If I wasn't the guy who was balling her, I'd be doggin' that shit myself."

"Then why are you breaking up with her?"

"Well, if I can quote brother Shel Silverstein, "After you've been havin' steak for a long time, beans, beans taste fine.""

"No offense, man," Jamie said as he stood up and made for the door, "but you are such an asshole."

"None taken," Mike said as he stretched out on the couch and grinned, "Oh one other thing I forgot to mention. Dr. Berman, Rachel's dad, is going to Indiana for the summer. Some academic thing. So they're closing up the house, Rachel and Angela are getting an apartment together, and Angela's looking for a job."

Mike suddenly barked out a laugh.

"What's so funny?"

"I just pictured you and Malcolm the Cowboy Hippie standing on the front porch of the chicks' apartment, fighting over who gets to ring the doorbell."

Jamie was shaking his head as he walked out the door.

"Tell Lisa I said 'Good Luck!'" Mike called after him.

* * *

After the last race, Jamie came out onto the track. Lisa saw him and jumped into his arms for a long and happy hug.

"You were just..." Jamie croaked and cleared his throat to try again, "You were wonderful." Jamie's voice sounded like he'd swallowed a Brillo pad.

"Oh poor baby," Lisa said, "you blew your voice out just for me. Thank you."

"I couldn't help it. It was really exciting. So who was the dude?

"What dude?"

"The guy you were talking to. Mr. Slacks."

"Oh, that was Walt Higgins, the track coach at CU in Boulder. He wants me to come to Boulder and train with him this summer.

"What did you tell him?"

"That I'd think about it. It's a great opportunity but... we need to have a talk, Jamie. But not now. I'm all sweaty and you sound like Bull-frog Bill."

She took his hands, gave him a quick kiss, and then followed the rest of her teammates as they headed for the showers.

Lisa and Jamie rode back to Colton in the back seat of Madeleine's car. They talked about the Meet, Lisa told stories about the girls on her team, and they all made bad jokes about Lisa's new trophy and ribbons, but the subject of the upcoming summer was somehow avoided.

Sixteen

Jamie came out of the Colton County Courthouse and started down the marble steps.

You don't run down steps like this, but you don't walk down either. It's sort of a tippity-tappity toe step.

He smiled as he tippity-tappitied down the rest of the marble steps. He carried two envelopes. Inside the large one was a brand-new Colorado license plate, inside the small one was a registration slip. His brother had finally done the paperwork and sent it to Jamie along with a snapshot of himself standing next to a kangaroo.

The walk from the Courthouse to the Fifth Street house was only half a dozen blocks and soon he was sitting in the weeds behind the little red VW. After giving the license plate's mounting screws the final twist with a screwdriver, Jamie sat back, admired his new, official Colorado ride, and thought about Lisa. There had been a note from Waltz when he got home that Lisa, visiting Madeleine at a house on Perkins Street, wanted to see him.

I hope her head is still in a good space. The last few days were pretty intense, but that whole concert scene Saturday had been such a far-out trip that she should still have some left-over mellowness.

The whole thing had started a few days before when they were in his new room together at the Fifth Street House. Anna had a little hammer and was driving a nail into his wall above the dresser. Jamie was lying on the bed enjoying the view. He didn't often get to see her body from that angle and he was making the most of the opportunity.

"Okay," he said, "I've figured out this 'secret present.' It's a nail to hang my underwear on when I go to bed. That's very thoughtful."

"Just wait, silly."

She opened the large carryall bag she'd brought with her, took something out, and hung it up on the nail. It was the mask of Little Bear.

Jamie, genuinely touched, stood up and put his arm around her. They both stood there admiring the paper mache mask.

"That's so sweet," Jamie said, "Thank you. But didn't your father say his job was to look after you?"

"He did. And Little Bear was as good as his word. But now, between the two of us, I think that with the people you hang out with and the things you get into, you need his attention more than I do."

This led to much hugging and exchanging of kisses.

"Speaking of the Fast Life," Jamie said, "I bought some acid this afternoon from Krenovich. It's called White Cloud. He said it was 'as smooth as a baby's butt,' so I bought two-one for each of us for the concert."

Anna had, very gently at first, refused. The more Jamie pushed, the deeper her heels dug in. Then Jamie said one of those things that you hear come out of your mouth that you can't believe you said, and that you'll never be able to take back.

"You used to be a lot of fun, but lately you've been about as much fun as a fart in a space suit."

And the flood gates opened.

When you're in the first serious romantic relationship in your life, that other person is absolutely perfect in your eyes. Any little flaws or faults are as if they don't exist, so you never see them. You just hide them in the dark. But there they accumulate like tiny weed seedlings deep in the soil of your flower garden, ready burst forth just at the wrong moment and choke the life out of your love.

No punches were thrown, no one struck anyone, but it was a no-holds-barred verbal donnybrook. The battle raged from red-faced and screaming to cold and snide. And quickly back again.

In such an emotional confrontation people usually react not to what is said, but to what they think is meant. All Jamie heard was that Anna thought he was a drug-soaked loser and a lazy bum. For her part, Anna thought she was being called a pushy, controlling harpy.

Eventually, the storm had passed. There were tearful apologies, promises to never fight again, and some amazing, emotionally-charged make-up sex.

The next day, Jamie had hot-footed it down to Melvin's Music Shop where he asked Harvey to swap his two Sunday tickets for two Saturdays.

"It's your trip," Harvey had said, "Saturday is a pretty far-out lineup, but Sunday is gonna be Hendrix."

"Yeah, I know. But Lisa is a big Tim Buckley fan and he's playing Saturday."

What they had been talking about was The Denver Pop Festival – eighteen of the best bands in the world spread out over three days and nights in Denver's Mile High Stadium.

The Festival had exceeded Jamie's expectations. The music was magnificent, the acid was first-rate. There had even been some drama as a group of crazies tried to break into the stadium and the Denver Police tear-gassed them for their efforts. But that had soon passed and later on, the Tim Buckley set made Lisa so emotional that she had to be held and squeezed for a long time afterward.

J* * *

amie pulled up in front of the house on Perkins Street, shut off the VW and started up the walk. There was what looked like the back seat of somebody's van next to the front stoop and a tall, thin, ridiculously handsome young man sat on it working with a pencil on a drawing pad. The fellow looked up and grinned.

"Hey brother, what's happenin'?"

"The usual, man. I'm Jamie."

"Phiz." The fellow put down the drawing pad, held up his open hand, and Jamie gripped it.

"Did you say fizz?"

"Yeah, I did. Weird, huh? My name is actually Phil but when my cousin Eddie was two he was having a hard time pronouncing L's, Phiz was the best he could do. And it stuck."

Phiz looked across the street at a cottonwood tree growing in a front yard, and then went back to his drawing. Jamie stepped up beside him and craned his neck to look at the pad. The tree across the street was being reproduced on the pad in startling detail.

"That is very cool work, Phiz. I'm diggin' it."

"Thanks, man. Some people can dance, or sing, or play music. I draw trees. Big whoop, huh?"

Jamie, continuing to watch the work progress, was suddenly aware of something flapping over his head. He looked up into a cloud of dust and bits of dirt falling on him. He jumped back at the same time Phiz bounced up shaking the grit off his drawing.

"Hey!" Phiz yelled. "What's going on?"

The throw rug that was the source of the dust was quickly pulled back inside and a female head popped out.

"Oh, I'm sorry," The girl said. She had long, straight brown hair that hung down over her face with only a narrow crack for her to look out of. "I didn't know you were down there."

Another female face appeared at the window. This face was round, pug-nosed, and generously freckled.

"Are you bitching again?" the second girl yelled at Phiz, trying not to laugh, "well, knock it off. Oh hi," she said to Jamie. "I'm Polly and this is Sarah."

"I'm Jamie."

"You're Jamie? Are you Lisa's Jamie?"

Jamie spread his hands, palm up, and shrugged his shoulders.

"We'll tell Lisa that you're here."

Phiz settled back into his drawing, filled in a few shadows, then glanced up.

"Oh, you can go in if you want. Sorry," Phiz held up the pad in explanation, "I can get wrapped up."

Jamie went into the house and stood in the middle of the living room. The furnishings were similar to those in the 5th Street house-second-hand, Salvation Army, and scrounged. A couple of mismatched overstuffed chairs and a couch surrounded an empty wooden spool coffee table. On the opposite wall, a stack of concrete blocks and wide boards acted as bookshelves. Hearing a noise, Jamie looked up to see someone coming down the stairs. It obviously wasn't Lisa, unless she'd decided to put on a large, ratty pair of hightop sneakers. A moment later and a young man with a goatee, a dishwater-blonde ponytail, and a familiar face came into the room. Jamie grinned and held out his hand as he racked his memory for a name.

"You're... Quentin, right? We met at Thanksgiving."

"Yeah. You're the guy with the big brother who came beating on the door. Good to see you again. Lisa and Madeleine are finishing up something upstairs. She'll be down in a sec."

They shook hands and Jamie sat on the arm of the couch while Quentin put a record on the stereo and set the needle. It was Janis Joplin singing "Down On Me". Jamie liked the song but was glad Quentin didn't turn it up too high. His ears were still ringing from the Festival.

"Nice place," Jamie said, "How many people you got living here?"

"Officially, four. But really anywhere from three to six. You met Phiz, and I think you know Aaron. A chick named Polly and her friend Sarah pay for the fourth bedroom. They have rooms up in a sorority on campus but also wanted a little pad for getting loose now and then."

"I met them just a couple of minutes ago. Is it a good set-up, living with chicks?"

"Better'n a poke in the eye with a sharp stick."

"That good, huh?"

Jamie heard noises on the stairway and turned to see Lisa and Madeleine come in. Both girls looked very nice in cut-off jeans and halter tops. Lisa wore a beaded headband around her blonde hair.

Jamie took Lisa's hands in his and kissed her on the forehead.

"You look great, Babe," he said. He expected her to smile and kiss him on the lips, but instead, she stepped back and said, "Jamie, can we go someplace? We need to talk."

Uh-oh.

"Like where? Do you mean like Campus Coffee? Are you hungry?"

"No. Let's go to Dietrich Park, it's just a few blocks away."

Aw shit. Here we go.

"Okay. We can drive over. I got my car back."

Not long afterward, Jamie was sitting on a picnic table, his feet on one of the benches, his chin in the palm of his hand. Lisa, hands clenched behind her, was pacing back and forth a few feet away.

"Coach Higgins said the sooner I get settled in Boulder, the sooner we can start my training. I'll take some Summer classes and if I do well on the track, I could be in line for a partial scholarship for Fall and Spring semesters."

"Oh, well that's great. But how does that work for me and you?"

Lisa took a deep breath, "Okay, straight out, this me and you whatever it is... it just isn't working for me anymore, Jamie. It's... it's just not. I thought about letting the long distance end it for us, but that would be dishonest. I'm still very fond of you and I don't want to hurt you, but I just don't see, the way we are now, any future for us."

"What if I said I could change? That I could figure out who you want me to be and then be that guy?"

"I don't want you to change. I'd hate it if you tried to do that." She reached out to touch him on the shoulder, and then drew her hand back, "We're each walking on our own path. We were so lucky that, for a while, our paths were the same. But they've been drifting apart. There are different people, different things, and different adventures ahead for each of us. You see that, don't you?"

Jamie didn't reply, just stared down at a dandelion puffball that moved gently in the breeze.

Later, the VW pulled up in front of the Perkins Street house. Lisa got out and then leaned down to the passenger side window as if to say one last thing. But her lips quivered, her mouth worked soundlessly, and rivers of tears began to pour down her face. Jamie started to get out, thinking he would go around the car to comfort her, but she turned abruptly and ran up the walk and into the house.

Jamie put the Volkswagen in gear and drove away.

* * *

Jamie sat in the living room, his feet up on the coffee table and his second can of beer in his hand. He had been thinking about going into the kitchen and putting his head in the oven. About the time it dawned on him that it was an electric stove, Waltz and Shoes came in the door.

"Jamie, there y'all are," Shoes said. When he had a story to tell, his voice sped up, he paced back and forth, and his eyes bugged out even further than usual. All this was going on even as he came in the door, so Jamie knew it was going to be a good one.

"Did y'all hear what happened last night over at Harvey's with Big Dan?"

"No. But I'm hoping you're gonna lay it on me."

Waltz had pulled a lid of pot out of his vest pocket and laid it out on the coffee table along with a packet of Zig-Zag papers.

"Big Dan came over and announced he was going to shoot up a San Francisco Speedball," Shoes said, "He put together a moosey hit of methedrine, a bunch of cocaine, and a couple of tabs of strong LSD. He cooked them up with water in a spoon, pulled out some big glass syringe he'd got from God-knows-where, pumped up a vein and mainlined it."

"No shit?" Jamie said. He'd heard about people shooting up, but nobody he knew in Colton was into it.

"Harvey said he watched him do it," Waltz said around the joint between his lips as he fished in his vest pocket for matches.

"After he pulled the needle out," Shoes went on, "Dan stumbled around the house twitchin' and shakin' and talkin' as fast as his mouth would fuckin' go."

"About what?"

"He said Hendricks had spoken to him in Denver through his music, that there was going to be a gatherin' in the Grand Canyon, and that a huge lightnin' storm there would light everybody up with love. And that was only a small part of a long string of weird, weird shit."

Shoes paused long enough to take a hit off the joint and pass it along. Holding his breath, he resumed in a high, squeaky voice.

"After a half hour, the acid started to kick in," He let out his breath with a whoosh, "He crawled into Harvey's closet and sat in there, by himself, squealin' and screamin' and makin' strange animal noises. After about an hour of this, he quietly came out of the closet and told the three of them-Harvey, Theresa, and Jacqueline-that he'd come to the realization that he was God.

"You mean like 'a' god? Like a being with godlike powers? Or like 'the' God?

"Jeez, Jamie, I don't know," Shoes said, "they've got him locked up down at the Colton Jail. Why don't y'all go down there and ask him?"

"In jail? How'd he get thrown into jail?"

"Harvey had to call the cops. About 3 am Big Dan, or 'God' if y'all buy that shit, went fuckin' nuts. He slapped Harvey and the chicks around some and then started rippin' all Harvey's stuff off the walls. He tossed most of Harvey's records on the floor and jumped up and down on them. The racket woke up the neighbors and Harvey, standin' out on the sidewalk with a fat lip, asked them to call the Police. When the pigs showed up they found Dan, stark naked, squattin' over the pile of Harvey's broken stuff. On top of the pile was... picture this... a big turd."

"Oh man," Jamie said, "That is so gross."

"It took six cops to wrestle the crazy bastard out of the house and into a patrol car," Waltz took up the story while Shoes hit on the joint. "As they dragged him along, they worked him over with their batons pretty good. I imagine God has got some fierce bruises on him today."

Waltz and Shoes looked at each other and then burst out in wild laughter. Jamie smiled, shook his head and got up.

"You guys want a beer? I got some in the fridge."

"Sure," said Waltz, "And a glass too. I like drinking beer out of a glass."

Jamie waved over his shoulder as he walked to the kitchen. On the refrigerator shelf behind the beer, Jamie noticed a paper cup from Frosty Muggs. It was half full of muddy brown liquid.

If she loved these root beer floats so much, why did she only ever drink half of them? And then leave the other half in the damned fridge?

Jamie carried the cup over to the sink, but couldn't bring himself to pour it out. He just stood there looking into the cup.

"Hey man, you okay?"

Jamie looked up to see Waltz standing in the doorway and realized that he'd been frozen there for some time.

"Oh, I'm cool, no problem." He poured the remains of the float into the sink and then tossed the cup into the trash bag. "Lisa just split for Boulder and she... well, I broke up with her. You know, different places, different people. I figured we both needed some elbow room."

"Well, I gotta admit I wasn't expecting that." Waltz got a glass out of the cabinet and two beers from the fridge "Are you cool with it? Should me and Shoes split for a while?"

"Oh hell no. Let's drink beer, smoke a little weed, and talk about God's Plan for the World."

Waltz laughed and led the way back into the living room.

SEVENTEEN

Jamie got to the end of the paragraph and realized he didn't have even a foggy idea of what the paragraph was about. He could vaguely recall seeing the words fly by-a distant flock of geese, honking faintly, on their way north for the Summer. He wasn't reading, he was just was staring at Plato's *Republic* and thinking about Lisa.

He squeezed his eyes shut, opened them wide, then started the paragraph again, "You know that the beginning is the most important part of any work, especially in the case of a young and tender thing..." And in his mind, he was holding Lisa close to him and feeling the incredible softness of the skin on her cheek.

"Shit," he muttered.

"Havin' a hard time, brother?" Phiz asked, "You and Plato not gettin' along?"

They were sitting across a table from one another in the Colton College Library. Jamie had decided that he wasn't that keen on breaking his hump for two dollars an hour at the sawmill this summer and had signed up for a couple of classes in Summer Semester. It was enough to keep his GI Bill checks coming in. Uncle Sugar's money wasn't much, but it was enough to pay rent, buy drugs, and sometimes a little food.

He'd taken *Introduction to Philosophy* the previous semester and had flunked it. Mostly because he'd gotten in an argument with the Instructor about the "Socratic Method." Jamie had maintained, in front of the class, that the Sophists were idiots who couldn't argue their way out of a wet paper sack. What good were Socrates' insights when they were gained by verbally walking all over some moronic stooge? Mr. Palmer-whose large head and little topknot of hair made him look like a turnip-didn't take it very kindly. Evidently, he'd written his Master's thesis on Plato and was eager to let Jamie know that he knew more about Plato than any smart-mouthed Freshman would ever dream of knowing. He was so unrelentingly sarcastic for the next month that Jamie didn't even bother going to the final exam.

So, when it came time to pick his summer courses, he took *Intro* over again. The Instructor this time was a guy that Mike had smoked dope with. Jamie was confident he could get his GPA back up a little, and he didn't have to buy the book. But he did have to read it.

"I'm just not into it tonight,' Jamie said, "How are you doing?"

"Not bad. Take a look." Phiz turned the drawing he'd been working on around so Jamie could see it.

It was a lovely pencil drawing of a beautiful girl, her naked back to the camera, leaning against a tall, turned post of a four-poster bed. It was done in the intricate style that Phiz gave to all his drawings.

"Nice work, man. Is this for a class?"

"Yeah. The assignment was to find three separate pictures and combine them. Here's what I started with."

The first was a four-poster bed cut from a newspaper, the second was a woman's naked back from a magazine ad, and the third was a Polaroid photo of the beautiful girl, her eyes made-up like the Egyptian Queen Nefertari.

"Who's the chick?" Jamie held up the picture, "You know her?"

"That's Jennifer. She's a dancer. Travels around the area dancing in bars and stuff. She has cassette tapes that the bartenders play. She likes it when heads on acid come in to watch her dance-she puts on a show for 'em."

"Sounds pretty flashy," Jamie said, "What's she doing with you?"

"She's doing what all the other women <u>wish</u> they were doing," Phiz smirked. "Actually, she has a little apartment here in Colton she shares with a girlfriend. She has me come over, ball her, and spend the night whenever she's in town. She can't sleep unless there's a man in bed with her."

"But when she's out of town?"

"There's some other guy in her bed. It's a little bizarre, but I'm cool with it."

The thought of this arrangement hit Jamie as simultaneously intriguing and repellant.

"The next time Jennifer's in town I'll introduce you," Phiz said as he began to gather up his things.

"Cool. I'd be up for it."

Jamie picked up his book and they walked out to his car.

As he opened the driver's door he asked, "Speaking of dropping psychedelics, have you ever tried to draw your acid hallucinations?"

"You mean, like, patterns and stuff?" Phiz said as he settled into the passenger seat.

"Yeah, all that shit."

"Well, no. I don't see any of that stuff when I'm high. I get way loaded, and there's all kinds of crazy crap running through my head, but I think my hallucinator is just busted. If I'm really fried, I can see trace lags, but that's about it."

"Bummer, dude."

"Yeah, for an artist? No shit. Hey, I've got a couple of numbers on me," Phiz said as he patted his breast pocket, "Let's go over to your house a fire 'em up. Would that be cool?"

"I don't see why not. Waltz and Nancy are at the movies. I think Shoes was going to tag along so there won't be anybody to bum hits off of us. I may even have a beer or two in the fridge."

"Cool."

As the Volkswagen chugged its way across Colton, Jamie was feeling oddly satisfied with himself. The day was, in fact, Jamie's twenty-first birthday and nobody knew. It wasn't that Jamie didn't like having a birthday; he just didn't like *celebrating* his birthday. His Mother had done all the work; he himself hadn't had anything to do with it. In fact, although he couldn't remember it, he was sure he was pretty pissed off about the whole thing at the time. So, since the whole "Happy Birthday to you" routine just made him uncomfortable, he decided to keep the damned thing a casual secret. When asked, he'd say "Oh, next fall" or "It's in the winter-a long time away".

Jamie, my boy, it looks like you pulled it off.

He pulled the car up to the 5th Street house. The house was dark and no other cars were parked in front.

In moments Phiz and he were on the front porch and opening the door. As he entered the house, Jamie clicked on the light switch next to the jamb. Nothing. The house remained steadfastly dark.

"The light must be burned out, I'll turn on a lamp."

Jamie had shuffled halfway across the Living Room when every light in the house snapped on and twenty people jumped up and yelled "Surprise!"

Jamie's eye's bulged, his heart stopped beating, and his body jerked in such wild spasms he almost fell down. He had to lean on the arm of a chair while his heart thundered back to life. Everyone there was laughing, pointing, and having a good time at his expense.

"Sit down, sit down," Shoes guided him into the chair, "you should know that we all think it was a shitty trick for y'all to try and keep your birthday a secret, but we've decided to not hold it against you. In fact, we all chipped in and bought you a present."

Lefty, holding a cardboard box, made his way through the crowd. Jamie reached out to take the box but Lefty pulled it away.

"Don't get grabby Dude, let me take it out for you."

Eager to see what it was, Jamie watched intently as Lefty reached into the box to get a grip on whatever was inside and then whisked the box away.

What the hell is that? It looks like a cream pie...

With a loud "plop", Lefty pushed the pie into Jamie's face and gave it a twist for good measure.

"Happy Birthday, Asshole!" Lefty shouted above a torrent of laughter from everyone there.

Jamie sat there stunned as the crowd sang "Happy Birthday", then he scooped a handful of chocolate cream off his face and threw it at Lefty. This set off a minor pie fight until Angela appeared with a damp towel and a bucket.

"What you need is a bath. Maybe we can fix that up later."

After helping him to clean himself up, she smiled, tapped him on the nose with her finger, and took the bucket away. Jamie was trying to figure that out when Phiz came up and opened his hand. In the middle of his palm was a gelatine capsule filled with a mottled green powder. There was a tiny red ribbon around the capsule that had been tied with a bow.

"I was feeling sorry for setting you up like that brother," Phiz said with a grin, "but that pie made it all worthwhile. Happy Birthday, man."

Jamie slid the ribbon off the capsule and held it up. "What is this?"

"Mescaline. Peyote cactus, man. I know a guy who has an Indian friend who came up from the rez in Texas with a gunny sack full of buds. Nearly everyone here has already dropped some."

"Well, in that case..." Jamie tossed the capsule into his mouth, choked it back and tried to work up enough saliva to swallow it down. When he finally succeeded he asked hoarsely, "Did you do one?"

Phiz shook his head, then smiled smugly and held up three fingers.

"Three? Jesus."

"Call it a Vision Quest, man."

"Good luck with that," said Jamie, "See you on Mars."

They shared a laugh, and then Jamie went to find a glass of water. He was halfway to the kitchen when Shoes and Waltz stopped him.

"Hold it right there, my friend," Waltz said then turned to the bedroom door and shouted, "Come on out, man!"

For the third time in about the last ten minutes, Jamie's mind sustained another jolt as Lyle Kirk walked out.

"Holy shit!" Jamie yelled, "Fuckin' Lyle."

Jamie stepped forward and grabbed Lyle in a big bear hug. Lyle smiled uncomfortably and patted Jamie on the back. Lyle was not a hugger.

"Hey, Hippie. Nice to see you." Lyle said.

"So what's your tale, man?" Jamie said, "I'm sure you've already told these guys, so now you get to tell it again."

"Not that much to tell, really," Lyle leaned back against the door jamb and lit a cigarette, "I finished Basic Training and got sent to Fort Dix in New Jersey, for Quartermaster School. Started hanging out with some guys who liked to get high. One of 'em had a cousin up in the City who'd send him rolls of cross-tops now and then."

"What are cross-tops?"

"Methedrine. Speed. Pharmaceutical quality. Drop a couple of those and it's like somebody shot a bolt of lightning up your ass. But that shit is rough on your guts, man, especially if you're not eating. Then we came across this junkie working in one of the kitchens who, in exchange for a few hits of speed, taught us how to cook that shit down and shoot it up.

"You mean like needles and shit? Fuck, man, did you like it?"

"Oh, yeah," Lyle said, "most amazing rush in the world. Zero to 60 in five seconds. If I can score some speed around here, I'll show you the trip sometime. Anyway, it wasn't but a few weeks later I got just sicker than shit. My eyes turned yellow, my piss turned brown, and I didn't have the strength to zip up my goddamn pants. The Docs told me I had Hepatitis and tossed me in the hospital.

"The lucky thing for me was that I'd found a nice vein up here on top of my arm," Lyle pulled his sleeve up and tapped on a place on his forearm, "and they looked for tracks down here in the crook of my elbow. Dumb shits. So they decided the Hepatitis was 'service-connected'. After feeling like Death Takin' a Shit for about a month, I got better. Then they discovered I had developed a heart murmur and Bingo! Medical discharge with all the trimmings."

"A heart murmur?" Waltz asked, "What's that?"

"Well… if you put your ear up to my chest you can hear a little voice in there saying, real quietly, 'Waltz is a faggoty asshole.'"

Nancy stepped up next to Waltz, put her arm through his, and said, "I'm sorry, I missed that. What did you say?"

"I said… um… Waltz is the nicest guy in Colton"

Nancy smiled at him and said, "Um hmm. You may be right."

"Nancy, this is Lyle," Waltz said, "I've told you about him."

Lyle put out his hand and Nancy gripped it.

"There's Madeleine," Nancy said, "I've got to talk to her. Nice to meet you, Lyle."

"Nice lookin' chick, Waltz," Lyle said once she was gone, "does she always carry that pair of nutcrackers around with her?"

A couple of hours later Jamie was sitting in the kitchen watching the cartoon show that was going on in the linoleum floor. It highlighted one of the differences Jamie had noticed between LSD and this mescaline. Acid hallucinations, for him, were about shapes and color and intricate patterns that pulsed and intertwined. But the visuals that the mescaline was inducing were more like old Walt Disney Silly Symphonies where constantly-mutating creatures dance to an unheard rhythm while odd faces with long droopy noses shimmy out from behind the scenery and wink at you. Strange looking animals morph into flowers that wilt and then re-bloom again. But like acid visuals, if things got too intense all he had to do was blink and look away and they'd be gone.

Another difference he noticed, between wild flights of fancy, was that where an acid trip was a more solitary experience, mescaline was more communal. He enjoyed talking to the various people who wandered into his space, shared something of themselves with him, and then wandered out again. Instead of judging people he was appreciating them.

Just as Jamie was spacing out on appreciation itself and seeing it as another shade of love, McNulty appeared before him. With a cigarette clamped in his teeth, fedora hat pushed back on his head, and his glasses sliding down his nose, it was the full McNulty going on and Jamie was, he had to say, appreciating it.

"Sit down, man," Jamie said. "What's up with you? Did you get off?"

"Oh yeah, like Gangbusters in fact. This is pretty good shit."

"True. Very good shit," Jamie said. "I can't imagine what's going through Phiz's head right now. He dropped three of 'em."

"Oh yeah, I was gonna tell you about that freak, man, but then I forgot."

"Funny how that happens."

"Yeah. So anyway I was just out in the backyard, you know, taking a breather, looking at the stars. And a UFO comes cruising by. Really, I'm not shitting you. It was kinda round and metallic with glowing lights flickering across it. I just about crapped my pants. Then it sorta shimmered and disappeared. And I'm thinking, "that was so far-fuckin'-out man, and nobody is gonna believe me.""

"Oh, I believe you," Jamie said, "At least tonight, probably not tomorrow, but you gotta take what you can get. Anyway, you were gonna tell me about Phiz."

"Oh yeah, Phiz. So I'm out there looking to see if that UFO might come back and I hear these grunting and rustling noises. I wander back there and see Phiz, sitting up against the house behind a lilac bush. He's got a branch pulled down and he's staring at the flowers on it. I say, 'Hey man, you okay?' and he says, 'Wait a minute, let me check...' and after a little while he says, 'Everything is in good working order, man. So I guess I'm okay.' And he goes back to looking at the lilac flowers."

"Woo," Jamie said, "Sounds like 'Lost in Space'. Maybe I'll go check on him."

They stood up. McNulty began flailing his arms and shouting in a mechanical monotone, "Danger! Danger Will Robinson!"

Jamie laughed himself all the way out the back door. He found Phiz right where McNulty said he'd be, sitting cross-legged behind a lilac bush with his back up against the house. He was holding both his hands up, fingers slightly bent, in front of his face.

"Watch this, man," Phiz said.

His right index finger bobbed up and down and Phiz laughed merrily.

"It's like it does it all by itself, man. All of them do!"

Jamie sat down on the grass next to Phiz.

"I take it you got off on those three caps, then."

Yeah, I did. Very smooth trip, man. Very mellow.

"Trace lags?"

Phiz moved his thumb quickly back and forth.

"Yep"

"Hallucinations?"

"Nope. Not a thing."

Jamie thought this was odd as there was a naked, green-skinned fairy with wings and a big yellow afro standing next to Phiz's knee. Then he blinked and the fairy had changed itself into a dandelion. Tricky bastard.

"You coming back in?' Jamie said.

"Maybe in a while. But right now this feels like my Power Spot to me. I tried moving a few feet over and it just wasn't right, you know what I mean? Like this is the spot I'm supposed to be in."

"I can dig it," Jamie got to his feet, "It's like everybody's got their own Power Spot, they just have to find it, right? It's something to think about. Check you later, man."

Reassured that Phiz was okay, Jamie went back into the house and found Angela standing in the middle of the Kitchen grinning at him.

"There you are! I've been looking all over for you, where were you? Never mind, you probably don't even remember. Come on!"

She grabbed his hand and led him down the little hallway and into the bathroom. The water was running in the tub and a small mountain of bubbles was growing under the stream.

"Is the water too hot for you?" Angela flicked off the light. Two candles on a far shelf were giving off a golden glow.

Taking time out from his birthday party to take a bath seemed like a pretty strange thing to do, but since it was Angela, Jamie decided that "going with the flow" was the order of the night. He put his hand under the spigot.

"Maybe we should make it a little bit hotter so it won't go cold too fast."

"Whatever you like," Angela smiled, "Now out of your clothes and into the tub."

Jamie had never been overly self-critical about his body, but taking his clothes off in front of Angela-THE Angela, the girl-that-everybody-falls-in-love-with Angela-made him wish that he had a little more sun-tanned muscle and a little less pallid flab.

He stepped into the tub, gave his feet a few moments to get used to the hot water, and then turned around. Angela had taken off her top, kicked off her sandals, and was dropping her jeans to the floor.

Holy Shit.

He sank down into the bubbles watching her breasts sway gently as she slipped her panties down over her hips. Then she gathered up all the clothing and threw it into a corner.

"Well move over," she said. "Oh, wait a minute..."

She ran back and pulled the door into the hallway open, then scurried back and jumped into the tub.

"Now we can talk to people as they go by," she said.

She scooped up a handful of suds and blew them at Jamie. The merriment was infectious and soon they were giggling like preschoolers playing in a mud puddle.

To the two of them in the tub, the doorway to the hall became a three foot by seven television screen. There wasn't much of a plot to this story, but the actors were so good at playing their characters that it seemed to Jamie and Angela that they had known these people for months.

The actor playing Lyle stopped and peered into the bathroom with such a believable what-the-hell-is-going-on look that Jamie and Angela cheered and applauded. The Lyle-character held the outside seams of his pants and curtsied, then walked off shaking his head.

Lefty walked by holding a corn-cob pipe and calling for a match. "It's the Villain!" Angela yelled. She and Jamie hissed and booed and threw handfuls of bubble-bath foam at the doorway.

"Jesus," the Lefty-character said, "you guys are fuckin' nuts." and he disappeared.

A few minutes passed, no one appeared in the doorway, and the audience grew impatient.

"Hey!" Jamie yelled, "on with the show!" and the two of them started drumming the bottom of the tub with their bare feet.

Then McNulty came into view walking slowly backward. He had the end of a piece of string in his hand and was shouting encouragement back down the hall.

"Keep it straight! Freeway coming through!"

He passed from view, but the string kept moving. A moment later Waltz was sidestepping down the hall, holding the string between two fingers and motioning down the hall with the other hand. By then Jamie and Angela were caught up in the drama, their chins practically resting on the edge of the tub.

Then Aaron was holding the string with one hand, his arm around Madeleine's waist. She was the helpless damsel being rescued and made appropriate whimpers and sighs.

Then, finally, the end of the string came into view. It was being held by McNulty again who waved his hat to the cheering audience of two.

After a few curtain calls, the players retired to the kitchen. Krenovich came walking into the bathroom, put the lid down on the toilet and sat down on it.

"There's some reefer out there goin' around. I didn't think you guys wanted to miss out, so I rolled you a bomber."

Krenovich pulled out an extra-fat joint and lit it with a wooden match. It was so oversized that little chunks of flaming marijuana and paper were falling from the burning end even as he inhaled.

After the joint made two or three rounds, Jamie felt that familiar fuzziness settle over his brain. The marijuana didn't mask the mescaline high, it complemented it, made it more comfortable somehow.

In the tub, most of the bubble-bath bubbles had disappeared leaving large patches of water showing. Angela turned those big green eyes on Krenovich and asked, "Hey Doug! Would you like Peenie to say hello?"

Krenovich looked mystified but said, "Uh... okay, sure."

A grinning Angela reached down between Jamie's legs, took hold of his penis and pulled it up so the head was above the water. She turned it a quarter turn, then, gently pulling on the skin with her fingertips, made the slit in the end open and close like a little mouth.

"Hi there, Dougie-boy!" Peenie said in Angela's voice, "How's about a little kiss?"

The first statement made Krenovich's eyes bulge. Upon hearing the second he jerked backward so violently that he fell off the toilet. He jumped back up to see Jamie and Angela splashing in the tub and howling with laughter. He picked the smoldering roach up off the floor, said, "Jesus Christ, you fuckers," and left.

A few minutes later Jamie was sitting on the edge of the tub, a towel in his lap, watching Angela dry off and put her clothes back on.

"Where's Rachel tonight? I would think she'd be here."

"Jeez, I haven't seen Rachel for more than a week. She got all giggly about Malcolm, balled him, and now she thinks she's in love."

"Malcolm the Cowboy Jew? I thought he was taking care of her horse?"

"He was. Now he's taking care of her little fuzz-clam as well. I'm a little worried about her."

"Is she okay?"

"Well, Malcolm's a decent sort of guy, but he's got some pretty hard-core friends. And Rachel trusts everybody. I think she gets it from her Mom."

Jamie sat quietly looking at his hands while Angela finished getting dressed then looked up at her and said, "Thanks for the bath. It was the most fun birthday present I've ever gotten."

She smiled, bent down, kissed him on the mouth, and left. While Jamie got himself dressed and then mopped up the water that had splashed on the floor, he wondered about that kiss. It was definitely more than sisterly, but not exactly "romantic." Did it mean anything?

We got naked and spent God-knows-how-long in a bathtub together. And she grabbed my cock. Of course, it meant something. Sure, maybe I am sort of a ridiculous clown, but it doesn't seem like Angela's figured that out yet. Maybe she never will.

With a confident smile, Jamie left the bathroom and walked into the living room. Looking around the room for Angela, he saw her sitting cross-legged on the arm of an overstuffed chair. She was talking to Lefty's friend, Scott, who sat on the other arm propping himself up with an elbow on the back of the chair. He was tall and broad-shouldered, with wavy black hair and smoldering dark eyes. Jamie's confidence evaporated further when he saw Scott say something to Angela that made her laugh delightedly. Then she reached out her index finger and tapped Scott on the end of the nose.

Jamie turned around and headed toward the back door. Looking for a Power Spot suddenly seemed like a good idea.

EIGHTEEN

Patrolman Sherman sat on the red leather couch in Chief Gaskin's office and listened as Sergeant Bill Crenshaw re-explained his latest bust to the Chief. Evidently, Gaskin had heard the first half, stopped Crenshaw, and sent somebody to ask Sherman to come in and join the meeting.

"Okay, so about nine o'clock, me and Goot... uh, Officer Guttierrez," Crenshaw indicated another officer who was sitting on the other side of the room with his hands folded in his lap and his hat pushed back, "we were cruising down 8th Street when we notice this kid walking along the sidewalk."

Crenshaw scratched his neck while he assembled his recollections. Although he was overweight, balding, and in his 50's, Crenshaw still had the kind of restless energy that made it difficult for him to tell a story while he was sitting down. So he stood in front of the Chief's desk and swiveled his head around to include all of his listeners.

"He was a hippie-type, you know-bell-bottom pants, long hair, and he was smoking as he walked. Now when I smoke a cigarette, I hold it between my middle and index fingers like this."

Crenshaw put his two fingers up to his mouth and took an imaginary drag to demonstrate.

"When the butt gets short, I drop it and step on it. But when a marijuana joint gets short, hippies pinch it with their thumb and index fingers like this."

He made what looked like an "okay" sign with his fingers, held the fingernails up to his mouth, and again took an imaginary drag.

"That's just what this kid was doing. It was dark so we could see the little red flare of the ash light up. So I told Goot to make a u-turn and I flicked on the lights. The kid had ditched the butt-end of his joint, or maybe eaten it, who knows? I patted him down, but he was clean. Then Goot says... well you tell it, Goot."

Officer Guttierrez cleared his voice and said, "Something was nagging at me and I said, 'you know, Sarge, I think he was wearing some kind of a red jacket when we first spotted him.'"

"So I told him to take a look around," Crenshaw picked up the narrative, "and stuffed behind a trash can just inside the mouth of the alley, Goot found this red windbreaker," he gestured to a thin jacket on the chair next to Guttierrez. "This was what was in the pocket."

Sherman got up off the couch to look at the small pile of things on the Chief's desk. There was a clear plastic baggie that contained a small amount of dried and crushed plant material as well as two hand-rolled cigarettes. Next to the bag were four aluminum foil-wrapped cubes, one of which had been opened to show a brown, tarry substance. Finally, there was a small plastic bottle that contained six pink pills.

"Sherman?" said the Chief.

"I'd guess, pending analysis by the Boulder Lab, we're looking at less than half an ounce of marijuana, four grams of hashish, and six hits of acid."

"Enough for Intent to Distribute?"

"If it pans out, absolutely."

"All right," Crenshaw turned to Guttierrez and stuck his hand out, "a felony bust." Guttierrez slapped his hand closed around the Sergeant's and shook it.

"Don't get too excited yet, okay?" Chief Gaskin said. "There might be a better way to play this. You did the Drug Enforcement Training, Sherman. What do you think?"

Well, sir," Sherman said, "the Course Leaders were pretty clear about the different ways of letting a small fish get away in order to net a bunch of bigger ones."

"Letting him go?" Crenshaw said, "Are you nuts?"

"No offense to Sergeant Crenshaw and Patrolman Guttierrez, sir. They did some excellent police work. But if we offer this kid a chance to walk in exchange for some help and information, it could give us an opportunity to really clean Colton up."

Chief Gaskin said, "Hmmm," and drummed his fingers on the desk. After a few moments' thought, he looked up at Sherman.

"Okay, Sherman, we'll do it your way. Don't screw it up, okay?"

Crenshaw and Guttierrez looked unhappy and the Chief turned to them, "Don't take it badly, Sergeant. There's a different kind of criminal out there these days and we have to use some different methods to catch 'em. If this works out, I'll make sure you two are in on it at the end. That's it. Dismissed."

The Colton Police Interrogation Room was small with a high, barred window and a heavy door. Against one wall stood a table bolted to the floor. A young man, brooding and uncomfortable, sat in one of several folding chairs around it. The door opened and Sherman, holding a clipboard and the red windbreaker, walked in.

"Hi, my name is Larry Sherman. I asked your arresting officers if they would hold off booking you for a while and let me have a chance to talk to you first."

The young man just stared at his hands folded on the table. Sherman sat down and hung the windbreaker on the chair next to him.

"Before we start, I've gotta read you something," Sherman said as he pulled a card out of his breast pocket.

"You have the right to remain silent. Anything you say may be used against you in a court of law. You have the right to an attorney. If you cannot afford an attorney, one will be provided for you without charge. Do you understand these rights?"

The young man almost imperceptibly nodded his head.

"Okay, here's the bad news. There was enough dope in the pocket of your windbreaker here to qualify you as a dealer. Intent to Distribute is a felony. That means up to five years in prison, a fine big enough to wipe out your parents' life savings, and a black mark on your record that will follow you for the rest of your life."

"What if I said I'd never seen that jacket before? That it was a plant or something?"

"I kinda think you'd have a hard time explaining this," Sherman said as he reached into an inside pocket of the jacket, pulled out a postcard, and dropped it on the table. "In case you haven't read it, your Aunt Dot in Arkansas congratulates you on completing your first year of college."

The young man muttered "shit," and looked away.

"There is, or can be, a possible upside to all this. We don't think you're a big-time dealer at all. We think you're just a guy who sells a little bit to his friends so he can get high when he wants, and have a little pocket money to boot. You, in other words, are not the guy we're after. So I'm going to offer you a deal. You work with us, help us get the guys we're really after, and you can walk out of here tonight like nothing ever happened. We put an 'Administrative Hold' on your records and a year from now, if you've been cooperating and we've made some significant arrests, those records go into that incinerator out back. And that will be the end of it."

"What do you mean by 'cooperating?'"

Sherman pulled a piece of paper off the clipboard and, along with a pen, set it down in front of the young man.

"You start by writing down the name of the guy who sold that stuff to you. Where he lives, how do you contact him, everything. After that, you go on about your life, hang with your friends, and if you get an opportunity, ask a few questions. If you hear about or meet someone we'd be interested in, let us know. Easy as that."

The fellow didn't move, just stared at the blank sheet of paper. As Sherman stood up, he picked up the postcard, the jacket, and his clipboard.

"I'm going to give you some time to think it over. If you decide not to work with us, I'll tell Sergeant Crenshaw he can go ahead and book you for Possession of a Controlled Substance with Intent to Distribute. Or you can fill out that paper and walk out the door. Your choice."

As Sherman left the room, the young man was still staring at the blank sheet of paper.

Nineteen

Jamie, carrying an army fatigue jacket and a paper sack from the CC Bookstore, came in through the front door of the Fifth Street house. Waltz, with his feet up on the coffee table, was listening to Cream's *Disraeli Gears* on the stereo. Nancy sat next to him leafing through a magazine.

"Whattya got there?" Waltz yelled over the music.

"It's a-

"I've Been Waiting So Long," Jack Bruce sang.

"What?"

"Lyle and I-"

"To Be Where I'm Going."

"What?"

"Jesus Christ!"

"In The Sunshine Of Your-"

Jamie turned the volume knob on the stereo down to 2 and turned back around.

"It's Lyle's Army-issue fatigue jacket," Jamie held up the garment, "the one that he brought back from New Jersey."

"What are you doing with Lyle's jacket?"

"It's mine now. You know that cowhide vest my Mother sent me for my Birthday? I could never get behind it, you know? Too much of my Mom goin' on with it. And Lyle's jacket had too much of an Army vibe for him. So we swapped. And now I'm gonna customize my new threads."

Waltz nodded and got up to turn the stereo back up. But now it was Nancy's turn to be interested.

"What do you plan on doing?"

"Secret shit, man. But if you want to watch, I'm gonna set up on the kitchen table."

A few minutes later, Jamie had the jacket spread out on the table, had a little jar of acrylic paint open, and was painting the jacket's lapels a bright red. Nancy sat across the table from him, watching what he was doing and asking questions.

"Will that paint wash off?"

"I don't know, really. It's acrylic. Isn't that a kind of plastic when it dries? Anyway, how often does a guy wash his jacket, anyway?"

"Not often enough, I'm sure. But what if there were a mud hole and I wanted to cross, wouldn't you put your jacket down so I wouldn't get my shoes muddy?"

"Ha! Dream on."

"You're cute, Jamie Shipman. You're rude, but you're cute."

Jamie grinned as he worked, periodically glancing up at Nancy and enjoying a rare moment of closeness. Round and plump and blushing like a peach ready for picking, Nancy was probably the most sensual girl he'd ever met. Enjoying Nancy's company was fine but whenever he caught himself fantasizing about working her panties down over her buttocks while her nipples ticked his chest, he'd convince himself to think about something else until his heartbeat settled down again. She was, after all, Waltz's Old Lady, and Waltz was one of his best friends.

The lapels were soon finished and Jamie got up to wash the brush out in the sink.

"Is that it?" Nancy said, "just red?"

"Better red than dead, right? No, I'm teasing. There's more to come. I wasted a whole class of American Literature this morning figuring out what I wanted it to look like and how to get there."

Out of the bag came a sheet of white cardboard, a protractor, a compass, a razor knife, and another little jar of acrylic paint-this one yellow. Using the protractor. he made a big circle and made a mark every 36 degrees around it. He got a bread knife out of a drawer and, using the back of it as a straight edge. drew five lines through the circle, then, with the compass, drew two smaller circles. Finally, by connecting intersections, he had drawn a perfect five-pointed star.

"Cool!" said Nancy, leaning in to look. Jamie was looking as well, but mostly at her heavy breasts resting on the table, the nipples pushing at the cotton of her t-shirt. To distract himself, he got up, pulled out a breadboard, and used the razor knife to carefully remove the star from the cardboard.

"There!" he said with a grin, "I wonder if Old Mrs. Smith, my Eighth Grade Geometry teacher, would be pleased or shocked? Now, what do you think, one yellow star in the middle of each, or a pattern of stars?"

"Hmm. One star each I think."

"I agree. A pattern would look like a shower curtain."

The red lapels were already dry and Jamie was able to hold the cut-out star right in the center of each and, with a sharp pencil, trace out an accurate outline. Then he carefully filled the star shapes in with yellow paint. When it was done he found a wire coat hanger and hung the jacket on the refrigerator to dry while Nancy boiled water for tea.

"Have you ever been to a leather shop?" Nancy said.

"You mean like fringy suede jackets and stuff?"

"Well sorta, but more like belts and hatbands and stash bags. You know-accessories."

" You're not talking about the belts cowboys wear with 'Bubba" stamped on the back, right?"

"Oh no, way hipper than that."

"Okay, yeah," Jamie said, "I know what you're talking about. Some of it is pretty cool."

"That's what my sister's husband, Ike, does-works in a leather shop, I mean. They live in Cambridge. Back East. Anyway, I think you could be pretty good at doing that."

"You really think so?"

"Well, look at that," she gestured at the jacket, "You pictured what you wanted it to look like, and then worked out what you needed to do to make it happen. Leather would be a similar process, just different tools, and different ways to work."

"You know, Nancy, I'm likin' this idea a lot. But I don't know how to even cut a piece of leather, let alone make a belt out of it."

"I've got a book I can loan you. Lots of pictures and step-by-step stuff."

"I'd love to see that. Please and thank you."

Jamie was still thinking about Nancy's idea a few minutes later when the phone rang. He didn't much feel like getting out of his chair, but the phone was on the wall out of his reach and Nancy had gone into the living room to see if Waltz wanted some tea. He sighed, stood up, and picked up the receiver.

"Hello?"

"Is that Jamie? Hey man, it's Mike."

"Mike! Far-fuckin'-out, man. What's happening?"

"Kind of a bummer on my end, Dude. I don't mean to bring you down or anything..."

"No, tell me. What's going on, man?"

"You know that guy in Denver that was sending me those books now and then? One arrived at my house here yesterday. The Postman who delivered it asked me to sign for it. Like a dumbass, I did. I'd barely got the door closed behind him when the bell rang again and two plainclothes cops were standing on the front porch holding their badges out."

Oh shit, man. That sucks."

"Yeah, it really does. The Old Man's lawyer thinks he can maybe get me off with a fine and probation, but I don't know... Anyway, the reason I called is to ask you to spread the word. I don't know if anybody in Colton is doing business with my Denver guy, but if so, they need to step back. Somebody narked him out and he may not even know it yet."

"Sure I'll do it, man. Just let us know what happens, okay?"

"I will, my friend. Sometime when we can talk. Right now the Old Man is pissed off and giving me the bad eye. Take care of yourself."

"You too, man..." but Jamie was listening to a dial tone.

* * *

Jamie turned onto Buchanan Street and pulled into a parking space near the end of the block. Nancy looked at an address on a slip of paper, then at the addresses next to the doors.

"One Fifty-Three," she pointed out a heavy door with peeling green paint, "That's it. Those must be their cars."

In parking spaces right outside the door sat a late-model pickup and a slightly seedy-looking mint green '57 Cadillac.

Jamie turned in his seat. "Tell me again how you met these guys."

"It was at a party last week. Jack and Tammy, a married couple from Casper and old friends of mine invited me over and said to bring Waltz. But you know Waltz, he's so shy around strangers. He managed to find a TV, fell asleep in front of it, and that was it for the night. So I started talking to these two guys from Nebraska."

"Bill and Charlie. Bill's the one with the money?"

"Maybe some, I don't know, but he did inherit this whole building. He didn't know what to do with it so he asked his friend Charlie to go into business with him."

Jamie sighed, picked up a spiral notebook, and got out of the Volkswagen. Nancy joined him and they started toward the green door. Then Jamie stopped.

"How can we tell them we're going to put a leather shop in there? How can we fill such a big space with a little leather business? And how can we say we're experienced leather-makers when you've sewed two vests and a purse and I've never made a damned thing?"

"I told you, Jamie. Don't freak out on me. They want to put a head shop in there, you know-candles and incense, hash pipes and posters-all that stuff. But, like you said, it's a big space. I suggested a little leather shop in the corner and they got all excited."

Nancy started walking again and Jamie quickly caught up.

"And as for not actually having made anything," Nancy said, "they don't know that. You've read the book, right?"

"Yeah. Twice in fact."

"They say half of any business is bullshitting. So think of this as your big chance to get started with that."

They had reached the entrance. Nancy waited for Jamie to open the door for her, and they entered.

They walked into a large, high-ceilinged space. The back wall was bare, red brick, the same as the exterior of the building. A young man who was sitting behind a couple of card tables pushed together stood up and said, "Nancy. I see you brought him. Come in. Come in."

Jamie noticed another fellow, who was off to the side pushing a broom, put the broom down and walk over toward his friend.

"Hi, Charlie. Bill," Nancy was all breathy smiles and sparkles, "this is Jamie Shipman, the guy I told you about. Jamie, this is Charlie Melman and this is Bill Snyder."

Before Jamie had finished putting his arm up and his hand out to shake, he knew who he was dealing with. He usually didn't try to size people up so quickly, but Charlie Melman and Bill Snyder were so wildly transparent that he couldn't help himself.

Charlie was something of a fraud and knew it. The tinted aviator glasses, the flowery, puffy-sleeved shirt, and the peace sign pendant around his neck all spoke of a desperate need to be accepted into the hip community. To Charlie, Jamie wasn't just a hippie, he was an artist-a far out, experienced hippie who'd had his praises sung by a beautiful blonde hippie chick. Charlie, in short, was prepared to metaphorically kiss Jamie's boots.

In that short moment, Jamie not only understood all of this but knew, instinctively, how to handle it. He hadn't been Mike Harding's roommate and best friend for nearly a year without learning how to add just a whiff of arrogance and condescension into an otherwise friendly conversation. When Jamie put his hand up, Charlie put his hand straight out, looked momentarily confused, then reached up and shook Jamie's hand in the hip-acceptable way. Normally, Jamie might have reached down to catch Charlie's hand midway, or said something lighthearted to allay any awkwardness but this time he only smiled and waited for Charlie to catch up.

The rest of the meeting proceeded along the same lines. Jamie was personable and friendly and yet kept the attitude that he was doing Melman and Snyder Enterprises a big favor. Charlie, with a mostly-silent Bill in tow, smiled and laughed and acceded to just about every request. Nancy and Jamie picked out a nice corner of the establishment to work in, Jamie opened the notebook and made a quick sketch of what they thought it might look like, and Charlie threw in the use of a display case. Jamie's leathercrafting experience, or lack thereof, was never mentioned.

* * *

Not long after, Jamie and Nancy sat together in the Full Moon Coffee House celebrating with a couple of cups of tea and a slice of carrot cake.

"I still can't quite believe it," Jamie said, "Free rent and only 10 percent of sales. We can just figure out what we'd like to get for our work, and add 10 percent to it."

"Or better yet, add 20 percent," Nancy added, "ten for Melman and Snyder Enterprises and ten for future needs. I'd really like to get a heavy-duty sewing machine made to sew leather; the one I've got can hardly do two seams without breaking a needle."

"So let it be written," Jamie said, and held up his tea mug, "So let it be done."

Nancy picked up her tea, clinked mugs, and they both drank.

Jamie smiled contentedly. Not only did he have a fun and interesting project to focus on, but he also had a fun and interesting partner. When they sat down, Nancy had not selected the chair across from him, but the one immediately to his left. She had then pulled it even closer to him until their shoulders were touching. Clearly, this was a woman who craved intimacy, and Jamie was all too happy to provide what he could.

Jamie opened his notebook to a clean page and began to sketch an idea for a sign. Rectangular, with a simple border, the sign read "Nancy and Jamie's Leathercrafting" in a kind of Old English script. At least, that's what he was going for, even though the writing looked more like "Old Yard Sale Sign."

Nancy had been leaning her head against his shoulder as he drew. When he was finished, she looked up at him and said, "You put me first."

"Well, sure," he said, "it was your idea, you set it up, and 'Nancy and Jamie' sounds better than 'Jamie and Nancy' don't you think?"

In answer, she gave him a squeeze and kissed him on the cheek. Jamie suddenly felt an animal lust stirring down deep at the base of his spine and quickly changed the subject.

"So we've got until Labor Day-which makes less than two months to teach ourselves the leather business. That reminds me, you've got a typewriter, right? Can you remember the points of the deal we made well enough to write it all up? Make a carbon, everybody will sign and we'll be set to go."

With a faraway look in her eye, Nancy just nodded her head.

On the way back to the 5th Street house, Jamie said, "I'll probably be getting my G.I. Bill check in a day or two. After I pay the rent, there should be enough left over to buy some blank leather and some tools and stuff. The book not only had lists of what to get but lists of some places that sell it, one of which is over in Fort Collins."

He parked the car in front of the house. "How'd you like to take a drive over there in a few days?"

He looked over at Nancy expecting an answer but saw she was kneading a wad of tissue paper while big fat tears rolled down her cheeks.

"What's wrong? Did I say something?"

She dabbed at her eyes, blew her nose, took a deep breath, and began to explain. She said she'd realized a couple of weeks ago that she'd made a mistake hooking up with Waltz.

"He's, a dear, sweet man and I'm very fond of him, but it became obvious to me that the guy I was really meant to be with was standing there just a few feet away."

"Who?"

"You, silly."

Jamie's heart seemed to turn sideways in his chest. It was both painful and exhilarating. The roaring in his ears made it difficult for him to hear his own voice as he said, "Uh... me?"

"The thing is," Nancy went on, "I haven't been able to figure out how to tell Kenny. I don't want to hurt his feelings or make him angry."

"Do you want me to talk to him?"

"No, no," she shook her head, "I got myself into this mess; it's up to me to find a way out. You see that don't you?"

Jamie, secretly relieved that he wouldn't have to lower the boom on one of his best friends, nodded his head solemnly.

"So until I can do that, you and I have to be just good friends, okay? As much as we may want to ball each other's brains out, we can't be sneaking around behind Kenny's back. It wouldn't be fair. Deal?"

Jamie took a deep breath, fought down a desire to grab Nancy right there, and said, "Deal."

It was only later that it occurred to Jamie that Nancy had never asked him how he felt about hooking up, she just assumed it was what he wanted-ed. Since her assumptions were correct, he decided not to worry about it.

The following week was, for Jamie, bordering on bizarre. If it wasn't the strangest he'd ever spent, it had to be among the top three. The trip to Fort Collins took a lot longer than it should have because every ten miles or so Jamie would pull over and he and Nancy would clutch at each other and trade spittle until she would push him away. Then they would drive on as tears and guilt slowly gave way to undeniable animal attraction and soon Jamie was pulling over again.

At home, they had put a chunk of plywood over the kitchen table and Jamie was cutting out belt blanks, dying and edging them, riveting hardware, and learning blind weaving techniques. With Nancy just on the other side of the table cutting and sewing the parts for a fringed suede handbag, the work was frustrating and satisfying both at the same time.

To make matters more freakish, Jamie was really feeling bad for Waltz. Although Nancy was smiling and talkative around Jamie, around Waltz she was silent and distant. When Waltz would ask her what was going on, she'd say, "Oh nothing," and walk away.

The tension was getting so thick around the 5th Street house that Jamie was feeling he was going to need hip waders just to walk through the living room. Then Waltz came up to him.

"Hey Jamie," Waltz said, "can I talk to you?"

One look at Waltz's haggard face and Jamie knew what it was going to be about. Since there were some other people in the house, Jamie said, "sure man, c'mon," and led the way out onto the porch.

"It's about Nancy," Waltz said as soon as the door closed behind him, "she's on some kind of a weird trip. She won't tell me about it, she just stares into space and cries and when I ask her what the matter is, she says she's fine and then clams up. It's driving me nuts. Has she said anything to you?"

"Okay man, she made me promise not to say anything," Jamie said, "But I'm going to go ahead and lay this on you."

While Jamie was pausing to try to get his thoughts together Waltz blurted out, "Is she pregnant?"

"No man, no," Jamie said, "She's not pregnant. She's just, well... fallen for another guy. Umm... well, for me, in fact. I'm sorry."

"She's fallen in love with you?"

"Well, I don't know about 'love', but yeah, somethin' like that. She's been afraid to tell you because she didn't want to hurt you or make you feel bad."

"Shit, Jamie, compared to how I've been feeling, this is nothin' but relief! Whew. I was thinking if she wasn't pregnant, then she had cancer or something."

"You're not pissed off?"

Waltz thought about that for a moment, then said, "No, I'm not. Maybe I should be, but I'm not. But I sure could use a beer. Let's go over to Ziggy's Saloon and you can buy me one."

"With pleasure, my friend. In fact, I'll buy you two. When Jamie Shipman steals a friend's girlfriend, he spares no expense!"

* * *

Partly because Jamie and Waltz came home that night as drunk and loud as one can get on 3.2 beer and partly because Nancy got her period and was sick with cramps, it was four more days before Jamie and Nancy found themselves alone together in Jamie's room. Jamie had lit a candle but Nancy blew it out after turning out the lights.

"I like the dark," she said.

With only the faint light from a streetlamp halfway down the block coming around the curtains, Jamie could barely make out the vague shape of Nancy moving in the darkness. He thought about reaching for her when he heard a zipper being unzipped and hurriedly began to undress. Just as he'd removed his underwear he felt Nancy's hands slide over his shoulders. As her arms wrapped around him, his mouth found hers. Tongues slid back and forth across each other alternately thrusting out and sucking in. His hands slipped down inside Nancy's panties, cuddled her generous ass, and then pressed her pubis up against his already-hard cock.

Nancy reached down, grabbed him, and squeezed. He gasped.

"Oh, look what I found," she said in a breathy, husky voice, "I wonder what it does."

Using his stiffened penis like a lead rope, she gently pulled him toward the bed. Feeling a little foolish being led like that, Jamie put his arms around her and together they tumbled onto the bed.

Within a few minutes, he had pulled her T-shirt up over her head and was pulling her panties down her legs. Both of them were soon hot and sweating and their breaths were coming in ragged gasps. Jamie began the stroking, kneading and caressing that Lisa had loved so well, but instead found himself being gently pulled up on top of Nancy until he was lying between her legs and running his fingers between her wet, engorged labia.

"Fuck me, Jamie Shipman," she groaned, "fuck me good."

Jamie sent an urgent mental order to his genitalia.

Okay you guys, this time hold off for a while. Don't get excited, stay calm.

Jamie managed to get the head of his cock into her but no further. She had to reach around and guide him inside.

As he began to slide in and out of her, Jamie desperately tried to think of something, anything else.

Rows of corn marching past the car window. Bare feet walking on a sandy beach. Standing at home plate staring down the pitcher as he winds... oh God, here it comes. Too soon, too soon...

Jamie made groaning noises as the little pump at the base of his balls sent hot gouts of semen out through his cock and into Nancy. She stopped moving, pulled her head back and looked at him.

"That was it? You're done?"

"No, no. I can keep going."

Determined to please her, Jamie hung on tightly and kept thrusting away, hoping that somehow he could hold on to his erection. But it wasn't long before he began to shrink and soften and then fall out of her.

"Sorry," he said, "It's been a long time. I guess I got too excited."

He reached for her, but she said, "Just a second," slipped out of bed, tucked a couple of Kleenexes between her legs, and then got back in. She turned her back to Jamie. He snuggled up against her and said if they wanted to wait for an hour or so, he'd like to try again.

"No, that's okay," she said, "I have to get up early in the morning. Maybe tomorrow or the next day."

Without turning around, she whispered, "G'nite Jamie."

He kissed her on the back of the neck, wished her a good night, and then lay on his back for a long time with one hand behind his head. He thought of when he had balled Lisa for the first time on that cold night on her parents' farm. There had been a few things that were the same with Nancy but he mostly thought about the many things that were different. Then he decided he wasn't being fair, that when they got comfortable with each other, sex would get better too.

When Nancy's deep breathing told him she'd fallen asleep, he got out of bed, pulled on his underwear, and padded across the hall into the bathroom to wash and take a pee. At one point he cupped his traitorous equipment in his hands.

Thanks, guys. Thanks a fucking lot.

For the next few weeks, Jamie and Nancy struggled along together. Sexually, their relationship was iffy at best. On days when he thought they were going to ball that night, he would slip into the bathroom in the afternoon to masturbate. It helped him to maintain some endurance when it came time to perform, but it also killed a lot of the anticipation and excitement. There were times when Jamie caught himself wondering if the sex was really worth the hassle.

During the day, on the other hand, the two of them seemed to be getting along fine. Nancy was smart, fun, and beautiful. She was very supportive of his leather work and together they designed a leather pony-tail holder cut into a butterfly shape and featuring a lacquered chopstick. She quickly sold half a dozen of them to students she knew. Coupled with a couple of belts and a wristband Jamie had sold to his friends, they had enough money to buy more supplies and keep working.

They were just cleaning up at the end of an afternoon when Lyle came in. He'd let his hair grow out some and had trimmed his beard into the beginnings of a nice pair of muttonchops.

Waltz turned off the stereo and soon he was swapping insults with Lyle as Jamie laughed. Nancy brought out three beers, and then snuggled up to Jamie on the couch.

"So I'm living in the basement, right?" Lyle was saying, "and my Dad-he refers to me as 'the Beatnik' so I call him the 'Daddio Gouger' just to piss him off-is freaking out about the music he hears coming up through the floor. So I'm down there listening to *Music from Big Pink* by The Band, and one of their songs, "Chest Fever" starts with this Bach organ thing. Now I'm thinking the Gouger digs this Bach dude..."

"Johann," Waltz throws in, "Johann Sebastian Bach."

"Oh, well fuck you very much Mr. Classical Music Expert."

"Just trying to be helpful."

Lyle gives Waltz the side-eye squint, then goes back to his story, "And I'm thinking this might be a cool way to turn him on to Rock 'n' Roll. So I get him down there, sitting comfortably, and lay the tune on him. The organ starts, builds up, he's diggin' it... then 'Bam!' the drums and bass kick in and the band starts to rock. The Gouger jumps to his feet, his face all red, and shouts, 'They can't do that!' Then he stomps back upstairs slamming doors all the way."

Everyone laughed. Even Nancy giggled and Jamie knew she usually didn't like stories about how irredeemably square some people were.

Lyle lit a cigarette and said, "As much as I like looking at Waltz's pretty little face, the real reason I came over is I've got a guy who'll sell me an Eight Ball of crystal meth for $30. He won't sell it in smaller quantities, too paranoid. I haven't got thirty bucks or I'd buy it and sell it myself. So I'm figuring if six of us each pitch in five bucks we can get really speedy together. What do you think? Waltz?"

With barely a moment's hesitation, Waltz pulls out his wallet, extracts a five dollar bill, and waves it at Lyle.

Lyle nods, then looks at Jamie, "So, you in?"

"Who else you got?" said Jamie.

"McNulty, Lefty, and Phiz."

"...and me," Waltz said. He was carefully folding the five dollar bill on the arm of the chair.

Ignoring Waltz, Lyle turned to Jamie and Nancy. "Have you guys got mice? I could swear I heard something."

"What about an outfit?" Jamie asked, "you know, syringes...?"

"I'll bring a couple of those over. And I've got some extra needles. You just boil 'em up a little in between and you can use 'em over and over."

Jamie thinks about it for a moment, then shrugs, and digs into his wallet for five dollars.

"Okay, cool," Lyle said, "That looks like enough to do..."

Something hits Lyle in the forehead and falls into his lap. It is a little green paper airplane made from a five dollar bill. Waltz grins and wiggles his fingers in a silly wave.

"And Waltz," Lyle laughs as he stuffs the money in his shirt pocket. "See you around eight."

* * *

Fascinated and a little shocked, Jamie watched Phiz pass a cigarette lighter flame under the bowl of the tablespoon. The little pile of white powder in the water in the spoon was quickly dissolving. As soon as the powder was completely dissolved, Phiz snapped the lighter shut and put the spoon down on the table. Since he'd previously bent the handle into a triangular shape, part of it was laying flat on the table giving the spoon stability.

"Let it cool a bit," said Lyle, acting the professor, "you don't want to shoot up boiling water."

After about 30 seconds, Lyle said, "Now drop a little wad of cotton in there... good. Now put the needle in the cotton and draw the water up."

When Phiz had done so, he held up the syringe, tapped it to get any bubbles to rise, then slowly pushed up the plunger until all the air was out and a small drop of liquid emerged and ran down the needle.

"Anybody got a tie?" Phiz flexed his left arm.

"Here's a belt, that should work," said Lefty, "but I don't think you're going to have a lot of trouble finding a vein."

Phiz was one of those guys with very little body fat and his veins stood out on his arms like fishing worms. Perhaps just for tradition's sake, Jamie didn't know, Phiz put one end of the belt through the buckle, drew it up to make a small loop, put his left upper arm through, and tightened the belt around it.

Holding the belt tight with his teeth, Phiz laid his forearm on the table, picked up the syringe with his right hand and gently pushed the needle into a likely vein near the crook of his elbow.

"Good," said Lyle, "now pull a flag."

While holding the syringe in place, Phiz reached back with his index finger and pushed the plunger out a little way. A bright red squirt of blood came up into the water in the syringe.

"You're in," said Lyle, "fire away."

Phiz reached up higher with his index finger and began to push the plunger down. When it was at the bottom and the syringe was empty, he pulled the needle out and dropped the belt.

"Holy shit," Phiz's breath came in big gulps. "Holy shit! What a fucking rush!"

He tried to hand the syringe to Waltz, but his hand was shaking and Waltz had to use two hands to make the transfer.

"Fuck man," Phiz stood up and rolled his shirtsleeve back down. "I've shot up a little speed a couple of times but that was like jerkin' off compared to this. Holy shit. It feels like every hair on my head is standing straight up. Is that what it's doing? My hair, I mean? I'd better go check..."

Phiz walked out of the room, patting his head and talking loudly to himself. Jamie picked up the syringe, rinsed it out in the sink, squirted some water through the needle, then separated the needle and the plunger from the barrel and put all three in a pan of boiling water that was on the stove. When he finished, Lefty was already heating up the next hit.

After Lefty had finished and was huffing and puffing, eyes bulging, it was Waltz's turn. Being a completely different body type than Phiz, Waltz's veins were all but invisible. Reluctantly, and at Lyle's insistence, Waltz had to get down on the floor and do half a dozen push-ups. This, coupled with the belt, gave him enough visible vein that he could successfully pull a flag and inject the speed.

McNulty, after two or three tries before he was able to pull a flag, shot up next and then it was Jamie's turn. He had been rotating the syringes and needles in and out of the boiling water, leaving the finished ones to sit on a clean towel to cool. He assembled one of them and, using only his right hand, slid the plunger back and forth to make sure it was working smoothly. It was, and he sat down in front of the spoon.

He'd already decided that his best vein was more on the top of his forearm rather than down in the crook of his elbow. He'd watched the others carefully and was able to hit the vein and inject the drug efficiently and without any coaching from Lyle.

He'd barely pulled the needle out of his arm when his heart lurched into high gear and shot forward so fast he could practically feel scorch marks on the inside of his ribs. The hair on his arms stood up and the gooseflesh spread up his neck and to the top of his head. His breathing deepened and sped up and thoughts began running through his brain at a rate almost too fast to follow.

"Whoa," he finally said, "I see what you guys are talking about. The rush, I mean. Damn."

Jamie stood up from the table. He found he had a strong urge to go find Nancy, tell her all about it, and reassure her that it was okay. The more she'd thought about what the guys were planning, the less she'd liked it. While they were in the kitchen she'd refused to watch, preferring to sit in the living room and worry.

"Hey, Babe," Jamie walked up to her, "The deed is done and everybody is fine. It's a great rush and a really interesting high, you know? It's like all these little thoughts that come along, and you just pick one and suddenly it has, like, weight and meaning and you just have to..."

Nancy looked up over Jamie's shoulder and Jamie could sense someone was standing there wanting to tell them something. Reluctantly he abandoned his monologue and turned to see McNulty.

"Don't mean to butt in. Sorry. But I thought you should know Lyle is in there getting ready to shoot up Mount Everest."

"Jamie," Nancy grabbed his arm, "you've gotta go talk him out of it. You know he has a heart murmur. Please?"

Jamie stood up and hurried into the kitchen.

Probably no big deal. I'll just go in and check and then reassure her that everything's cool.

Lyle was sitting at the table with the bent spoon in front of him. In the bowl of the spoon sat a pile of speed that was easily four or five times bigger than the portions everybody else had mixed. Lyle was using the syringe to draw up water from a glass when Jamie decided to intervene.

"Hey, Lyle. I don't mean to be a downer or anything, but are you sure that shooting that much speed at one time is, you know, safe? You did tell us about this heart thing you had."

"Oh fuck off, Shipman. I've been doing up this shit for a while now. I know what I can take."

"Have you done this much at one go before?"

"Well not yet. But I'm planning on it."

Phiz had been watching and said, "I was at a party not long ago in Denver and some guy there over-amped on speed. Couldn't stand up, he was just sitting in the corner twitching and shaking. When he started puking on himself, some cats decided they better take him to the hospital."

"What happened?" Waltz asked.

"I don't know. Those guys just opened the door of the Emergency Room, pushed him inside, and took off. I heard a rumor later that the kid's parents had committed him to the State Hospital at Fort Dodge."

"Isn't that what happened to Big Dan?" Waltz said.

"Yeah, that's where he ended up," said McNulty. "They gave him electroshock treatments. Lit him up like a lightbulb."

"Okay, okay. Jesus Christ," Lyle said as he picked a dinner knife up off the table and began using it like a spoon to shift some of "Mount Everest" back into the plastic bag, "you fuckers sure know how to bring somebody down."

"I'm glad to see it, man," Jamie said, "Even though you're pretty much of an asshole, we've all gotten used to seeing you around here, you know?"

"Like I said, Shipman," Lyle dribbled water onto the reduced pile of methedrine, "fuck you. And you can tell Nancy to quit worrying too."

After a few hours, the high end of the speed began to wear off. The ideas that came thick and fast didn't seem quite so brilliant as before and the desire to share them with any and everyone had slackened. Since the plastic bag still had plenty in it, everyone-including Jamie-decided to shoot up again. Nancy went into Jamie's room "to rest" and fell fast asleep.

The sun had been up for hours when Jamie squinted down the length of the couch at McNulty, sprawled at the other end. Then he looked around the room at Phiz and Lefty.

"Jesus," Jamie said, "being strung out after dropping acid is bad enough. Now I find out that that's just a stroll down fuckin' Happy Lane. The only good thing is that if you fuckers all feel as bad as you look, then I'm not the only one."

You're not, man, you're not," Lefty smacked his parched lips together, "I feel like shit that's been pressed, folded, and hung up to dry."

McNulty looked around the room and said, "What happened to Lyle and Waltz?"

"They shot up the last of the speed and went out looking to score some pot," said Phiz.

"Yeah, I know. But that was, like, hours ago," McNulty looked at his watch, "or twenty minutes. Fuck."

During the ensuing silence, Jamie made a decision. The decision, simply put, was that he didn't much like speed. Even allowing for the depression he was going through at the time, he just wasn't thrilled with the effects of the drug. He liked LSD because it seemed to decorate the natural world like you'd decorate a Christmas tree-with bright lights and colorful surprises. With speed, you just lit the tree on fire and let yourself be convinced that all that light and heat came from your own intellect.

The weird thing was that the part he liked best was the shooting-up. He liked the whole ritual of it. He liked the bright red flag that let you know you were in the vein, he liked the almost sexual penetration of the needle, and he liked the wild climax of the rush as the drug hit the system.

So I just need to find something that breaks down easily in water, that's fun to shoot, fun to be high on, and that won't leave me feeling low, tired, and worthless like this. That should be easy.

TWENTY

Jamie hammered away at the nail he was driving through the face of one two-by-four and into the end grain of another. Waltz had easily finished driving in the two nails at his end and was holding the board steady while Jamie tapped away. Jamie finally put the nail in flush.

"Okay, Waltz, what the hell am I doing wrong?"

"It's like hitting a baseball. Swing with your body, snap with your wrist. But like my Dad always said, 'don't go apeshit on it'. If you bend the nail it takes twice as long to straighten it back out before you can hit it again."

"I'm jealous, man. All I ever learned from my Dad is how to sit around and gripe about shit,"

They flipped the half-built frame over and aligned the next piece. They were working in the corner of what was to become Charlie and Bill's new Head Shop. Jamie had asked if they could start setting up a workbench and some other things and Charlie was pleased to oblige. Waltz had volunteered to pitch in with tools and whatever knowledge he'd gained from building sheds and fences with his father.

Before long they had the frame set up and had trimmed a bit off one leg to keep it from wobbling. They picked up a large sheet and set it on the frame.

"What is this stuff?" Waltz asked.

"The guy at the lumber yard said it was called 'Particleboard'. It's cheaper than plywood and doesn't have any grain to throw my knife off."

Waltz was getting out smaller nails and the hammer when Jamie said, "Wait a sec. Is there some way we can attach this without big ass nail heads for me to run my tools into?"

"Hmm. Maybe some finishing nails and some kind of punch to drive the heads down into the top. I haven't got any, we'll have to go to the hardware store."

"Good thought," said Jamie. "What about lights? It's kinda dark back in here. And I haven't got the bucks to spring for some fancy-ass light fixture."

"Light bulbs and wire are cheap. You could just hang 'em from the ceiling."

"And maybe I can get some funky old shades from the Starvation Army Thrift Store. Slide me five, dude."

Waltz slid his hand across Jamie's outstretched palm and then they both snapped their fingers and made the clenched-fist power salute.

Jamie opened a door and yelled into a back room, "Waltz and I are going out to get some things. We'll be back in an hour or so. Cool?

"Sure, no problem," came Charlie's muffled voice, "I mean, 'Cool."

They went out through the front door which had been scraped, sanded down, and the window had been covered with a sign that said, "Future Home of the Electric Rainbow Head Shop."

"The place is starting to shape up, you know?" said Jamie, "I was hoping Nancy would come down and check it out, but she says she's busy."

Waltz rolled his eyes. "That sounds familiar."

"What are you saying? That she'd... nah. If something weren't cool she'd tell me."

Waltz just ducked his head, held his palms up, and walked to the car.

It took a few more days before Jamie could get Nancy to come down to the building and look at their shop space. He showed her the new work table with the funky lights overhead, the desk with the lockable drawer he'd also found at the thrift store, and how the display cabinet Charlie had offered them would also serve to keep the customers out of the work-space. She did not seem excited by any of it.

"And from this post Waltz said he'd help me brace up a horizontal board, kind of like a hangman's gibbet, where we could suspend our sign," Jamie explained with exaggerated arm movements. No reaction, no smile.

"And the sign would read, 'Nancy's Leather Shop' and under that in small letters, 'with possibly a little help from Jamie.' What do you think?"

"Whatever you want," she said in a wan voice.

"Okay," Jamie said as he hitched himself up to sit on the table, "to be honest I was expecting just a little more excitement. Are you getting cold feet or something?"

"I... I don't know. It suddenly seems like such a lot to take on. You know, like drop out of school and everything. It's just such a lot..."

"Are you having some kind of trouble? Something I can help you with?"

"No. It's nothing, really," she said with a sniff, "I can take care of it. Can we go back now?"

The next day, as Waltz was helping Jamie cut out the plywood for the sign, Jamie said, "Tell me something, Waltz. Have you seen Nancy goin' around with some other guy?"

"Why do you ask?"

"Well, remember how she was with you a few weeks ago, all distant and uncommunicative and 'I don't know" and 'nothing's wrong?' I think she's laying the same trip on me, man. Makin' me nuts."

Waltz stopped working and lit a cigarette.

He blew out a cloud of smoke and said, "You didn't hear anything from me, okay? But if I were you, I'd talk to Lyle."

"Lyle? You're kidding, right? Lyle Kirk?"

"How many other Lyles do you know?"

"Well, son-of-a-bitch," Jamie said.

* * *

The following evening Lyle's car came slowly down the alley behind the Fifth Street House. A chain hitched under the back bumper was attached to a beat up Pontiac Station Wagon. The little procession stopped behind the house and Lyle and Phiz got out to undo the chain. A hippie couple got out of the station wagon and undid their end of the chain. Then all four pushed the Pontiac into the weedy parking place behind the house.

Lyle and Phiz brought the strangers in.

"We were out on the highway and saw these folks broken down by the side of the road," Phiz said. "Jeff here thinks it's the generator."

Jamie, Waltz, and Shoes stood up and the introductions began. Jeff was tall and thin, clean shaven, and kept his blonde hair in a long ponytail. The woman who seemed to be permanently tucked under his armpit, Suzie, had curly platinum blonde hair that hadn't seen a brush since the Johnson Administration.

Shoes, wondering how he was going to study for Summer Finals, reluctantly agreed to let the two crash. Periodically during the summer, various traveling hippies had stayed in the house for a day or two. There had never been any trouble and usually the visitors provided a good reason to organize a party.

Lyle was helping the new folks bring in stuff from the wagon. Jamie took a deep breath and went out into the yard.

"Hey Lyle," he said as his friend came toward him with a rolled-up sleeping bag over his shoulder, "got time to talk?"

"Sure, man, what's up?"

"Well, I'm not pissed off or anything, just curious. Do you and Nancy have a thing going on?"

Lyle put the sleeping bag down. "Did she say something to you about it?"

"No, not a word other than 'I'm fine, it's nothing.' But let me guess, you offered to talk to me and she said, 'no, the fair thing is for me to tell him. I got into this; it's up to me to get myself out.' Is that about it?"

Lyle rubbed the back of his neck, "How did you know?"

"Dude, she laid the same trip on Waltz and me a few weeks ago. She's a good woman, man, she just needs to come up with a better way to handle her rejects."

"I'm sorry, Jamie. But I like her. I like her a lot."

"I'm cool with it," Jamie picked up the sleeping bag and handed it to Lyle, "and you can tell me about it tonight. Waltz and I started a tradition, you see. It's your job now to get me drunk or stoned-preferably both."

Lyle laughed and put a hand on Jamie's shoulder as they walked to the house, "I'll do my best, man, I'll do my best."

* * *

An hour later, after Shoes had split the five remaining beers in the refrigerator up among seven mugs and glasses and handed them out, everyone was sitting around the living room nursing their drinks.

"The hassle is this," Jeff said, "we bought a rebuilt generator from a guy in Omaha and he gave me a 90-day warranty. We haven't got the bread to buy another one here to get us down to New Mexico. If I could find someone to charge up the battery in the Pontiac-"

"We call it 'Ponty!'" Suzy earned herself a few puzzled looks.

"-I could drive it on the battery to somewhere in Nebraska like North Platte, After a night on a battery charger the car could get me to Omaha. Then I just get my guy there to put in a new generator and I could be back here in three or maybe four days."

"Seems like it could work," Phiz said.

"Would you guys be bummed if Suzie stayed here while I'm gone?" Jeff asked, "she tends to get carsick.'

"Jeffy just hates it when he has to stop and let me throw up," Suzie said, almost proudly.

"Sure, I think we can make room," Jamie said, glancing at Shoes and Waltz for confirmation.

"Let me drive around and we'll pull your battery and take it down to the Conoco station," Waltz said. "I've got a friend who works there who'll put on a charger for you overnight."

A few minutes later Waltz had loosened the clamps on Jeff's battery and was gently prying the cables off the terminals. Jeff was inside the car and Waltz heard some odd scraping and popping noises. Just as Waltz lifted the battery out onto the fender Jeff sidled up and slipped him a lid of marijuana.

"Share this out among your friends, okay? You guys have been great and I just wanted to show some thanks. But don't tell Suzie where you got it, okay? She doesn't know I'm holding more than a few J's. She tends to get kinda freaky."

* * *

It had taken Jamie all the next day to recover from what he called "The Great Nancy Transference". When Lyle picked him up he'd brought along not only a pipe and a nickel bag of weed, but also a little bag of lime wedges, a salt shaker, and a pint of Tequila.

Before they went into Ziggy's Saloon, they each knocked back a Tequila shooter, then shared a bowl. Then they went inside to bullshit, listen to the band, and drink beer for an hour. Then they slipped back out to the car for another round of shooters and pot.

On the third trip coming back from the car, Jamie had had to hang onto a parking meter while he emptied his stomach into the gutter.

Back in Ziggy's, Jamie was only a few swallows into his beer when he turned and announced to Lyle that he was going to bail on him.

"You need a ride?"

"No. I think I'd rather walk. It's only a few blocks. In fact, I'd advise you to do the same."

"I'll think about it," Lyle said as he put out his hand and Jamie shook it. "No hard feelings?"

"Feelings? What the fuck are feelings?" Jamie laughed, "Sometimes I wonder if I've got any."

Jamie put up two fingers and shouted to the noisy room in general, "Peace, you assholes!" and ambled out the door.

TWENTY ONE

It was a busy afternoon when Angela walked in the door. Jamie had a large piece of Masonite on the kitchen table and, armed with a yardstick, a compass, a book of Fonts from the library, and a sharp pencil, he was laying out a "Jamie's Leatherworks" sign. Krenovich, and Suzie, now known as "Suzie Weird Chick", were kibitzing. McNulty was rooting in the refrigerator for something to eat.

Out in the living room, Lyle and Nancy were helping Shoes move out while Waltz was helping Phiz move in. Shoes had decided to find a place to live that was a little quieter and study-friendly just about the same time that Phiz developed a desire to live somewhere that was crazier and, as he put it, more "creative."

Lyle and Shoes had just carried a beat-up chest of drawers out the door and Waltz and Phiz were maneuvering a mattress in over the threshold. Just behind them, Angela came through the blocked-open door, took three steps into the room, and stopped. Her face seemed to crumple in on itself and tears rolled down her cheeks.

Nancy put down the cardboard box she was carrying and gathered Angela into a big bear hug. Angela hung on and began to sob.

Within a few minutes, everyone had gathered in the living room. Nancy had settled Angela into a chair, dispatched Jamie to the kitchen to boil water for tea, and sent Shoes to find a box of Kleenex. It took Angela a little while to calm down enough to tell her story.

"My mother lives in Denver," Angela said in a still-shaky voice, "she's always had this weird idea of who she thought I should be instead of seeing and loving who I really am. We fought a lot. That's why I moved up here to live with the Bermans."

Jamie came in with the cup of tea, put it on the side table next to Angela, then leaned against the wall to listen.

"Mom has a friend here in Colton-they went to school together," Angela said, "and this... woman-Martha somebody-is a dried up old gossip and passes along lurid stories of my behavior to my Mom. Anyway, a couple of days ago Krenovich was walking down the other side of the street, shouted, pulled down his pants, and flashed me a moon shot. Naturally, I pulled up my shirt and shook my titties at him. An asteroid, you know?"

"Made me laugh my ass off," Krenovich said.

"Nasty old Martha was in her car, saw the whole thing, and couldn't wait to get home and call my mother to tell her what a slut I was. Totally wigged out, my mother drove up here today while I was at work, broke into my apartment, and ransacked the place. I came home from work and there she was, sitting in a chair in the middle of the room, holding my journal in her lap."

"What kind of a journal?" Waltz asked.

"You know, like a diary. Where I write down all the stuff that happens to me and what I think about it. If I'd known she was going to break in and read it, I'd have hidden it better."

Knowing Angela, I'll bet she didn't spare any details. Mrs. Tucker probably had to put on oven mitts to read it.

"After she shouted at me for a while, she calmed down enough to lay the Big Ultimatum on me. She said I was to stop seeing or talking to all of my friends, quit my job, move into Martha's house, and agree not to go anywhere unless Martha went with me. In other words, volunteer to be imprisoned by horrible old Martha."

"And if you tell her to stuff it?" Nancy said.

"Then she'll have me committed to Fort Dodge."

"The loonie bin?" said Waltz, "can she do that?"

"I don't know. She said that until I'm twenty-one she's my legal guardian and she can do whatever she thinks is best. What am I gonna do?"

She began to cry again as people tried to comfort her and make suggestions. Chief among these was that she quickly pack up and run away.

"But I don't have any money, I don't know anybody who'd take me in, and I want to stay here in Colton. I like it here. I like my life. I don't want to give it up just because my mother has flipped out and decided to fuck things up."

"There is a way," Jamie said loudly over the ensuing clamor.

Angela turned her tear-stained face to him and everyone quieted down.

"You're eighteen aren't you?"

Angela nodded.

"In Colorado, I'm pretty sure that if the woman is at least eighteen and the man is at least twenty-one, they can get married without parental consent. If you did that, then your husband would be your legal guardian, not your mother. There's nothing she could do."

Angela had stopped crying and looked thoughtful.

"That might work," she said, "but then I'd have to deal with a stupid husband who'd want to order me around. I'd still be fucked."

"Not necessarily," said Jamie, "you'd just have to marry someone who didn't want to get married either. Someone to whom a marriage certificate would be just a piece of paper to keep your mother off your back and nothing more."

"But who's over twenty-one who'd do that?"

"Me."

There was a pause while everybody there mentally chewed this over. Suzie broke the silence. "Cool!" she shouted, "can I be a bridesmaid?"

"That's very sweet of you, Jamie..." Angela started.

"But I'm not exactly husband material?" Jamie laughed. "The point is Marriage is just a phony institution being pushed on us by the churches and the uptight middle class. What better way to throw it back in their teeth than to do it and then totally ignore it? You continue to be Angela and do your thing, and I'll be Jamie over on the other side of town doing my thing. Make sense?"

Angela laughed, had to stop to blow her nose, and then said, "No, it doesn't make any sense at all. I guess that's why I like it. Thank you, Jamie."

Now that some kind of an Emergency Exit had been found, Angela was back to being Angela and everyone relaxed. Waltz rolled a couple of numbers and as they worked their way around the room, ideas were discussed and several things were decided.

Since Angela was afraid to sleep in her apartment, she would temporarily move in with Jamie. Phiz would call his mother in Montrose. She was a family lawyer and he could ask her not only about the commitment thing but the marriage thing as well. A friend of McNulty's from High School did janitorial work at the Courthouse and McNulty would ask him to keep an eye out for any large Italian women looking for legal help.

Suzie Weird Chick quietly asked if she could move her mattress into Jamie and Angela's room. She thought she'd seen Waltz giving her "funny looks" and didn't want to sleep by herself in the living room. Although he knew it was ridiculous, Jamie said okay.

If, as Angela thought, it was all a bluff on her mother's part, then nothing would come of it and it would all blow over.

Two days later, Jamie was inside the Electric Rainbow hanging up his new sign when Waltz knocked on the door.

"We just got a call from McNulty," Waltz said, "and his friend told him that a big woman with black hair and a loud voice came into the Sheriff's Department. He overheard her asking to talk to someone who could give her advice about her daughter."

"Holy shit. It's going down. Does Angela know?"

"McNulty was going to call her at the radio station as soon as he hung up with me. Did you walk down here?"

"Yeah. Just give me a minute to lock up and you can give me a ride back to Fifth Street."

When Jamie walked into the house, Angela was already there looking pale and nervous. Suzie sat on the couch next to her and held her hand.

"You ready to take a drive to Fort Collins and get hitched?" Jamie said.

"I called Mom's house in Denver. There was no answer. Do we need a witness?"

"I'm not sure. Phiz said his mother the lawyer agreed that we were right about the age thing, also about the whole guardian trip, she even said that we could do the license and the ceremony on the same day, but he didn't think to ask her about witnesses."

"What about taking Rachel?" Waltz asked, "If she's your best friend, wouldn't you want her there?"

"I haven't seen Rachel for several weeks now. I wouldn't even know where to look for her," Angela said then turned to Suzie, "Well honey, you said you wanted to be the bridesmaid, are you still into that?"

"Wow. How cool is that?' Suzie said, "What are we waiting for?"

She jumped up and ran to the door, then looked back expectantly, "Well?"

Jamie and Angela shrugged their shoulders and got up to leave. Waltz and McNulty shook Jamie's hand and hugged Angela on their way out the door.

* * *

When he looked back on it, it always surprised Jamie how little he remembered of that trip to Fort Collins to get married. Perhaps because in the back row of his personal Parliament there was a Jamie who was dancing on the seat of his chair and singing, "I'm gonna be hers and she's gonna be mine! The girl we never thought we'd ever have. Forever and ever!" All the while the other Jamies who had made the vow to ignore the vows were trying to tie him to his chair and gag him.

Among the few details Jamie did remember was being relieved at the Clerk's window that he hadn't spent the $20 he'd saved for the license, that the man performing the ceremony was Judge Smoke, that no one seemed concerned when they said they wanted to get married without rings, and finally, he remembered the words themselves. The gravity of those words was such that neither he nor Angela goofed on the sentiments or answered disrespectfully. Even Suzie Weird Chick kept herself mute.

The mood inside the little VW as it chugged back to Colton was somber. Conversations got started then quickly collapsed. Jokes fell flat.

They were barely two blocks into town when a car at a cross street started honking its horn and flashing its lights. It pulled in close behind them.

Angela turned around and said, "It's my Mom."

"What do you want me to do? Should I ignore her?"

"No. Better pull over."

Jamie parked the car next to the curb and a Buick pulled up next to them.

The woman driving the Buick had dark hair pulled back in a bun and several chins that quivered as she yelled through the open passenger window, "Well I hope you're proud of yourselves!"

"Mom, I..."

"I'm not going to discuss this here in the street. I'll be waiting in your apartment."

The electric window hummed back up as the Buick took off toward town.

"I guess we'd better go talk to her," Angela said.

"Yeah, I guess so. What can she do? Sticks and stones and all that... she doesn't throw things does she?"

"Can I come?" Suzie said, "If she tries anything I'll kick her ass!"

Having their honor defended by Suzie Weird Chick was an interesting thought, but Jamie said, "No. I think I'd better drop you off at Fifth Street. And you know, Jeff might have called while we were gone."

"Oh man, that's true. Yeah, Fifth Street will be cool."

* * *

The apartment was a one-bedroom with another bed in the living room that doubled as a couch. Mrs. Tucker was seated on the bed and the two kitchen chairs had been pulled out from the table and were facing her.

Jamie walked up to her and said, "Mrs. Tucker, I'm Jamie Shipman"

She looked at his proffered hand as if Jamie were holding out a dead carp, then looked at Angela who, refusing the chair, leaned against the kitchen sink and folded her arms.

"What have you got to say for yourself?" said Mrs. Tucker.

"What do you expect me to say to someone who broke into my apartment, went through my things, stole my journal, my diaphragm, and God knows what else!"

"I'm a mother who found out her only daughter is hanging around with immoral hippies, taking drugs, and acting like a cheap trollop!"

"Now wait a minute," Jamie said, "that's my wife you're talking to. Let's keep it civil."

"So you did it." Mrs. Tucker looked stricken. "Oh my God, my God! What have you done? I heard you were going to get married and I got down on my knees and begged, begged God to stop you."

"Was that," Jamie said, "before or after you were in the Sheriff's office trying to get her committed?"

"You stay out of this," Mrs. Tucker shook a finger at Jamie, "I'm talking to my daughter!"

Jamie started to form a snappy reply but Angela put out a hand and Jamie kept quiet.

For the next half hour, or so it seemed to Jamie, Mrs. Tucker trotted out every emotional appeal she could think of, starting with swearing on Angela's dead father's grave that she would never actually commit her only beloved daughter to a horrible place like that, that it was all a bluff to save Angela from throwing her life away. Then Guilt became the main theme as she reminded Angela how much her suffering mother had sacrificed to give her daughter the best life she could.

In true Italian diva fashion, Mrs. Tucker stalked up and down the little room, beating her breast, calling on God and the Saints with grand gestures, and turning her tears on and off seemingly at will.

"But it's not too late," Mrs. Tucker said to Angela, "You can go to the judge, tell him you made a mistake, and ask for an annulment. If you do that and agree to stay with Martha for a few months, I will pay for you to go to any college or professional school in the country that will accept you."

"And as for you Mr. Shipman, if you agree to get an annulment I will write you out a check for $500 on the spot. But if you don't agree then I will go to the Colton Police and tell them you are a drug pusher. They will find out where you live, they will surround the place, and they will arrest anyone who comes in or out. You wouldn't like that very much, would you?"

Angela straightened up and said, "Are you finished now? If so, Jamie and I are going home."

Angela started for the door and Jamie jumped up to follow.

Mrs. Tucker shouted at their retreating backs, "I'll give you 48 hours. If I haven't heard from you by then, I'm going to the Police."

Angela ignored her mother and walked out of the apartment. Jamie stopped on the threshold and gave the older woman a saucy wave.

"See ya," he said, "but I wouldn't wanna be ya," and he shut the door behind him.

Twenty Two

The telephone rang in the Colton Police Group Office.

"Colton Police," Larry Sherman said, "Sherman speaking. How may I help you?"

"Hello, Officer Sherman," said the voice on the other end of the line, "This is Jamie Shipman. You may not remember me. A few months ago you wrote me a ticket for driving with expired plates. A red VW?"

"I think I remember... yes?"

As he spoke Sherman scrawled "Jamie Shipperman(?)" on a scrap of paper.

"Anyway, at the time you gave me your card and asked me to call you if I wanted to talk about illegal drugs and stuff."

"Okay. I'm glad you called. What's on your mind, Jamie?"

Well, I haven't seen any illegal activity-I'm a student at the college and they keep me pretty busy studying and all, but I have a question that's kind of related."

"I see. What's your question?" Sherman wrote "student at college" and "drugs?"

"A friend of mine has been having some trouble with his girlfriend's mother. She wants to break up their relationship and has threatened to go to the Police and swear he's some kind of a big-time drug dealer. She says she can get him arrested."

"And is he a big-time drug dealer?" Sherman asked.

"No, sir. Nothing like it."

"Well," Sherman checked his notes for a name, "... Jamie, I'd tell him not to worry. Cops can pretty much tell the difference between a mother with a grudge and someone with genuine information. As long as he stays well within the law he has nothing to worry about."

"Thanks. I kinda thought that was the deal, but I told him I'd check."

"No problem. And keep your eyes peeled. If you see something you know how to find me, right?"

"Yes, sir. I do. And thanks again."

Sherman shook his head and smiled as he hung up the phone and then dropped the scrap of paper into the wastebasket.

"Hey, Sherman," Captain Gaskin said from the doorway into the office, "got a moment?" Without waiting for a reply, Gaskin came into the room and sat on a corner of Sherman's desk.

"Anything new from that kid we turned a couple of months ago?"

"No, sir, I checked in with him last week and he maintains he's keeping his nose clean and that one time is the only time he's gotten involved in the drug scene."

"Do you believe him?"

"I don't know, sir. He's still got all that hair and everything. My gut tells me he's still up to his chin in it, but there's no way to tell, really."

"No, there's not. If we could arrest somebody based on how they looked, we'd be trying to book half the College. Anyway, I'm thinking there's a way we could use him again."

"Well, the information we got the last time was gold, sir, especially for the Denver PD. They not only nailed a really heavy hitter but parlayed that bust into several more-including one as far away as Phoenix. What we're holding over the kid may be getting a little stale, though. And if he doesn't have any other leads..."

"I've got a whole different tack in mind," Gaskin said, "a young couple came into my office a couple of days ago and told me they wanted to help us 'nail the drug dealers.' Probably watching too many movies, but they volunteered to go 'undercover' to catch the bad guys. I thanked them and told them I'd be in touch. But then last night it occurred to me that if we hooked them up with our young friend, he might be able to give them enough credibility that they could make a buy or two."

"Hmm... it might just work, sir. Do you have something in mind we can offer to get him to sign on?"

"Tell him that as soon as we make an arrest, all pending charges will be immediately dropped. I'm dumping this whole project in your lap, okay?"

"Yes, sir. I'll get right on it."

TWENTY THREE

Jamie used a fork to flip over the odd-looking chunks of bacon he was frying, opened the oven to turn two pieces of bread over, and then slid them back under the broiler. A few minutes later he was eating a fresh-ly-made bacon ends-and-pieces sandwich when the phone rang.

"Hi Jamie, it's Angela."

"Hey, Sweet Tart, what's going down?"

"I just got off the phone with my Mother."

Jamie put the sandwich down and gave the phone his full attention. Mrs. Tucker's deadline had passed the night before unacknowledged, and when Angela had left for work that morning, both she and Jamie were waiting for the other shoe to drop.

"What did she say?"

"She leaned on the guilt for a bit, then said that she was giving up the fight, that she was going back to Denver, and that she wished us all the best."

'So everything is cool, then? Our crazy-ass plan worked!"

"Yeah, I guess so."

"You're not sounding too happy about it."

"Well, it sorta made me sad for her. When she was pissed off and ranting and raving it was easy to stand up to her. But today she just seemed smaller, you know? Like, defeated. And when she wished us 'all the best and every happiness' it kinda broke my heart."

"She's still manipulating you, Babe. You gotta stand strong."

"Yeah, you're probably right. Oops, Aaron's giving me the heads-up. The Boss must be coming in. Gotta go. I'll see you tonight."

Jamie heard a click and then the dial tone. He hung the receiver back up on the wall and took another bite of sandwich.

* * *

As Jamie parked the VW in front of the Fifth Street House and shut off the engine, Angela said, "I still don't feel much like going to this party tonight."

"To be honest, I don't either," Jamie said. "Maybe we're just feeling a letdown after all this drama. But McNulty looked so bummed when I told him we were thinking of staying home that I said we'd come."

"I suppose you're right," Angela opened the door. "And thanks for standing guard while I showered and changed. I had a feeling Leona was going to come storming up my stairs after I got home from work."

"Sometimes not having a premonition work out can be a good thing."

"You can say that again."

"Sometimes not hav-"

Angela shut him up with a dangerous warning finger. Then they both laughed and walked up to the house. The first thing they saw when they walked in was Suzy Weird Chick sitting on the couch weeping.

Angela immediately sat down beside her, took her hands, and asked what the matter was. Jamie just stood there shifting his weight from foot to foot. Crying women made him uncomfortable.

"He's not coming back, that lying bastard."

Angela produced a Kleenex from somewhere. "You mean Jeff?"

"He just called. From a truck stop in O-fucking-hio. He's on his way to some big deal rock festival in New York!"

Between stops for sniffing, hiccupping, and blowing her nose, Suzy managed to get the story out. It seemed that while he was in Omaha waiting for his generator to be fixed, Jeff had gotten friendly with the cashier at the garage. So friendly that he'd spent the time getting high and balling the girl. They'd heard about this giant three-day rock festival somewhere North of New York City and as soon as the car was ready they took off together heading East.

"He had the balls to tell me I should go ahead and hitchhike down to the commune in New Mexico and he'd meet me there in a few weeks. Whether he was going to bring Grease-Monkey Girl with him he didn't say."

"What an asshole," Angela said as she hugged Susie.

"Can I get you anything?" Jamie offered, "a glass of water or something?"

"I'd prefer a pint of cheap whiskey, but I guess water will have to do."

By the time Jamie got back with the water, Angela and Suzy had decided that they'd go to the party tonight, that Jamie would buy a small bottle of booze so Suzy could get herself righteously bombed, and that in the morning Suzy would move into Angela's apartment with her until she could figure out what to do.

* * *

Jamie parked the car in front of a split-level home in one of Colton's nicer neighborhoods. Suzy, clutching a paper bag-wrapped pint of Old Crow, looked up at the house in disbelief.

"This is McNulty's house? What is he, some kind of secret rich guy who hangs out with a bunch of poor hippos 'cause he thinks we're trippy?"

"No, this is his parents' house," said Jamie. "They went out of town for the weekend and left him in charge."

"Cool," Suzy observed as she headed for the front door. "I hope they have one of those front-load dryers. I like to watch the clothes go around."

* * *

It turned out to be a strange evening for both Jamie and Angela. Although they had tried to make it clear to their friends that they were not really a couple, that they were still just two members of this big family and no more than that, people were treating them not as Jamie and Angela, but more as "Jamie'n'Angela"-a single entity. It probably didn't help that Jamie, knowing that Angela was feeling out of sorts, stayed next to her most of the evening. And Angela, when she wanted to go talk to somebody, would tell Jamie first.

Once the party was well under way, Shoes came into the room, called for quiet and produced a box with a ribbon on it. He said that everybody had chipped in. Wondering if it was another pie, Jamie watched carefully as Angela opened it. He was relieved to see it was a nice little blue tea kettle with flowers painted on it.

Jamie took the kettle from Angela and held it up.

"Thanks a lot, guys," he said, "Now we have joint property. When we get divorced we'll have to hire lawyers to fight over our tea kettle."

The general laughter was interrupted when Waltz stuck his head in the room and said, "Hey, you guys should come and see this."

Everybody went into the family room where Waltz, in true Waltz form, was watching television.

"It's on the Ten O'clock News," Waltz said. "Check it out."

On the screen was a long shot, obviously taken from a helicopter, of a huge crowd out in the countryside. On one edge of the crowd was a large platform stage surrounded by towers of speakers.

An announcer was saying, "...The Music and Art Fair near Woodstock, New York. There are three or four hundred thousand young people here and thousands more are on their way. All roads and highways in the area are closed because so many people who were stuck in traffic decided to abandon their cars and walk the rest of the way."

Everyone in the room was saying, "Far out! How cool is that? Wow. What a trip it would be to be there," except for Suzie Weird Chick who shouted at the screen, "If you see that asshole Jeff, tell him to go fuck himself!" Jamie could see that she considered throwing her nearly empty bottle of Old Crow at the television, but then she stamped out of the room.

* * *

"Jamie, I think we made a mistake."

Jamie looked at Angela over a nearly-empty plate of spaghetti. He chewed quickly, swallowed, and then wiped the sauce from around his mouth with a paper napkin.

"Things have gotten a little crazy, haven't they?" he said.

She poked at the food on her plate for a few moments then said, "Someday I want to get married for real, you know. I want to be all magic in love and stand up there with a guy who is as crazy about me as I am crazy about him. And say 'forever' and really mean it. I'm really, really fond of you Jamie..."

"But not magic in love," he said.

"No," she said, looking at her plate.

Then she looked up at him and said, "Please don't be angry at me."

"Not even close to it. I've been hearing that clank of chains in the distance myself and it's been scaring the shit out of me too. But what can we do about it?"

"If it's okay with you, I can call Leona and tell her we want to get an annulment. She'll know what we have to do."

"Okay, but on one condition. I want to be sure she won't try to throw you in the nut house again."

"I don't think she will," Angela said, "but I'll make her say it out loud. Do you want some more spaghetti? There's plenty left in the pot."

"Well, as long I can have a little bread and butter to mop up the sauce, I could probably force some down."

Angela grinned and took his plate to the stove. A slight groan came from the other room, followed by a thump and then some sharp swearing.

"Sounds like Suzie is finally rolling out," Jamie observed.

"With a hell of a hangover, I'll bet," she said as she put his overloaded plate down in front of him.

"Thanks, lady."

"No," she said, "Thank you. I mean it. For everything."

Jamie smiled and shrugged as he picked up his fork.

* * *

Six days later, Jamie was sitting in the living room of the Fifth Street House and telling his friends the story of his Day in Court.

"There was a judge, of course, and a lawyer which Mrs. Tucker had been happy to pay for, me on one side and Angela on the other. And Suzy Weird Chick was sitting in the audience."

"So what happened, man?" Lefty said.

"Now this is just the oddest shit," Jamie said, "but the way the Law looks at it, marriage is a kind of contract. The woman promises to cook and clean and keep house, and in return, the man promises to do his best to get her pregnant as quickly and as often as possible. Since I didn't try to 'consummate the marriage,' the judge found me 'In Breach of Promise,' and granted the annulment."

"But dude," Phiz said, "you slept with her every night for four nights. And you didn't dip the wick even once?"

"Nope. See, I don't know how many guys she might have been balling before we went to Fort Collins, I only know I wasn't one of them. So if we weren't balling before we got married, and we didn't get married to be married, why would I try to jump on her after?"

Nancy looked confused and asked, "But how would the judge know whether or not you two were getting it on?"

"Well just look at him," Lyle pointed at Jamie. "Doesn't he look like the guy with the worst case of blue balls in history?"

Jamie laughed along with everybody else, then said, "Don't forget Suzie Weird Chick was sleeping on a mattress on the floor next to us every night we were in bed. The lawyer said she would be willing to testify that Tab A never went into Slot B."

Waltz blew out the cloud of smoke he'd been holding in, passed a smoldering pipe to McNulty, and said, "What I want to know is who gets the fucking tea kettle?"

TWENTY FOUR

Jamie had to admit it. He was feeling pretty damned good. It was a sunny day, the water in the quarry was clean and cool, most of the people he'd come to call his "Family" were here enjoying the party, he was tripping along on some very mellow mescaline, and his friend Mike was sitting on the next rock.

Mike had taken off his shirt and was squinting into the sun.

"Man, I got to get some color back," Mike said. "Six weeks in the Maricopa County Jail with no sunshine and I look like a freakin' albino."

"Just learn some Johnny Winter songs and you'll be fine."

"Wouldn't that be a trip?" Mike laughed. "I go to Malcolm Tingley and say, 'hey man, thanks for putting me in your band. Now let's toss out this Country shit and play some down-home Southern Blues. Would that be cool? Why? Because I look like Casper the Friendly Fuckin' Ghost."

It wasn't a funny line, but Mike delivered it with just enough self-deprecating bitterness that it made Jamie laugh.

There was a long moment of quiet broken only by the buzz of an insect hoping for sex. Then Jamie said, "Remember last Spring when I said you could have your old room back when you wanted it?"

"Yeah. You offering?"

"If you want it. But I'm thinking there's something that may be better suited to your needs. You interested?"

"No, I'm stone bored. I can barely keep my eyes open. Kidding, man. Lay it on me."

"So these two guys, Charlie and Bill are going to open this head shop downtown..."

Mike rolled his eyes. "Yeah, the Electric Rainbow. I heard"

"They own the whole building. It's got some little rooms upstairs that they're eventually going to rent out, but the plumbing's shot and needs a lot of work, so that'll take a while. But it's got..." Jamie paused for dramatic effect, "a full basement."

"And..." Mike prompted.

"And having my little leather shop already ready for Opening, and knowing you were gonna show up, I put some time in and cleaned the place out. Even built a platform for a bed down there. Just so if you wanted your room back, I'd have a place to move into."

"Where would you pee?"

"Charlie said I could use the head shop's bathroom. But when I was rapping with him about it, I flashed on something and asked him how he'd feel about a band using the space down there to practice."

Mike sat up and began to pay close attention.

"What did he say?"

"He was cool with it as long as the band didn't practice during business hours. In fact, he said that since the neighborhood is practically deserted at night, the noise would be no problem. And dig this. The basement has its own outside entrance."

"How much is the rent?"

"Thirty bucks a month. But if the band agrees to play a little concert upstairs in the Head Shop every couple of months-no charge."

"Holy shit man," Mike jumped up, "I gotta go talk to McNulty."

He scrambled down to the next rock, and then scrambled back up again.

"McNulty and I are putting a band together, he's got a line on a drummer-a new kid in town-we really need a place to practice."

"I thought you and McNulty were going to play with Tingley?"

"Oh definitely. Malcolm and the Prairie Rangers. For a while anyway 'cause I need the bread. McNulty and I will have to work around that. When can I see it?"

"Tomorrow okay?"

"Tomorrow?"

"Well we're not goin' over there today, my freaky friend," Jamie laughed. "In case you forgot, we're both pretty well loaded. And we've got a thing goin' down here right now and a Cinnamon Roll Party over at the Perkins Street House tonight."

"You're right, man. I was just trippin'. Tomorrow will be cool. And anyway, I've got to get a couple of lids to a couple of people."

"Wait a sec, man," Jamie said as he leaned back against a rock and gave Mike the Eye. "You're dealing again?"

"Don't worry, it's cool," Mike said, "I stopped in Boulder on my way up here to see an old friend and he fronted me a kilo. I'm only going to sell it to people I know, okay? And no more hollowed-out books in the mail."

Mike was back to his old swaggering self as he leaned against a rock next to Jamie and pulled a rolled joint out of his breast pocket.

"This is some pretty good shit here. Jungle weed. South American. Care for a toke?"

Jamie pulled out a butane lighter and handed it up to Mike. In a short time, Jamie was drawing in a deep lungful of the earthy-smelling smoke and within moments those warm and fuzzy clouds were rolling up in his head.

Jamie giggled a little and said, "Good shit indeed, my friend. As long as you're going to risk your dumb ass selling it, put me down for a lid, okay?"

* * *

Jamie saw Angela sitting near a little campfire. Rachel and Scott, Lefty's roommate, sat on either side. They were fiddling with some long willow sticks and a bag of marshmallows.

"Oh no," Jamie called to Scott as he approached, "you've got to hide me! It's my ex-wife and she's trying to hit me up for more alimony."

Scott looked confused until Angela replied, "It's not about the money, you idiot. It's about the kids. You have to take the little bastards, they're driving me nuts!"

Jamie and Angela laughed, while Scott just shook his head. Rachel managed a smile and a chuckle but Jamie could see the pain underneath.

"So, Rachel," Jamie said, "you want to take a walk while these two Master Chefs work their magic?"

Rachel got up and together they started away. Jamie turned to yell back at Angela and Scott, "About the time you get your mushmellow technique down pat, we'll be back to help you eat them."

"How are you doing Rachel?" Jamie and she stood on a rock pitching pebbles into the water. "Are you okay?"

"Not too good, but better than I was a few days ago. Definitely getting better."

Jamie looked at his friend closely. Her hair was lank and needed washing, her face looked pale and drawn, and there were pimples on her forehead and cheeks.

"I haven't seen you for a few weeks," Jamie said, "what happened to you?"

"There's a guy named Walter but everybody calls him 'Motion', you know him?"

"Biker dude, right? Sawed-off jean jacket, fu-manchu mustache."

"Yeah, that's him," Rachel said, "Tries to come off like the coolest of the cool, but he's controlling and mean. He never hit me, but he... well, what's done is done. He sells smack and a week and a half ago he threw me out. He said I was snorting up all of the profits."

"Shit. That's harsh. Did you pick up a habit?"

"A small one, yeah. It was just as well he threw me out, my parents are coming back this week and I had to kick before they got here. Angela and that slightly-strange girl Suzie have been holding my hand."

"Achin' and shakin'?"

"Something like that. But I'm, like I said, definitely getting better."

"Good to hear. If you need anything, call me, okay?"

"Okay. I'm ready for a marshmallow I think."

"Me too," Jamie pitched his last pebble into the water. "Let's hope they haven't burnt the snot out of 'em."

Jamie leaned against his car, smoking a number, and enjoying the sunset. The lowering sun was lighting the big, puffy clouds over the mountains a burnished gold at the tops and pink in the middle while lending a dark purple shade to the bottoms. Someone slid up next to him and a feminine hand took the joint away. He finally tore himself away from the light show to look over at the girl as she took a deep drag on the joint.

"Hello, Patty," he smiled. "Nice sunset, huh?"

"Yeah," she blew out a cloud of smoke. "It's breath-taking."

They just stood there together for the next few minutes as the golds turned to pink, and the purples moved up the clouds. Another minute and the clouds went dark.

"I'm gonna need a ride back into town," Patty said. "Are you cool with that?"

"Absolutely. The old VW would be honored. Did someone ditch you or something?"

"Mostly something," Patty said then turned and pointed to an old pickup that carried a homemade wooden camper. The whole rig was gently rocking back and forth, its rusty springs squeaking in rhythm.

"That's Wisconsin Juan's rig isn't it," Jamie asked, "the photographer?"

"You met him?"

"Only briefly when he hit town a couple of days ago. He said he was taking pictures of 'the counterculture.' He seemed like a decent dude in a geeky kinda way."

"He drove Suzie and me out here today, said he wanted to get pictures of both of us. He thought the quarry would make for some far-out shit."

They walked around the car and he opened the door for her.

"I take it neither one of them ever got out of the truck," Jamie observed.

Patty laughed and shook her head. Jamie climbed in the driver's door, got the car started, and soon they were out on the road headed back to Colton.

"Well good for them," Jamie said. "But I'm thinkin' he chose the wrong chick. If I was him, it would be you and me back there makin' that camper rock."

"Oh," she said, "that's so sweet."

She leaned over, put her face in front of his, and kissed him on the mouth. Fortunately for them both, he was able to see just enough over her ear to keep them on the road.

He had to wait a few minutes for the adrenaline rush to wear off, and then said, "I'll bet you don't remember the first time you kissed me."

"I've never kissed you before."

"Au contraire. It was almost a year ago after Mike's band had played for a dance and I was rolling up cables. You came up and gave me a long, sexy kiss and said I should pass it along to the band."

"And I did that? How flashy. You remember it, huh?"

"It was a pretty amazing kiss."

She sighed happily, snuggled up to him, put her arm through his, and just like that, Jamie had acquired a new Old Lady.

* * *

When they got to Perkins Street, they had to park halfway down the block and walk past the cars of the people who'd gotten there before them. Jamie carried a gallon jug of apple juice and Patty had a tall package of paper cups.

As they got close, they noticed someone climbing up the angle of the roof and taking a position at the peak, just back from the edge. He raised an odd, spikey, pink and white thing to his mouth, filled his lungs, and blew.

Having never heard a conch being sounded before, Jamie was enchanted. Between the tail-end of the mescaline, and the joint they had just smoked, the sonic experience was deep. The long, eerie drone seemed to reach back into his consciousness even to a prior life where, armed with spear and machete, he prepared for battle.

Simultaneously, he and Patty both said, "Wow!"

After sharing a laugh and listening to two more blasts on the conch, they went inside.

There are many wonderful smells that exist on this planet. Jamie liked the smells of sagebrush after a rain, Jasmine and Lilac flowers, and the curling smoke of sandalwood incense. But for him, little else could compare with the fragrance of cinnamon rolls baking in the oven. And that was the sweet odor that assailed them as they walked through the door. Immediately he began to salivate. He glanced over at Patty but she was already headed toward the kitchen. Next to the kitchen door was a table made of plywood and two sawhorses that was surrounded by a crowd of hungry people.

Phiz came out of the kitchen carrying a bowl that had two pounds of butter in it that supported three table knives sticking up at different angles. As he put down the bowl, Phiz announced, "They're cutting the first batch now, guys. Make sure you've got a plate."

He gestured to a stack of small paper plates, a pile of plastic forks, and a couple of rolls of paper towels. By the time Jamie and Patty had put the apple juice and the cups on a nearby folding card table and armed themselves with plates, Quentin was coming out of the kitchen carrying a large baking pan, obviously liberated from one of the college kitchens, full of freshly baked and iced cinnamon rolls.

After an initial uncontrolled grab-and-run by some of the craziest, the rest of the party formed themselves into a rough line that shuffled past the tray of rolls, the butter bowl, and then the drinks table.

A few minutes later, Jamie and Patty were sitting next to each other on the floor, leaning up against a wall, and making low ecstatic moaning noises as they chewed and swallowed.

"Holy Mother of God, this is good," said Patty in between bites.

Jamie could only grunt and nod his head emphatically as he chewed.

As they finished and got to their feet, Patty glanced over at the now-empty serving pan and said, "Thank God they're out. I couldn't eat another one, but I probably would do it anyway."

"Well don't toss your plate away," Jamie said, "Phiz said that was the 'first batch' which pretty much implies-"

Before he could complete his thought, Polly and Sarah came out of the kitchen. Sarah picked up the empty pan and Polly replaced it with another pan, this one full.

"-a second batch," Jamie finished.

* * *

With a half-empty beer bottle in his hand, Jamie wandered around the party saying hello to old friends and meeting new people. Because the new semester would be getting underway in a few days, there were a lot of fresh faces in the crowd and Jamie thought he may as well meet some of them.

Two friends of Nancy's, Robin and Tammy, had come down from Wyoming to go to school and Nancy made them promise they would come by the Electric Rainbow in the next few days to see Jamie's leatherwork.

Jamie noticed Mike and McNulty deep in conversation with a curly-haired, Italian-looking guy who wore tight, tailored bell-bottoms and had a long flowing scarf around his neck.

"Lemme guess," Jamie stuck his hand out, "you're the drummer they've been telling me about, right? I'm Jamie."

"Anthony," the fellow said. "How'd you guess?"

Mike said, "He's psychic. It's a side-effect of dropping too much LSD. Next thing you know his brains will catch on fire and start oozing out of his ears like melted wax."

Jamie clapped a hand over one ear, took a step away, and said, "Oh my God! I've got to go find a cork!"

He grinned at Anthony over his shoulder as he left. The drummer shook his head and returned the grin.

In another room, he found Patty telling a story to a spellbound group of people. He had heard some of Patty's stories before. Not only were they well-told, but they were invariably hair-raisingly freaky.

"So here I am," she said, "living in Venice, California with a junkie. I've been running speed for four days so I'm nuts anyway. I come into the apartment and he's looking in the mirror at the bottom of his tongue. He's got it pressed up against the roof of his mouth so he can see the bottom. He says, 'look at that. I've got a really mean vein under there. I decided to hit it. Watch this.'"

"He picks up a syringe full of smack and jabs it into that vein. I'm watching this about to piss my pants. He pulls a flag and pushes the plunger in. He only gets about half a hit in there before he makes this weird yodeling noise and falls over backward. Like a tree in the for-est-bam! I'm thinking he's dead for sure. Five minutes later I still haven't decided whether to call an ambulance or just pack up my shit and leave when he puts his head up and says, 'Damn, now <u>that</u> was a fucking rush!'"

There was scattered laughter, some of it genuine, some of it shocked and nervous. Patty stepped up to Jamie and pressed herself up against his hip. In a low voice that no one else could hear, she said, "I could use a good fucking right now, how about you?"

"Your pad or mine?"

"I didn't say later, I said now" She caught his earlobe between her teeth and gave him a gentle little bite.

He gave her what he hoped was a sexy look and said, "Keep that little fuzz clam warm for a few minutes while I scout the place. I'll see if I can come up with something fun." She slid her hand across his ass, gave it a squeeze, and walked away. He turned to see Krenovich, Phiz, and two strangers all looking at him.

Krenovich handed Jamie a smoldering joint, not one of his usual huge bombers, this one was only about twice normal size. Jamie took a hit and handed it to one of the two strangers, a short woman with mouse-brown hair and large, thick granny glasses.

"Got a thing going with Patty, eh?" Phiz said. "Pretty flashy company, my friend."

"Oh yeah," Jamie answered, "Seems like I'll be turning up the volume on the crazy in my life."

The joint had moved from the woman to the man next to her, then on to Phiz.

"This is my cousin, Moira," Krenovich said, "and her husband Victor. Victor's a Graduate Assistant over at the Sociology Department. They just moved down here from Oregon."

Victor was pallid and stoop-shouldered. He had thinning hair, long and over his ears, that was retreating around a bald spot on the back of his head. His hand, when Jamie shook it, was damp and soft and caused Jamie to let go as soon as he could.

Jamie decided they were geeky but harmless. "It was nice to meet you folks. Sorry to toke and run, but I'm looking for something. Welcome to Colton."

Jamie headed for the stairs but made a quick detour over to Mike, McNulty, and the new kid, Anthony.

"Hey Mike," he said, "can you guys wait until like One tomorrow afternoon to see the space?"

Mike grinned at him, gestured with his head to the other side of the house and said, "Patty, huh?"

"Yeah, somethin' like that."

"You and I are going to have to have a talk young man."

"Thanks, Pop," Jamie headed for the stairs. "Maybe later."

As Jamie got near the top of the stairs, he had to make his way through a group of people deeply involved in a conversation about college politics. Although most of them were folks he didn't know, he did notice Polly among the most vocal and Sarah quietly listening and nodding her head. He caught their eyes for a moment and smiled a greeting as he edged past them. Then Jamie saw Quentin sitting on the top step and he squatted down next to him.

"Great party, man. And the cinnamon rolls were out of freakin' sight."

"Thanks," Quentin said. "It was mostly Polly and Sarah and good ol' Betty Crocker. I was just "Manuel Labor.""

"Manuel! Just up from Mexico, eh?"

"Oh, si."

They both laughed, then Jamie said, "Okay, let's say there's a chick who's lookin' to get laid and there's a guy-me-who's quite willing to fill up her crevasse. Have you guys got like a little spare room or something?"

"A nookie nook, huh? Sorry, I couldn't help myself. The last door at the end of the hallway is my room. There's another bathroom in there you can only get to by going through, so not many people here are going to try to use it. But don't ball her on my bed, okay? I've got enough cleaning up to do in the morning without having to sleep on your hootenglobben."

"You're my hero, man," Jamie shook Quentin's hand. "Thanks, and we'll clean up after ourselves. In fact, I'll come over tomorrow about eleven and help you swab out the place. Cool?"

"Cool."

Jamie made his way back down through the crowd on the stairs.

* * *

Patty looked around the bathroom and smiled.

"The bathroom?" she said as she unbuttoned her blouse, "that's pretty twisty. But I can dig it."

Jamie had snagged a candle off a chest in Quentin's room as they passed through. He finished lighting it and turned the hot water handle on the tub to full.

"When Jamie Shipman invites a woman to ball, only the best will do."

"Oh yeah. I heard you had a thing about bathtubs."

Earlier, on their way back up the stairs together, Jamie had had a rude premonition.

What if it's one of those tiny bathrooms and we end up wedged between the toilet and the shower, grunting and sweating on a little bathmat?

He needn't have worried. It was a good-size room in which some thoughtful soul had installed a large, corner bathtub.

"Cast ye not aspersions upon bathtubs, my little kumquat," Jamie slipped her blouse off her shoulders and draped the garment over the toilet tank. "Some of the great dudes in History have been partial to the tub."

"Like who?" she pulled his T-shirt over his head.

"Like Archimedes..." he gently squeezed her breasts and licked the nipples, "...and Jean-Paul Marat."

Then, as he unbuttoned her jeans, slipped his hands inside her panties, and slid his hands around to grip her ass, he said," And of course Winston Churchill spent most of the Second World War soaking in one tub or another."

No more conversation was possible as lips and tongues found other uses.

Shortly thereafter the two of them, naked, were squeezing and tugging at each other's reproductive parts. Jamie slid away from Patty to shut off the incoming water. The tub was not quite full, but what was there was keeping them warm and wouldn't slosh over the rim as easily.

He leaned back to enjoy the pleasant sensations of Patty's fingers fondling his stiffened cock.

Why is it I can sit here and wallow in a good hand job without coming? But wrap a hot pussy around Junior and it's instant whoop-de-doo.

"Tell me something," Patty said as she rested her head on his chest, just out of the water. "Has anybody ever given you decent head?"

"What is...? Oh. I dig. Um... no, not even indecent head."

She gave him the same look of shocked disbelief that a film freak will give you when you say you've never seen *Citizen Kane*.

"You've never had anybody suck your cock, before?"

"Nope. Not so much as a lick or a kiss."

"Get your little butt up here," she slapped a flat triangle of decking between the tub and the corner, "and I'll show you what you've been missing."

Jamie did as he was told and soon his shoulders were against the walls, his legs wide, and his scrotum was hanging over the rim of the tub. Patty had slid up between his legs and had her right arm draped over his thigh.

By then, his penis was losing its erection and as it softened, it bounced up with every heartbeat and drooped a little lower in between. Patty gently wrapped her fingers around it and tugged down rhythmically while she ran her tongue in circles around the head. Jamie felt his heart rate pick up and his cock stiffen again.

"Hello, soldier," Patty said, then looked up at Jamie, opened her smiling lips, and sucked his member into her mouth.

To Jamie, the sensation was astonishing. It was grotesque and vulgar while at the same time enchanting and beautiful. A vagina with a tongue inside! And teeth!

Good Lord, this is amazing! What do I do with my hands? Hold her head? Grab her shoulders? And what if I start to come, should I warn her? Oh, oh God, here we go...

Jamie groaned and said, "I think I'm coming, I'm gonna come..." and made as if to push her away, but she waved him off and kept going. Two more surges in and out of her mouth and Jamie was making little animal screeches as his jizm was pumping into her mouth and down her throat.

She sat back on her heels and gave him a warm smile. A drop of pearly white liquid started to trickle down her lip. She licked it up and swallowed it.

Jamie slid back down into the tub with a splash and wrapped his legs and arms around her. He kissed her and hugged her and told her how amazing she was.

"But now the little guy has curled up and gone to sleep," he said, "how are you going to get yours?"

"In a little while, we can get in the car and trundle on over to my place. By the time we get there, I'll bet the little guy will be standing up and ready for another round."

Jamie kissed her grinning face, stood up, and stepped out of the tub. "Where're you going?" she asked.

"The sooner we get there, the sooner we can get it on." He tossed her a towel. "I got a lot to do tomorrow, and if I'm not gonna get any sleep, at least I want to spend the night getting righteously laid."

* * *

It was only a few minutes after eleven the next morning when Jamie knocked on the front door of the Perkins Street House.

"Hey Jamie!," Quentin pushed the door open wide, "come on in. You actually showed up."

"Is that weird?"

"Must have been five people last night said they were going to come and help us clean up. Madeleine and now you are the only ones who showed."

"Madeleine? Was she here last night? I didn't see her."

"Dude, I don't think you saw anybody last night who wasn't in the bathroom playin' hide the pickle with you. Sarah's up there now trying to scrub cum shots off the walls."

"Oh horseshit! There may be some moosey spots on the ceiling, but none on the walls."

Quentin, laughing and grabbing his crotch, stumbled around in a circle yelling, "Help, help, it's out of control! Oh, the humanity!"

Jamie, having never seen a bad joke that couldn't be dragged out even further, began his own loud lament, "Now I'll never have children! They're all running down the bathroom walls!"

After more bumbling around and whooping from both of them, Quentin suddenly stopped. Jamie kept yelling, "Save them, save the..." then also stopped. Madeleine and Polly were standing in the Kitchen doorway with their arms crossed.

"You kids had better quiet down," Madeleine said. "You'll wake up Grandpa."

"But Mo-om," Quentin whined, "We hate Grandpa."

Polly shook her finger at Quentin, "Don't you start crying young man, or we'll give you something to cry about."

Unable to contain themselves any longer, all four of them gave up to raucous laughter.

It wasn't long before everyone had gone back to work. Jamie was making his way around the living room with a plastic trash bin, picking up paper plates, cups, napkins, and empty beer bottles. As he picked up an ashtray from the spool table and dumped its contents into the bin, he noticed a newly opened package containing what looked like posters. He pulled one out and studied it.

Most of the space was taken up by a head-and-shoulders, black and white photograph of a dark-skinned man, presumably Indian, with high, strong cheekbones flanking a hawk-like nose. He wore a white beard and his long, gray hair was swept back and fell behind his ears to an indeterminate length. A cotton robe was pulled loosely around his shoulders and a necklace of dark beads hung around his neck.

But it was the man's eyes that caught and held Jamie's attention. Though it was only a photograph, Jamie could see a stern, bright intelligence, deep wisdom, and compassion in those eyes.

Whatever this guy has, I want what he's got.

Across the top, the poster read: LEARN THE LAAGHAVA MEDITATION TECHNIQUE. Under the picture was the man's name: *Swami Shri Bhaktinanda*. Below that it only said: *Free Introductory Lecture*. There were blank spaces for the place, date, and time of the presentation.

"Hey, Quentin," Jamie carried the poster toward the kitchen, "What's the deal on this lecture thing?"

Quentin came out of the kitchen carrying a broom, saw what Jamie had in his hand, smiled, and set the broom aside.

"The LM Course? The lecture will be a week from Thursday at the Colton Bank Community Room."

"Yeah, okay, but is this guy actually coming here to Colton? And what are you doing with all these posters?"

"First, no. A different guy is coming. A guy who went to India and learned how to teach the technique from Bhaktinanda. Second, we asked the LM Center in Boulder if someone would come up here to do a course. They said, 'sure, as long as you can guarantee at least five people will want to start.' We said, 'got 'em,' and they sent us posters, press releases, all that stuff."

"So who've you got?"

"Me, Polly, Sarah, Aaron, and Madeleine. As soon as we finish cleaning up, we're going to fill out the info on these and then divide them up."

"Tell you what," Jamie put the poster back on the pile, "I have to split soon, but if you'll fill out a couple of these before I leave I'll put 'em up at the Electric Rainbow. They-and I guess me-are having our Grand Opening in a couple of days."

"Far out. Is there a black Magic Marker over there? I'll do them for you now."

While Quentin carefully filled out the place, date, and time spaces on several posters, Jamie went back to picking up trash. Only when the living room was cleaned up and back to its funky normalcy, did Jamie relax on the arm of the couch.

"I've got a question for you"

Quentin looked up.

"Do you guys ever hear from Lisa?"

"Madeleine talks to her now and then. The last thing she heard was she wasn't real happy with the Track program at Boulder. She's thinking about maybe transferring to someplace in New Mexico."

"New Mexico?"

"That's what Madeleine said. But who knows, really? Anyway, thanks for helping out." Quentin stood up, "Come by any time. Bring food and the chicks will cook it for us."

They shook hands and Jamie picked up the posters. He took a step for the door, and then turned back.

"One more thing," Jamie said, "you can put my name on that meditation list of yours."

"Don't you want to hear about it first?"

"Don't need to," Jamie smiled and held up a poster. "The picture was enough."

* * *

Jamie wondered if Charlie Melman had heard much at all of what was being explained to him. Charlie was intently looking over Jamie's shoulder at the small crowd of people who were standing in the middle of The Electric Rainbow and looking around.

There you go, Charlie. You wanted a store full of Hippos and that's what you got.

Jamie had been expecting to show Mike, and possibly McNulty, the basement space. Instead, half the Family had tagged along too. Anthony, the kid drummer, was here, so were Lyle and Nancy, Harvey and his girl-friend Jacqueline, Phiz was there, and Krenovich had even brought along his Oregon relatives.

Suzy Weird Chick was off to one side leaning against a tall, boney-kneed guy with a thick beard and a camera around his neck. This, Jamie assumed, was Wisconsin Juan.

Mike had explained earlier that he had stopped by Harvey's house to pick up McNulty and Anthony. All the others were already in there eating pancakes and laughing at the Sunday Morning TV preachers. Hearing where Mike was going, everyone demanded to come along so they could see the inside of the new head shop.

"Think of it as a good thing, man," Mike had said. "If the cat doesn't dig a crowd of us hanging out, we don't want to be down there in his basement anyway."

"So," Jamie said to Charlie, "you want to meet Mike?"

"Oh yeah, that'd be cool."

Jamie looked at Mike and jerked his eyebrows up. The guitarist walked over with a friendly smile on his face.

"Charlie Melman, this is my main man, Mike Harding. Mike, this is Charlie."

Charlie put up his hand in the proper position and Mike grasped and shook it.

"Mr. Melman..." Mike began.

"Please, call me Charlie."

"Charlie, I really dig the space here. Very Trippy. Very... psychedelic, you know?"

Jamie hoped that Charlie didn't hear the faint, sarcastic edge to the statement and was relieved when the businessman smiled proudly.

"Why, thanks, Mike. We've tried to make it as groovy as possible. Good for sales, you know?"

"Jamie tells me you're thinking about making your basement avail-able. Mind if we take a look?

"No. I mean, yes, sure. Check it out. Two keys-the gold one fits the padlock on the outside entrance. The silver one is for the door at the top of the stairs-in case one of the customers comes out of the bathroom and takes a wrong turn."

Charlie handed Mike the key ring. "Are all these people in your band?"

Mike grinned and said, "Only three of us. The rest are the Family. It's like... okay, here's a story. I once knew a guy who owned about twenty gerbils. He kept them out in his back yard and they all browsed around the lawn together in a big group, like this."

Mike put out both hands, palms down and fingers extended. He slowly moved them around together in a flat plain, gently wiggling his fingertips.

"That's us. Dig?"

Jamie led the whole group out of the shop while Charlie stood there, looking at the backs of his hands.

The rear entrance was a large steel door that had been installed at an angle to the building. Once unlocked and opened, it revealed a flight of cement steps that led into the basement space. One by one, everyone trooped down inside to have a look.

"The ceiling is like a good eight feet," McNulty said, "I had pictured you having to scrabble around in here stooped over to keep your head from banging on the floor joists."

Lyle and Nancy were looking up at two small, grimy windows. "Not exactly flooded with natural light, eh?" Lyle said. "But what do you want for nothin'?"

There was a furnace on one end of the space with octopus-like ducts going up through the ceiling and three storage rooms along one side. Two of those were locked for the head shop's use; the other was a little bedroom.

"What's the electrical like?" Mike asked.

"When I first came down here it was doodley-squat," Jamie said. "Since they were doing some electrical work upstairs, I got them to add a twenty amp circuit and some plugs and stuff down here. Not great, but you should be able to make some noise without blowing the breakers out."

While Mike checked out the bedroom, Jamie walked up to Suzie Weird Chick.

"Suzie," Jamie said, "you haven't introduced me to your friend."

Suzie's head turned to him but he couldn't see her face under a tangled mound of snow-colored hair. She pushed the mass aside, looked confused for a moment, then grinned.

"Oh, I dig! Juan this is Jamie. Jamie this is Juan, my new Old Man."

Jamie gripped Juan's hand. "Take good care of Suzie, man. She was my Maid of Honor you know."

"Oh, that's so sweet!" She wrapped her arms around Jamie and squeezed him. "I'm gonna miss you guys so much."

"You're running off on us? Where are you going?"

Juan cleared his throat. "A friend of mine in Marin County knows of a little cabin up on a hillside there. It's not very big, but it has an extra little room I can make into a darkroom."

"Isn't he cute?" Suzie said. "He got up this morning while it was still dark so he could go up on the pedestrian bridge over the tracks and take pictures of the trains and stuff with the sunrise."

"It's the best light of the day," Juan said.

Jamie mock-shuddered. "I guess I'll have to take your word for that."

* * *

A few minutes later Jamie and Mike, leaving everybody else down in the basement arguing over what the band should be named, were walking back around the building to tell Charlie that Mike would take the deal.

"I'm pretty jazzed about this place, man," Mike said. "It'll be a great place to practice, a safe place to store our equipment, and a cheap crash for me. So, thank you."

"My pleasure, dude."

"I am a little freaked out though, I've got to admit it. After I got out of jail, I swore I'd never live in a place again that didn't have nice, big windows. With sunlight and blowing curtains and shit."

"Sure you don't want your old room back? Last chance."

"No, here is cool. If you were down there, you'd throw us out by midnight so you could sleep, right?"

Jamie shrugged.

"Thought so. Let's go find this Charlie dude and sign on the dotted line."

"Any time you get to feeling freaky, you're welcome to crash at Fifth Street." Jamie opened the head shop's door, "You may not be aware of it, but we've got the least comfortable sofa bed in Colton."

Twenty Five

Jamie sat in a chair in a room of the Weary Traveler Motel. The single bed had been pushed up against one wall and a chair or two added to the room. Sarah sat behind the little motel table/desk with an appointment book and a cash box. Quentin had been there when Jamie arrived and he had welcomed him in a quiet voice, and then suggested that he remove his shoes and have a seat. Quentin turned to a woman who had been waiting, asked her to follow him, and led her through an adjoining door into the room next door. When he reappeared, he took Jamie's three carnations, two apples, and a white handkerchief and left the room again.

Jamie caught Sarah's eye. "So, have you been initiated yet?"

"Not yet," she said in a near-whisper. "We go this afternoon."

She then went back to writing a receipt for Jamie's $30. A little slow on the uptake, Jamie finally got the message that he should just wait quietly. He sat back and let his mind wander over the previous two weeks.

There had been only a few requirements to begin Laaghava Meditation. Most were easy to comply with-get plenty of rest; take care of any personal things that might distract or worry you; when you come bring a handkerchief, two pieces of fruit, and some flowers. But the last requirement proved to be a lot tougher to hold to than it had first sounded: "We ask that you refrain for at least two weeks before Initiation from the use of any non-prescription drugs."

Jamie had spent those two weeks declining frequent opportunities to get loaded. It seemed that suddenly everyone was eager to share their stash of Lebanese hash or Yucatan Blue. The town was suddenly and apparently awash with every mind-altering substance known to man. But Jamie felt he had made a commitment and he kept to it.

Then there was Tuesday night. I still don't know what to think about that.

It actually began on Sunday two days earlier. Jamie and Patty had packed some sandwiches and a bottle of wine and drove up into the foothills to have a picnic. They were looking for a private little place that Patty had been to once before.

After parking the car, they followed a narrow deer trail around one hill, up and over another, and came out into a little clearing. There were soft grasses there, wildflowers, and a couple of leafy bushes growing next to a little brook that gurgled down into the woods.

Jamie busied himself opening the wine while Patty spread a blanket. When he looked up, she was removing her clothes and piling them neatly on a rock. Jamie shrugged, unbuckled his belt, and kicked out of his jeans. Soon his own clothes were in a not-so-neat pile and the two of them stood there naked in the sunlight with silly grins on their faces.

Patty took the wine bottle, filled two paper cups, and set the bottle on a rock.

Carrying some branches he had cut from one of the bushes, Jamie sat down on the blanket and showed them to her.

"Do you think those are willow bushes? I've heard that in Finland they whip themselves with willow branches, like this." He swung the handful of branches over his head and hit himself across the back a couple of times. There was a slight sting, but it was more interesting than painful.

"Why the hell would they do that?" Patty asked.

"I don't know," he said. "Come to think of it, they don't really do it in summer. It's like in the middle of winter, way below zero; they get in hot saunas until they can't stand it, then run out, roll in the snow, and beat themselves and each other with willow switches."

"You are such a liar. Rolling around in the snow and beating each other with switches."

"Don't knock it 'til you've tried it." He waved the branches at her in a threatening way.

Patty looked defiant."You wouldn't dare," she said.

Then she dipped her fingers into her cup and flicked a spray of wine droplets in his face. He tried to grab her but she spun away and then poured the rest of her wine on top of his head.

After wrestling on the blanket, Jamie managed to get one arm behind her shoulders and force her down across his knees. He picked up the handful of branches and swatted her across the butt several times. She was still struggling so he gave her a couple more, and then let her up. She sat there, breathing hard and staring at him. He was trying to frame an apology when she crawled up, settled her lips on his and pushed her tongue deep into his mouth. She shoved him onto his back, and pressed her pubis into his hip bone, hard.

"Fuck me, Shipman! Fuck me now!"

She straddled him, reached down and pushed his cock up into herself, then began to rock back and forth and moan. The rhythm steadily increased until she was bucking back and forth, her breasts slapping against her belly. The moans had become a loud continuous wailing.

Just as Jamie felt his own climax building up, a spasmodic jerk rocked her body and she screamed, "Oh God!", then came another, bigger spasm, and, as Jamie came too, her body jerked and quaked a third time.

Their cries still seemed to echo off a distant hillside as Patty fell on top of him, hugged him, and covered his face with happy kisses.

They lay twined around each other for some time as their heartbeats slowed and the warm sun and a gentle breeze evaporated the sweat from their skin.

"The big 'O', man, three times," she exulted, "what a trip."

Jamie had a smug smile on his face. For the first time since that Mexican whore had popped his cherry, the girl he was balling had come before he did.

Patty had appeared at the shop on Tuesday and was itching for another go at him, but he had to apologize and put her off.

"Tonight's just not happenin', Babe, and I'm sorry about that. But I've got to do my books tonight. I've been making shit and selling shit for two weeks and now I'm out of leather, brass rivets, buckles, you name it. I'm going to drive down to Denver tomorrow on a buying trip and I haven't got a clue how much money I have to spend on stuff. Plus my meditation fee and a little left over for luxuries like, you know... food."

"Come on, man," Patty said, "Don't be such a drag. I scored a couple of hits of that 'Deep blue' from your pal Shoes. You know what they say-'The family that drops together bops together."

"Nope, not a chance." Jamie held up two fingers and counted off, "A. I took the Pledge, made a pact, and signed the contract in blood. Cold turkey on everything. And B. I've gotta work tonight."

"God, you are such an asshole."

"I'll be getting back too late tomorrow night but I'll cook spaghetti for us Thursday night, how does that sound?"

"I'll think about it."

"Don't go away all pissed off."

Without looking at him she held up her middle finger and let it trail her out the door.

That night Jamie was in the kitchen making lists.

Rivets, rawhide lacing, belt leather, suede (colors?)...

He'd already balanced his checkbook and entered every transaction onto a sheet of ledger paper. Charlie had shown him how it was done and, he had to admit, it was much easier to see what was going on with everything listed on a neat page rather than a scattered across a wad of carbon copies of receipts. He even had a separate column for the sales tax he had charged.

"Sales tax?" he'd said to Charlie. "Why would I want to collect money for a bunch of fathead politicians in Denver who'll only use it to raise their salaries and buy trinkets for their mistresses?"

"Because it's against the law if you don't. And before you can collect the taxes you have to get a tax license from the State of Colorado. For a fee."

"What? I have to pay them money for the right to send them more money? Seriously?"

"Seriously. But you can't buy your material at wholesale unless you have a tax license to prove you're a business. That alone makes it worth the expense."

Charlie's advice turned out to be right on. Jamie had to admit that his opinion of Charlie had changed markedly over the past few weeks. At Charlie's suggestion, Jamie had gone to the library and found several outfits in Denver that sold leather and findings "to the trade only" at much better prices than the "hobby" place he'd gone to in Fort Collins.

...dye, knife blades, peace-sign punch or finding...

He kept getting requests for peace signs on things. He personally felt that the symbol was overused to the point of embarrassment, but if some tweek wanted a leather wristband with a peace-sign on it, who was he to tell them to fuck off.

Just then the front door opened and Jamie looked up to see if it was Waltz or Phiz back from the party. It was neither. It was Patty. She was giggly, shy, excited, and very stoned. He'd long before gotten used to looking only at her good right eye, which was presently so dilated as to have no visible iris at all, and to ignore her glass eye which was always looking up and over his shoulder.

He grinned at her right eye and said, "Patty! Come in here. You're not pissed off anymore?" He stood up and held his arms out wide. She scurried up to him and snuggled into his bear hug.

"Oh, Jamie. I'm sorry for being such a cunt. No, I wasn't really pissed off. I was just trying to jerk you around a little. Don't be mad, okay?"

"Not even a tiny bit. So why'd you leave the party?"

"Well, I'm sitting there and everybody is grooving out but me. I'm all weird and just thinking about the picnic on Sunday and then I had a flash."

"A flash?"

"Oh, this is so cool." She took him by the hand and pulled him into the bedroom.

"What I was thinking about was, like I said, the picnic and you beating my ass with those switches-"

"I wouldn't say beating..."

"-And then us balling and like earthquakes and skyrockets and shit went off. Don't you see?"

"See what?"

"Maybe I'm a masochist."

Not knowing what to say to that, Jamie just stared at her open-mouthed.

"You know, like I can't really get off on sex unless somebody knocks me around first. So I wanted to, like, explore that. You dig?"

"You want me to go cut a switch or something?"

"No, no. Nothing small-time. I want you to beat me with a belt."

It wasn't long before Jamie, naked and feeling a little foolish, was standing next to his bed. Patty was lying face-down on the bed, her naked body wriggling with anticipation. Jamie held the buckle end of his belt and wondered how to go about this.

Should I leave it long and take a big windup like the boson's mate in that pirate movie? Or should I double it over like my Dad used to do to me and Jack?

"Come on, Baby. Let's get it on! Make it hurt!" Patty yelled with excitement, kicking her feet against the bed.

Jamie flipped the end of the belt behind him, braced his feet, and then hesitated.

Once again he found himself standing at a fork in the road, looking down two different paths... and one was just too dark and creepy. He dropped the belt on the bed.

"I can't. I'm sorry. I just don't have the stomach for it."

They put their clothes back on in silence. Patty shrouded herself with disappointment while Jamie was feeling only relief. They came out of the bedroom, Patty holding Jamie's belt. The front door opened and Waltz and Phiz came in.

"Hey you guys," said Phiz, "what's up?"

"Well I hate to say it, but your roommate is a pussy."

Phiz said, "Jamie! Bad boy." Turning to Patty he said, "What did he do?"

"I came over all nice as could be and asked him to beat me with a belt and he freaked out and wouldn't do it."

"You asked him to beat you with a belt?"

"Yeah. And he wouldn't do it. Would one of you guys?" She held out the belt.

Waltz took a step back and put up his hands, "No way, not my thing."

Patty looked pleadingly at Phiz, "Phiz, please? I just gotta know what it feels like."

Phiz shrugged his shoulders and took the belt.

Happy again, Patty practically skipped back into the bedroom, pulling off her top as she went.

Phiz looked at Jamie and Waltz, elaborately rolled his eyes, and followed her.

A few minutes later, they heard a sharp "crack", and after another few minutes, a subdued Patty and Phiz came back out into the living room.

"You okay?" Jamie asked her.

"Yeah, I'm fine. I think I'm going to go home now."

"Do you want me to go with you?"

She gave Jamie a sad, faraway look and said, "No, I'd rather be alone. You stay here. I'll be okay."

She opened the door and walked out into the night.

When Jamie called her on Thursday, he wasn't surprised, or particularly saddened, to hear she thought they ought to cool it for a while.

* * *

Jamie heard someone quietly calling him and his attention snapped back to the motel room. Quentin was standing in the doorway to the adjoining room. As Jamie stood up, Sarah held out a tray that contained the carnations, the apples, and the handkerchief his mother had bought and packed for him more than a year ago. A one-page form that Jamie had filled out two weeks before was folded over and wedged between the two apples. Jamie took the tray and followed Quentin into the other room.

Through a thin haze of incense smoke, Jamie saw Richard Hanover, the guy who'd interviewed him, standing next to a small table that was covered with a white sheet. On the table was an arrangement of little brass trays and bowls and a gold-framed picture of Shri Bhaktinanda. Hanover was wearing a reddish-gold robe that covered him to his knees. The cloth was wrapped around him and thrown over one shoulder.

Hanover, smiling kindly, took the tray and set it on the table, gestured Jamie to one of two chairs, and nodded to Quentin, who withdrew. He opened the form, studied it for a moment, and then put it down on a side table with several others.

"Welcome, Jamie," he said in a soft, almost musical voice. "I am going to perform a short ceremony of gratitude to Swami Shri Bhaktinanda, my master, for giving us this teaching. You are required only to sit quietly and witness."

Hanover began the ceremony. It was half sung and half chanted in an exotic-sounding Eastern language. The things he'd brought, plus pinches of rice and sprinkles of water, were all lovingly placed, one-by-one, in front of the picture. A candle and several sticks of incense were lit. To complete the ceremony Hanover got down to his knees and touched his forehead to the ground. Jamie felt a strong impulse to bow down himself but decided to remain in his chair. Hanover rose up and sat next to him.

"Become aware of your breathing," Hanover told him. "On every inward breath, the presence that is you spreads a little further outward into the room. You feel that?"

Jamie nodded his head as he listened to his breathing.

"Now repeat after me, very softly, the sound 'ham-sah."

Jamie said, "ham-sah." Seeing that Hanover was gently rotating his hand he repeated, "ham-sah, ham-sah, ham-sah."

"Keep repeating, but with almost no sound."

"Ham-sah, ham-sah, ham-sah."

"Very good. Now repeat mentally without moving tongue or lips."

Ham-sah, ham-sah, ham-sah...

Jamie could feel his body relax and, simultaneously, his senses sharpen. It occurred to him that he had probably parked his car just outside this room. Since he had been in a hurry, he wasn't sure if he had parked in someone else's reserved spot.

"Now open your eyes, slowly," Hanover said.

When Jamie had complied Hanover said, "Very good. Did you notice that at some time thoughts came up and the mantra was lost?"

"Actually, yes. That happened. I guess I wasn't concentrating very hard."

"No, you were doing it perfectly. Thoughts are a normal part of this meditation. Concentration is not. All you have to do is when you realize you are thinking a thought, just let that thought go, listen for your breathing, and then come back to the mantra. You understand?"

Jamie nodded his head and said, "yes."

"Now close your eyes, listen for your breathing and then start the mantra again. I will meditate here with you and tell you when to stop."

Jamie did as he was told. As he meditated, the darkness in front of his eyes grew deep and silent. Small points of light would appear, grow into gently swirling areas of soft color which would grow and then slip past him just as other small points of light would appear. Then he would realize that he was thinking about lights in the dark, so he would let the thought go, listen for his breathing, then start the mantra again. After what seemed like two or three minutes (he found out later it had been ten) he once again heard Hanover's voice.

"Very good, now take a minute or two to come out of meditation slowly, and then open your eyes."

When he saw Jamie's eyes were open Hanover asked, "Was it effortless? Did you have any difficulties?"

"No, no difficulties."

"And you feel good?"

"Oh yeah. Really good."

"Excellent. Now I want you to meditate on your own once this evening before dinner for twenty minutes. The same tomorrow morning before breakfast. Find a place that's comfortable to sit and private. And please remember-what you learn in silence retains its power only when it is kept in silence. Do not speak your mantra out loud to anyone."

Hanover picked up a flower, the handkerchief, and an apple from the tray and handed them to Jamie.

"These are for you. There is one last thing-there will be a meeting for all of you who started practicing LM today. It will be tomorrow at 11 am in the community room at the bank. You'll be able to attend?"

Jamie said he definitely would.

"Good. I look forward to seeing you there." He put his hands together palm-to-palm and said, "Namaste. Enjoy your meditations."

Jamie turned and saw Quentin wearing a big smile as he held open the door to the hallway. Jamie was feeling light, almost buoyant, and calmly satisfied as he floated out of the room.

* * *

Jamie sat in the community room next to Shoes and looked around at the other brand-new meditators. There was a light, peaceful vibe in the room and he was feeling particularly close to the people who were generating it.

Even the usually serious Shoes had a grin on his face when he had gotten into Jamie's car earlier.

"So how were your meditations?" Jamie had asked.

"Truthfully? Boring as hell, but I feel pretty damned good, and I guess that's what matters. How about you? How are y'all feelin'?"

"Like you said-'pretty damned good."

Richard Hanover, dressed in a brown suit this time, came into the room and thanked them for coming. Jamie had the feeling that something or someone was missing. He took a quick headcount.

Since Aaron was sitting right in front of him and Hanover was taking a minute to set up a little cassette player, Jamie put a hand on Aaron's shoulder and leaned forward.

"Hey Aaron," he said softly, "where's Madeleine?"

"In Kentucky, Emergency trip, I'll tell you later."

When he was ready, Hanover sat down in a chair facing them and said, "Let's start with a ten-minute group meditation. Everyone close your eyes and listen for your breathing. When you feel settled, start the mantra. I'll tell you when to stop."

During the meditation and in between thoughts, which were many, Jamie felt a pleasant expansiveness. The possibility that the others in the room, on some level, were sharing the same feeling was intriguing.

Hanover then said something that sounded to Jamie like "Jay Accordion."

Then after a moment, "Take your time and open your eyes slowly... It was effortless..? Any difficulties..?"

When no one responded, he nodded, "Very Good... Today I want to cover all, or at least most, of the practical problems that may arise in your meditations. But first, there is a short recording that Shri Bhaktinanda made recently and he asked that it be played for all the new meditators." So saying, Hanover pushed a button on the little tape player.

"My congratulations to you who have begun practicing the Laaghava Meditation Technique," said a rich baritone voice with a strong Indian accent. "As you continue to meditate, you will find yourself on a path that will lead you to more and more bliss, more and more deep experience of Pure Consciousness, and eventually to the Awakening of the True Enlightened Self.

"Why do we always start by listening to our breathing? The mind is so restless it is hard for it to focus on the absence of everything, on just the silence. So we give the mind something to focus on-the breathing.

244 | TIM PELTON

For every breath begins and ends in silence. And the mantra does its job best in silence.

"Now what is this job the mantra does so well? To understand, I would ask you to imagine your self-personality, conscious mind, unconscious mind, all those many levels-as a beautiful musical instrument with many, many finely tuned strings. But now imagine that musical instrument, over a long time, has been subject to jolts and stresses. Some big jolts, some small ones. Every time this happens a little twist or a knot comes into some string or another and the music that it plays is no longer so perfect. If you find a way to untie that little knot, the string vibrates and makes a sound as it regains its original shape in that place. Now here is our metaphor. During meditation, the job of the mantra is to untie the knots, to release those small stresses and strains. And the act of releasing makes some vibration which we experience as a thought.

"So one may have a meditation that is nothing but thoughts from beginning to end. That is very good! Many and many of those stresses and strains are being released. At some other time, one may have a different meditation where there are hardly any thoughts at all, just deep silence and peaceful feeling. That is also very good! One is experiencing the finer and finer depths of consciousness and becoming comfortable there.

"Here is another metaphor for you to consider. Your daily practice-two twenty minute meditations-is like taking a bath every day. You take a bath to clean the outside of yourself, and you meditate to clean the inside of yourself. You do not wonder, "Should I change the temperature of the bath water? Am I washing myself correctly? Where did this dirt come from that I am washing off?" No, you just take your bath and go about your life feeling better because you have done so. It is the same with Laaghava Meditation. We do not look for results within our meditation, we look for results within our daily lives.

"Once again, my great congratulations. Remember, to live a happy and fulfilled life, to eventually come to a state of full spiritual awakening, all that you need is this: twenty minutes meditation every morning and twenty minutes meditation every evening. Jai Acarya."

Hanover turned off the tape player and faced his small audience with a wistful smile. It seemed apparent to Jamie that although he must have listened to this tape many times before, just hearing the sound of his Master's voice still touched Hanover deeply.

Before Hanover could begin, Polly's hand went up. "Excuse me, Richard, but what does 'Jai Acarya' mean? You said it at the end of the group meditation and Bhaktinanda just said it at the end of his talk."

"It is Sanskrit. Two words-'Jai' means 'hail' or 'all glory to...', and 'Acarya' means 'Spiritual Master.' So together they mean 'all glory to the Spiritual Master." When Bhaktinanda says it, it is a way of honoring his master, Govinda Satguru Maharaj. When we say it, we are honoring Bhaktinanda.

"Now I'm going to tell you about certain things that may arise as you proceed with the practice, most of these are questions that have but one answer-whatever is simple, easy, and helps you to stay with regular practice, that is what you should do."

For much of the rest of the meeting, Jamie felt that everything covered was just an elaboration of this basic rule. Then there was a period when Hanover answered people's questions-or at least some of them. The more abstract, philosophical questions like "what is Spiritual Enlightenment and how long does it take to get there?" he gently declined to answer but instead invited as many of the group that were interested to come down to the LM Center in Boulder to attend advanced lectures on this and on other topics.

Before he left, Richard took the time to talk to everyone personally, to make sure they were comfortable with the teaching, and to reassure them they were ready to practice the technique on their own.

Quentin and Polly stopped Jamie and Shoes before they could leave and invited them to a little group meditation and dinner that evening at the Perkins Street house. Later, over a bowl of vegetable soup, Jamie asked Aaron about Madeleine.

"Four days ago, Madeleine got a phone call from her Mother. An American patrol had been ambushed East of Da Nang. Her brother Tyler was among those who were killed. I drove her down to the Denver airport Friday morning and put her on a flight to Louisville."

"Ouch. Terrible news. Is it a big family?"

"No, her Dad died of Cancer only two years ago. Now it's just her and her Mom."

"When you talk to her, tell her we're all sending her the best vibes we can generate."

"Thank you. I think she'll appreciate that."

* * *

Jamie sat on his bed, eyes closed, with a pillow between his back and the wall. For the last few days, during his meditations, he had become used to hearing his roommates' footsteps clunking up and down the hall along with periodic rumbles of conversation. But the sounds he was hearing now were different. The footsteps were quieter and seemed to stop outside the door. Then came the rustling of paper, some muffled giggles, and many footsteps heading back toward the living room.

Jamie put his curiosity aside and opened one eye long enough to glance at the clock. Ten minutes to go. He listened for his breathing for a few moments, and then started the mantra.

Ham-sah, ham-sah, ham-sah…

When he had finished resting after meditation, he rolled off the bed and opened the door. A cartoon on a sheet of typing paper had been taped there. The drawing was of a man with long hair, presumably him, sitting cross-legged. He had a halo above his head and lines of brightness shooting away from him in all directions. At the top was the lettering, "This is the cave of THE BUDDHA MAN!" Underneath the drawing it said, "Hold onto your aura! This Dude is KOZMIC!" It wasn't signed, but McNulty's style was unmistakable.

Putting on a mock appearance of indignation, Jamie walked into the living room. He was greeted by hoots of laughter and loud taunts from the crowd of his friends.

"The Buddha Man puts in an appearance!"

"All hail the Buddha Man!"

"Tell us, oh master, the meaning of life!"

Mike, McNulty, Lyle, Nancy, and all the usual Family members were passing around a hose connected to a big hookah pipe, a bowlful of grass smoldering on top of it.

"The meaning of life?" Jamie said. Then he put up his left fist, the back of it facing the room. "Here it is!" With his right hand, he twirled a small imaginary crank on the side of his fist. As he did so, the middle finger slowly rose up to a vertical position. There were more hoots of friendly derision.

Jamie sat down on the arm of a chair next to Robin or Tammy, one of Nancy's Casper friends between which Jamie had not yet learned how to tell the difference. He was offered a turn on the hookah pipe's hose but declined.

"Hey, you know," Mike said, "why don't you guys come over to the Hellhole tonight. We've been working on an original song. It's pretty rough, but we'd like to hear what you think."

Although he said it to include the whole group, Mike was looking at Jamie, who grinned and said, "Okay. But it had better be rockin'. The Buddha Man don't listen to no second rate shit."

Twenty Six

"Pull in here and park," Larry Sherman said to the uniform driving the car. "Block these cars in and stop crossways to the entrance."

"Yes sir," the officer did as requested.

Technically, the driver didn't have to call Sherman "sir," they were both the same rank, but Captain Gaskin had asked Sherman to lead this team and to wear a suit rather than his uniform, so he didn't correct the officer.

At the station, they had divided up into eight teams of three, and each team was given an arrest warrant to execute. The Colton force was not big enough to do this by itself, but rather than turn the whole investigation over to the State cops, they had pulled officers from the Colton College Police and some nearby towns.

Sherman glanced at the officer in the back seat. He was a College cop who'd been sent out early to reconnoiter and they had picked him up at the entrance to the alley. "They still down there?"

"Yes, sir. The Suspect, along with a group of friends, left a house on 5th Street at 7:45. They came over here in two cars, and went in that door." The officer pointed at a steel door angled to the side of the building.

"Good," Sherman said. "Why don't you go around to the front door and make sure no one tries to slip out that way." He turned back to the driver. "You ready? Let's go bust this guy."

Standing next to the steel door a few minutes later, Sherman rubbed the sore knuckles on his right hand. He had knocked on the door as loud and forcibly as he could, but there had been no response. Although the rock and roll music he could hear coming from the basement of the building was somewhat muffled by the thick concrete walls, it was still remarkably loud.

"It must be deafening inside there," he said to the uniformed cop. "Get your baton out and we'll wait for a pause."

The cop unsnapped the club from its belt loop and a couple of minutes later there was a sustained feedback wail from the guitar that quickly descended into a short power chord and the music stopped. Sherman nodded to the cop who thumped loudly on the steel door with his baton four times.

Less than a minute later, he heard the bolt shoot back inside the door and then saw someone pushing it open.

"Jesus Christ, you guys," said whoever was opening the door, "you don't have to scare the crap out of... oh shit."

The hippie with the mutton-chop sideburns who'd opened the door just stood there dumbfounded. The uniform quickly reached out and secured the door while Sherman flipped open a leather wallet that contained his badge and ID.

"My name is Sherman and I'm with the Colton Police Department. Please step away from the doorway."

The hippie turned and walked back the way he had come. Sherman heard him say, "Bummer guys. It's the pigs." After a quick skip down the stairs, Sherman turned the corner and strode into the basement.

There were nine or ten people there, three of them were musicians, and the rest were young people, all of them about the same age, all of them hippies of one kind or another in colorful clothes, fringy vests, and long hair.

Sherman, having studied the pictures and descriptions of the suspects, immediately picked out his man. The lead guitarist saw him approaching, smiled ruefully, took off his instrument and handed it to his bass player.

Sherman said, "Are you Michael Harding?"

"Yes."

"I am placing you under arrest. Please step over there." Sherman gestured toward the wall next to the bedroom door. Harding complied.

"The rest of you, please move over to that side of the room and have a seat. Frank, ask Officer Adams to come down and give us a hand."

The uniform produced a walkie-talkie and spoke into it.

Sherman read Harding his rights, handcuffed him, and had the two uniforms take him up and put him in the back seat of the squad car. Then he did a quick search of the basement. In the bottom drawer of an old dresser in the little bedroom, he found three clear plastic sandwich bags, each one about a quarter full of a dried green plant that smelled like marijuana. Since they were in a brown paper bag, he picked up the bag and went out into the main room.

He looked carefully at each of the hippies sitting on the floor. He did not have the manpower or desire to search and question everybody, but he did want to familiarize himself with each one before he left. He recognized three of them. Two he knew from High School-the guy with the muttonchops who'd opened the door and the fellow with the round face and flat-brimmed black hat. The other one was the kid who looked like Keith Moon that he'd picked up a few months back for an expired plate. The kid's dark hair had gotten longer, almost to his shoulders, so the resemblance wasn't so striking, but Sherman was pretty sure it was the same guy.

Sherman addressed the group. "Although it is against the law to knowingly enter a residence where a marketable quantity of a controlled substance is being stored," Sherman held up the bag to illustrate his point, "and I could arrest each of you, I'm going to let it go. Next time we won't be so lenient. My advice to each of you is to go home, take all of those things out of your pockets that you've been afraid we were going to catch you with and flush them down the toilet. The best way to stay cool is to stay clean."

Sherman turned and walked toward the stairs that led outside.

TWENTY SEVEN

"That's good to hear man," Jamie said into the phone. "We've got some other calls to make. No. Only Phiz was holding and he's taking care of it. If we hear anything more we'll let you know. Later."

Jamie hung the phone up and looked at Waltz, Lyle, and Nancy. "Lefty says nothing is going on over there. Scott said Angela is okay too, but I wasn't worried about her. She's never tried to sell anybody anything except the punchline to a bad joke."

"So it wasn't just Sherm the Sperm out busting people," Waltz said, "they must have had several crews out. Harvey says they also picked up that kid, Willie Something..."

"Willie Stardust?" Nancy said.

"Yeah, that tweek," Lyle said with a roll of his eyes. "And that guy McNulty calls "Newton von Tripp.""

"Oh, you mean Eugene Brown," Waltz said. "Has anybody heard from Shoes?"

"Lefty said they got the same thing we did when they called-no answer."

Lyle picked up the phone. "I'm gonna call Krenovich. He's still living at home isn't he?"

Lyle dialed a number and waited a bit while it rang. "Hi Mrs. K, this is Lyle Kirk. Is..."

Jamie, Waltz, and Nancy could overhear a woman's angry voice yelling vehemently on the other end of the line. Then there was a click and an obviously shaken Lyle hung up the phone.

"She said don't try to find him or talk to him. He's gone somewhere where filthy scum like me can no longer screw up his life."

"What the fuck does that mean?" Waltz said. "Not the filthy scum part, she knows you pretty well, but the part about him 'going somewhere?"

Lyle held up a fist in front of Waltz's face and pointed at it. Waltz gave him a slitty-eyed grin in return.

Then Nancy said, "Maybe he narked everybody out and decided it was time to split."

* * *

By the next afternoon, folks who'd been arrested were getting out on bail and filling in the gaps in the story. Moira and Victor, the couple Krenovich had been introducing around as his cousins, were actually a couple of drug-hating do-gooders that had been working with the police from the beginning. The cops had evidently had something to hold over Krenovich to make him co-operate. As well as Mike, Shoes had been pulled in. Four High School kids that Krenovich knew had gotten busted. When Eugene Brown and Willie Stardust were added in, eight people had been arrested and charged with selling drugs. The amounts purchased never exceeded two tabs of acid or one lid of weed.

Among the Hip Community, they became known as The Colton Eight.

Most of the defendants had asked parents or family to bail them out. At their arraignment, the Judge had set bail at $5000 for each of them. By the end of the day, everyone had gone home except Mike. Shoes had talked to Mike before getting out and told Jamie that Mike's prospects of getting sprung on bail looked pretty bleak.

"Mike's old man, on the phone, basically informed his son he could rot in jail for all he cared," Shoes had said. "When Mike tried to reason with him, his Dad hung up on him."

Jamie had asked, "What about his Mom? Or maybe there's another family member he might ask?"

"No help there. Mike said his mother would never think of crossing his Dad. There's an older sister, but if a lynch mob ever came after him, she would be the one holding the rope."

While Jamie was trying to figure out how to spring Mike, Angela must have gone over to the Berman's house after work and talked to Grace. The next day about noon as Jamie was making breakfast for himself and Phiz, Mike walked through the front door. Jamie put some more bacon pieces into the pan and two more slices of bread under the broiler.

In between bites of a bacon sandwich, Mike said he was fortunate the judge hadn't had time to check other states for priors or the bail would have been ridiculous.

"I guess I'm going to have to take a Public Defender for my lawyer," Mike said. "Since I haven't got a phone over at the Hellhole, I'll have to check in next week to see who they've got for me."

"How long before you go to court?" Phiz said.

"Damned if I know. In Arizona, I pled Guilty and found myself in the Slam before the judge could fart. Once I get a lawyer I'll probably go for Not Guilty here so it could take a while."

"It was nice of Grace Berman to go to bat for you."

"Yeah, no shit, she's the best. She not only bailed me out, but she and Angela took me home and fed me pancakes. With blueberries."

"Was Rachel there?" Jamie asked, "Is she okay?"

"She's still a little spooky around the edges, but she looks better than she did out at the quarry. Grace has got her seeing a Shrink twice a week. She's even started riding again."

That evening most of Jamie's meditation was taken up by thoughts of Sherm the Sperm and the long, hard look he'd given Jamie the night before.

Obviously, he recognized me from last Spring. Did that look mean, "Oh it's you" or was it "Ah-ha, it's that snotty punk who jerked me around. Well, you're next, Pal."

When Jamie finally realized he was thinking and he should get back to the mantra, he was five minutes over time. He scooted his butt down until he could stretch out full-length for a few minutes.

Wait and see, I guess. Just wait and see.

Twenty Eight

The Fall and Winter of 1969-70 seemed to slip by Jamie. He was determined to stay straight and sober, keep up his meditating twice a day, and put in his hours at the leather shop Tuesday through Saturday. Not that he was making a whole lot of money at his trade. After a busy first few weeks, almost everyone who had wanted to buy a belt or a headband had done so. But after that, there still remained a slow but steady trickle of customers and they kept generating enough business to barely pay the rent and keep him in cheap bacon sandwiches. He kept at it because he liked the work. It gave him someone to be. He felt much better about himself being "The Leather Guy" than he did when he was just "the dude who hangs out with Mike the Guitar Player" or "the cat that drives that funny-looking Volkswagen."

Mike was a little concerned after his arrest that Charlie Melman might evict him from the Hellhole. But since business not only did not drop off after the incident but actually picked up a little, Charlie decided, as he said to his partner Bill, to "go with the flow."

The second Friday Night in October, Jamie, Waltz, and Lyle helped the band move their equipment up the stairs and get it set up in one corner of the Head Shop for the agreed-upon mini-concert.

Several days earlier Mike had explained to Charlie that they'd only be able to play for about forty-five minutes. It wasn't from lack of desire, but what with both Mike and McNulty practicing and playing with Malcolm and the Prairie Rangers, they'd only had time so far to learn four songs.

"We can do some extended jams on a couple of blues lines and pad things out a little, but three-quarters of an hour is about as far as we can push it."

Charlie said that they would be "cool with that" but he did make one demand. Since he was going to do some publicity, the band had to come up with a name for themselves.

Mike asked the Family for suggestions, and the names proffered provided mostly merriment: The Dirty Rats, The Doorknobs, The Russian Army Chorus and Band, The Exhaust Pipes, and The Slime. Finally, a decision was made and the announcement went out that The Skid Marks would be playing a free mini-concert Friday Night at the Electric Rainbow.

As they positioned McNulty's bass amplifier and plugged it in, Waltz said, "Hey, Jamie, I didn't know Mike was a singer. Is he any good?"

Jamie looked confused but followed Waltz's gesture and saw Mike attaching a microphone to its stand in the front and center where he'd be standing.

"News to me," Jamie said. "He never sang with the Daffodils when I was working with them. But it being Mike and all, I'd be surprised if he sucked."

And he didn't, in fact, suck. Mike had a clear tenor and he could add a little vibrato on the ballads and a throaty rasp when he was singing the blues.

The four songs they had learned included Grand Funk Railroad's "Are You Ready?" Cream's "Sunshine of Your Love", Hendrix's "Foxy Lady", and Mike's Original Song "Steppin' In It." The band inserted one long blues jam after the first two songs and another at the end.

During the little concert, Charlie prowled around the store with a 35mm camera taking flash pictures of the band.

Throughout the last song, the three musicians took turns playing extended, freestyle solos. Mike beat on his instrument with his fist, played behind his head, and, suggestively, down low between his legs. McNulty's bass solo included a phrase from the Pink Panther Theme and the Roto-Rooter jingle and Anthony's drum solo featured a lot of flowery stick-twirling.

"I wonder if the Colton Marching Band wonders what happened to their Majorette?" Phiz yelled in Jamie's ear.

Just then a drumstick came sailing through the crowd just missing several people and left a permanent mark in a wooden wall panel.

"What the fuck was that?" Lyle shouted.

"Broken drumstick," Jamie shouted back. "Anthony once saw Carmine Appice throw a broken drum stick into the crowd during a Vanilla Fudge concert and thought it was cool."

Then the concert was over and Mike was thanking everyone for coming.

Jamie and Phiz had set up a small card table by the door and put a glass bowl on it with a sign that read, "Colton 8 Legal Defense Fund. Please donate." As people left, most of them ignored the bowl, a few made surly comments like, "Fuck that, man. A stretch in the Pen will do them good," But a few dollars did make their way into the collection. After the equipment had all been carried back downstairs, there was enough in the bowl to buy a little weed for the band and their friends.

Once again, Jamie declined the several joints that were being passed around and did so with an easy smile. But he had to acknowledge a slight, but growing, feeling inside himself that maybe the Family was just putting up with him.

Why do I keep going to the Amusement Park if I never want to ride the rides?

Telling everyone that he had to work in the morning, Jamie left early and went home alone.

About once a week Jamie would find himself at the Perkins Street House. Sometimes he'd be invited, sometimes he'd invite himself. Sometimes he'd bring Shoes along and sometimes he'd come alone. He was always welcome, especially when he'd bring some vegetables to contribute to the dinner table. He went not only because he enjoyed their company, but because he felt his meditations were deeper in the group than they were alone.

Now and then he'd ask Aaron how Madeleine was doing in Kentucky and then, almost idly, wonder if she'd heard anything from Lisa. The answer was usually that Madeleine was so busy taking care of her

Mother, who'd fallen apart at the news of her son's death, that she didn't have much time to stay connected with friends.

"That's such a drag for her," Jamie said, "and for you too. I imagine you're missing her a lot."

"That I am, my friend. That I am."

* * *

Jamie put the cap back on the bottle of dark brown leather dye and tried to clean his fingers with a rag. Ever since he'd started working with leather his hands had been stained with an ever-changing palette of earth-tone colors.

"I can't find anything that'll clean this shit off," he said.

Mike, perched on a stool on the other side of the worktable, laughed and said, "It's leather dye and leather is just another kind of skin, dig? If you really want to get it off, sandblasting would probably work."

Jamie gave his hands one last, disparaging look, then leaned back in his chair and put his feet up on the table.

"So, Mr. Harding," he said. "How are things going with that lawyer of yours? Have you managed to inveigle your way into her panties yet?"

When Mike had returned from his first meeting with his court-appointed attorney he was as giggly and awestruck as a schoolboy at a carnival. Instead of some hick local lawyer with a beer gut and an intolerant attitude, he found himself shaking hands with a tall, beautiful woman in a business suit with lots of leg coming out from under a short skirt. He became obsessed with the notion that to properly handle his case, she should sleep with him first.

"Biding my time, my friend, our day will surely come."

"When do you go to court?"

"It'll be a while. The Luscious Linda said she wants to wait until all the other trials have taken place so she can better tell what strategies play well with the different juries."

Mike switched to a cartoon-evil voice. "All the more time to spin my inescapable web, ah haha."

"Ah, the Master Plan, mwah ha ha," Jamie added in his own evil voice and both of them smirked and snickered as they rubbed their hands together in a slow, Vincent Prician way.

"What the fuck have you two been snorting?" Phiz said as he walked up.

"The crushed bones of small puppies," Jamie answered in the same voice.

Mike said, "if you want some you'll have to provide your own puppy," with an evil leer.

"Okay, I'll just go over and look at the hash pipes for a while and then come back again."

"No stay, stay," Jamie said. "What's up? And what's that in your hand?

"Check it out."

Jamie took the paper from Phiz, unfolded it, and read aloud.

"Order to Report for Induction" from the President of the United States Richard M. Nixon. Greetings..."

"Aw shit, man, that's a bummer," Jamie said, looking up. "When do you have to go?"

Phiz tapped a place on the letter, "November 10th. A little more than two weeks"

"What was your lottery number?" Mike said.

"Ninety-Three. In most places, that's high enough to skate by, but I registered in Montrose and they must have run short of bodies with lower numbers. But I'm not overly freaked. I've just got to come up with a good way to flunk the physical."

"Peanut butter," Mike said. "I heard about a guy who took about a teaspoon of peanut butter and covered his asshole with it. After a bunch of other stuff, they came to the part where all the draftees were told to line up, drop their underwear, bend over, and spread their cheeks. A doctor went down the line with a little flashlight thing looking for hemorrhoids. When he got to this guy, the Doc looked at the peanut butter, stood up, and said, 'Is that shit in your ass?' The guy scooped some out with a finger, stuck the finger in his mouth, and said, 'Yep.' He was on the first bus home."

Charlie Melman had wandered over to hear the story. When the laughter died down he said, "My brother swears he knows a guy who stuffed a mouse up his ass and left the tail hanging out. He was out of there and 4-F in a hurry."

More laughter and then Phiz said, "I ran into Motion on my way over here. I told him the deal and he suggested that I wait till I'm on the bus and then shoot up a near-overdose of smack. 'Don't do enough to kill yourself,' he told me, 'but close enough so when the bus pulls up to the Customs House, you'll be on the floor unconscious and foaming at the mouth. If they so much as touch you, you'll throw up. I guarantee they won't take you."

There was laughter again, but this time much more subdued and queasy.

Charlie again spoke up, this time directly to Phiz. "You know you could apply to be a Conscientious Objector. Colorado is one of the states that are cool about that. You'd have to agree to do two or three years of Community Service, though."

"You mean like cleaning turds out of bedpans at the Old Soldier's Home and shit jobs like that?" Phiz said. "I'd rather just get high, make art, and have them leave me alone. But thanks. I'll think about it."

Over the next couple of weeks, Phiz was thoughtfully listening to advice from all quarters that varied from hilarious to weird. Being a roommate, Jamie heard a lot of these suggestions, most of which Phiz discarded, but there were a few things that he wrote down and carefully considered.

On November 9th, most of the Family were grouped together at the bus stop to wish Phiz goodbye. The Government was paying not only for his bus fare to Denver, but for a bed overnight in a cheap hotel, and then a ride down to the Customs House where the Physical Exams were held. Although Phiz maintained that he'd be back in Colton in two days, there was much hugging with tears from the women and brusque takecare-ofyourselfs from the men.

Finally, Phiz jumped up on the first step, grinned, held up two fingers in the Peace sign, and then disappeared onto the bus.

* * *

Later that night, Jamie and Waltz were sitting in the living room listening to Crosby, Stills, and Nash when someone knocked softly on the door. Jamie flicked on the porch light, opened the door and a familiar-looking girl with blonde hair in a braid down her back was standing there.

"Hi Jamie," she said in a soft and slightly quivery voice, "I know it's late, but can I talk to you?"

By then, Jamie had recognized her as one of Nancy's friends from Casper. Not being sure if her name was Robin or Tammy, he said, "Why hey, how are you? Come on in. No, it's no problem, Waltz and I are both, like, doing the night owl thing. Come on into the kitchen, pull up a chair, and I'll make us a cup of tea."

Without a word, she headed for the kitchen. Jamie looked back at Waltz, winked, and followed the girl.

After he put the flame on under the little blue tea kettle, Jamie sat down across from the girl. She was red-eyed and trembling.

"Kinda bummed out, huh?" Jamie said, "You want to tell me about it?"

She started to cry and talk at the same time, so Jamie went to the storage cupboard, got out a roll of toilet paper, and set it down in front of her. She unrolled a good-size chunk, dabbed at her eyes and blew her nose.

"Sorry, this probably is going to sound stupid, but I went to the movies tonight with Tammy and a couple of other girls..."

Ah. So it must be Robin.

"...the movie was Easy Rider. Have you seen it?"

"Yeah. Very heavy film."

"Well, that's just it. When that terrible stuff happened at the end and these two guys I really liked got killed just like that... Anyway, I sort of lost it. I got back to the dorm and I couldn't sleep. I just kept thinking 'What are we doing? We think we can bring love and peace to the world and then these people will just shoot us.'"

The tea kettle started to whistle and Jamie busied himself making the tea. He put down two mugs of hot water on the table with a tea ball in each, then a saucer, spoon, and a plastic bear half full of honey as well. He sat back down, bobbed his tea ball up and down a couple of times, and then looked up at her.

"I told you it was stupid," she said.

"No Robin, it's not stupid, not at all. Tell me something though. Were you high when you saw the movie?"

She shrugged and said, "No. Well, maybe a little. Tammy and I had agreed to split one tablet of mescaline between us. But after I took my half, she chickened out. About twenty minutes later, I didn't feel anything so we went off to the movies. Then after the movie started, I began to feel a little weird but I didn't say anything."

Jamie nodded and finished for her, "and it wasn't until that heavy ending that you freaked out."

She nodded. Jamie smiled as he pulled the tea ball out of the cup and put it on the saucer, and then stirred a generous dollop of honey into his tea.

"First of all, it takes at least half an hour, sometimes longer, to get off on psychedelics, so I think you were definitely high by the time the movie got going. Second of all, psychedelic drugs turn the volume way up on the things you are feeling. But those feelings weren't stupid, they were, and are, absolutely honest and true. To live the way we choose to live is threatening to some small-minded people and in certain circumstances, it could get violent. But the thing is-you can't change the world without having courage. To stand for what we stand for is a brave thing to do. You see what I'm saying?"

Robin seemed to brighten up as she said, "You mean like David Crosby sings on the album your friend is listening to. You know... 'I felt like letting my freak flag fly."

"Exactly. Now say those last three words three times, quickly."

"Freak flag fly, freak frag fry, fleek fag fly..." she broke into happy laughter.

For the next half hour, they made silly jokes and did goofy improvisations. She did an impression of Nancy that was spot-on and made Jamie laugh. Then Jamie asked her if she was seeing anything that wasn't normally there and she said that other than the colors of everything seeming brighter, the world was pretty much the same.

"Are you, by any chance, an artist?" Jamie asked.

"Well, that would depend on the definition of 'Artist', which is a whole head trip by itself. But I would like to be one. That's what I'm studying in school. I love what color can do."

"Now that's very interesting. Do you know Phiz? He's an artist-mostly a pen and ink guy. But when he drops psychedelics, he doesn't see the crazy shit that the rest of us see. He says his 'hallucinator must be busted.' And then here you are and it seems like the same deal."

"What connection could that have?"

"You're both Art majors," Jamie said," maybe it's something parallel to the fact that most of the mentally unstable people on campus are Psychology majors."

"But that would mean... no, it might be... whoa!" she cried, holding her head as she shook it back and forth. "Too much information! Cannot compute!"

They laughed together and then Jamie said, "Sorry if I did your head. It was just a flash."

The phone rang and Waltz picked up the extension in the living room. A couple of minutes later, Waltz, holding his big black hat, came into the kitchen.

"That was Lyle. He's got a piano to move and needs my help."

"Good luck with that, man," Jamie said to Waltz's already retreating back.

"They're moving a piano?" Robin said, "At midnight?"

"Actually, it's Waltz's code for 'Nancy has gone home and now he and Lyle are going to get loaded.' Probably on speed."

When Robin showed a slightly shocked expression, Jamie added, "And don't mention it to Nancy, okay? She wouldn't be pleased."

"You guys... Jeez. Okay, mum's the word. You know, before tonight I thought that getting high all the time was kind of silly. Like, there's more important stuff, you know? And then tonight I got really scared, but now I feel really good and I can kind of see it. Am I making sense at all?"

"Enough I guess. If I were high too, it would probably be crystal clear."

"How often do you, what's the expression, get loaded?"

"For about two months now, I've been straight as an arrow. I've popped no pill, nor smoked no joint. I've got my head into a new space and in order to stay there I'm thinking I have to stay unstoned."

Jamie put more hot water into the mugs, put the tea-balls back in to steep, and told her about Laaghava Meditation and how the two-week drug-free period had turned into two months.

"The first month or more was pretty cool. My meditations were really nice, like settling into a soft, silent, warm blanket. And there was a sweet, alls-well-with-the-world feeling afterward. Lately, I guess I've been going through a rough patch. My meditations are boring and restless. I can't seem to settle down. I feel okay afterward, but not as good as before. My meditating friends Quentin, Polly, and Sarah say I'm just working some stuff out and it'll get better but what do they know? They started on the same day I did."

Jamie went silent and was making little circles with his finger in a drop of spilled tea. Robin reached over and covered his hand with hers. When he looked up and gave her a crooked smile, she bent to him and kissed him softly on the mouth.

Jamie cleared his throat and said, "Listen. I know they lock the doors of your dorm at what? 11-11:30? Would you like to spend the night here? With me?"

She nodded and kissed him again. He stood up, took her hand, and led her to his bedroom.

* * *

When Robin had appeared on his doorstep that night and for the first few minutes she was with him in the kitchen, Jamie saw her only as somebody who needed some company. But after she had relaxed and begun to laugh and smile a lot, a desire to have hot, monkey sex with her had started to glow in his groin and from there grew only stronger.

But now that most of her clothes were off and she'd shaken her hair out of the braid, in his eyes, she had become enchanting and delicate. He mostly wanted to admire her, touch her, and to kiss her gently. Her body he found delightful. Her breasts were small and shapely, but the aureoles were not flat pink circles, they were convex and rounded with the nipple sitting on top like a jaunty little party hat.

He cupped her face in his hands, kissed her, and let his fingers trace around the curves of her body. The tips of their tongues touched, caressed each other, and then shyly retreated.

A thought came to Jamie and he sat back against the headboard. "Do you have any, like, protection? You know, from pregnancy?"

Robin looked confused and then brightened up.

"Oh, I see what you're saying. Yeah, I do. And I'm glad you mentioned it, I would have spaced out on it for sure. One of the girls in the dorm gave me a birth control pill and I've been carrying it in my purse, just in case."

She turned to get out of bed, but Jamie put his hand on her shoulder and turned her back around.

"Robin, wait a second. We need to talk. You don't know a lot about how birth control pills work, do you?"

Robin shook her head.

"When a woman gets pregnant, her body releases hormones which are like messages to the ovaries. They say 'Stop sending those eggs down, guys. We've got something going on here.' And the woman stops ovulating and as long as she's pregnant, the hormones that say 'no eggs, please' continue to be released. The Pill mimics those hormones and their messages. But you gotta take one every day for a month to make sure no eggs are coming down the chute right when you want to have sex. I'm sorry but one pill isn't going to have any effect at all."

Robin was looking disappointed. "How do you know so much about it?"

"I had a girlfriend a few months ago who told me to read up on it. She said it was just as much my responsibility as it was hers. And she was right."

"So you're not going to ball me?"

"No. We are not going to ball each other. At least not tonight. I don't have any rubbers so..."

"So what do we do?"

"That mescaline isn't going to let you fall asleep for a few hours and I'll try to stay up with you as long as I can. We could start with you telling me your life story."

"No way. That'll put you to sleep with boredom. Do you have a deck of cards?"

Jamie scurried out of bed and dug through his bottom dresser drawer. He stood up holding a pack of cards and a cribbage board.

"You play cribbage?"

"My family has a little cabin up on Casper Mountain. We go up there and have cribbage marathons. I'll mop the floor with you."

"Oh, ya think so, eh? But what you didn't know is we're going to play Backwards Strip Cribbage. We start naked and every ten hands we stop and whoever is behind has to put something on that belongs to the other person."

"Okay, Mr. Crazyman," Robin laughed. "I'll set the board up and you shuffle."

As Jamie pulled the cards out of the pack he looked at her and said, "I'll tell you the truth. The way you look right now... I hope I lose."

* * *

It was pushing noon when Jamie finally dragged his butt out of bed. Robin had, as she predicted, beaten him badly at cribbage. He had ended up with her bra on his head like a double beanie, her top slung rakishly around his neck, and her bell bottoms tied around his waist like an apron. She had to chase him, giggling, around the house to get them back. He put on the Little Bear mask and tried to chase her, but the eyeholes were too small and he kept running into things. Finally, they cuddled under a blanket while they played the Crosby, Stills, and Nash record several times, especially "Guinevere" and "My Lady of the Island."

The last thing he remembered was seeing a soft light growing in the East. He had promised her he'd make her some breakfast; he just needed to rest a few minutes.

There was a note on the dresser.

"Jamie," it said, "Thank you for all the sweet fun. I had a wonderful time. Robin. 675-8832."

* * *

Jamie had been home from the Electric Rainbow for about half an hour that evening when Phiz came walking through the door.

"Hot damn, man!" Jamie whooped. "They didn't take you!"

"Not even my little pinkie!"

Waltz and Lyle came hurrying from the kitchen to shake Phiz's hand and slap him on the back. Both of them, still speeding from the night before, were simultaneously asking him how he'd managed to do it.

It wasn't until everyone was sitting comfortably and Waltz was rolling a joint, that Phiz told his story.

"First I tried to flunk the hearing test. A guy had told me to do one ear as best I could, but then on the other ear only push the button now and then on the high tones and never on the really high ones. They stopped the test in the middle and told me they knew I was faking it, so fuck me and they were going to give me a passing grade. I wasn't too worried because I thought I'd for sure flunk the urine test. I had a pin stuck into the waistband of my underwear. All I had to do was pee in the cup, poke my finger with the pin, and squeeze in a few drops of blood. So what did I do? Old Fumblefingers drops the fucking pin into the urinal. About then I started to hear the whine of bullets in the jungle. There was only one chance left for me and I took it. I told them I was a fag."

"Wait," said Lyle, "you told them what?"

"A fag, you know, a queer. A homosexual."

"What happened?"

"They took me aside and had me fill out another form.'Do you feel sexually attracted to men?' Yes. 'Have you had sex with other men?' Yep. 'Do you blah blah blah... I signed it and half an hour later I was walking out the door."

Jamie and the others were a little taken aback.

Waltz leaned forward, "I heard that they take all the guys that say that and lock them in the same room for a night. They knew the fakers will soon be beating on the door begging to be let out."

"That's such bullshit," Phiz rolled his eyes. "That's just straight people scared of what they don't understand and making up stories."

"But won't that follow you for the rest of your life?"

"More bullshit. 4-F is 4-F, and nobody will ever ask why."

"Unless you ever wanted to run for office," Lyle said. "Somebody'd dig it up and then everybody would flip out."

Phiz put an agonized look on his face. "And I wanted to be the fucking Grand Poobah of the Western Slope! I'm so bummed."

"Well man, congratulations!" Jamie said. "I think we should get some hippos over here tonight and have a party!"

* * *

Though perhaps not among the Great Parties of 1969, the party that night at Fifth Street was crowded and loud enough to be considered for Honorable Mention. Almost all of the Family had shown up to celebrate

Phiz's rejection from the US Military. Even Harvey and his Old Lady Jacqueline were there and they rarely went anywhere.

So why am I not enjoying this as much as I think I should be? I feel like I've backed up a step and I'm looking at my friends from a distance like I'm some kind of fucking anthropologist. Well, fuck that.

He finished his beer, set the can down on the coffee table, and noticed that Phiz had just taken a big toke on a joint and was passing it to Lefty. So Jamie casually walked over and stood next to Lefty. When Lefty had taken his lungful of smoke, he passed the joint to Jamie who, instead of just passing it along, put the number up to his lips and drew in a good-sized hit.

The smoke sidled into his bloodstream like a ne'er-do-well Uncle into a chair at Sunday Dinner. He had passed on the joint and was relishing the old familiar changes in his consciousness when he looked up and noticed several people staring at him.

"It's a special occasion," he explained. "The Buddha Man hasn't split the scene entirely; he's just taking a break for a night."

"And leaving Mr. Mushbrain in his place," Lyle reached for the joint.

Everyone laughed, Jamie along with them. After he'd had a few more hits, Jamie was feeling stoned enough to notice his mouth was drying up and he made his way to the kitchen for another beer. He'd just pulled the pop top and tossed it in the trash when he realized Nancy was standing in the doorway looking at him.

"Hey Nancy," he said. "How's your beautiful self?"

"I talked to Robin this afternoon. She told me what a good time you guys had last night."

"Yeah, she's fun."

"She was a little hurt you didn't invite her to this party. She thought you liked her."

"Well, I did. I do. But last night was just kidding around, you know? Like I didn't ball her or anything."

"Robin is a dear friend of mine, Jamie Shipman. If you break her heart I'll kick you so hard you'll be wearing your testicles for earrings."

The threat created some truly horrific mental images that Jamie was still trying to get out of his head when he came upon Mike talking with

Shoes and a tall, lanky guy with half-closed eyes and a wispy goatee. The latter was in the midst of making a point.

"...my Dude says we'll find out at the trip."

Mike said, "The what?"

"The trip. You know, man, the trip. The Preliminary Hearing."

Jamie realized this must be Eugene Brown, and why McNulty called him Newton VonTripp.

"Ah, that trip," Mike said. "Yeah, the Luscious Linda told me the same thing."

Mike noticed Jamie looking puzzled, "Because they're not sure how many trials there'll be, they have at least a couple of judges lined up. Who gets which judge could be important."

"How about you, man?" Brown said to Shoes, "What's your Dude say about the trip?"

"If y'all mean my lawyer, I haven't really signed one yet. I made some phone calls, talked to some people and I came up with a name. Ronald Bascomb. He's a hotshot defense attorney. I've heard he's never lost a case. His office in Denver has the information, they say he's looking at it and I should know soon."

"Bulldog Bascomb?" Phiz said. He'd heard the name as he was going by and stopped. "My parents know him. They say he eats Prosecutors for breakfast."

"Yeah, they told me that, too," Shoes said. "Your Mom was one of the people I called for a referral."

Jamie noticed Angela, Scott, and Rachel had recently arrived, and he went over to say hello. Just as he got there a stranger with curly hair and thick glasses came up from the other direction carrying two glasses and a giant clear plastic bottle of Pepsi.

"I found a couple of glasses in the cupboard," the stranger handed one to Rachel. "There doesn't seem to be any ice so we'll have to drink it warm."

As the guy was filling her glass with Pepsi, Rachel looked up at Jamie and smiled.

"This is my friend Asa Rothman," she said. "Asa, this is Jamie."

"Glad to meet you, Asa," Jamie said. They shook hands. "I've never seen a giant bottle of Pepsi like that. Where'd you get it?"

"Safeway," Asa filled his own glass. "The stockboy said it was a brand new thing. It seemed easier than trying to schlep around a bunch of glass Coke bottles, so here we are." He handed the bottle to Jamie for inspection. "We figured there'd be nothing here to drink but beer and Rachel and I are teetotalers now."

"Well, Scott and I aren't," Angela said." And I could use a beer, where are you keeping them?"

"In the fridge," Jamie said. "Help yourself."

Scott carried all four coats into a bedroom while Angela headed for the kitchen.

"Asa and I met at the 12-step meetings." Rachel said. "He's an alcoholic, I'm an addict. He keeps me clean and I keep him sober."

"I'm a Graduate Assistant in the Physics Department here at Colton," Asa said. "They nearly booted me out for showing up to teach a class drunk. But instead, they said 'Get thee to a 12 Step Program.' That was five months and fifteen days ago."

"So are you guys, like... you know, together? Or just mutually supportive pals?"

"We don't know," Rachel said as she took Asa's hand and squeezed it. "We're just taking it one day at a time."

"So how's Grace doing with all this?"

"Are you kidding?" Rachel laughed, "He's Jewish. Mom's over the moon."

Hours later when the beer and weed had run out and everybody had gone home, Jamie sat in the darkened living room in his underwear, finishing off the last of the Pepsi from the big plastic bottle.

He wasn't feeling very good about himself after talking to Rachel and Asa and carrying on about how proud he was of their sobriety while all the while he himself had just taken a swan dive off the wagon.

On the other hand, it's not like I'm a stumbling drunk or a hopeless junkie. Why can't I be a meditator who just happens to smoke a little pot? On the weekends, maybe, while I meditate during the week. Nothing wrong with that. I've heard there are monasteries in India where the monks smoke hashish day and night. It's like a sacrament for them to help them get Enlightened. So that'll be me-no women and a little weed-the stoned monk.

Feeling somewhat cheered up, he tossed the empty bottle into the trash and went off to bed.

* * *

It was nearly two weeks later that Jamie gave Robin a call. He'd been hoping that she would give up on him and move on, but that afternoon he'd gone to lunch with Waltz and Phiz and afterward found a note from Robin on his work table.

"Well," Robin said when she heard his voice, "what a surprise. It knows how to use the phone after all."

"Ouch. I deserved that. I should have called earlier. Sorry. No excuse. Can I see you tomorrow?"

"I'm leaving tomorrow afternoon to go back up to Casper for Thanksgiving with my family."

"Then how about tomorrow morning at Campus Coffee? About Eleven?"

When Jamie walked into the little coffee shop, Robin was already sitting in a booth stirring cream and sugar into her cup. He took off his fatigue jacket with the gold stars on the collar and slid into the seat across from her.

After the waitress had taken his order, Jamie said, "That night when you were feeling bad and couldn't sleep, how come you picked me to talk to?"

"Nancy," she said. "When you and Nancy were together last summer, she told me what a good guy you were. Kind and caring and a good listener. So I got your address from the phone book. I must've stood outside your house for ten or fifteen minutes getting up the courage to knock on the door. I wasn't disappointed."

"Yep, that's me. Kind and caring. And Nancy dumped me for a surly speed freak within a few weeks."

"Well, maybe that's just Nancy."

"And every other girl I've gotten next to since I came here. Most of them I've been able to get over and move on. One of them hasn't been that easy."

"The one you married?"

"You mean Angela? You heard about that, huh? No, actually both of us pretty quickly figured out we'd made a mistake. But there was still a lot of emotional craziness to go through. We're still good friends. Like a couple of old war veterans who had made it through the Battle of the Bulge together."

Robin smiled at that. Then a sad look came into her eyes.

"So you're just going to throw us out the window without even giving it a chance?" she said.

"I just know that sooner or later I'd let you down, Robin. Sex, for instance. I'm not very good in bed. I come too quickly. No matter how much I try to control myself it's 'Slam, Bam, Thank you, Ma'am' and nothing left for you but disappointment."

Robin just looked down into her coffee while she stirred it, but she didn't take a sip.

"Speaking of sex," Jamie asked, "did you find out about the pill?"

"Yes, I read up on it and I decided I didn't want some weird chemicals messing up my body..."

"But-" Jamie started and she held up a hand.

"...so I went to a gynecologist in Boulder and got fitted for a diaphragm."

"Well good. Good for you."

"I'm going to go now," Robin said, "thanks for talking to me and letting me know what's what."

She stood up, put her coat on, and wound a scarf around her neck."

"One more thing," she said. "That problem of yours? I think you might be able to do something about it. But first, you have to find a girl who'd be willing to work on it with you. And then you'd have to have the courage to ask her to do so. Kindness and caring are good things to give, but you also have to be able to receive them back. Goodbye, Jamie."

Jamie watched her walk out the door. Long after she had gone, he was still staring at the empty doorway.

TWENTY NINE

"With us, it's potitsa," Waltz's new girlfriend Katie Potochnik said. "Every year my grandma rolls out this thin dough until it's about six feet long. Then she sprinkles cinnamon and sugar and chopped nuts and stuff on it and rolls it up tight. The dough is so thin that rolled up it's still only about as big around as your forearm. A slice of that, fresh-baked and still warm will just about curl your toes up."

The mere thought of it made Jamie's mouth water and the grunts of assent around the room let him know he was not alone.

"My mother," Lefty said as he reloaded the little soapstone pipe with a dark brown chunk of hashish, "makes Santa Claus sugar cookies every year. When they're fresh, and you have a glass of cold milk to dunk 'em in, they are so freakin' good."

"Jesus Max! You guys are killing me," Mike complained, laughing. "Here's a room full of stoned heads in a house completely empty of food, and what do they talk about? What their families' favorite treats at Christmas are! Well, every year my Mom makes sticky pecan rolls and my Old Man, the asshole, eats about half the pan and then bitches about how they make his teeth stick together."

When the laughter died down, Jamie said, "If my Grandmother wasn't old and senile, I'd be happy to treat you folks to the best goddamn fudge in the universe-Grandma's Secret Fudge."

"What does her feebleness have to do with it?" Phiz asked. "Did she drop it or something?"

"Or maybe that's the secret," Waltz said. "She kicks it around the floor a few times to give it that extra crunch!"

"No, asshole. I think she sent it to the wrong address again. Last year I told her I was here in Colton, but she sent my box of fudge to Iowa and my Dad ate it. I wrote to her a month ago and again explained that I had moved and what my address here in Colton was, but... no Grandma's Secret Fudge. And that shit is really good too."

Katie broke into Jamie's lament. "Is her name Hartman?"

"Yeah."

"And she lives in Minnesota?"

"Yep. Pelican Falls."

"Yesterday Kenny and I were here only he was in the bathroom and there was a knock on the door. You remember, Kenny?"

"I remember being in the bathroom for a while."

"Well it was the Postman and he gave me a package for you, Jamie. It had Christmas stamps on it so I put it under the tree."

A few days before, Jamie, Phiz, and Waltz had come across a funny little pine tree in the back yard of what looked to them like an abandoned house. So they'd cut it down, dragged it home, and decorated it. Phiz had made folded paper ornaments, Jamie had cut stars out of scrap leather, and Waltz had found a string of colored lights in his parents' garage.

It took a few moments for Jamie's foggy brain to connect the words that Katie was saying, but when the gears finally meshed, he lurched over to the tree and scrabbled at the packages underneath it. Knowing that they probably weren't going to get many presents, they'd wrapped some empty boxes with colored paper just for effect.

Jamie had found the package and was ineffectually pulling at the string tied around it when Mike opened a pocket knife and handed it to him. Once the string was cut and the package opened quickly; there, arranged around pieces of nougat and dried figs with blanched almonds stuck in them, were nine pieces of Grandma's Secret Fudge.

There happened to be nine people in the room and if any of them wondered at the coincidence, the thought was soon drowned in astonishing, chocolaty goodness. Those who had popped the pieces whole into their mouths found themselves wishing they had taken measured bites instead and looked lustfully at the remaining parts held by those who had. The fudge was quickly gone and only groans of pleasure remained.

"Okay," McNulty said, "I give up. Why is it called Grandma's Secret Fudge?"

Jamie licked his fingers and then dried them on his pants. "Because she won't tell anybody just how the hell she makes it."

* * *

Lyle, Nancy, Jamie, and Mike were standing near the door.

"I hear you two are moving in together," Mike said to Lyle and Nancy. "When's this supposed to happen?"

"We've got to find a place first," Lyle said.

"And being this close to Christmas, it may not be so easy," Nancy added. "But it would nice to be all moved in before school starts again in January."

After they had left, Jamie turned to Mike, "Didn't I see Shoes here earlier talking to you? When I came over to say hello he'd already split."

"Yeah, he was here. Laid a bizarre thing on me about his lawyer. Then he went over to talk to what's-his-face Brown."

"What was this thing?"

"Uh... What thing? Oh, you mean the lawyer thing. It seems Shoes went down to Denver today to meet with Bulldog Bascomb. He must be a busy dude, man. It took a month for Shoes to get in to see him. But here's the deal. Bascomb told Shoes he'd take his case. He said he'd read the documents, he was royally pissed off, and it was obvious to him that some fat old farts, like the local Police Chief and the D.A., were doing this solely to score political points and were happy to ruin the lives of eight local kids in the process.

"Bascomb said that he'd take all of our cases, all eight of us, for free. All except Shoes. He has to pay the full fee because he was the one who made the original contact."

"What did you say?"

"I asked him to give me some time to mull it over. It's an intriguing thought, man. This Bascomb guy is a showboat. Like he wears western suits with cowboy boots and a ten-gallon hat. He's a big, loud, opinionated dude who'd turn the courtroom into a circus. Nothing like the Chicago Seven Trial, but still it could be, like, national news. And that wouldn't do my career any harm at all, you know?"

"But first you'd have to be acquitted."

"Yeah. That's the fuckin' scary part. With this Bascomb cat, I don't think there'd be any quiet fuckin' plea deals. I'd have to get on his stagecoach and ride it to the end of the line. I'd either walk free or do hefty time in the Pen. No middle ground.

"The Luscious Linda, on the other hand, thinks there's a good chance it could all go away. The Judge we were assigned to is Harley T. Buford. He's an old-time Socialist who started by lawyering for the Unions back in the Depression. He's like 70 years old or so, but still thinks that bright, repentant, young people can rehabilitate themselves on parole, but not in prison."

"So she wants you to plead 'guilty,'" Jamie said, "and throw yourself on the mercy of the court."

"I'd have a big old felony on my record, but I wouldn't have to do any time. I may have mentioned before how it wasn't any fun being in jail? Well, the truth is way worse than that. Six weeks just damn near killed me. If I had to do a year or two, I'd go stark, fuckin' mad. I can't go back inside, man, I just can't."

* * *

Several days later Jamie fished the last square of nougat out of the box that his grandmother had sent and popped it into his mouth. When he tossed the empty box in the trash, he noticed that there was a handwritten note tucked under the bottom layer of tissue paper.

"Dear Jamie," the note read, "I hope you enjoy these Christmas treats and are having a lovely Holiday. I'm afraid this year will be the last time I will be able to make and send the candy. I've got the Arthritis in my hands and it hurts too much to do all the work. So from now on, you'll have to make your own fudge. If you want to know the recipe, just buy a bottle of Marshmallow Creme at the grocery store. The recipe is on the back label. Love, Your Grandma."

* * *

Jamie got out of the Volkswagen, zipped his parka up and headed for the barn. There wasn't much snow on the ground, but it was cold enough to make the hoarfrost crunch under his feet and his breath form clouds of steam in the air. He opened a side door in the barn and stepped inside. It wasn't as cold in the structure and there was a pleasant earthy smell to the place.

He walked down a central aisle admiring the horses in the stalls on each side. Suddenly a large bale of hay dropped to the wooden floor next to him and made him jump back and scream.

"Whoa! Sorry, man, I didn't see you." A voice came from above him, "You okay?"

Jamie looked up to see a tall, young man with a droopy mustache. He had long hair coming out from under a cowboy hat. He was standing at the edge of a loft and there was a big stack of hay bales behind him.

"Yeah, I'm okay." Jamie checked himself for injuries and found none. "But I'm probably going to have to hose out my shorts later. You're Malcolm Tingley, right?"

"That's me," Malcolm lowered himself down a wooden ladder.

"My name's Jamie. Angela wanted me to come out and see you."

"You're the guy that makes the leather stuff down at the head shop, right? Check it out."

Malcolm held up his arm. A heavy leather wristband was buckled there. Jamie could remember making it and then adapting it to hold a watch face. He smiled and nodded.

"So what's Angela up to?" Malcolm slung the hay bale into a wheelbarrow and cut the twine. "I haven't seen her since before she pulled that damfool gettin' married stunt."

Jamie quickly ran through his list of snappy comebacks, couldn't come up with anything appropriate, and decided to just let it go.

"It's about Rachel. She's disappeared and Angela thought, because you're taking care of her horse, she may have been out here."

"No, she stopped comin' out here once it got cold," Malcolm said. "Since you're here you want to give me a hand? See how the bale can be separated into two-inch chunks? They're called flakes. In the far corner of every stall with a horse inside there's a hay trap, put three flakes in each one."

As Malcolm walked down the aisle with three flakes under his arm he yelled back, "What happened with Rachel?"

Jamie pulled three flakes from the bale, popped the catch on the nearest stall with a horse in it, went in, and closed the door behind him. He waited till the animal had moved to the other side of the stall, then crossed to the hay trap and stuffed the flakes in from the top. All the time he did so he was murmuring reassuringly to the horse.

"Atsa good boy, atsa good horse, yes."

When he came out into the aisle and latched the stall door behind him, Malcolm was already back at the wheelbarrow.

"She'd moved out of her parents' house and in with a guy called Asa Rothman," Jamie reached for more hay. "Two days ago they had a fight, Rachel walked out, and nobody has seen her since."

Malcolm gave him an appraising look. "You ever worked with horses before?"

"Not for a long time. When I was a kid in Iowa I went to Camp Wah-Nee-Ay-Gah every summer. I hung around the stable as much as they'd let me."

"Wah-Nee-Ay-Gah, eh?" Malcolm laughed and peeled off three more flakes. "Can you ride?"

"I s'pose I still can. Angela said she tried to call you but got no answer."

Jamie had to shoulder an over-eager horse out of the way as he tucked three more flakes into a feeder.

"No phone in the barn. I've been working out here most all morning. See that bay mare in the number two stall?"

Jamie walked up and looked over the top of the stall door. A beautiful brown horse with a black mane, tail, and legs looked back at him.

"That's Missy, Rachel's horse," Malcolm said. "A trained riding horse needs to be ridden at least once a week or they go all froggy on you. I try to get on her when I can, but it's not often enough. If you ever have an hour or two sometime you'd be welcome to come out and ride her."

"Really? Thanks, man. But the thing is I don't know how to put on a saddle or a bridle."

"Come out sometime and I'll show you how. It ain't rocket surgery. But for now, I think you'd better go back into town and tell Angela that I saw Motion on that big 750 Norton of his yesterday afternoon. Rachel was hanging on behind him."

* * *

Jamie, Waltz, Katie, Harvey, and Jacqueline, taking up more than half a row of seats in the small County Courtroom, were listening to Bulldog Bascomb cross-examine the first witness, Fiona Blair. During her testimony, she had related how she and her husband had gone to the apartment of Winslow Schumacher and purchased two tablets of LSD for which they had paid $8.00.

"Just for the record Mrs. Blair," Bascomb said, "Winslow Schumacher is presently in the courtroom. Would you point him out for the jury?"

Just before the trial began when the defense team seated themselves, Jamie tried to catch Shoes' eye to let him know they were there. He realized that the guy who'd sat down next to Bascomb wasn't his friend at all. This guy had long, straight, black hair and a scraggly beard just like Shoes wore, even had on Shoes' old jacket, but it sure wasn't Shoes.

Jamie mentioned it to Waltz who finally spotted Shoes sitting in the front row. He had gotten a short, conservative haircut, was clean-shaven, and wore a dark suit with a tie.

Fiona Blair sat fidgeting in the witness chair and when Bascomb asked her to point Shoes out, she made a show of squinting carefully around the room before she pointed a finger at the unknown fellow next to Bascomb.

"That's him."

"Let the record show that the witness pointed out Mr. Ralph Teesdale, lately of Denver, Colorado."

The Prosecution objected, the Judge let it stand, and the Witness watched with nervous indignation as Teesdale and Shoes switched places.

"Now then Mrs. Blair, would you mind telling the court what happened once Mr. Schumacher let you into his apartment?"

"He got out a little bottle, tapped two blue tablets into a baggie, we gave him eight bucks and he gave us the stuff."

"And nothing was said?"

"Oh. Well, Danny K introduces us, says we're okay, then we say 'have you got any stuff?' and he says 'no' and we say 'c'mon man, we really need to get high." And then Danny K takes him aside..."

"I'm sorry to interrupt Mrs. Blair, but who is this 'Danny K?'"

The Prosecution again objected and was again overruled.

"Danny K?" Bascomb prompted.

"He was a guy who was a friend of Schumacher's but was secretly working for the Police. We never knew his full name."

"Oh, I see. It took three of you, all secretly working for the Colton Police, to convince Mr. Schumacher to sell you the pills?"

"I guess you could say that."

Bascomb took a long pause to look around the courtroom with an apologetic smile, especially to the jury, before he said, "Mrs. Blair, are you aware of the legal term Entrapment?"

The courtroom buzzed as the Prosecutor jumped up to object that the witness was not a lawyer. The judge agreed with him and asked that the last question and answer be stricken from the record.

The Prosecutor and his assistant put their heads together with the Chief of Police and then asked the Judge for a sidebar in his chambers.

"There will be a ten-minute recess" the Judge announced. Then he, Bascomb, the Prosecutor, and the Recorder all filed out through a back door.

"What's all that about?" Katie asked Waltz and Jamie.

Waltz just turned his hands palm up. Jamie said, "I'm not sure but the Prosecution must be freaked out. Bascomb is kicking that little narc-chick's ass up and down the courthouse steps."

Harvey leaned around Jacqueline and said, "Hey, man. Where's Lyle and everybody?"

Waltz answered, "Lyle's selling somebody a car over at the lot. He couldn't get off. McNulty and Lefty are freezing their asses off out at the sawmill."

"Mike's lawyer told him to stay away," Jamie said. "Judging by this so far, I think he's going to wish he'd gone with Bascomb."

Katie looked puzzled and said, "Where would he go with Bascomb?"

Waltz carefully explained Bascomb's offer of an all-inclusive deal.

"Mike decided to turn the offer down and stay with his original lawyer," Waltz said. "The other six did the same."

A couple of minutes later, the missing people filed back into the room and took their seats. Bascomb turned to Shoes and began explaining something to him. After a couple of minutes, Shoes smiled, nodded

280 | Tim Pelton

his head and said "yes." Bascomb nodded to the Prosecutor who stood and addressed the Judge.

"Your Honor, with the approval of the Defendant and Counsel, The State moves for an Open-Ended Continuance."

"Motion granted," said the Judge. "Ladies and Gentlemen of the Jury, you are released from duty, thank you for your service. Court is adjourned."

The Judge banged his gavel down and everyone got up and put on their coats and mufflers.

Jamie and his friends made their way up to the front of the Gallery behind the Defendant's Table. Shoes was shaking hands with Bulldog Bascomb who then snapped his briefcase shut, put his Stetson on his head, and walked for the exit.

"Dude," Jamie said to Shoes, "what's an Open-Ended Continuance? Is it good?"

Shoes was grinning as wide as his mouth would go. "The best," he said. "It means that if I stay out of trouble for a year, they'll drop the case entirely. Like it never happened. My record will be squeaky clean."

"Wow! That's great! Congratulations, man!" everybody shouted at once. There were hugs and handshakes and beats on the back.

Then Shoes said, "It's too bad for Mike and the rest though, as part of the deal Bascomb had to agree to go back to Denver and to not represent any of the other seven.

After a pause, Harvey said, "Party tonight at my place?"

"How about instead all y'all take me to Ziggy's tonight. I feel like getting happily, and legally, shitfaced," Shoes said. "I've made up my mind I'm going to Law School someday. I want to be able to do... that."

He gestured to the courtroom. Everybody knew what he meant.

THIRTY

Missy was back in her stall. Jamie had taken the saddle and blanket off and, remembering Malcolm's instructions, had swapped the bridle for a headstall and was brushing the horse down.

The ride had been pleasant as it wound around the town and by the campus, then back again. It was a warm day for March, enough so that Jamie had even had to take his jacket off and tie it around his waist. Most of the time he'd held the horse to a walk. He wasn't a big fan of trotting, the gait bounced him up and down right on his balls.

Next time I come out I've got to remember to wear a jock strap. No wonder cowboys wear tight jeans.

He let the reins out one time and Missy responded with enough speed to scare him into pulling her in again. Thinking of gopher holes and broken legs, he had walked her back to the barn.

When Jamie came through the door of the little farmhouse, Malcolm and Mike were noodling on guitars, Mike on electric and Malcolm on flat-top, throwing little riffs back and forth.

"Hey Jamie," Mike said, "Listen to this." He turned to Malcolm and said, "From the top, okay? One... two..."

"With every lie you tell,
With every dream you sell
You know you get yourself in deeper.
I only wanted you,
Someone who'd love me true
And not a phony or a cheater."

The music segued back to the beginning of the verse, then stopped.

"What do you think, man?" Mike grinned. "Harding and Tingley – Songwriters."

"I dig it," Jamie said. "It's like Poco or The Flying Burrito Brothers. Very cool."

"Oh yeah, damn near ready to record!" Malcolm said. "All it needs is a chorus with a strong guitar hook, a good release in the middle, a tasty instrumental break, maybe some clever lyrics. No problem. Speaking of lyrics, I'm not too crazy about that last line. Phony and cheater are two different things, you know?"

Jamie looked thoughtful and said. "How about 'and not a storytellin' cheater?'"

Malcolm and Mike looked at each other with eyebrows raised, strummed their guitars and sang the last lines with Jamie's modified lyrics.

"Shit," Malcolm said in mock-exasperation, "Now we've gotta fit 'Tingley, Harding, and Shipman' on the record label."

"Nah, forget it, man. Sing it with my blessing. Just remember to give me a pair of well-worn panties from one of your groupies to pull over my face when I sleep."

Malcolm laughed and shook his head.

"So how'd you and Missy do?"

"Really well," Jamie answered. "I've been kinda bummed for the past few days. There was some harsh shit. The ride picked me up."

"You mean the Rachel thing? You were there?"

"Yeah, I went along, but I didn't go inside. I stayed out in the car with Grace Berman. Angela was afraid she might freak out and run inside. Angela, Scott, and Asa went in. Evidently, Motion just sat there watching TV like he could give a shit while they dragged Rachel out of bed, got her dressed, and walked her out the door. Just as they were leaving Motion demanded eighty bucks for the smack Rachel had snorted up and Scott told him to go fuck himself."

Mike barked a laugh. "Man, if Scott Mallory told me to go fuck myself, I'd be saying 'yes, sir' and pulling down my pants. He can be a scary dude."

"Being six-three and a Golden Gloves boxer can give a guy that vibe."

"So what's going to happen to Rachel?" Malcolm fitted his guitar into its case.

"The Bermans found a clinic down by Colorado Springs called Sunny Hill. They specialize in addiction rehab. She'll probably be there for at least a couple of months."

Jamie had his hands in his pockets and was looking down at his feet.

"I thought being on that horse made you feel better, man. What's with the long face?" Malcolm asked.

"I don't know, maybe I'm fuckin' crazy. But with all this shit going down about heroin, rather than making me want to avoid the stuff, I'm thinking I'd like to do some up."

"You've never done heroin?" Malcolm seemed astonished.

"Nope. I've dropped a ton of acid, shot up speed, done reds and yellows, smoked some shit a lyin' asshole swore was opium, but no smack."

Malcolm looked at Mike, "What about you?"

Mike just smiled and slowly shook his head.

Malcolm got all folksy and said, "Well don't you young fellers fret about it none. Yer old Uncle Malcolm is gonna fix you up."

Jamie cut short his laughter and said, "I don't want to do any junk that comes from Motion. Sorry, but that yellow-eyed fucker gives me the willies."

"Not a problem, my friend," Malcolm said. "I've got a buddy who's coming back from a stint in Vietnam. If all goes well, he's bringing back a couple of ounces of Vietnamese smack. It's sparkly white, man, not like that Mexican brown shit that's been stepped on so much you can practically see the boot prints on it. A balloon should get seven or eight of us off."

Mike looked concerned. "One good hit of this stuff isn't going to turn any of us into junkies, is it? I mean, that's all I need at this point."

"One hit? Nah. You've gotta run for two or three days straight before you start pickin' up any kind of a habit."

Malcolm stood up and opened the door for them. "I'll let you know when and if. Bring your own works, I ain't sharing needles with anybody. And bring your own goddamn spoons too. I don't want my family silverware gettin' all bent up."

Jamie and Mike chuckled as they left the house.

"Hey Jamie," Malcolm called from the doorway, "come back and ride any time. And Mike, don't forget we've got a gig. I'll see you at 7 o'clock on Friday night at the Roundhouse in Fort Collins."

"Yassuh, Boss!" Mike yelled back as he got in the car, "Jes' don' beat on me no mo'."

On their way back to town, Jamie asked Mike if he'd talked to Aaron lately.

"No. I've seen him a few times, but not for much more than a 'hey, how are ya doin'? Why do you ask?"

"I drove by the Perkins Street House the other day and there was a big van out front and a family was moving their stuff in. So I was just wondering what happened to Quentin and the rest."

"No idea, man," Mike said. "But Aaron still works at the local radio station. You can always stop by and ask him."

* * *

Jamie sat on a cushion in the corner of a strange living room and looked around at the eleven other people there. Other than Shoes, who was sitting next to him, he didn't know anyone in the room. They looked pretty much like the people of the Family-the men with long hair and beards, the women with headbands and bell-bottoms-but to Jamie, they seemed almost painfully earnest. Jamie's friends rarely took themselves that seriously and didn't think much of people who did.

These were Campus Revolutionaries, and as Shoes put it, "pretty hard-core." After the trial, Shoes, who had always been political, seemed to become even more so.

Jamie had gone over to Shoes' apartment earlier to meditate and have dinner with him. Halfway through a plate of spaghetti, Shoes asked him if he'd like to go to the first meeting of the Colton Revolutionary Council that night. He said they were an offshoot of a larger campus group that Tom Nicholson, an English Professor, was leading.

"Leadin' them around in circles," was Shoes' opinion. "'Let's make committees, and let's make proposals, but let's not make any waves.' Fuck that. Makin' waves is how you get somebody's attention. That's why we're gettin' together. Y'all interested?"

More out of curiosity than revolutionary zeal, Jamie agreed to go.

* * *

A large man with curly hair and wearing blue denim overalls stood up and cleared his throat.

"Okay people," he said, "Listen up a minute. Olivia has got some news."

A small, pale woman with mouse-brown hair got to her feet.

"For work-study, I do typing over in the basement of Big Red. They asked me to type up a press release for a bigwig who's coming to give a speech on the 20th. Only Board Members and Tenured Faculty will be invited. Now get this, the bigwig is David Packard, the US Deputy Secretary of Defense."

An excited buzz went around the room. Shoes turned to Jamie with conspiratorial raised eyebrows. Jamie smiled and gave him a "thumbs up" sign.

It must be tough to be a radical back up here on the ass-end of nowhere when all the action is on the campuses of the big schools. Now, look at 'em. They're like a hungry pack of wolves seeing a fat sheep blithely strolling into their patch of forest.

"What's a big cheese like that doing in Colton?" someone asked.

"I think he was born somewhere near here," Overalls said, "Favorite son and all that shit. They'll give him some dippy award, he'll tell them what a great job the Military is doing in Vietnam, and then he'll ask them to re-elect Nixon in '72."

A tall, thin, red-headed man with what Jamie could only describe as "crazy eyes", jumped to his feet.

"We can pretty much figure that Nicholson and his namby-pambies will get a permit to stage an orderly and peaceful protest on the sidewalk out front of wherever it's going to be-"

"In the small auditorium in the Arts and Sciences Building." Olivia interrupted.

"Right," said the redhead. "I say we blend into that protest, and then when the Pigs aren't expecting it, we rush past them, into the building, and fuck up the meeting."

The buzz around the room was sharper now, varying from "Damned straight!" to "It'll never work." Then everybody quieted down, turned, and looked toward Jamie's corner of the room. He realized that Shoes was standing up.

"I dig what y'all are sayin', Art. We need to get in there and let Mr. Packard and all those folks know that the people don't support this war. But there will be cops there and y'all don't want to have to fight your way through. So how about this? I'll be over on the left-hand side of the demonstration, along with Jamie here, and all y'all over on the right. You give us the signal and we'll start a ruckus. Then when the Pigs come over to see what's happening, y'all can run in there and give that bastard hell."

There was general assent and shortly thereafter the meeting broke up with the agreement to meet again three days before the event to firm up plans.

"Thanks a lot, man," Jamie said as soon as they had walked out of earshot of the rest. "Did you just volunteer me to get worked over by the cops?"

"Au contraire, mon frere," Shoes grinned. "Whatever we do-start a fight, light a string of firecrackers-the Pigs will just be gettin' there when they'll realize that Art and the rest of the CRC have run by them and into the building. They'll all turn around and give chase while we just melt into the darkness."

"You sure?"

"If I get busted for rioting, I lose my Continuance. I'd better be sure."

After a couple of blocks of thinking about it, Jamie broke the silence, "Okay, I'll do it but on one condition-I want Scott to be there with us. He doesn't have to do anything, just be ready to back us up if anything goes weird."

"I think that's a fine idea. And y'all can be the one to ask him."

* * *

The call from Malcolm had come on a Monday before Jamie had left the house for work. His soldier friend had come through and everything was set for that evening. Before opening up the leather shop, Jamie had gone down into the basement and got Mike out of bed with the news that that night was going to be "Smack Night."

Now, as pastel twilight turned to darkness, Mike's Econoline van was bouncing its way on its bad shocks out to Malcolm's ranch on the edge of town.

"You remembered the spoons?" Mike asked.

"Got two of them. Also brought some cotton balls and a length of surgical tubing to tie off with. You got works?"

"Yeah. Four needles and two syringes. That's all my friend Wendell could come up with on short notice. It'll be enough. Who's coming?"

"As well as you, me, and Malcolm," Jamie counted the names off on his fingers, "Phiz, McNulty, Waltz, and Lyle." He looked at the eighth finger for a minute then remembered, "Oh yeah. Harvey is coming too."

"Harvey? I thought he was scared of needles?"

"He wants to snort his share up. I told him to bring his own dollar bill."

Mike pulled up to the buck fence that ran around Malcolm's yard. "If Malcolm's soldier friend is here and wants to hit up with us, I'm guessing he'll go into his own stash."

"Well, if he's expecting us to buy it off him and then share, that'd better be a damned big balloon."

* * *

"How was what? You mean Smack Night?" Jamie asked as he stirred a blob of honey into his tea. "I guess I'd have to say both amazing and frightening at the same time."

Scott, imperturbable as always, just looked at Jamie calmly and sipped his beer. Angela, on the other hand, obviously wanted details.

"The heroin," Jamie began, "was not like what I thought it was going to be at all. I'd pictured something between Novocain and ether. Something that would make you sort of numb all over. Way different. It's like a big filter in your brain that only lets the physical sensations through that are going to make you feel comfortable and only lets the thoughts and feelings in that are going to make you feel happy."

In case he wasn't expressing himself well, Jamie said, "It's like when I was a kid and we would go up to Minnesota to visit my Grandmother. She had a cabin up in the woods and she'd always make me a little bed out on the screened-in porch. One morning I woke up to the quiet sounds of bird songs and a babbling creek. I wasn't really awake and I wasn't asleep either. I was totally comfortable, not too warm, and not too cold. If I wanted, I could drift off to sleep for a while and have the most amazing dreams. Or I could stay awake and enjoy the warmth of the morning sun on my face. No problems, no worries, no pain. That's what heroin feels like."

Angela said, "So what was frightening?"

"Just that. Having been there once, in some way I'll always want to get back to that place again. And again. And that's not even figuring in how godawful sick you get when you try to stop. I used to think that junkies were weaklings and just needed a little willpower if they really wanted to kick. I've only hit up once and I can see that it's not a slippery slope at all. It's a fuckin' cliff."

"Poor Rachel," Angela sighed. Then she looked up at Scott and said, "What are you laughing about?

Scott grinned around his beer can. "I'm just picturing eight of you guys strewn around Malcolm's house like dirty laundry."

"Yeah," Jamie chuckled. "Throw a little blood around and you've got yourself a horror movie. Except for Jackie. He's the guy that smuggled the shit back from 'Nam. Maybe because he's been using for a while, but for him it was kind of like speed. He was chugging around the place, chatting up anybody awake enough to listen. He cleaned up the kitchen, washed the dishes, and even swept the floor. It was bizarre."

"Tell me something, Jamie," Angela said. "How are you doing? Not just the other night, but, you know, how's your life?"

"Why do you ask? Do I look a little ragged or something?"

"Not so most people would notice. But maybe just a little to those who know you best. We're concerned, that's all."

"The truth?" Jamie took a breath. "For some reason, I'm just not into it anymore. The drugs and the life, know what I mean? Ever since I started meditating last fall, all that has seemed kinda empty for me. But I love the people and the fun. I even thought for a while I could lose the drugs and just have the fun, but it was kind of like trying to stay celibate in a whore house. "Wake up man. Here, have a toke of this shit. It'll set your day up right." or "Hey Jamie, we're going to drop some Psilocybin and go out ice-skating at the quarry."

"Yeah, it's a hard thing," Angela said. "I was lucky. I found this big bozo."

She hooked a thumb at Scott who rolled his eyes.

"Jesus, listen to me," said Jamie, "I sound like a contestant on Queen for a Day. Sorry for the tearjerk. I came here to ask a favor."

"I remember," Scott said as put down his beer, "what's on your mind?"

Jamie told them about the Colton Revolutionary Council and their plan to confront the Deputy Secretary of Defense. He also explained the scheme that Shoes had come up with for a diversionary tactic.

"There shouldn't be any real violence, just Shoes and me faking it. You know, pushing, shoving and yelling, grabbing demonstrators' signs and generally knocking each other around. We'll be trying to make enough of a commotion that the Cops will run over to break it up. I'm only worried that some guys in the crowd might take offense and jump us, you know? I'd feel a lot better if you were there for us, just in case."

"You want me to start a fake fight?"

"No, no. That'd just be Shoes and me. Unless you <u>want</u> to get in. The more people the more noise."

"I'll just stand on the sidelines if you don't mind. I'm not sure I'd know how to fake a fight."

"That's great, then," Jamie said. "The Arts and Sciences Building at around eight o'clock tomorrow night. Do you need a ride?"

"No, I'll walk over."

"You mean <u>we</u> will walk over," Angela said. "I'm not missing this for anything. In fact, I may even add a little something myself."

* * *

On the wide sidewalk in front of the Arts and Sciences Building, the protesters walked up and down in a long loop shape. Many of them carried signs demanding Us Out Of Vietnam, and Yankee Go Home! In the middle of this loop stood a portly, bald man holding a megaphone. Earlier he had yelled through the device, "What Do We Want?" and the protesters had yelled back, "End The War!" Then the megaphone blared, "When Do We Want It?" and the answer came, "Now!"

Now he was leading his flock in the chant, "We Are Cool, We Are Calm, Soldiers Out Of Vietnam!"

"That's Nicholson I take it," Jamie said over Shoes' shoulder. They were among the thirty-odd protesters that were walking in the loop.

"That's him," Shoes replied. "Did you notice Wally and Art and the others gatherin' down at the South end?"

"Not yet. Wait 'til we make the turn."

As well as the walking protesters, at least as many more spectators had gathered behind them and on the sides. So as soon as they had walked around the North end of the loop and were headed back, Jamie could step enough to the right to see around Shoes, down the line, and scan the crowd. Redheaded Art and Overalls were standing next to each other studying the Police that were guarding the building.

On the sidewalk leading up to the building, three pairs of uniformed Colton Cops stood with their thumbs hooked in their belts.

The lined moved along and soon they were passing in front of Art and Overalls.

"You ready?" Shoes muttered.

"Wait a little. Look what just arrived." Overalls replied.

A van labeled "Channel 9 News" had just parked and a TV news crew were jumping out and hustling equipment across the street. It took two full circuits of the loop for the TV crew to be up to speed, lights on, and shooting tape.

Nicholson, visibly preening for the camera, had changed the chant to "U.S. OUT OF VIETNAM!" The protesters were bouncing their signs and their fists up in the air in rhythm. Many in the crowd were also pumping their fists and chanting.

As Shoes and Jamie passed, Overalls said, "We're ready. Go."

On their way back down to the end, Jamie studied the police officers standing guard. Because of the floodlights, Jamie could now see them more clearly. He noticed something familiar about one of them and realized it was the same policeman who had busted Mike. Sherm the Sperm.

There was no more time to think more about it because they were turning the corner of the loop. Jamie took two giant steps and walked on Shoes' heels.

"Hey!" Shoes shouted as he turned around. "Watch where y'all are goin' asshole!" and he shoved Jamie into the person behind him.

"Fuck you!" Jamie yelled and bull-rushed Shoes, pushing him into several other bystanders. People around them began to swear and scream as the two of them grabbed each other's windbreakers and jerked and pushed each other while they yelled the vilest threats they could think of.

Suddenly something hit Jamie above the ear and cracked in two. Somebody had just broken a protest sign over his head. Astonished, he turned to see Angela holding the broken handle.

"Let go of my boyfriend you bastard!" she yelled and threw the stick at him.

Jamie let go of Shoes, took Angela by the shoulders, and pretended to shake her. "You stay out of this, goddammit!"

Shoes hit Jamie, open-handed in the chest. It was a harmless blow, but Jamie staggered back.

Just as he was about to have another go at Shoes, he heard a hard voice say, "Come here, bitch!" Jamie looked in disbelief. Motion had appeared with two thuggish friends beside him.

Motion, with the shoulder of Angela's jacket in his fist, was jerking her around, and not gently as Jamie had done.

"You owe me eighty bucks!"

"Back off, Motion!" Jamie yelled and moved toward him, but one of his buddies stepped in front, his fists balled.

With barely a thought, Jamie swung his leg as hard as he could, hoping to kick the goon in the balls. Instead, he caught him square in the shin. The guy screamed in pain and began to hop around on one leg.

A huge hand came out of the shadows, grabbed the other thug by the shirt front, picked him up, and threw him into his hopping friend. They both went down in a tangled heap. Motion spun around and looked into the angry face of Scott Mallory.

Motion jumped back a few feet, reached into his pocket and produced a shiny metal handle. He flicked his wrist twice and he was suddenly holding a knife.

The crowd, which had pressed in to watch the fight, tried to surge away as people screamed, "A knife! He's got a knife!"

Motion swung the knife at Scott, who merely leaned back to let it go by harmlessly. Then with a short, hard, straight right fist, Scott punched his assailant in the face. Motion's eyes were rolling back as he left his feet and when he hit the pavement five feet behind him, he was unconscious.

Jamie noticed that policemen were pushing into the crowd. Assuming Shoes had already left, he grabbed Scott's arm and yelled, "Cops coming! Gotta split!" and pulled him away. He saw that Angela had Scott's other arm. They slipped into the crowd and disappeared.

THIRTY ONE

Officer Larry Sherman stood on the sidewalk in front of the Arts and Sciences Building, scanning the people protesting and the crowd behind them. He was glad that the lights of the Television crew had turned back to the crowd and away from him and his fellow policemen. For a short while, the glare had made it difficult to keep watch.

Next to him, Sergeant Crenshaw muttered, "Oh, that's nice."

"What's that, Sarge?" Sherman said.

"Over a little to the left, there's a tall girl with long, blonde hair and a tiny little miniskirt. Really decent legs. Now I'm more of a boob man myself, but-"

"Something going on over there," Sherman said.

On the right side of the demonstration, the orderly march had dissolved into some kind of melee. It was difficult to tell, but it seemed two men were pushing each other around. While the left side of the crowd was still chanting, people on the right side were yelling 'Fight! Fight!" and pressing for a closer view.

"Take a man and go check it out." the Sergeant said.

"Paulson!" Sherman yelled, "Come with me!"

He started for the area of the disturbance and then saw a picket sign swing in a big arc and crash over the top of one of the fighter's heads. The volume of the crowd noise climbed, all the chanting stopped, and the people pushing to get a better view were stopped by the people trying to back away. He started to run.

Suddenly the crowd's shouts of encouragement turned to yells of dismay. There were people screaming, "A knife! Look out, he's got a knife!"

Sherman unsnapped his nightstick and held it in front of himself with both hands to push people out of the way.

"Police! Step back! Step out of the way!"

Officer Paulson, his own nightstick out, came up beside him to help clear a path. The people were not reluctant to let them through, they were just packed together too tightly and stumbling over each other as they tried to move aside.

Sherman suddenly broke through and into a small open space. He turned slowly around, searching the crowd for anything or anyone threatening. He saw two young men with long hair and sawed-off jean jackets disappearing into the onlookers. On the ground, another of the same type was laying on his back, not moving. Paulson was bending over him, checking for a pulse.

Sergeant Crenshaw and two other cops burst into the little circle. Before he'd had time to say anything, Crenshaw heard Guttierrez's voice shouting from the edge of the crowd, "Sarge! A bunch of protesters just ran into the building!"

"Aw shit!" Crenshaw swore, and then yelled back, "Stop 'em, Goot! Don't let 'em get in there!"

"Sherman," he barked, "you and Paulson secure the area. You're in charge here. Come on, you two!" he yelled to the other cops and took off running.

"How is he?" Sherman asked Paulson.

"He's alive, somebody just cold-cocked him. Look at that face."

Sherman noticed the puffy redness on the right side of the face and the trickle of blood running out of the nose. Then he looked closer and realized the face was familiar.

"I know this guy, or at least, who he is," Sherman said, "His name is Fellser. Walter Fellser. He's on the Narcotics Watch List. Search his pockets, then go back to the cruiser and call for an ambulance. I'm going to get some names and addresses."

Sherman looked around at the crowd, "If you saw what happened here please wait for a few minutes. I'd like to talk to you."

Sherman pulled out a handkerchief and used it to wrap up the knife that had been lying next to Fellser. Then he took out a pad and pencil and walked up to the first of the three or four people who were waiting to make a statement.

* * *

Sherman was standing at attention in a short line consisting of himself, Sergeant Crenshaw, and Officer Guttierrez. Behind them stood the other three officers that had been on duty earlier. In front of them, a red-faced Captain Gaskin was sitting on the front edge of his desk with his arms crossed.

"What the bloody Hell happened out there tonight?" Gaskin said. "All you had to do was keep a few protesters from entering a building. Instead, you end up clubbing several of them into bloody submission in full view of every bigwig in Colton. And you, Sergeant Crenshaw, run up behind a kid who is addressing the Deputy Secretary of Defense and hit him over the head with a nightstick. Gave him a concussion."

"Something happened, sir. We ran to investigate and they slipped past us. It was a planned diversion, sir."

"You think a drug pusher and his biker pals were working with a bunch of peace-queers?"

"We haven't quite worked that out, sir."

"And you, Guttierrez," Gaskin turned to the hapless officer. "You have several of them corralled in the lobby when a girl makes a break for the auditorium. A 90-pound little girl and you break her jaw with a nightstick."

"I just put the baton out to stop her and she sort of... ran into it."

"How clumsy of her. And all this in front of TV news cameras. Congratulations, you're all movie stars. In living God-damn color!"

Gaskin got to his feet, took a breath, got himself under control, and then continued in a quieter tone. "Sergeant Crenshaw and Officer Guttierrez, please leave your badges on my desk. You are both on suspension pending further investigation. Dismissed."

The six policemen began filing out of the room when Gaskin said, "Sherman, wait a few minutes."

When the room had emptied Gaskin said, "Well, you and Paulson were about the only ones who kept their heads tonight. Good work recognizing that punk. Paulson found two packets of what looks like heroin in his pocket.

"In a month or two, when all this blows over, we'll probably slip Crenshaw and Goot back into the lineup. But in the meantime, the men are going to need a little leadership. You haven't got enough time in grade to qualify for Sergeant so I'm promoting you to Corporal. There isn't much call for that rank in city police forces, but it's there if we need it. Think you can handle that?"

Sherman popped to attention, saluted, and said, "Yes sir. And thank you, sir."

"Congratulations, Corporal Sherman. Here..." Gaskin went around his desk, pulled a cellophane packet out of a drawer and tossed it to Sherman. "...have your wife sew these on before duty tomorrow."

Inside the packet were two patches, each with a single, embroidered blue chevron outlined in white.

THIRTY TWO

Phiz settled into the living room armchair and put his feet up. "What you're saying is that good ol' Motion isn't getting out of the jug any time soon."

"That's the way it looks," Jamie said. "Huge bail. They say he's a flight risk."

"I heard his buddies were trying to sell his motorcycle for him."

"You didn't hear? They did sell it. Then kept the money and split town."

"You're shittin' me!"

Jamie put one hand over his heart and held up the other in the three-finger Boy Scout salute. Then he laughed and took a sip from a cup of herb tea.

"Waltz probably told you that he's decided to move in with Katie," Jamie said.

"Yeah, he did. He said they had a little basement apartment over on Hickock."

"And that means that you and I have to come up with another roommate. You got any ideas? I already asked Mike about it, but he says he kinda digs living over in the Hellhole. He says the grunginess of it matches his depressed state. Plus he's not sure what's going to happen to him. His trial comes up in a few weeks and things could change in a hurry."

Phiz shifted in his chair and put his feet back on the floor. "There's something I need to tell you, Jamie, but I'm not sure how."

Jamie had never seen Phiz, normally easy-going and sure of himself, suddenly seem this uncomfortable. Jamie's first thought was that it was about that lid of weed Phiz had left on the coffee table and Jamie had smoked half of.

"Look, if you're still tight-jawed about that pot..."

"No, no. It's got nothing to do with that," Phiz said, "Just promise you won't get pissed off. At least not until I've finished."

"Okay, I promise," Jamie said. "So what is it? Lay it on me."

Phiz took a breath and said, "You remember what I told them to get out of the draft? About me being a queer? Well... it's true."

Jamie didn't say anything, just waited for Phiz to say more.

"I like boys. I like girls too, I'm not turned off by girls like some guys I know, but I like balling a man better."

Jamie just stared at Phiz while his whole world began to mutate and shift. There was something like a rattling sound in Jamie's head as things that he thought were true clicked over to become false and things he knew to be untrue turned around and became reality. It was, to use his own phrase, quite a rush.

"Really? No shit?" Jamie finally said, "You're a... Jesus, I don't know what to call you. Homosexual is too clinical. Fag, queer, homo... those are all insults."

"Try 'gay' or 'gay man', those seem to be labels we can accept." Phiz said, "So you're not pissed off? You seem okay."

"Well... yeah, I guess I'm okay with it, I'm just still trying to get my head around the whole thing. Like, how the Hell did I miss it all these months? Now that I think about it and other than that dancer, Jennifer, you never had a woman stay over. But I just thought you were slipping out and banging some married chick."

"Actually, I was. Only it wasn't a chick." Phiz grinned.

"Why, you dog! Did this guy's wife know?"

"He didn't say and I didn't ask. But that's all over now. I've found somebody. He's single, he's really cute, and he loves me."

"That's great, man," Jamie said. "Are you two talking about moving in together?"

"Both of us really want that, yeah. But how could I talk to you about moving out and in with him if I hadn't come out to you first? I can't tell you how relieved I am that you're okay with it. I figured you'd want to punch me out or maybe just kick me in the shins."

Jamie winced, "Has anybody not heard about that?"

"Well, if you had kicked me in the shins, then at least I'd have had a good reason to split. Now I don't. So both Waltz and I are moving out at the same time and we're leaving you here to shift for yourself. That's a shitty trick I know, but I don't know what else to do."

"Have you got a place?"

"No, Raoul lives in the dorm right now. The hard part is going to be finding a landlord who won't slam the door in our faces."

"I've got an idea," Jamie stood up. "But I'm carrying a load of water. Let me go cop a squirt while I think about it."

When he got back from the bathroom he asked Phiz, "Can you and Raoul handle a hundred and fifty bucks a month rent between you?"

"I think so. Raoul's family is loaded and his Mom sends him whatever he wants."

"Cool. So why not have Raoul move in here with you?

"You'd be okay living with two gay men?"

"Not really, no," Jamie said. "Don't take it personally, but I really don't think I could handle the squishy noises in the middle of the night. I'm talking about me being the one to hit the trail. And I think I already know of a little place that would be cheap and close to work."

"Where is it?" Phiz asked.

"I don't want to say right now," Jamie said. "I'll check it out tomorrow, and if it's cool, I'll let you know. Shit, man, we could have this whole deal done in a week or less."

* * *

"Morning, Charlie," Jamie said, "Pretty busy today, huh?"

Charlie Melman closed the cash register and looked at all the customers in the store.

"No shit, man," Charlie said. "Ever since the news broke about the riot last Wednesday, kids are coming in looking for something to show what side they're on. Clenched-fist buttons, Peace signs, anti-Nixon posters all selling like crazy. Hardly anything left. I wish these anti-war people would give me a heads-up before they start something. But, no. And on a weekend too."

"You mean that little scuffle up on campus?" Jamie said, "I didn't think it was that big of a deal."

"Jesus, Shipman, get a television," Charlie said. "Channel 9 News in Denver broke the story Thursday with lots of video featuring cops beating up protesters. There were close-ups of a guy half-conscious with blood running down into his eyes, and a girl with a smashed and bleeding mouth. Then Nixon announced we were invading Cambodia, and suddenly college campuses all over the country started going nuts.

So ABC picked up Channel 9's story and featured the footage on their national broadcast with all the other craziness. Now every network and newspaper in the State has a crew in Colton. The Radicals have called a Press Conference for tomorrow afternoon. Excuse me..."

A girl with a scarf tied around her head pointed out a "Make Love Not War" poster on the wall. Charlie reached into a partitioned cabinet, pulled out a rolled-up version of the poster, and rang the girl up.

"Only two of those left. Jesus." Charlie said.

"Not much call for leather from those in a revolutionary fervor, I guess," Jamie said. He'd been keeping an eye on his little showcase and nobody was looking.

"Wait a Minute!" Jamie suddenly perked up. "I just had a flash. Do you know Frank, that guy that does silkscreen printing for you? Can he work fast?"

Charlie looked over his shoulder at some T-shirts hanging up that had the Electric Rainbow logo printed on them. "Once he gets the artwork it takes him about a day to set up and a day to print per color. Why?"

"My friend Phiz is a freakin' amazing graphic artist. He supplies the artwork, Frank does the screen printing, I do the running around, and by Monday you have T-shirts that say "Pigs off Campus!" and "Colton Students Say U.S. Out of Vietnam!"

Jamie could practically see the pupils in Charlie's eyes turn into dollar signs.

"I like it, man," Charlie said. "If you're supporting the cause, there's no harm in making a little scratch on the side, right?"

"It's the American Way."

"If you can get me some cost estimates and some preliminary sketch-es from Phiz, I'll talk to Frank and my partner Bill. Can you meet me back here this afternoon?'

"Cool!" Jamie grinned at Charlie and headed for the door. Then he stopped and went back.

"I got excited and spaced something out," Jamie said. "A few months ago you said you and Bill had some little apartments upstairs and when you got the plumbing fixed, you'd be renting them out."

"Yep, that's true," Charlie said. "We've had tenants in there for a couple of months now. You know somebody who's looking?"

"Yeah, I do. Me."

"Oh. Okay, great. We've got two small rooms available without win-dows for $25 a month, or there's one larger one with windows for $35."

"Can I look at them?"

"I'm the only one here right now," Charlie said as he opened a draw-er and got out two keys. "But here are the keys. Number Eight is one of the small ones and it's ready to go. Number Four is the larger one. Fair warning: the guy had to move out of Number Four in a hurry and it needs a good cleaning. You might have to use your imagination a little."

Jamie found the outside entrance-a door marked "Hormel Apart-ments"-and went up the stairs two at a time.

Number Eight was a small room with a bare light bulb hanging from the ceiling and an old, water-stained sink on the wall in the corner. A sudden, fierce memory came to him of the dingy little room in Juarez where a Mexican prostitute had once relieved him of his virginity. Feeling a cloud of depression beginning to descend, he quickly stepped back out of the room, locked the door, and went looking for Number Four.

He followed a carpeted corridor around several turns, past a niche with a pay phone, and past the common kitchen. He found Number Four next to the back door and across the hallway from a common bath-room. As he was warned, the room was messy and needed a good scrub-bing, especially around the sink. There were patches of something pink and brown growing on the porcelain along with cream-colored, dried-out blobs that Jamie could only hope were toothpaste.

But all-in-all, he liked the room. It was bigger than Number Eight and had two large, double-hung windows that looked out on a fire escape platform. Once the windows were clean, he was sure there would be a nice view of the featureless back wall of the warehouse across the alley. There was a serviceable area rug the previous tenant had left behind and the place even had a little closet.

Jamie left the apartment, going out by the back door and down the fire escape, just to check out the best moving-in route. He was feeling he had found his new home.

* * *

The next afternoon Jamie and Shoes were standing together off to the side of the little platform where the press conference would be taking place. The members of the CRC were arranged tightly around the platform along with a lot of other serious-looking young people.

"There's been a truce called between Nicholson's group and the CRC," Shoes said. "The Council thinks that solidarity is important and Nicholson wants to get his share of the publicity. A marriage made in Heaven."

"How come the University is letting them do this right in the middle of the Quad?" Jamie asked. He had been running around getting Phiz's final drawings to Frank the screen printer and had only just arrived.

"A political football game," Shoes explained. "Neither the City or the College wanted to give them a permit, but because some people got hurt, neither one wanted to appear publically to be anything but magnanimous. It was sort of a stalemate. Then Art and Olivia threatened to talk to the press from their hospital beds and the College caved. It was a bluff of course; both of them had been released on Friday. Here we go."

The Press had formed a tight semi-circle around the platform; reporters with microphones stood in front, camera operators in back. Four people mounted the platform and stood in a line. Overalls was on the right, next to him stood Art with his hair shaved in a patch near the top of his head and a heavy white bandage stuck in the middle of the tonsure. Next to him was Nicholson trying to look grave and purposeful, and on the end was Olivia. The whole lower left side of her face was a livid green and purple bruise and when she tried to smile the sun glinted off the wires on her teeth.

"Thank you all for coming..." Overalls began as seven or eight microphones were pushed in his face. He read a prepared statement that put forward three main points of the activists' agenda. The first was a call to the students of the College to go on strike on Tuesday, the 5th of May. The second point unveiled plans for a Protest March through the streets of Colton on the same day. For the third point, he passed the paper to Nicholson.

"As representatives of CCAWM-the Colton College Anti-War Movement," Nicholson intoned, "we invite Governor John Arthur Love to come to Colton and meet with us in an open, frank dialogue about the direction of this State and this Country. If Governor Love agrees to come here, we will call off our activities. If he does not agree, we will have no choice but to persevere."

That, as Jamie heard it, was the gist of the presentation. There was a lot more said, of course, but it was all the usual anti-war, anti-establishment rhetoric that made Jamie wish he'd brought a book to read.

As the reporters asked questions that the activists answered with the predictable platitudes, Jamie turned to Shoes and said, "Shit, man. Why didn't you tell me about the Strike? We could have had T-shirts on the street and made a killing!"

"Who the fuck are you?" Shoes asked. "Y'all look like Jamie Shipman but talk like Charlie Fuckin' Melman."

"Sorry, man, you're right. I've been letting this T-shirt thing overload my head. Okay, I'm back now. Who do you want me to kick in the shins?"

Shoes laughed and said, "Y'all can start with that dipshit Nicholson. That whole Meetin' with the Governor trip is his personal obsession. The crackpot thinks that if he can just have this 'debate with the Governor' we can turn Colorado and then the whole country around."

"That's just crazy on so many levels."

"Yep. It is. But the guys are pretty sure that Love will never agree to it, so they're letting the Professor demand it. Then when it doesn't happen they'll be free to keep raising hell and fighting the good fight."

"Didn't Lenny Bruce say that fighting for peace is like fucking for virginity?"

"So what else do y'all suggest?" Shoes said. "Lie down and let the bastards run over you?

"No, but I'm just thinking there has gotta be other ways to get people's attention."

* * *

It was a little after one o'clock Monday afternoon when Jamie banged through the front door of the Fifth Street house.

"Hey you two!" he shouted, "I hope you're up and around. I got something to show you!"

"We're in here," Phiz called from the kitchen. "We're eating lunch. You hungry?"

He and Raoul were watching a small, portable TV as Jamie came in waving a fistful of white fabric at them.

Raoul was nearly as tall as Phiz, had skin the color of hot chocolate, wavy black hair, and the longest eyelashes Jamie had ever seen on a man.

"What is it?" Phiz asked.

"Ta-daa!" Jamie unfolded and held up two T-shirts.

One shirt had a heavy line drawing of a raised fist in front of the lettering, "No More War!" The other was of an ugly, cartoon pig wearing a policeman's hat and a badge and carrying a bloody nightstick. Underneath was the phrase, "Pigs Off Campus!" both drawings were signed with a small and simple "Phiz."

"Wow!" said Raoul. "Lover, you are a genius!"

"I dropped four dozen off at the Rainbow and Charlie had sold two before I even got out the door," Jamie said.

"Raoul," Phiz said as he admired his own work, "have you got enough stuff left to make Jamie one of those sandwiches?"

"It's called a Croc Monsieur. I'll do it, but my Soap is coming back from commercial so you have to pay attention and tell me if I miss anything."

Raoul busied himself at the stove and Phiz grinned at Jamie. "The man is an unbelievable cook."

Suddenly the TV network cut into the show.

"We interrupt this program for a Late-Breaking NBC News report. On the Kent State University campus today, during a large, unpermitted student demonstration, Ohio National Guardsmen opened fire. Using live ammunition, they shot indiscriminately into the crowd killing four students, two of them women. We will have more on this story as information becomes available. We now return you to your regularly scheduled program."

The soap opera returned and Raoul ran back to the stove to save Jamie's sandwich from burning.

"Holy shit," said Phiz.

"They shot them?" Jamie asked nobody in particular. "That's what they do now to people who demonstrate against the war? Shoot them? What the bloody blue fuck! I was thinking about blowing off the March tomorrow, but after that crap, try and stop me."

Still seething, Jamie bit off a chunk of the sandwich Raoul had put down in front of him. His expression instantly softened.

"Damn, Raoul. That is really good. Thank you."

* * *

Grace Berman was walking down the middle of Main Street holding up a sign that read, "Bring The Troops Home Now!" Close around her were two or three thousand people, all marching in the same direction, many holding similar signs. Jamie, who was moving between several groups of marchers, slowed down to walk beside Grace, Angela, and Scott. On Grace's other side were several other faculty wives.

"This turnout is amazing," Grace said to Jamie, "Where did all these people come from?"

"I've heard there are people here from Fort Collins, Greeley, even Boulder," Jamie said. "After Kent State, a lot of folks wanted to get out and do something and Colton already had this march planned. It's great isn't it?"

Grace smiled, threw back her head, and pumped her sign up and down to the rhythm of the ongoing chanting.

It was a sunny, warmer than usual day and people made the most of it. Since the route of the march passed by many student apartment buildings, people had set their stereo speakers into open windows and loud rock 'n' roll serenaded the marchers. A man on one corner had a pan of bubble soap and a large wire hoop and was creating huge bubbles that floated over the march. Others had hoses and sprinklers out to cool the demonstrators with a fine mist.

When the crowd gathered in front of the courthouse and various speakers began lining up to use Nicholson's bullhorn, Jamie found Mike and together they slipped away.

An hour later, they had backed Malcolm's pickup up to the kitchen door of the Fifth Street house and were loading Jamie's stuff into it. They already had the mattress and box springs standing up in the truck bed and they were slowly maneuvering the armchair through the kitchen and toward the back door.

"Wasn't it almost exactly a year ago we were moving shit into this house?" Jamie asked.

"Yep," Mike said, "same truck too. We don't have to move that heavy, god-forsaken sofa bed do we?"

"Nope. Not unless you want it."

"Nah. It wouldn't look good in my jail cell."

Jamie put his side of the chair down on the back porch. "You aren't giving up hope are you?'

"Just a little gallows humor. Don't let it freak you out."

When they had gotten the chair settled in the truck, Jamie said, "So how's it going with the Luscious Linda?"

"Nothing so far. Not even a quick hand job in the back of my van."

"I meant with your case."

"Oh, that. I talked to her this morning and she said there was some brouhaha with my judge. It seems His Honor, Harley T. Buford, announced yesterday that he was going to march in the protest today. The Governor told the Press it was "unseemly" and threatened to ask the State Judicial Oversight Committee to take action."

"Will that affect your case at all?"

"It shouldn't. Even if they do something called "sanctioning" him, it would take months and my trial is in a couple of weeks."

Soon they had Jamie's dresser, suitcase, duffel bag, and a couple of boxes of Jamie's stuff packed up and ready to go.

"Oops," Jamie said. "Just about forgot ol' Little Bear." He plucked the paper mache mask down from its nail and tossed it into an open box.

They carried the dresser out to the truck and then tucked the rest of the things into open spaces.

As he put up the tailgate, Mike said, "Don't Phiz and Raoul care that you're taking some of this?"

"Not at all. They're downtown right now buying some snazzy new furniture with Raoul's parents' money."

THIRTY THREE

Jamie came back up the backstairs of the Hormel Rooms. Since Mike had left his van out at Malcolm's when they swapped for the truck, he was taking the truck back out to the stable, leaving Jamie to unpack.

As soon as Jamie came in the back door he stopped, unbelieving. He and Mike had left his armchair out in the hallway when they'd carried everything up to Jamie's new room. Now the armchair was gone.

After checking to see if it had somehow got into his room, and seeing it hadn't, Jamie went looking for his chair. It had to be someone in one of these rooms, if they'd tried to take it down the long front stairs, they would still be noisily at it.

I'm not thrilled with having to bang on doors and get all huffy with my new neighbors but... dammit that's MY fuckin' chair!

When he'd gone past the kitchen and the phone and made a couple of turns, he heard music and laughter coming from one of the front rooms. The door was unlocked and ajar so he just pushed it open and tried to strike a threatening pose.

"Jamie!" called a familiar voice and everybody in the room was suddenly coming toward him, grinning and holding their hands out. It was Quentin, Polly, Sarah, and Aaron.

"Hey, man, "Quentin pumped Jamie's hand. "What are you doing here? Where have you been? Haven't seen you in, like, forever. Look what we found."

They dragged Jamie over to look at his own armchair.

"It was just sitting in the hallway like someone was just going to throw it out," Aaron said. "It'll be great for meditating."

"I know," Jamie said, "because it's mine."

Polly looked confused and asked, "Well, how did it get up here?"

Jamie just laughed and shook his head. "It got up here because my friend Mike and I carried it up here. I'm moving into Number Four. We left it in the hallway and I went back down the fire escape to thank him for his help. When I came back up five minutes later it was gone! How was I to know I was moving into a nest of chair thieves?"

After a few more rounds of good-natured jibes, mock heartfelt apologies, and loud and happy comments of "Welcome to Hormel Rooms," Aaron and Jamie carried his chair back to Number Four.

It would have taken Jamie an hour or so to unpack, arrange his room, and hang his clothes up, but instead it took most of two hours to do so with visitors from the front rooms repeatedly walking in to offer him a cup of tea (Polly and Sarah), to perform a skit featuring two highly opinionated interior designers (Quentin and Aaron), and to make sure he knew when group meditation was happening (everybody).

When Jamie asked to be shown the layout, the whole crew, of course, had to go along. Quentin took on the role of stuffy docent. "This bathtub was once used by the stable boy to Louis the Fourteenth's Eleventh Mistress to wash his feet. Look closely and you can still see the stains of 300-year-old horseshit."

"Mmm," said Aaron, "and smell 'em too."

They showed how Quentin, Polly, and Sarah had rented two adjoining rooms in the front of the building and had designated the large one with windows out onto the street as The Living Room. The smaller one was The Bedroom which had three single cots in it. Aaron had rented a smaller room next door for himself and Madeleine. She was, he explained, down in Boulder, finally learning Laaghava Meditation.

"It took her months to get her mother settled in a nice Senior apartment complex, Aaron explained. "Her mother was pretty freaked out about it until she found a whole group of ladies lived there who loved to play Mah-Jongg. After that, it was 'Jeez, Madeleine. Are you still here?' So it was just getting the house ready to rent and Madeleine was on a plane to Colorado."

Later, after evening meditation, Jamie was given a bowl of vegetable stew that the girls had made. There was no invitation or special deal made of it, Sarah simply handed it to him. And just like that, he had been welcomed into the group.

In the future, Jamie would look back on this moment with a mixture of wonder and gratitude. It was almost as if some power greater than himself-God, Nature, or Mother Devine-had said, "Okay, that will be quite enough of that," picked him up by the scruff of the neck, and dropped him here. There are many small turning points that delineate a person's life but, for Jamie, this would be a major one.

Knowing a mawkish speech would just make everyone uncomfortable, Jamie said, "Rather than leaving me to deal with these terrible guilt feelings about pulling my chair out from under you guys, how about we go over to the Starvation Army tomorrow and if they've got a comfortable chair for cheap, I'll buy it for all of us. All you guys have to do is carry it back."

"The fact that you won't have to sit on the floor when you come over to meditate doesn't have a thing to do with it, right?" Aaron said.

"Oh, not a thing,"

* * *

The next day Jamie spent the morning delivering Phiz's latest artwork to Frank the screen printer. Then while Frank prepared the screen, Jamie drove to Fort Collins to buy four dozen sheets of poster board. In the midst of selling a lot of T-shirts, Charlie had also had many requests for a poster that could be held up during a march or hung on a wall. The poster Jamie and Phiz came up with featured a similar clenched fist to the one that was on the shirts, but the lettering was changed to "Students Strike for Peace!"

As Jamie came back into Colton, he purposely drove through the college campus to see if anything was going on. There were groups of students picketing in front of almost unoccupied classroom buildings and a makeshift memorial to the Kent State Four surrounded by a dozen students holding a vigil.

He also saw a fairly large group marching in support of the war. Cowboy hats and boots were common among the men, and among the women, big puffy hair and heavy makeup were the norm. They held up signs that said, "Victory!" and "God Bless President Nixon!"

But most of the Colton Students were enjoying the unscheduled vacation by lying out in the grass under a warm sun or gathering around someone with a guitar and singing Peter, Paul and Mary songs.

Jamie made his deliveries, and then met up with the rest of the Hormel mob for the trip to the Thrift Store. They considered, and took turns sitting in, several armchairs.

Quentin scooched his butt back and forth in a chair and said, "I like this one the best. It's not too lumpy and has room for my arms."

"But look at it," Polly complained, "It's as ugly as a dog turd!"

The chair was oddly shaped and its upholstery was faded green and purple, threadbare, and had stuffing trying to escape in several spots. They were looking at it dubiously when Sarah appeared. She was holding a yellow bedspread decorated with white cabbage roses.

"Check this out," she said as she tossed it over the chair. "A few tucks and folds, and what do you think?" The disreputable chair had become entirely reputable.

Everybody cheered, Jamie paid three dollars for the chair and fifty cents for the bedspread, and they happily carried their new acquisitions home.

*   *   *

Jamie was sitting in his little leather shop buffing the edges of a new belt when Mike came in the door. Jamie looked up and grinned a welcome, but Mike's return smile was wan and pallid.

"Hey, Dude." Jamie used his foot to hook a stool out from under his desk. "What's up? No offense, but you look like shit, or at least its second cousin. Did somebody die?"

"No," Mike sat down heavily. "But they may as well have. I told you a couple of days ago about my Judge wanting to march in the Protest?"

"Yeah. The Governor had his tits in a twist over it."

"Well, he marched. He was right up front next to Nicholson and the others. The Governor publically asked the Judicial Oversight Committee to see if they could remove Judge Buford from office. And Buford said, in effect, 'Fuck You, I Quit!'"

"He quit?"

"Yep. Resigned. Effective immediately."

"So where does that leave you?"

"Up Shit Creek. With no sign of a paddle."

"What does Luscious Linda-?"

"I met with her this afternoon. She said that we would now get pushed into Judge Chandler's court. Judge Earl Chandler is an ultra-conservative bastard and proud of it. He firmly believes that the only reason there is a 'drug problem' in this country is that the courts have been too lenient."

"So you're fucked."

"My lawyer says if I plead guilty, the best I can hope for is two to five."

"Years?"

"Yep. If I plead not guilty and the jury doesn't see it that way, it could be five to ten. This is worse than fucked."

"Jesus, man," Jamie put his hand on Mike's shoulder. "That truly sucks."

"If those stupid fucking cops hadn't beaten the shit out of those protesters, I'd have been okay."

"Oh shit," Jamie paled. "If Shoes and I hadn't started that diversion, then the cops would have stayed in place and stopped those crazies from running into the building. So this is my fault."

"Now you're just tripping out, man," Mike looked up with a rueful smile. "If I started thinking like that, the freakin' list would be endless. No, there's really only one person I can truly blame, and that's me. I knew what might happen and I did it anyway. I guess after all those times of hearing people tell me to go fuck myself, I took their advice to heart."

"Is there anything I can do?" Jamie said. "You don't have to even ask, just tell me what you want and I'll do it."

"There is one thing you can do," Mike said after a long pause. "You can tell me why we did this."

"Did what?"

"Grew our hair out, smoked pot, dressed up in funny clothes, told our parents and their whole generation to go to hell. You know, this whole 'hippie' thing. Think about it, man, we are risking our health, our sanity, our freedom, even our lives. And for what? What do we hope to get out of all this crazy bullshit?"

Jamie leaned back in his chair, obviously considering the question as he turned his burnishing tool over and over in his fingers.

"Krenovich once told me that he was only doing it for the pussy," Jamie finally said. "Others, like Charlie over there, desperately want to be cool, so they find people who are really only putting up a better facade than they are and try to fall in step with them. But there are a lot of us who, as tweeky as it may sound, genuinely think that the world can be changed. We see all this hate and envy, violence and greed. And fools that we are, we think that love, understanding, and maybe a little humor, can turn all of that around."

Jamie flipped the burnishing tool back up on his work table.

"You ask a good question," Jamie said. "So what about you? Why did you take up this crazy hippie-bullshit?"

"I don't know, man. I look back and I can't think of any one point where I made a conscious decision to do this and to not do that. I just went the way the current was carrying me. And along the way maybe things just came too easy for me. Like I said, I don't know."

"Well, now you've got my head full of all sorts of shit to process," Jamie smiled. "Thanks a lot."

Mike stood up and shoved the stool back under the table. "Don't mention it, man. Anytime you need a good bummer, you know where to find me."

Jamie walked Mike to the door.

"There are some other people I'd better tell about this," Mike said. "Grace Berman and Angela. Maybe Shoes if I can catch him."

Mike reached for the door handle and then turned his head back.

"I don't know if you know this," Mike said. "But I always looked up to you."

Jamie tried to answer but the words got stuck in his heart.

Mike smiled that Mike Harding smile and said, "I love you, man. I do." And then he was gone.

* * *

Upstairs at Hormel Rooms, Jamie mopped up the last dribble in the bowl of vegetable soup with the last bite of a crusty roll and popped the whole thing into his mouth.

Earlier, everyone was already sitting in the Living Room for meditation when he had gotten there. He had been trying to make up his mind between the only remaining chair, a straight-backed wooden desk chair, and a cushion on the floor when Quentin decided to run to the bathroom, leaving the new chair unoccupied.

Jamie had been well settled among the cabbage roses and listening for his breathing when he had heard someone loudly clearing their throat. He had opened one eye to see Quentin standing in front of him and giving him an evil stare. Everyone else in the room had laughed merrily as Jamie had made a show of yielding the chair back to Quentin and scuttling across the room to the cushion on the floor.

Holding his empty soup bowl, Jamie got up and started picking up the others' bowls and spoons to carry them to the kitchen.

"Excellent soup," he said to Polly and Sarah. "And I loved the crusty rolls, where did you get them?"

Polly grinned at the compliment and handed him her empty bowl. "At the Hometown Bakery. Half price because they were a day old."

That morning, Jamie had noticed the big cookie jar on a shelf in the corner of the Living Room labeled "Food Fund" and asked what his contribution should be.

"Whatever you can afford," Aaron told him. "It usually works out to around five bucks a week. If you want anything special, put a little extra in with a note."

Balancing five bowls and spoons, Jamie headed for the kitchen, then stopped and said, "I've got a jar in my room of some herb tea, chamomile I think. Also a couple of tea balls and a little blue teapot. Anyone interested?"

Four hands shot up and a chorus of voices yelling, "Me, me, me, me!"

Jamie put the dishes in the kitchen sink and then went around the corner to Number Four. There was a piece of paper thumbtacked to his door. It was a page that had been torn out of a spiral-bound steno pad, folded in half, with "Jamie" on the outside in Mike's handwriting.

Jamie opened it and read, "Remember me telling you about The Big Statement? I've decided it's time. Watch the sky."

Forgetting about the tea, Jamie ran back to the pay phone in the hall, fishing in his pocket for dimes.

Twenty minutes later, as much of the Family as Jamie had been able to round up sat around Shoes' apartment waiting for Jamie to tell them why he had called so urgently.

"Thanks for coming," Jamie said, "I found this attached to my door with a thumbtack sometime about eight o'clock." He passed the note around the room. "The Big Statement was a rap of Mike's from last summer. He said something like, 'When things seem to be sliding away, that's the time a dude has got to make a Statement!'"

"So what's the big deal?" Lyle asked.

Jamie looked at the people around the room and said, "When he said it he was holding a stick of dynamite."

"Where would he get that?" Shoes said.

"His Father builds golf courses out in the Arizona desert," Jamie said. "Mike ripped off a stick. And he knows how to use it."

After a short discussion, the consensus was that there were three possible places that Mike might want to blow up. The ROTC hutch on campus, the local Draft Board office downtown above the hardware store, or the Police Station.

"I'm thinking we should divide up," Jamie offered. "Some of us at each of those places. Shoes stays here by his phone and we call in from pay phones every hour or so."

Waltz put up a hand. "What do we do if we see him?"

"I guess try to talk him out of it."

"Here's a thought," Scott said."Why not just let him do it? As long as nobody gets hurt, why not let him make his Statement?"

"I admit it would be hysterical to see the ROTC hutch go sky high," Lefty said, "but chances are really good they'd catch his ass and tack another twenty onto his sentence."

After some discussion, it was agreed that they would try to stop him. They left Shoes' apartment and headed for different cars. Phiz had just gotten into Jamie's Volkswagen when they heard a car horn honking repeatedly. Jamie stepped out of the VW and saw Waltz standing next to the open driver's side door of his own car.

"Turn on your car radio!" Waltz yelled. "Local station. There's news."

Not having a radio in the VW, Jamie and Phiz ran over to Waltz's car and put their heads into an open window to listen.

"To repeat: There has been an explosion out at the old quarry ten miles North of Colton. The Sheriff's Department has sent two cars to investigate. News crews are on their way."

Deciding that it must be Mike and that they did not want to just sit around and wait for any news, all three cars, including Shoes in the back seat of the VW, were soon on the road to the quarry.

When they got near, a Sheriff's Deputy was blocking the entrance road and they could go no further. Lyle got out of Waltz's car and walked over to the VW as Jamie rolled down the window.

"It's bad, man," Lyle said. "One person blown to bits. No one else around."

They could see down into the little meadow and parked there, illuminated by the flashing lights of several emergency vehicles, was Mike's old, white Econoline van.

"I suggest," said Shoes from the back seat, "we go back into town and get thoroughly drunk."

The seven of them started with two fifths of Tequila. They alternated stories of funny things Mike had said or done with shots of the fiery liquor. They had just run out of Tequila when Scott and Angela came in with a case of beer and two bottles of cheap whiskey.

Jamie didn't remember much after that, only getting through the front door of Hormel Rooms and then deciding that stairs were much more comfortable than their reputation.

* * *

Jamie woke up in his own bed with a piercing headache and a mouth so dry and rank he didn't want to breathe the air that had to pass through it. Someone else, he realized, had put him to bed. His undershorts were still on him and normally he slept naked.

He rolled out of bed, stumbled to the sink in the corner, and vomited.

After cleaning out the sink, taking three aspirins, and brushing his teeth, he felt minimally better.

Once dressed, Jamie opened the door and watched a note that had been stuck in the jamb flutter to the floor. He opened it with some trepidation. The last note on his door had eventually brought his world crashing down.

"Jamie-Sorry for your loss. He was a good guy and we'll all miss him. When you feel up to it, come down to the store, I have a project for you.-Charlie"

As he ate a peanut butter and jelly sandwich in the kitchen, washing it down with a glass of milk, he considered telling Charlie to fuck off and spending the rest of the day in bed. Although his hangover was somewhat better, a gray mantle of grief still draped itself over his shoulders. Not wanting to deal with it was what finally prompted him to go downstairs and see what Charlie wanted.

"Hey, Jamie," Charlie said, "I'm glad you came down. I was worried about you. News like that can really mess a guy up."

"Thanks, man, I appreciate it," Jamie said. "What's this project?"

"You haven't listened to the radio or read a newspaper, right?"

"No, don't know a thing."

Charlie pulled out a copy of the local paper, The Colton Coloradan. The headline was "Local Musician Takes His Own Life."

"First," Charlie said, "there's no picture of Mike. The college didn't have a photo. But I do. Remember that first night that The Skid Marks played in here? I took a bunch of photos of the band that night. This morning I took several of the pictures into Quigley's Photos and George the darkroom guy and I picked this one out."

Charlie put several black and white photos of the band down on the counter and tapped his finger on one that had had a frame drawn in ink around Mike's upper body.

"I gave him the negative and he blew that part of the picture up to this."

He opened a wide, flat paper bag and withdrew a couple of large sheets of paper that had been taped together along one edge. He flipped the top one over to show a grainy, fifteen-by-sixteen, black and white photograph.

Jamie sucked in his breath and a sharp pain clutched at his heart. There was Mike tossing his head back, hair flying, as he hit a power chord that would drive him into his solo. It was a one-in-a-thousand shot and Charlie and his friend in the darkroom had found it.

"Wow, man," Jamie said, "that's just beautiful."

"I had time to drop by Modern Printers on my way here," Charlie continued. "I showed them this and asked them if they could print it up on these 17 by 22 sheets by late this afternoon."

He put a large sheet of paper on the counter and, holding the photograph by the edges, put it down and adjusted it until there was a one-inch border on the top and sides and a five-inch space at the bottom.

"If we get it to them by one o'clock, along with the lettering that goes on the bottom, they can print 250 sheets by four o'clock."

"What lettering?"

Charlie just looked at Jamie for a moment, and then said, "Oh shit. I forgot to tell you about the quote."

He picked up the newspaper and turned it over as he said, "they found a little notebook in Mike's van. It was open to a page where Mike had written what seemed like a goodbye note, a sort of summing-up of his life-at least that's what everybody is saying."

"What did it say?"

Charlie tipped up the paper and read out loud.

"There are a lot of us who genuinely think that the world can be changed. We see all this hate and envy, violence and greed. And fools that we are, we think that love, understanding, and maybe a little humor, can turn all of that around."

What Jamie wanted to do was say, "He didn't say that. I said that." But he kept his mouth shut and solemnly nodded his head.

"So, can Phiz do lettering?"

"He can, but I think I can do it for you faster," Jamie said, "The College Bookstore sells sheets of Press-and-Apply lettering. I can probably get you a nice 3/4" font and have the whole thing laid out and ready to go by noon. One problem though. I'd feel really crappy about making money on Mike. Especially this soon."

"Listen, man," Charlie said, "I'm not planning on selling these, I want to give them away. For Mike. I wanted to do something for him and this is the only thing I could think of. If you'll do the lettering, I'll put up the money for everything else."

"You've got yourself a deal. I'm on my way," Jamie said. "Thanks, Charlie." Jamie put up his hand, gripped Charlie's hand warmly, and headed for the door.

"I don't know what we're going to do with them once we've got them," Charlie called after him.

"Just leave that part to me," Jamie said and walked out the door.

The lettering sheets came with multiples of common letters and Jamie, standing in the College Bookstore, did some quick math. He bought three sheets of Bookman Italic type and drove back to the Rainbow. On the way, he once again drove through campus. The students were still striking, and it seemed like there were more of them on the picket lines and the shouts were louder and angrier.

Then he saw something hanging from several high windows on Hargreaves Hall that made him stop his car to get out and look. It was a bedsheet lettered in red and blue paint.

MIKE HARDING

1950-1970

WITH LOVE AND

UNDERSTANDING

RIP

Not far away he saw sixty or seventy students surrounding a home-made monument of flowers, stuffed animals, and personal notes. At the center of the pile was an old guitar that had been covered with carnations.

Later, Jamie sat at his worktable and applied the lettering to strips of white paper. To keep things straight and square he used previously drawn blue pencil lines He finished the quote and added another line to go at the bottom-"Michael Harding 5/7/70."

When he had all the parts assembled, he stood back from the mock-up and let a wistful smile play across his face for a few seconds.

Well, my friend, you always wanted to be famous.

True to his word, Jamie got everything to the printer by Noon. Then he went to see Shoes.

Shoes was at home and looking a little worse for wear. As soon as Jamie came in, he pulled a couple of bottles of beer out of the fridge and handed one to Jamie.

"Thanks, man," Jamie said. "How are you holding up?"

"Well, let's see," Shoes counted off on his fingers. "I'm hung over, I'm bummed out, and I'm afraid I'm gonna flunk my finals because I haven't been to class in three or four days. Other than that, I'm just fuckin' ducky."

The beer was cool on Jamie's vomit-burned throat and he took another swig.

"I drove through campus a while ago. Did you know they're turning Mike into some kind of Martyr for the Cause over there?"

"No shit?" Shoes said, "I always thought Mike was strictly a music, drugs, and chicks guy. He didn't give a rat's ass about politics. But what the hell, if it gives the Resistance a local focus, all hail Saint Mike!"

"It's good to hear you say that," Jamie said, "because I'm working on something along those lines and I need your help."

Jamie explained what Charlie and he were working on. Half an hour later, He and Shoes were in Overalls' apartment explaining the project to Olivia and him. Art was called and all of them soon found themselves crammed into Nicholson's tiny campus office. Nicholson welcomed them but seemed distracted by the recent announcement that Governor Love was coming to Colton the next day.

Seeing that Colton was not, in fact, cooling off but instead was getting angrier, angry enough that a young man had committed suicide, the Governor said that he had changed his mind. Then he had announced that he would meet with any students, faculty and town citizens who were interested. The event was to take place at one o'clock within the confines of the Colton College Football Stadium.

"He mentioned me by name." Nicholson puffed, "He said he would gladly have a constructive conversation with me about the wants and wishes of the Colton community."

"That's great news, Professor," Overalls said, "Now; can you help us out this evening?"

"Oh, not me," Nicholson said, "I have to prepare for tomorrow. This could be a turning point, you know. But Katherine here..." He gestured to the young woman next to him taking notes, "...knows everyone and will be happy to connect you."

After a while, Jamie excused himself from the meeting and drove down to the printer to wait.

He had the posters in hand by four o'clock and by four-thirty he and Shoes were handing out bundles of ten posters each to a large collection of CRC radicals and Nicholson true-believers. Jamie was happy to see the volunteers armed with hammers, tacks, pins, clear tape, and staple guns.

By six o'clock, when Jamie climbed the back stairway of the Hormel Rooms, every bulletin board, phone pole, and empty wall in Colton featured Mike Harding sending out his message of Love and Understanding. And, of course, a little Humor.

* * *

Jamie did not sleep well that night. He kept coming back to the thought that there was something he still had to do. He could almost see Mike's ghost tapping him on the shoulder and saying, "Come on, Dude. Get your ass in gear. Just one more hill to climb."

Eventually, he pulled on his jeans and went out in the hall to make a phone call to Malcolm. When he got back to his room he pulled out a Big Chief writing tablet and opened it to the first blank page. Then he began writing down notes, drawing sketches, and making lists.

After an hour of this, Jamie, satisfied, dropped the notebook on the floor, snapped off the light and dropped off to sleep.

The next morning he spent some time driving around town picking up the various materials he had on his list. He went to Frank's shop for a couple of sheets of blank posterboard, then to the lumber yard, and finally to the Colton Bookstore for acrylic paint and a brush. After he'd checked off everything on the "Materials" list, he drove around the Colton Football Stadium several times, trying to get an idea of where the entrances and exits were, what the Police presence was like and where their cruisers were parked. He also looked for which gates were locked and which left unlocked.

Not entirely content, but not wanting to be conspicuous, he decided that he had enough information and turned the VW toward the road that led to Malcolm's stables.

Thirty Four

Corporal Sherman stood on what would be, during the season, the sideline of the Doc Watson Football Field and faced the crowd. His back was turned to the platform that had hastily been erected in the middle of the field. He and other local Policemen, along with some College Cops, stood ten yards apart all down the edge of the field and watched the crowd for any disturbances.

Governor Love had been introduced and was already well into his speech. Sherman didn't bother to check the area of the platform; the Governor was well protected by a squad of State Troopers from the Executive Security Unit.

Sherman was glad of a job that didn't require much analytical thought. The last two days had put a terrible strain on him, a strain that he had to keep entirely to himself. Both at home and at the Station, people depended on him to keep a clear head and an even keel. How could he tell them that he was being suffocated by guilt? A young man, not yet twenty-one, had decided to kill himself rather than submit to the System, a System that he, Corporal Larry Sherman, had never questioned, a system that he had represented when he arrested that young man, a System that rewarded him for doing so. And all for one little bag of marijuana. Ten dollars.

Snap out of it, asshole. Do your job and eventually it will all go away.

If the "Powers that Be" had had time to better organize this event, he was sure they'd have found a way to put the loud and obnoxious students in the upper deck and let the more composed local citizens have the ground level seats. Unfortunately, the students, with their signs and their catcalls and their rude chants had rushed in to take up most of the prime seating.

As part of the arrangement, Someone named Professor Nicholson had said he would ask his followers to act as "Monitors" to help control the crowd. These people, wearing white armbands to denote their authority, were doing their best to keep things civil, but were mostly ignored.

As the Governor droned on, chants arose spontaneously from the crowd. "U.S. OUT OF VIETNAM!" "KENT STATE, KENT STATE!" and most ominously for Sherman, "MIKE, MIKE, MIKE..." All the noise made it nearly impossible to hear Governor Love's speech and those who wanted to hear it started loud disagreements with those that didn't. It was total cacophony. Violence was in the air and Sherman felt the breaking point was coming soon. He had no idea what to do if it did.

Suddenly quiet spread over the crowd. Everyone in the stands had stopped in mid-chant and was looking in wonder to their right. Sherman spun to see what they were looking at and could barely credit what he was seeing.

Someone on horseback was trotting across the adjoining field toward the end zone fence. It was almost certainly a man in the saddle because he was wearing only boots and a jock strap. The jock strap had been painted Day Glow Pink. There was a bouncing ponytail on each side of the rider's head, each ponytail tied up with a bright pink bow. A red, white, and blue peace sign decorated the rider's chest.

Sherman shook his head to clear it and shouted, "Paulson and Eddings with me!"

A quick hand signal to tell the others to hold their position and Sherman was running toward the fence. He caught up with Paulson who yelled, "What do we charge him with?"

"Trespassing, Disturbing the Peace, Indecent Exposure. I don't know. We arrest him and get him out of there first, and then we'll worry about the rest."

The three policemen arrived at the fence just as the horseman did. Sherman looked frantically for a way over or around but the fence was nine feet tall and made of heavy chain link. There was a gate down at one end, but it was padlocked.

Sherman tried to make an identification, but the man was wearing some kind of mask over the bottom half of his face. The mask had high cheekbones, a giant hawk nose, and heavy lips. Everything above that had been cut away.

"We could just shoot him," Eddings suggested.

"Oh, great thought," Sherman snarled. "Cold-blooded murder in front of three thousand witnesses. just shut up and give me a boost!"

The rider turned around, untied something that had been lashed behind him, turned back around and held it up. It was a large, posterboard sign attached to two cross-staves which were themselves attached to a six-foot wooden closet pole. The lettering on the sign read, "A VOTE FOR JOHNNY IS A VOTE FOR FUN!"

As Sherman put the toe of his shoe into Paulson and Eddings' cupped hands, reached up, and began to climb the fence, he could hear gales of laughter sweeping across the crowd in the stands.

The climbing was slow and tortuous. His round-toed shoes had trouble finding purchase and the wires were cutting into his fingers. Though it only took ten seconds, to Sherman it seemed like ten minutes before his hands finally reached the horizontal bar at the top of the fence.

When Sherman made one more heave and pulled his shoulders up over the top, the rider stood up in his stirrups, tipped his head back, and shouted something. Because of the mask, nobody could make out what he had yelled. Nobody but Sherman, who happened to be only a few feet away.

"There, you Sonofabitch!" he heard the Rider scream, "Are you fucking happy now?"

The man on the horse rammed the sign into the ground. Since the end of the pole had been sharpened, A VOTE FOR JOHNNY IS A VOTE FOR FUN! stuck fast. The rider dug his heels into the horse's flank, wheeled the beast around, and let her run.

"Come back here!" Sherman shouted. Then when he realized how foolish he sounded, he lowered himself back down to the stadium side.

"Squad Cars!" Sherman ordered and began to run along the fence. As he ran, the other two close behind him, he watched the horse and rider gallop out through an open gate in the practice field, then turn right.

"East! He's heading East!" he yelled. Then he heard more laughter and booing from the crowd and realized that he and the other two Policemen had become the Keystone Cops. His cheeks burning with embarrassment, he got to the first exit door in the stands and jerked on the handle. It was locked. In full view of the hooting and boisterous crowd, he had to turn and run to the next exit door which, thankfully, was open.

When they reached the area where the Squad Cars were parked, Sherman yelled, "Eddings, go with Paulson!"

Jumping into his own car, Sherman backed out and, with a squeal of tires, sped off to track down the Mystery Rider.

THIRTY FIVE

Missy was running full out down Wicker Drive. The speed and power of the animal took Jamie's breath away. The terror about what he was doing kept it from coming back. He had no doubt that most of the Colton Police Force were only seconds behind him. If he slowed down at all, he was sure they would pull him over, drag him off the horse, and take him down to the station.

Then Sherm the Sperm would walk in holding a short piece of rubber hose.

Up ahead he saw the sign for Heron Lane, the road he was supposed to turn north on. He glanced behind him, saw no one following, and let the horse know he intended to turn left by pressing his left knee into the animal's side as he pulled back and left on the reins. Obediently, Missy made the turn and then sped back up to her previous running speed.

The mask was bouncing around on Jamie's face. After Jamie had cut the top half off the Little Bear mask with a coping saw, Malcolm could only find some short but heavy rubber bands, so they had used two of them tied together. It had worked fine for the slow trip from the stable around the back side of the campus to the stadium. But the mask was loose now and getting looser with every stride. Jamie wanted to take it off, but there was nowhere to put it.

I guess I should have bought a jock strap with a pocket.

Jamie only noticed the oncoming pothole when it was too late to swerve the horse around it. Without hesitation, Missy jumped over it.

The shock of landing made Jamie's head snap down, one of the rubber bands broke, and the mask fell into the street.

Jamie's disappointment in losing the mask was overshadowed by his relief that he was still in the saddle and not bouncing down the pavement himself.

Two more blocks, then a right turn on Dinwiddie, and he saw the County Fairgrounds coming up on his left. And there was Malcolm's truck, with a horse trailer hitched to it, parked as planned behind the Show Ring stands.

Malcolm was brushing down his old gray, Domino, when the sound of Missy's slowing hoofbeats made him look up and then shake his head with a weary smile. As Missy slowed to a near-stop, Malcolm got a hold on the reins under the horse's chin to steady her while Jamie jumped off.

"Okay, in you go," Malcolm said. "I got that dark blanket already pinned up so when you've got her tied up, just drop it behind you. There are some clothes in there and a hat to hide your hair. And take down those God-damned ponytails and ribbons."

The tailgate of the trailer was folded down to make a ramp and Jamie led Missy up into the trailer. A few minutes later Jamie reappeared wearing jeans, a western work shirt, and a cowboy hat. He'd stuffed his hair up under the hat, and after he'd found a pocket knife in the toolbox and picked up a stick, he sat down on the fender of the trailer and started whittling.

Malcolm ran the brush down the length of Domino's back and out onto the hip.

"How'd it go?" he said.

"Pretty good actually," Jamie said without looking up from his stick. "When I turned and bolted, everybody in there except the Governor and Professor Nicholson was whooping and laughing. It was pretty cool."

"I still think you're nuts. Uh-oh. Looks like we got company."

A Colton Police squad car pulled up next to them and stopped. Larry Sherman got out, put on his hat and said, "Afternoon."

"Officer," Malcolm replied. "What can we do for you?"

"You haven't seen anybody riding a horse down the street here have you?"

"No, sir. We've been working Domino for a while, but we haven't been out in the street."

"This horse would be brown, with black mane and tail. The rider had long hair with pink bows in it. Other than those he was damn near naked."

Malcolm laughed. "Sorry, sir. If a man was to ride by wearin' nothin' but pink bows in his hair, I think I'd remember it."

Sherman moved over and addressed Jamie directly. "What about you? You see anything?"

Jamie looked up. Trying to ignore his thundering heart, he said, "No sir. I ain't"

Sherman looked at Jamie for a moment, and then one side of his mouth twitched up in a funny little half smile. He turned around and went back to his car. Instead of getting in, he picked something up off the seat and carried it back to Jamie.

"I found something of yours," he said as he dropped the bottom half of the Little Bear mask into Jamie's lap. "Better tuck it away somewhere safe. And it would be good to close up the snap on your shirt while you're at it."

Jamie and Malcolm watched in silence as the Policeman went to his car, opened the door, and put one leg inside.

"Gentlemen," Sherman said. "Have a pleasant day."

He started the car and drove away. Both Jamie and Malcolm looked down at Jamie's shirt. One of the pearl snaps, near the top of the placket, had not been fastened properly and the shirt sagged open. A white arc, part of the peace sign that Jamie had painted on his chest, was visible through the opening.

* * *

"So, did they find the guy?" Quentin said.

"Nope, not a trace," Shoes said with a grin. "It's been four days now. I, for one, hope they never find him. People love to groove with that mysterioso shit."

Jamie chuckled. "The Governor is saying that it must have been a professional that the Democrats hired to make him a laughingstock. A professional what I couldn't say."

"A professional chain-yanker?" Quentin said. "What a great job. Where do I go to apply?"

Jamie laughed along with the others as he thought of the two halves of the Little Bear mask hidden under the clothes in his bottom dresser drawer not fifty feet away.

"So what happened to you, man?" Quentin asked him. "We saved a seat for you but you never showed up."

"I had some stuff to do and I got there late," Jamie said. "They wouldn't let me in on ground level, said it was full. I had to go sit in the upper deck. I ended up right next to a bunch of rednecks who were pissed off about the guy on the horse. I had to bite my cheeks to keep from laughing and getting my ass kicked. Hey Aaron, when is Madeleine supposed to get here?" Jamie said, changing the subject.

Aaron, carrying a bouquet of flowers wrapped in clear plastic, had been nervously pacing between the Kitchen, where Polly and Sarah were cooking, and the Living Room.

Earlier, Jamie had gone to Safeway with Aaron to buy long strips of white butcher paper and a magic marker or two. Now there were two banners hanging on the walls of the Living Room. One said, "Welcome Home Madeleine!" and "Jai Acarya" was on the other.

"Any time now," Aaron said. "She called this morning around eleven o'clock and said that she was leaving Boulder and bringing a friend up with her. It shouldn't take more than an hour and a half, should it?"

"She's here!" Polly shouted from the hallway. "She's coming up the stairs!"

Aaron ran out of the room closely followed by everyone else. A noisy little crowd gathered at the top of the stairs with much hugging and hallooing. Jamie, not knowing Madeleine as well as the others, held back a few steps.

All at once the group moved off toward the Living Room. There, standing a couple of steps down, was Lisa. Jamie drifted a few feet toward her as she came up to the top of the stairs. They paused, and then rushed into each other's arms and clung together for a long while.

"Lisa, Lisa," Jamie whispered, then pulled his head back to look at her. "It really is you, isn't it?"

She gave him a shy smile and nodded her head. Then she kissed him.

"But how did you... I mean, why..." he stammered.

"What made me come back to Colton to find you?" she said. "I saw your picture in the paper and I just knew."

"What picture?"

"The picture of you on that horse holding up that silly sign."

"How did you know it was me?"

"You couldn't expect me to spend all those years being watched over by Little Bear, and not be able to recognize the bottom half of his face, could you?"

Jamie looked over his shoulder toward the Living Room, then said quietly, "Let's talk about it in my room, okay?" And he walked her around the corner to Number Four.

Once they were inside he said, "You didn't say anything to Madeleine, did you?"

"No," she laughed. "I thought you might be keeping it secret, so even though I was dying to tell her, I didn't."

She was sitting in his armchair and he on the end of the bed. She reached out and took both of his hands in hers. He started to say something and she put a finger up to his lips.

"Me first, okay?" she said, "I've had a few days to think about what I want to say and you've only had five minutes. Fair enough?"

He nodded and she began.

"I had lost touch with Madeleine. I thought I'd never see her again. But then three weeks ago I saw a poster for Laaghava Meditation and decided I had to go to the lecture. And there was Maddy. As the course went on she told me about this place, and Aaron and the others. Then a few days ago she heard from Aaron that you had just moved in and she asked if I would like to drive up to Colton after the course. And I said no. It wasn't because I didn't love you, Jamie, it was because I did love you. Maybe even more than I did a year ago.

"But here's where all the sappy love stories have got it wrong. You can't build a life with someone based only on the fact you love them. Even if you have a truckload of good bricks, you'll never be able to build a house out of them without mortar, and wood, and roofing, and a thousand other things. I couldn't see the other stuff that holds the love together. Until I saw that picture and I read the story.

"The Jamie Shipman I knew a year ago would be sitting around with his buddies, smoking pot, and saying, 'wouldn't it be cool if I found a horse and rode up on it? You know, like with a sign?' And that Jamie would never actually get up off the couch. But then there you were in that picture, nearly naked, holding up that sign. And I know you didn't do it on a whim. It obviously took a lot of work and planning, not only on how to get there but then on how to disappear afterward. It was a crazy-assed, foolhardy, nearly pointless stunt and I was so proud of you I could just pop."

Jamie said, "I guess I don't get how doing that would make you want to come back to me, but I'll take it."

"What I'm trying to say, Sweetie, is I don't care what star you decide to chase." She caressed his cheek with her thumb. "It doesn't even matter if we succeed or fail, just as long as you take the journey and take me with you; I'll be by your side every step of the way."

Jamie kissed her. It was a long, sweet, and sensual kiss. Jamie felt the glow of rising heat at the base of his spine but chose to let it go. Ahead of them, he could suddenly see all the time in the world.

They resettled themselves both in the armchair and snuggled up together.

"I've been told that I have a problem with asking for kindness," Jamie said. "So I'm asking you for that. For all those times that I will act like a jerk, say something thoughtless, or fall flat on my face, I'm asking you now for kindness. Even when you have every reason to walk away, I'm asking you to, instead, help me up, dust me off, and let me apologize. Because I love you, Lisa Cunningham. I understand that's just, like you said, a load of bricks, but together I think we can build something out of it that will last.

"Hey, you two!" Polly's voice came from out in the hallway. "Unhook yourselves and come on. We're all ready to meditate, just waiting for you."

With a laugh, Jamie and Lisa walked out into the hallway and closed the door behind them.

The End

Acknowledgments

I saw a painting once, I can't remember where, that affected me deeply. Since the advent of The Internet, I've searched for it, but to no avail. It shows a tribal group of early hunter-gatherers around a campfire at night. Meat roasts on a spit, the successful hunters and their women gorge themselves in celebration. Their attention is focused on one man who is standing and telling the story of the hunt. How the head man planned it, how the fastest chased the beast down, how the bravest dragged it to the ground. This man is a little spindly and pot-bellied, obviously not one of the alphas of this pack, but he is an honored member of the tribe, for he's the one who knows how to tell the tale. He knows not only how to tell it, but how to polish it up here and there so it gleams. The title of this painting is *Storyteller*.

I would like to thank the people who acted as Beta Readers and whose feedback on early drafts I found invaluable. Carolina Carter, Jane Caton, Peggy Benedick, Ian Gersten, and Deb Blachowiak. Thanks also to Greg and Jan Thatcher who coached me through the crowdfunding process.

I bow in gratitude to the folks who truly went above and beyond the call in backing this project – Greg and Susi Benes, Jean Morrow, James Stubbs, David and Irene Linn, Debra and Ernie Blachowiak, Randy C. Bunney, Deborah Sanchez, and Ross and Maureen McConnell.

It is said that love is just appreciation but carried to its highest degree. All that and my deepest thanks go to my editor, my partner, my friend, and my wife – Michelle Benes.

Coming in Late 2021

THE BRAIDED RIVER

An astonishing journey of discovery and healing as a mid-century housewife explores seventeen of her previous lives.

by

HELEN PELTON

and

TIM PELTON

Coming Soon

THE STREETERVILLE WAR

A Novel Based on a True Story

In 1890, bootlegger and flim-flammer Cap Street-
er stumbles upon a way to turn the lakewater
next to Downtown Chicago into buildable land.
The Moneybags and Robber Barons of the city
decide to take it away from him. And the battle
for Streeterville begins.

BY
TIM PELTON

Made in the USA
Las Vegas, NV
08 May 2023